SARAH BETH DURST
Vessel

MARGARET K. McELDERRY BOOKS
New York London Toronto Sydney New Delhi

For my daughter and my son,
my Liyana and her Jidali

✻　✻　✷

Acknowledgments

Every book is a journey, and many wonderful people trekked across the sand with Liyana and me. I'd like to thank my spectacular agent, Andrea Somberg, and my magnificent editor, Karen Wojtyla, as well as Justin Chanda, Paul Crichton, Emily Fabre, Siena Koncsol, Lucille Rettino, Anne Zafian, and all the other amazing people at Simon & Schuster for believing in this journey. Many thanks and much love to my family, whose support makes every quest possible. Huge thanks to my mother, who showed me the way by teaching me to love books and to dream of dragons; to my daughter, who named nearly every character that Liyana and I met; and to my husband, who shares every step of every journey with me.

Chapter One

On the day she was to die, Liyana walked out of her family's tent to see the dawn. She buried her toes in the sand, cold from the night, and she wrapped her father's goatskin cloak tight around her shoulders. She had only moments before everyone would wake.

She fixed her eyes on the east, where the sky was bleached yellow in anticipation. Shadows marked each ridge, rock, and sand dune. Overhead, a few stubborn stars continued to cling to the sky, and a raven, black as a splinter of night, flew into the wind before angling toward the dark peaks of the distant mountains. Liyana felt the wind caress her cheeks and stir her hair. She'd left it loose last night, and she'd counted the strands when she couldn't sleep. The wind stirred the sand at her feet, and it whistled over the dunes and rocks. She listened to it so intensely that every muscle in her body felt taut.

She had wanted to be calm today.

She'd heard a tale once about a man who had caught the first drop of sun. He'd kept it inside his lantern, and he never felt fear again. In his seventieth year, he was struck by a cobra, and he embraced the snake and called him brother—and then he died. Liyana thought he should have sliced the snake's head off so at least the cobra wouldn't bite the man's family, too, but then again Mother always said Liyana had a decidedly practical streak in her.

On the horizon, the first drop of sun looked like liquid gold. Liyana stretched out her hands and imagined she were cupping it in her palms. As the light spread, it ran up her arms across her tattoos. She refused to look at the markings, and instead she marveled at the beauty of the sand dunes. In the dawn light, they blazed red.

Behind her, the tent flap was tossed open. Aunt Sabisa burst out of the tent, her chest heaving as if she'd run miles instead of the five steps from the sleeping rolls. "You! You want to kill me!"

A goat bleated at her.

"I wake, and you're not there. In, in, in!" Aunt Sabisa fluttered around Liyana, shooing her toward the tent.

Liyana murmured the traditional apology to an elder whom one has deeply wronged, and then she commented, "You have a lizard in your hair."

Aunt Sabisa's hands flew to her head.

Liyana grinned as her aunt shrieked, danced, and flung the tiny lizard onto the ground. She stomped, still shrieking, as the terrified lizard burrowed into the sand and escaped. By the time Aunt Sabisa quit, at least a half dozen people had emerged to watch the spectacle, and another dozen had poked their heads out their tent flaps.

One of them was Jidali, Liyana's four-year-old brother, who was stuffing a corner of the tent flap into his mouth in an effort not to laugh. His shoulders shook, and his eyes watered. Liyana winked at him, then pointed to a bare patch of sand and said in an innocent voice, "Over there, Aunt Sabisa."

Aunt Sabisa pounded the sand, stomping so fast that she looked like a rabid jackrabbit. Jidali broke into peals of laughter that shook his whole body. Aunt Sabisa looked at the little boy who now writhed laughing half in and half out of the tent. She twitched her lips, and then her face broke into a smile. Laughter erupted from the nearby tents, and soon the desert rang with a mix of bell-like laughs and deep-bellied laughs. Liyana laughed with them.

Now *that* was a far better start to her last day.

Liyana let her aunt shepherd her inside. She squeezed Jidali's hand as she passed, and his face seized up. She knew he'd remembered what day it was. She wanted to stop and embrace him, but as soon as she crossed the threshold, all her female relatives swarmed her, and she was swept to the back of the tent. She let the chatter wash over her—consternation over the state of her hair, the condition of her skin, the length of her fingernails—as they pushed her behind a blanket that had been strung up for privacy. Still clucking at her, the women removed Liyana's night-shirt and positioned her, naked, in the center of a shallow, silver basin. Sponges were passed around and then dipped into a clay bowl of milk and honey. Liyana shuddered when the first sponge touched her skin.

"You'll warm again fast," one of her cousins told her.

But it wasn't the cold that caused her skin to prickle. Only newborns and those near death were bathed in milk and honey. She smelled the sweet honey and the oversweet goat milk mixing together in a cloying scent that invaded her nostrils and filled her throat. She closed her eyes and waited for the bath to end.

Dabs of water washed the milky residue off her skin, and she was wrapped in cloth and dried as if she were a child. As they rubbed her so dry that her cinnamon-colored skin developed a pink tinge, her aunts and cousins chattered over her, touching on every topic but today's ceremony.

When they finished, Liyana's mother lifted her chin so that Liyana's eyes would meet hers. "You will wear your dancing dress all day today. Do try not to dirty it." She held Liyana's gaze a moment longer than was warranted.

Liyana understood the message: *Don't disgrace us.*

"I must attend to the goats." Mother strode out, knocking aside the privacy blanket. Aunt Sabisa readjusted the blanket, and in the minute that followed Mother's departure, no one spoke.

Liyana broke the silence. "And I thought the dress was for Jidali." She knew it was a pathetic joke, but it was the best she could manage today. As if they knew that too, her aunts and cousins broke into gales of laughter. As they laughed, Liyana wondered if she would be spending today comforting her family, instead of the other way around.

She was presented first with the finest undergarments that she had ever seen. She fingered the fabric. It was as light and white as a cloud. "My work," her aunt Andra claimed. Everyone cooed over the intricate weave. Liyana lifted her arms, and the slip was pulled over her head. It floated down around her body. She felt as if she were wearing a piece of the sky.

Next, the ceremonial dress. Aunt Sabisa brought it from the chest where it had lain, sealed against the desert dust. Everyone gasped as she displayed it, though everyone had seen it many times. Over the last year, every woman in the tribe had added seventy stitches of gold thread, and every man had tied seven knots, completing the pattern that matched Liyana's tattoos. Liyana forced her face to curve into a smile and she put as much enthusiasm into her voice as she could muster. "It is more beautiful than the sunrise."

Everyone murmured in agreement at this, and Liyana fought

the urge to grab the dress, run outside, and thrust it into the clan fire. She felt her face grow hot, even though no one could hear her thoughts. Truly, the dress was beautiful. The bodice was a masterwork of embroidery, and the skirt was composed of twenty panels, twice the usual number, each dyed a brilliant, jewel-like color. It would swirl around her when she danced. The sleeves would billow as well, her dress magnifying her every movement. Slits in the sleeve would cause the fabric to fall back and expose her decorated arms when she reached toward the sky. It fit her perfectly, and by tradition it would never be worn by another. Hers was the only skin it would ever touch. "The sun and the stars will be jealous of me," she declared.

Her aunts and cousins liked that compliment, and Liyana saw only smiles as the dress was pushed over her head. She was caught inside the fabric, momentarily alone in a swirl of blue, red, and green so deep and rich that her head swam. It smelled of sage. A moment later the dress was cinched around her waist. Aunt Andra fitted shoes on her feet. They were of the softest leather but strong for dancing. Like the dress, these were finer than any shoes her toes had ever touched. She felt as if her feet were being caressed. She hoped the goddess wore these shoes often. They'd never cause a blister. That thought calmed her. She'd prepared her body well—her limbs were strong, her back was straight, her teeth were healthy—and now she wore fine shoes.

"Hair!" one of her cousins cried.

"Watch for lizards," another said.

More laughter. Even Aunt Sabisa joined in.

Pushing aside the privacy blanket, the aunts and cousins swept Liyana to a stool by the cooking fire pit. All the men, including Jidali, had left the tent during the dressing. Six hands grabbed chunks of her hair, and Liyana did her best not to yelp as they raked combs through it. Once every knot was yanked to everyone's satisfaction, more hands dove in to braid. By the end, Liyana felt as if every strand had been plucked out of her scalp. She touched her head to check that she still had hair. She felt dozens of braids. Each braid ended in a tiny silver bell. She jiggled her head, and the braids danced around her face. Her hair sang as crisply and clearly as a bird in mating season. "I am a hunter's worst nightmare," Liyana said.

One by one, her aunts and cousins kissed her cheeks. She'd be left makeup free so that the goddess could see clearly what her new face looked like. Liyana clenched her hands together on her lap as she received the kisses.

She would not allow a single tear.

Others would come soon, and she would not disgrace her family. Positioning herself on the stool, Liyana spread her skirt to display the elaborately embroidered panels so that her family could admire it as they departed. Two of her cousins flung the tent flap open and secured it on either side. Already, men and women milled outside. Her relatives filed out of the tent.

As the others left, Aunt Andra knelt next to Liyana. "You will be asked by many to take messages into the Dreaming. Do not accept, but do not refuse."

Liyana nodded. She knew this.

"But if you have the opportunity, please . . . tell my Booka that his herd fattens well and his son . . . Tell him we are well, and we miss him."

Liyana swallowed. Her throat felt thick. "I am certain Uncle Booka is waiting for you."

Aunt Andra half smiled. "Of course he is. That man never did anything without my permission, except die." She left the tent, the last of the aunts and cousins to exit.

Liyana was alone.

Chapter Two

The tent smelled thick with her family's sweat and the greasy tinge of last night's dinner partially masked by a layer of burnt sage. Her own skin smelled sweet, and she felt stickiness behind her ears and in the pits of her knees where her relatives had missed rinsing the honey milk. She'd been left these few moments to meditate, but instead she fetched a damp rag from her bath and wiped the last of the sticky bits away. She'd never seen much point in meditation anyway, and she saw zero point in attracting flies with dried milk and honey. When she finished, she resumed her position on the stool.

The first visitor entered.

Kneeling at her feet, the man—her mother's third cousin—turned her wrists over to view her tattooed arms and then kissed her palms. "You will be honored in the Dreaming, and we will not waste your gift."

By tradition she was not required to respond, but she tried anyway. "Thank you. It is my honor and my joy to know you and yours will thrive."

He squeezed her shoulders and kissed both her cheeks as if she were his closest relative, instead of merely a distant one who he had spoken with only a handful of times. Tears were bright on his cheeks, and he scurried out of the tent without another word.

Her hands shook, and she clenched them tightly together. For the next visitor, she merely nodded her acceptance of the ritual words. After two more hours of farewells, she was grateful for the tradition that allowed her silence.

Others like Aunt Andra had messages for loved ones to take with her. A few of them shared memories they had of her so she could take those with her too. She'd forgotten that she'd burnt her first flatbread so badly that her cousins had used it to knock dates out of a tree. Also there was the time she'd wrestled a boy twice her age and won because she'd dropped leaves down his shirt and he'd thought they were a snake—this was several years before her dreamwalk had determined her fate and she was no longer permitted to risk herself in such games.

The children, having completed their morning chores, were allowed to visit her next. She endured their questions without throttling a single child, which she considered an achievement, especially since their questions included "Will it hurt?" and "What if your soul doesn't reach the Dreaming?" Some of them were old enough that they should have shown more discretion, and she privately hoped the rich feast tonight would cause them massive indigestion. But in truth, the children were hardest because Jidali was last among them.

Escorted to the tent by their mother, Jidali walked inside alone with the measured pace of a grown man. His chin was lifted high, and his shoulders were flung back so far that Liyana half expected him to pitch backward. He knelt at her feet and kissed her palms exactly as tradition dictated. She felt a surge of pride followed quickly by a sharp pang. She'd never see him as the man he would become.

All of a sudden it was hard to breathe. The air in the tent felt stiflingly hot. It pressed against the inside of her throat. She touched her brother's still baby-plump cheek, and with a cry, he flung himself forward and wrapped his arms around her waist. She bent over him and hugged his head and shoulders. He sobbed great, heaving sobs. His body shook against her. She didn't trust herself to speak.

At last he quieted. He sucked in air and then exhaled. His body stilled, though his hands were fists against her back as he continued to hold her. His voice was muffled by the fabric of her dress. "Why you?"

Liyana stroked his hair, soft as the finest carded goat's wool.

He knew that she had been born in the first Year of No Rain, and he knew that her dreamwalk had showed her connection to the Dreaming. But that wasn't what he meant, and she knew it because she'd asked that question too, silently in the night, over a hundred times since the day her fate was tattooed on her arms—the tattoos that said she was a vessel. "Did I ever tell you the story of the spider who wanted to fly?"

He shook his head and then sniffled.

She didn't dislodge him. No one would notice that a child's tears had dampened the elaborate embroidery. "She spun her web in the branches of a tamar tree, and day in and day out she watched the birds fly to and from their nest with food and water for their young. When she laid her own egg sac, she determined that that was how she would feed her children. If she fed them only what her web caught, then a mere quarter would survive. But if she could fly and fetch the scorpions and beetles that scurried on the desert floor, then more of her children would survive. Perhaps even all."

Jidali curled up at her feet and lay his head on her lap. For an instant, her voice caught. He'd done this a thousand times, and this would be the last. She got control of herself and continued. "And so, the spider spun herself wings from her finest thread. She wound them around her back legs, and she stretched them with her front legs. When she was ready, she climbed to the top branch of the tamar tree, and she spread her silk wings. The wind blew

Sarah Beth Durst

against them, and they puffed behind her. Pushing off the branch, she leapt into the air."

She heard a rustle in the doorway and glanced over to see her father. It was his turn next. Liyana nodded to him so he'd know she'd seen him, but she kept stroking Jidali's hair.

"But the desert wind battered her wings with sand, and the threads broke apart. She fell down, down, down into the tamar tree, and she died as she hit the branch where her egg sac lay. At that moment, the egg sac hatched, and with the food from her web and the food from the mother spider's own body, all of her children survived."

Jidali lifted his face toward her. "That is a horrible story."

"Of course it is," she said, "for the spider. But it's good news for you."

His cheeks were stained with tears and smeared with the dye that had leaked from her skirt. "What do you mean?"

"At least you don't have to eat me."

From the doorway, her father roared with laughter. Her brother started to smile, just a little. "Liyana, you have the strangest sense of humor ever," Jidali said.

"I love you, too, Jidali," she said. She hugged him again, wiped his face, and whispered into his ear. "I'll wait for you in the Dreaming. You will never be alone."

He wasn't crying when he left, and she knew the clan would pretend not to notice the puffiness of his eyes or his dripping

nose. He could remember the day with pride at his strength—
and at hers.

After Jidali left, it was her father's turn. He knelt and kissed
her palms.

"It feels strange for you to kneel before me," Liyana told him.

"I will honor you every day of my life, as I always have." He
kissed her cheeks and then departed. Her mother entered the
tent next.

Mother halted by the cooking fire pit. She put her hands on
her hips and pursed her lips. Unlike the others, she didn't kneel.
Instead, she briskly nodded once. "You'll do," Mother said, as if
approving a cut of meat for dinner.

"Of course I will," Liyana said. "I'm your daughter."

Mother's lips twitched. "A valid point." Solemn again, she
studied Liyana a moment longer. "I am proud of you." She then
swept out of the tent before the tears caused by that unexpected
compliment could prick Liyana's eyes. Liyana blinked fast, sucked
in the increasingly hot air, and composed herself to face her family's midday meal.

She was given a lunch of sugared dates, flatbread, and dried
mutton. Aunt Sabisa added Liyana's favorite yogurt to dip the
bread and meat in, and one of her uncles contributed his finest tea,
steeped in mint water. Her cousins draped her in napkins, which
turned out to be a good thing since they caught drips of the tea
and a smear of yogurt. Every time she thought of anything but

eating, it became impossible to swallow. So she focused with deep intensity on the gritty sugar in the dates that stuck to her teeth and the spices in the yogurt that pricked her tongue. Clustered around her, her family ate sparingly. They'd feast tonight, after the ceremony was complete, to welcome the goddess to their clan. The feast would also serve to remind the goddess of what it felt like to eat and that she would need to feed her new body in order to live. Liyana wondered if someone would have to show the goddess how to chew. Or how to perform other basic functions. She doubted that deities in their transcendent form ever had to pee.

She got herself through the day that way, thinking of mundanities and focusing on the needs of the moment. At times the heat inside the tent threatened to choke her and ruin her careful placidity. At every opportunity she drank water from a silver pitcher that a cousin continually refilled. She did not have to ration herself today.

At last it was dusk. Talu, the clan's magician and Liyana's teacher, came to claim her. Liyana's knees creaked as she stood— she'd sat for too long. She was more used to scrambling after the herds, hauling water from the well, and helping out with the myriad of tasks that kept the camp functioning. As a vessel, she had no specific responsibilities aside from preparing for the summoning ceremony, so she had poked her nose into everyone else's business. She'd never had a day like today. But then again, she supposed that no one in the clan had ever had a day like today, at least not in the last hundred years.

Talu rushed to Liyana and clasped her hands to her own heart. "Oh, to think I am here to see this glorious day!" She hooked Liyana's arm under hers and led her out of the tent. "I was there on the day you were born. You nearly died. The cord was wrapped around your neck." She drew a line across Liyana's neck to indicate where the umbilical cord had strangled her. "I sliced it away. Your first breath was an indignant scream. You were so angry that the cord had dared to stop your breath that you screamed for three hours. Your poor, tired mother nearly put you out with the goats so she could sleep."

"What calmed me?" Liyana asked, even though she had heard the story at least a dozen times. Up ahead, she saw that the torches were lit in a ring. Voices drifted through the evening air, as if buoyed by the heat that still filled the breeze.

"A sandstorm," Talu said with a chuckle. "You heard the wind batter the tent and the sand wolves howl, and you fell fast asleep."

Picturing her mother threatening her with the goats, Liyana was able to smile as she was led to the heart of the oasis. The entire clan waited for her around a bare circle of sand. Her smile faltered as she stepped into the circle, ringed by everyone she knew and would ever know.

"Breathe, child," Talu whispered in her ear. "You are strong. You are ready." She kissed both of Liyana's cheeks. "Honor us."

Seated north of the circle, the elders beat drums with the heels of their palms. Slow and even, the drumbeats spread across the darkening desert. With measured steps, Talu walked in a circle around Liyana. Liyana rotated with her, watching as Talu dragged her toes to etch a line in the sand, symbolically separating Liyana from the rest of the clan. As she turned, Liyana saw familiar faces. Cousins. Aunts. Uncles. Friends. She lingered on a boy's face, Ger's. He'd also been born in the Year of No Rain, but his dreamwalk had showed only desert horses racing across the sand. He'd been apprenticed to one of the riders, and she'd heard he rode well. Beside him was Esti. She and Liyana had been friends as children. They'd chased sandfish lizards in the shade of the date palm trees, and they'd made necklaces of woven dried leaves for each other. Liyana noticed that Esti held tightly to Ger's hand. She'd heard they planned to announce their claim at the next festival. She should have remembered to wish them well. Continuing to turn, she focused on other faces in the crowd, family and friends. She wanted to shout over the drumbeats. She regretted her silence during the farewells. There were so many things she hadn't yet said! She'd thought she'd had time before, but now it didn't seem like she'd had any time at all. Days had slipped away. Squeezing her eyes shut, she tried to think of one day, an ordinary day, and fix it in her memory: waking in her sleeping roll in the cold dawn, breathing the scorched air of the afternoon, playing ball with Jidali by the goat herd, taking lessons with Talu, sharing the evening meal with her family, tasting the night tea. She imagined holding that day inside her as she opened her eyes.

Talu had completed her circle.

Oh, sweet goddess, I'm not ready! Liyana felt her muscles lock. She'd trained every day. She knew the steps in her sleep. But she looked into her mind, and it was a void, as if the memory of one sun-drenched day had seared away all her training.

In the center of the circle, the magician lowered herself to her knees. She crossed her arms and began to chant. "Bayla, Bayla, Bayla. *Ebuci o nanda wadi,* Bayla, Bayla, Bayla. *Ebuci o yenda,* Bayla, Bayla, Bayla. *Vessa oenda nasa we.*" Around the circle, the clan joined in the chant, repeating the ancient words to summon the spirit of the goddess Bayla. Their voices didn't matter, though. Only a magician's voice could reach the Dreaming, the home of the spirits of the clan gods. "Come and breathe the desert, Bayla," the words said. "Come and be. Your vessel is ready for you."

The drums beat louder.

Listening to them, Liyana felt her muscles loosen. Her feet, encased in the soft shoes, rocked forward and then back. She lifted her arms, and her sleeves fell to her shoulders, revealing the markings. She flicked her palms toward the darkening sky. The air was still hot on her skin, sucking out moisture and wicking away the sweat left over from a day inside the stifling tent. She swung her hips.

Thud, thud, thud. The drumbeats were footfalls. She matched their pace. Forward two steps, back one, she danced around Talu. The woman's voice was as strong and clear as a herder's horn. "Bayla, Bayla, Bayla. *Ebuci o nanda wadi . . .*" Liyana spun, and her skirt spun with her, spreading like a bird's wings. Blue, red, and green flickered in the torchlight, and the gold thread glittered. Forward two steps, back one . . . forward and back. Arms raised, she spun faster. "*Ebuci o yenda,* Bayla, Bayla, Bayla!"

Her clan, her family, cried to the sky. "Bayla, Bayla, Bayla!"

She was the dance. Her body knew it; each step had been drilled into her muscles by hours of daily practice. Her legs whipped beneath the skirt as she spun, arms open wide. Her feet flew over the sand.

Faster . . . *Thud, thud, thud.* "*Vessa oenda nasa we!*"

Overhead, the sky deepened to azure, and the desert darkened. Stars materialized as if someone were flinging shimmering droplets across the sky. Liyana's breath burned in her throat, and her lungs ached. She felt her muscles strain, but she welcomed it. She'd danced to this point and far beyond in her training. She had only begun to dance.

The bells in her hair sang between the drumbeats. Her feet beat staccato on the sand as her arms beckoned the goddess's soul. She sang the summoning words with her people. "*Ebuci . . . ebuci . . .*" "Come! Come! Your vessel is ready!"

As the hours passed, her feet felt the sand cool through the soles of her shoes. She had ceased to notice the faces outside the circle. The drums continued to beat, and Talu continued to chant.

Stars watched cold from the sky above. The torches threw their light into the circle. Her feet stabbed the cold sand, worn from the pattern of her dance. She heard whispers between the drumbeats, voices from beyond the circle.

One carried itself to her ears. "She hasn't come."

Liyana's feet faltered. Quickly she caught the step, and she twirled and spun in time with the drumbeats. But the words wormed themselves into Liyana's mind. By now, the goddess should have come. Her soul should have filled Liyana's body, and Liyana's soul should have been displaced. She should have been drawn to the Dreaming while the goddess breathed her first breath with Liyana's lungs.

Talu's voice was hoarse, but still it echoed across the camp. Liyana noticed that someone had draped furs around the old woman's shoulders. The night wind whipped past the tents and chilled Liyana's skin. Her bells continued to ring, and she continued to dance, but each move felt stiff. *She hasn't come,* Liyana thought. *She should have come!*

The moon etched a path across the sky. Still, Liyana danced. And still, her goddess did not come.

Chapter Three

At dawn the drums ceased.

Liyana collapsed forward into the sand. Sky serpents circled above her, their glass scales catching the rose and gold rays of sunrise, and scattering them like a thousand jewels onto the desert below. Songbirds called to one another from the tops of the date palm trees. Chest heaving, Liyana tried to swallow. Her throat felt raw from breathing so hard for so long. Her braids were plastered against her cheeks and neck with her dried sweat. On hands and knees, she dug her fingers into the sand. These were still her hands. This was still her body.

Talu's voice died, and Liyana raised her head and felt the first kiss of sunrise on her face. Dawn dyed the sand dunes red as it had yesterday. She shouldn't be here to see it again.

Around her, the clan was silent. She noticed only a few children remained, and young men and women had replaced the old as drummers. Their hands rested limply on the skins of their drums. A few covered their faces with their hands.

Someone in the clan keened.

Liyana looked at her parents' faces. Her father's was ashen, his eyes sunk deep, dried tears etching his cheeks like scars. Her mother's face was frozen, as if she had forgotten how to feel.

"She didn't come," Liyana whispered. "Talu, why didn't she come?" Her body was shaking like a palm tree in a windstorm. She wrapped her arms around herself. Every muscle screamed, and her bones felt like liquid. She wasn't supposed to feel anymore. "Talu . . ."

"My children, my children!" a woman wailed. She was the master weaver, a woman with five daughters and three sons. "You have killed their future!" Two of her children huddled behind her skirt. Eyes wide, they looked like spooked horses.

Liyana could find no words in her throat. Once a century, the goddess of the Goat Clan walked among them and ensured that her clan could survive the next one hundred years. She used a human body to work the magic that would fill the wells, revitalize the oases, and increase the herds. Without this infusion of magic . . . In an ordinary century, this would be a disaster. But now, in the time of the Great Drought, it meant death. Already this oasis was a tenth the size it once was. Others were worse. Many of the desert wells held only a few buckets' worth of undrinkable salty brine, and most of the others had dried up a full month earlier than they used to. Half the herd had sickened over the last season. Children were too thin, and they had lost far too many of their elders to illness. They needed Bayla more now than they ever had.

Others took up the master weaver's cry. Liyana felt each voice as if it were a whip on her skin. Talu raised her arms in front of her face as if to ward off invisible blows. Shoulder to shoulder, the clans people pressed forward, crowding together outside the circle that Talu had drawn in the sand. Their shouts overlapped until Liyana could not distinguish individual words. Startled, the birds fled the trees, darkening the sky with their bodies.

"Silence."

The word rolled over the clan.

All voices faded, like wind falling in the wake of a sandstorm. All eyes fixed on their chief, Chief Roke. It was his bellow from a chest as broad as a horse's that had cut through the cries.

Chieftess Ratha, his wife, drew herself up to her impressive full height. With her headdress of feathers and leaves, she towered over those around her. She spoke into the silence. "Talu, tell us what has occurred." Her voice was soft, yet it carried across the oasis like a rumble of thunder.

"I sent my words to the Dreaming," Talu said. Her voice cracked and splintered. "Bayla should have come!" Tears poured down the wrinkles in her ancient cheeks.

Murmurs spread around the circle. Talu could not heal a broken body, but she could ease its pain. She could not summon water to the wells, but she could sense how little remained. She couldn't work miracles, but this . . . this was a small magic. She could not have failed.

Chieftess Ratha turned to Liyana. Her face was as expressionless as the sand itself. "You danced true. Yet the goddess did not fill you. Why did she not come to you?"

Unable to explain, Liyana shook her head.

Talu's voice was broken. "Liyana, what did you do?"

Liyana flinched at her teacher's words. She had done all she'd been asked! She had eaten only the food Talu had approved, she had strengthened her muscles every day, she had protected her unblemished skin from the scorching sun, she had preserved her purity, she had perfected the summoning dance . . . But it hadn't been enough. Bayla hadn't come. Her eyes hot with unshed tears, Liyana could only shake her head again.

"She was unworthy!" a woman cried.

The clan erupted into shouts. Each shout felt like a spear hurled at her body. "Unfit! Unworthy!" Pressing closer, the clan crammed together at the edge of the circle. One hand—Liyana didn't see whose—threw a rock. It smacked the sand beside her.

Louder than them all, Liyana's mother roared, "My daughter is more than worthy! Bayla has judged *us*! We, her people, are unworthy! Bayla punishes us!"

Another rock hit the sand.

Talu cried out. And then a rock smashed into Liyana's back. Liyana dropped onto the sand and curled into a tight ball as rocks rained around her and Talu. One hit Liyana's shoulder. Another, her thigh.

A high-pitched shriek split the angry shouts, and a small form darted over the line in the sand. Liyana felt a warm body hurl itself on top of her. Her little brother wrapped his arms around her, covering her body with his. "Stop!" he yelled. "Stop, stop, stop! Don't hurt my sister!"

The rocks stopped.

The clan fell silent.

Liyana unwound herself, and she embraced Jidali. "I am sorry, Jidali," she whispered into his small shoulders. "I failed you. I am so sorry." For the first time in weeks, she cried. Her tears fell into his hair. Holding him, she rocked back and forth.

"People of the Goat Clan, your elders will discuss this matter," Chief Roke said. He strode to the council tent, and he raised the tent flap. Slowly the elders filed into the tent.

Chieftess Ratha addressed the clan. "Leave here and begin your day. You have tasks that will not complete themselves." She fixed her formidable glare on each of them, as if her eyes could burn them like the noonday sun.

Slowly the clan dispersed.

Rocking Jidali, Liyana listened to the footfalls as her people retreated from the circle. Ordinary noises returned. Above, wind rustled through the dry leaves of the parched palm trees. Across the camp, the herd bleated for breakfast. Inside a tent, a baby cried.

She lifted her head and met the eyes of the master weaver. The woman spat into the circle, and then the weaver's sister forced her to leave. On the opposite side of the circle, Ger led Esti away, and Liyana's childhood friend kept looking back at Liyana. At last only Liyana's family remained.

Checking right and left, Aunt Sabisa scurried across the line in the sand and into the circle. She pried Jidali's arms off Liyana. Liyana let him go. Clucking to the boy, Aunt Sabisa led him beyond the circle and away toward the family tent. Liyana's cousins, aunts, and uncles trudged after them.

Her parents did not move.

Liyana couldn't bring herself to speak to them. She laid her cheek against the sand. Talu still sat cross-legged a few feet away. She hadn't moved from that position, even when the stones were thrown. Liyana wondered if she sat by choice or if her old bones had betrayed her. As her student, Liyana knew she should help her mentor stand, should fetch her cane, should seek to make her comfortable. But Liyana felt as if she had melted into the sand.

Talu didn't speak. Neither did Liyana.

Overhead, the sun bleached the sky. As it rose higher, the heat soaked into the sand and rocks. Liyana felt it searing her skin, the skin she had been so careful to protect because it wouldn't always be hers. She let it burn until her father brought a makeshift shelter, a blanket propped up on two sticks, for her and Talu. He also pressed a waterskin into each of their hands.

"Drink," he said.

Talu let the waterskin drop from her fingers.

Her father replaced it in Talu's hands. "Drink," he repeated.

Three more times, they repeated this, with Talu letting the waterskin fall out of her fingers and Liyana's father patiently replacing it. At last Liyana raised herself to her knees, drank her own water, and then leaned over and lifted Talu's water to her lips. "The elders will know what to do," Liyana said. "You must drink so that you're ready to do it."

Talu sipped once and then withdrew. Liyana tilted the water to her teacher's lips until the precious liquid poured out over her chin and Talu drank. Liyana persisted until half the water was gone. She then let the old woman rest. She didn't look at her father.

"You don't need to stay here on display," her father said. "Come inside our tent."

Liyana shook her head so hard that her vision tilted. She steadied herself with a hand on the sand. Her palm landed in one of the depressions she'd made as she'd danced.

"Let her stay if she wishes," Mother said.

Her father retreated to outside the circle, and he sat with

Mother in the shadow of the council tent. Side by side, they kept vigil over the circle. And the sun moved on in the sky.

Late in the afternoon, as the heat baked the oasis and the wind failed to stir the sand, the elders emerged from the council tent. Chief Roke placed a goat horn to his lips and blasted a single note. As the note died, it was replaced by the sound of footsteps in sand and over rock as the clan returned. In minutes, everyone that Liyana had ever known surrounded the ceremonial circle. Kneeling, Liyana bowed her head and waited.

"Talu," the chief said. "Hear our verdict."

The magician lifted her head. Her face was lined with deep creases, as if she'd aged another decade during her time in the circle. She looked so sunken that Liyana feared her bones would collapse inward.

"We heard you chant the words of our ancestors. Indeed, we chanted with you," Chieftess Ratha said. "And so, we know your words were pure and true."

"My words were pure and true," Talu said, "and they journeyed far."

"You have never failed in your magic," Chieftess Ratha said. "Yet Bayla did not come."

Talu lifted her chin higher. Some of the shadows faded from her face, and her voice strengthened. "Bayla would never forsake us. We are her people."

Murmurs spread through the crowd. The chieftess inclined

her head to show that she'd heard Talu's words as the chief said, "Liyana, hear our verdict."

Chieftess Ratha addressed Liyana. "Talu's words flew true and far, and we do not doubt the goddess's love. Therefore, there is only one explanation: Bayla has deemed you an unfit vessel." Her voice was kind, though her words were knives.

Unfit vessel.

Other elders spoke, echoing this verdict, but Liyana did not hear them. She felt the weight of the words press her against the sand. She wanted to sink deeper and deeper until the desert poured into her ears and her mind, and erased the horror of her failure. *Unfit. Unworthy.* She was so broken and so soiled that the goddess had chosen to condemn them all, rather than come to her.

Her mother's voice broke through the downward spiral of Liyana's thoughts. "You saw my daughter dance. She did not falter. All night she danced beyond any reasonable expectation. She does not deserve your blame." Mother's fists were planted on her hips.

"Whom do you blame? Our goddess?" The chief's voice was like the rumble that preceded a lightning storm.

Liyana's father laid a hand on Mother's arm.

"This is not about blame, and we do not act to punish," Chieftess Ratha said, her voice smooth but expressionless. "We act only for the good of the tribe. We will travel to Yubay without

Liyana. There we will dreamwalk anew and hope to discover the true vessel."

Liyana felt as if her blood had congealed within her veins. Every breath hurt.

"We travel on, and she remains." Her father's voice was flat. "She'll die. You want us to abandon our daughter to death."

"If Bayla chooses her, then the goddess will claim her body here and rejoin us. If Bayla does not, then we will be free of the taint of an unworthy vessel and can try again."

"There is no 'try again'!" Aunt Sabisa said. She wagged her finger at the chief and chieftess, and also at Talu. "You read the dreams. You consulted your hearts. You said Liyana was our vessel!"

Shakily Talu pushed herself to her knees and slowly, painfully she rose to her feet. "The verdict of the elders is for the good of the tribe. We must try to find another, or else we are all doomed."

Liyana felt as if Talu had stabbed her. For years Talu had trained her. For hours every day, she had lectured her and coached her and prepared Liyana for her sacrifice. She had waxed poetic about her pride in Liyana, and she had bolstered her every time Liyana had felt any doubt.

"But I am your vessel!" Liyana raised her arms so that her tattoos were displayed. "In my dreamwalk, Bayla chose me!"

Talu met her eyes. "In the ceremony, she did not." Deliberately, ceremonially, she turned her back on Liyana.

"In Yubay," Chieftess Ratha declared, "we will draw a new circle and weave a new untainted dress for a more worthy vessel." Others turned their backs on Liyana as well.

"I can dance again!" Liyana jumped to her feet. She felt pain shoot through her aching leg muscles. Her breath hissed out. She mastered it and continued, "If we made another circle now . . . or tried another oasis . . . or chose another night . . ."

"The night does not matter. The place does not matter. And the circle is tradition, not necessity," Talu said, still facing away from Liyana. "The goddess comes when a vessel dances and a magician chants. But the chant must be magic, and the vessel must be worthy."

"Please, then let me come to Yubay," Liyana begged. "Let me dreamwalk again. Let me prove my worth to you and to Bayla!"

"Child, listen to me," Chieftess Ratha said. "If Bayla has rejected us, then you will be spared suffering with us. But if she has only rejected *you*, then your sacrifice here will spare the clan by removing your impurity. And if she has *not* rejected you or us, then she will come to you and all will be well!" She smiled as if that would sweeten her words.

"She'll die of exposure," Mother said. "Her death will be on your hands."

"If that is Bayla's will, then so be it," Chief Roke said, his voice a rumble. "Your daughter is lost to you regardless. If we leave her here, you may have a chance to give your son a future."

His words felt like a stab. Jidali! Liyana looked across the camp toward her family's tent where her little brother was. Only yesterday she had been prepared to sacrifice herself for his future. Could she do any less today?

"Please, do not do this," Father begged.

"It has been decided," Chief Roke said.

Already, throughout the camp, families packed up their tents and belongings. She heard the sound of hammers and the clang of pots. No one spoke, but the goats bleated as the herds were gathered for departure. *They are right to leave me,* her practical side whispered to her. This could save the clan. She still had a chance to save Jidali and her parents and everyone. She felt the fight leach out of her, and she bowed her head.

"Then we will remain with her!" Father said.

The chief and chieftess spoke in unison. "You may not." There was pity in the chieftess's voice as she added, "We understand your wish to protect your daughter. But the clan must act as one, or it is as if we did not act at all."

The master weaver pushed to the front. "She failed! You must see that. It's time to look to the good of all our children, not merely this one!"

Father's face flushed purple. His hands curled into fists. Beside him, Mother stood as straight as a palm tree. Her chin was lifted, and she looked as if she were a chieftess. Their posture said: *We will not be denied.*

"Without Bayla, how much longer will we survive the Great Drought? A handful of seasons? Less? You cannot risk us all for one!" the master weaver said. Her voice was shrill. "If we must, we will drag you with us."

"Try," Father growled.

Liyana held up her hands. "No."

All eyes turned toward her.

"I accept my fate," Liyana said.

Mother opened her mouth to argue.

"Please," Liyana said. "I failed you once already. I won't fail the clan again."

In the end, it took Talu leading her parents by the hands as if they were children before they would leave the circle. Talu did not permit them near Liyana. They had said their good-byes, she told them. More would be too difficult for all of them.

Liyana was grateful for that kindness. She didn't think she could face another day of farewells, especially feeling the full weight of her failure and the uncertainty of the clan's future. She retreated beneath the blanket shelter that Father had set up earlier. She drank a sip of water. Curling around the waterskin, she lay in the sand in the shade.

Around her, tents were lowered and rolled. Supplies were compacted and stowed away. The oasis was stripped of dates and palm leaves and any other material that would be useful on the journey. As the sun marched its way toward dusk, the clan loaded everything onto carts and wagons and horses. No one spoke to Liyana. No one even looked at her. She closed her eyes so she could not see her clan treating her as if she were already dead. She may have even slept.

She woke to a tickle by her ear. "Shh," Jidali whispered. He pressed something cool and smooth into her hand.

Blinking her eyes open, she looked at her palm. She saw a clear crystal-like knife with a carved bone handle. "I can't take this!"

He shook her. "I said, 'shh'!"

"But it's your inheritance." This knife was made from the scale of a sky serpent. It had been passed through the family for generations. Though it looked like glass, it could cut through anything, even rock, even bone. "No, Jidali."

"Yes," he hissed. "I won't leave unless you take it."

She glared at him for threatening her, and he scowled back. She warred with the thought of calling out. Any adult who was nearby would intervene and give the knife to Father. Jidali would be hauled back to the tent and forced to leave.

She couldn't do that to him.

Someday he'll reclaim it, she told herself. She'd leave it where he could find it, perhaps by the well or near the first date palm tree that Jidali had ever climbed—she'd shown him how, and he'd followed her up without hesitation, scampering as if he'd been born in a tree. She swallowed hard, choking back the memory. "Thank you," she said.

He wrapped his pudgy arms around her neck and whispered into her hair, "I am glad you are still you."

"*Jidali!*" Aunt Sabisa's voice cut across the camp.

"Go," Liyana said. Other words stuck in her throat. She'd said them all yesterday.

Fiercely Jidali said, "Stay alive."

He ran across the camp without looking back.

In another hour, the oasis was bare. The Goat Clan was ready. Judging by the low sun, they would have about two hours of dusk travel before they'd be forced to stop. If this were a usual move, they would have left at dawn. And if this were a usual move, Liyana would have been scurrying around her family's packs, ensuring that every knot was tight and that nothing was forgotten. She hoped her family had remembered everything they needed. And then she tried not to think at all. Curled underneath the shade of the blanket, she listened to her family and her people leave the oasis as the sun sank toward the western horizon.

Chapter Four

A lone, Liyana stroked the cool blade of the sky serpent knife. *Stay alive,* her little brother had said. But this blade could promise her the opposite. One quick slice, and her soul would (finally) leave her body.

She spent several minutes imagining a confrontation with Bayla in the Dreaming. First she'd ask, "Why?" And then she'd shame the goddess into selecting a new vessel. She'd tell her about Jidali, who deserved a future; about Talu, who honored Bayla with every breath she took; about Ger and Esti, who wanted to marry and start a family; and about Liyana's aunts and uncles and cousins, who all had their own hopes and dreams.

She laid the blade against her neck. It chilled her skin.

"Idiot," she said out loud. She lowered the knife. Her reflection flashed across the glass-like surface. If Bayla had truly rejected her, then the goddess would refuse to speak with her. And if Bayla had *not* rejected her, then the goddess would be extremely put out if Liyana slit the throat of her new body.

Besides, Liyana planned for Jidali to find his gift again some-day. He shouldn't find it pressed against the throat of his sister.

She tucked the knife into her sash. The desert could take care of killing her if it wanted to. She didn't have to help it. In the meantime, since she wasn't about to slit her own throat, she also wasn't going to allow herself to freeze to death in the night. Liyana pushed herself to standing. Her muscles protested, and she felt as if they were shrieking. The bone handle of the knife dug into her rib cage.

As the desert sank into dusk, Liyana used a flat rock to dig a shallow hole. Testing its length, she lay in it. The sand within was chilled compared to the surface. She rose. Dead leaves were matted under a date palm tree. She spread the leaves in a thick layer in her hole. She then stacked rocks to block the night wind. She stopped only when her arms ached too much to continue.

By now the temperature had plummeted. She retrieved the blanket that had been her shade earlier, and wrapped it tightly around her as she crawled between the dried leaves. She pulled several of the leaves over her head. Looking up through the slits, she counted the stars and listened to the wind and tried not to think. She felt the knife hilt against her ribs, its solid pressure comforting her. Eventually she slept.

She woke stiff and cold as dawn peeked over the edge of the world. Stretching, she shifted, and the leaves rustled around her. She felt a dry rope glide over her ankle, and her eyes popped open. She didn't move. She didn't breathe.

Snake, she thought.

She felt its scaled body resettle against her leg. Her heart pounded hard within her rib cage. A scream built up in her throat. *Don't move,* she told herself. Soon the desert temperature would rise, and the snake would want to sun itself on the rocks, rather than press against her body for warmth.

Liyana lay motionless. She breathed shallowly and slowly. Her bladder ached to relieve itself, and her muscles felt knotted. Soon her tongue felt thick and dry from thirst, and her stomach rumbled and rolled. The snake didn't move.

She watched through the palm leaves as the sun inched its way higher into the sky. She had a view of the sliver of sky above the stone mountains. Light spread over the barren peaks. Slowly her nest heated. She began to sweat within her blanket. Still the snake didn't budge.

Perhaps Bayla had sent it. Instead of the knife, this was to be Liyana's death. *Or perhaps the snake was merely cold,* she thought. She shouldn't assume divine intervention. She'd never heard of any story in which a god sent a snake to kill. According to all the tales, deities couldn't influence the real world while they were in the Dreaming—that was the reason they needed vessels.

After what felt like an eon, the snake stirred. Liyana held her breath as the snake slithered down her leg toward her foot. It crossed over her beautiful shoes, and then the palm leaves rustled as the snake poked through them to greet the sun.

Slowly, very slowly, Liyana withdrew her legs and tucked them beneath her. Reaching into her sash, she pulled out the sky serpent knife. The snake had exited near her feet. Most likely it was sunning itself on the rocks she had gathered. Liyana inched backward, and the bells in her hair tinkled. She halted and listened for the snake. Her palm sweat, and the knife blade felt slippery. She didn't hear anything. She scooted out of the pile of leaves.

Watching for the snake, Liyana grabbed one of the poles that Father had used to prop up the blanket. She held it like a spear as she scanned the rocks.

Sweet Bayla, it's a cobra.

Curled on a rock, the diamond cobra raised its head. Its tongue flicked in and out. It hadn't pinpointed her location yet. For an instant, she stared at it, frozen by the knowledge that its venom could kill a grown man in three hours of exquisite pain.

One, two, three . . . The bells in her hair rang as she lunged toward the snake and slammed the tip of the pole into its neck. Fangs out, the cobra struck the pole as she pinned it against a rock. Quickly she sliced its head off with the sky serpent knife.

The blade slid through the snake as if she were slicing sand, and the head toppled into her makeshift bed.

Her heart pounded painfully hard as she grabbed the second pole and used the two to lift the still-venomous head out of the palm leaves. She laid it carefully on a rock. Its fangs were open, and the yellowish venom oozed over the snake's chin. The snake's body twitched. She picked it up by the tail and held the body in the air until it quit writhing. She then laid the body on another rock, sat back hard on the palm leaves, and tried to remember how to breathe.

If she had rolled while she'd slept, if the snake hadn't crawled out, if she'd been slower to spear it, if it had reacted faster to her movement or to the sound of the bells in her hair . . . With shaking hands, Liyana used a leaf to clean the blood off the sky serpent blade, and then she sliced off the tips of her braids, letting the tiny silver bells fall to the ground.

If her family were here, Mother would have skinned the cobra in two seconds, and Father would have peppered it with spices and cooked it until crispy. And then Aunt Andra would have sneaked her share to Jidali, who would have gobbled it up and told all his friends that his sister had killed it with her bare hands and teeth. A half laugh, half sob burst out of her lips. She scooped the bells into her hands. Since she wasn't ready to part with the knife yet, perhaps she could leave the bells for her family to find.

Carrying the bells, she crossed to the circle that Talu had

drawn. She halted and stared at it. Already the wind had begun to erase it, as if it were erasing all hope. Liyana wanted to redraw the circle and stay inside it. She had never expected to leave this circle. Losing the line in the sand felt . . . *She's not coming,* Liyana told herself. Wallowing in false hope was stupid. She'd leave the bells by her family's tent site, and then she'd . . . She had no idea. The horrible emptiness of that thought seized her.

Just complete this task, she told herself. *Leave the bells. Say your symbolic good-bye.* Then she'd figure out what to do next. Liyana stepped out of the circle.

She strode through the remains of the Goat Clan's camp. Walking over the indents left behind by tents, she felt as if she were walking over graves. Wind swirled sand over her feet. She tried not to think about how alone she was. In a few days, the wind would erase all traces of the tents, leaving only the stones from the cooking areas. That was where she intended to leave the bells.

Halfway across camp, she lost her bearings. She turned slowly in a circle, surveying the oasis, orienting herself with regard to the distant mountains and the sun. At last she spotted the vestiges of her family's goat enclosure. Her family had taken the posts and rope, but the holes were still visible. She located the cooking stones.

Obscured by sand, a sack lay next to the stones. It was a hunter's pack, designed to blend in with the desert. Her family must have overlooked it. Except . . . why was it by the cooking fire? Her family always kept packs by the front tent flap for ease of access. Pots, pans, and dishes belonged in the fire area. Indeed she could see the indent from Father's favorite teapot. Squatting next to the pack, she brushed off the sand that had settled on it overnight, and she opened it.

Liyana rocked back on her heels as she ogled the contents: a second waterskin, strips of dried meat, fire-starting flint from the desert mountains. . . . Reverently she took out the items one by one and spread them in front of her. A knife, one of her father's best. Clothes, her own sturdiest set. Herbs for healing. Spices for cooking. A sling and snare wire to help her hunt. A length of gauze-thin cloth to wrap over her face to protect against the sun and sand. Needle and thread inside one of her mother's embroidery pouches. Her father's favorite travel tent, consisting of a tarp and a set of flexible poles. Liyana cried as she touched each item. Even if Bayla had rejected her, her family hadn't. They wanted her to live.

She left the bells in place of the pack—as a thank-you, rather than the intended good-bye—and she carried the pack back to the ceremonial circle. She dumped her precious new supplies next to her makeshift shelter.

Renewed, she bustled into action. First she needed water. Taking the two waterskins, she crossed to the oasis's well. It was protected with a thick stone that prior generations had carted there ages ago. She laid her back against it, braced her feet, and pushed. It scooted an inch. She took a deep breath and pushed again. Another inch. She shoved again. Inch by inch, the stone scraped across the top of the well until she could see inside. Panting, she swallowed, and her tongue felt like wool in her mouth. Nearly at its zenith, the sun blazed down on her. She felt for the rope that held the bucket and lowered it. The bucket scraped bottom, and she pulled it up slowly, careful not to spill any of the precious liquid. She drank, draining half the bucket, and then lowered it again. She filled the waterskin Father had given her yesterday and the new waterskin from the pack. Leaving the stone off the well so she could fetch more water later, she returned to her little camp.

Carrying rocks from nearby fire pits, she built her own cooking area beside her nest of palm leaves. She located a pile of sun-dried goat dung and carried it over to be her fuel, and she crumpled a dried palm leaf for kindling. She struck the flint and started her fire. Once she had a steady blaze, she skinned the snake, wound it around one of her poles, and laid it over her fire to cook. She buried the snake's head.

While the snake cooked, she focused on enhancing her shelter. Keeping her same shallow hole (but checking it for snakes and scorpions), she set up Father's tent and secured it with rocks around the outside.

By now the sun was directly overhead and felt as harsh as a fist. Liyana ducked into her tent with her snake meat and waterskins, and she ate and drank. She then stripped off her ceremonial dress, washed herself with the smallest amount of water she could spare, and dressed in more practical clothes. Carefully she folded the dress and placed it at the bottom of her pack. She felt as if she were laying bones to rest.

When her tasks were done, she lay down in her tent to wait out the heat of the day. Perhaps in the evening, when the air wouldn't choke her, she'd climb one of the trees and pick any dates that the clan had missed. She'd also need to fetch more water, maybe hunt for more snakes or a desert rat. And then . . . she could survive today and tomorrow. Maybe a week.

And then what?

She was nearing the time of year when this oasis dried up. In three weeks, she wouldn't be able to stay here. But it would take a miracle for one girl, alone, to cross the desert and reach the next well. . . . And assuming she did, what next? What was she surviving for?

She wasn't supposed to live past yesterday. Ever since her dreamwalk, she had been the girl with no future. Others, like Ger and Esti, had made plans. Others looked ahead. She never had. She'd known her fate. But now . . . her future was as empty and terrifying as the desert that stretched around her in all directions.

* * *

Two hours later, Liyana heard the howls in the wind.

She slid the glass-like knife out of her sash and held it against her chest. The sand wolves sounded close. That meant a sandstorm would hit soon, and the wolves would run freely through camp. . . . Except there was no camp anymore. There was only her.

Clutching the knife, she huddled inside her tent. The tarp billowed and rolled. Usually during sandstorms, the clan huddled together in the center tents, using the outer tents as a buffer. The sheer number of people served as a deterrent to the wolves. She'd heard them often enough, but she'd never seen them. Tales said they were made of sand.

"Bayla, is this how you'll kill me?" she asked out loud. "There are easier ways. You could send another snake. I am sorry I ate the first one." Hearing her own voice made her feel braver. "He was delicious, though."

As sand pelted the tent, she told herself that this wasn't a punishment—Bayla couldn't punish her, not from within the Dreaming. Like the snake, this storm was merely a natural occurrence. She only had to ride through it, and the wolves would be swept away with the winds.

She repeated this to herself as the world darkened, as if day had switched with night. Sand slammed against the tarp. The tent swayed sideways and then snapped sharply back upright. The poles shook, and she wondered if they'd snap. She cringed each time the wind knocked the tent back and forth. She wished she'd left rocks inside. She could have used them to brace the poles—or simply to be doing something other than listening to the howls of the wind and wolves.

The wolves were much too close.

Sand wolves hunted within sandstorms. In children's tales, they carried away boys and girls who did not obey their parents' warnings to hide from the storms. In adult tales, they slaughtered any goat, sheep, or horse that was not sheltered or guarded. They killed hunters who failed to outrun the storm and anyone foolish enough to be out alone.

She had to hope that they didn't notice her tent. It was all she could do: hope and wait. The paralyzing helplessness was almost worse than the storm itself.

Sand slipped through the gaps in the seams, and it swirled inside the tent. Liyana wrapped the facecloth around her head to keep the grains from stinging her eyes. Each inhale was filled with grit. She breathed only through her nose. It didn't help. She felt as if her lungs were coated with sand.

Outside, the howling came closer.

She saw a shadow surge past the door flap, and then she saw it again, darker than the already dark shadows that squeezed the tent. Her heart hammered in her chest. She crouched, knife in hand.

Another shadow ran past. This time the tent swayed as the shadow brushed it. She saw it pass again. *It's circling*, she realized. *Oh, sweet Bayla!*

The sandstorm screamed. Wind hit so hard that the tent shook as if it were about to collapse. The roof bent in on her, and she braced it with a hand as she ducked. It then billowed up before bending down again. The walls shuddered, and the rocks that had pinned the edges outside rolled and crashed against one another.

Suddenly the tent wall split.

Claws of sand raked through the tarp, and a wolf jabbed his head into the tent. His face was hardened sand, and his eyes were holes. Sand sloughed off his muzzle as he tilted his head back. Liyana scrambled backward as he howled. His jaws . . . As he spread them wide, she saw his teeth were sharp rocks. He lunged toward her.

She dove to the side—too slow. Hard as stone, sand claws raked her arm. She felt pain shoot up to her shoulder, and she screamed. Twisting, he snapped his jaws at her, and she rolled backward. His teeth closed on air.

Wind whipped into the exposed tent, and sand flayed her. She saw the shape of the wolf, blurred by the swirling sand. He leaped for her again, and she struck toward his throat as she ducked beneath his jaws.

She felt the blade slide in.

And then sand, only sand, fell over her as the sand wolf disintegrated around the sky serpent knife. Coughing and spitting, she wiped the sand away from the cloth over her face, and then she lunged for the hole in the tent. Yanking it closed, she held it shut against the wind.

Outside, the wind roared. She heard other wolves. Squeezing the tear shut with one hand, she readied her knife with the other. She'd heard no weapon could kill a sand wolf. She guessed no one had tried a sky serpent blade before. "Come and get me," she said. "Come and try."

She listened hard, every muscle tense. Slowly the howls retreated. The tent walls shook less. The sand inside the tent began to settle, and the world lightened as the blackness of the storm receded.

Her arm throbbed. She released the tarp and tucked away the knife. Her throat felt raw from the sand that she'd inhaled. Unwrapping the cloth around her face, she vomited on the floor of her tent. The sandy bile tore the inside of her throat. She wiped her mouth with a sand-crusted sleeve.

She felt sand clinging to her hair and sticking to her sweaty skin. Piece by piece, she peeled her clothes off her body and shook them out. Searching the pack, she found a clean cloth and wiped away as much of the sand as she could. Left alone, the sand would rub her skin raw. She poured a little water on the cloth and washed her face. Her fingers shook, but she forced herself to attend to one task at a time, and she avoided thinking.

Unable to delay any longer, she examined her arm. The rock-hard sand claws had raked through her skin, leaving four deep gashes. Sandy blood clumped around the wounds. She washed them out as best she could, which caused more blood to run down her arm and stain the sand. She pressed some of Mother's herbs onto the gashes, and she hissed through her teeth as the herbs stung. Leaving the herbs in place as she'd seen Mother do, she wrapped a clean cloth around the wounds and tied it. Blood stained the cloth.

One day alone and she was wounded. *Oh, goddess, if it becomes infected . . .* Liyana told herself firmly that she'd been lucky. If the wolf had broken through the tent behind her or if more wolves had followed, then all the herbs in the desert would not help. *Quit complaining,* she told herself. She'd use the herbs, and she'd keep her wounds as clean as she could.

Deliberately ignoring her aching arm, Liyana turned her attention to the tear in the tent, her next problem. If she couldn't seal the hole, then she wouldn't be safe from the next sandstorm. Or from ordinary wind. Or from any snake, scorpion, or spider that wanted to visit her for warmth. Liyana could patch it up. Yet another task to help her avoid thinking about her future. Between fixing her shelter, finding food, and fetching water—

Water! The well! She'd left the lid off! Liyana burst out of her tent. Outside, the oasis had been wiped clean. All the indents from the Goat Clan's camp had been smoothed away, and all the trees were coated in a layer of reddish tan. Sand choked the air, billowing and blowing. Afternoon sunlight filtered through, scattering off the particles so the oasis seemed to glow with an eerie light that appeared to come from everywhere at once. In this hazy half light, Liyana stumbled across the oasis for several minutes before determining the location of the well. She hurried toward it, and she tripped over the edge of the lid and sprawled. Her knee hit the stone, and pain shot through her. Tears pricked her eyes as she clutched her knee, and she whimpered.

After a moment, the pain receded to a throb that matched the throb in her arm. She tested her leg. She could stand, *thank the goddess*. Leaning over the edge of the well, she looked down. She saw only blackness. Hands shaking, she found the rope and bucket. The knot had held, which was one bit of good luck. She lowered the bucket. It hit bottom. Had it hit sooner than before, or had she just lowered it faster? She didn't know.

Please, Bayla, she silently begged. She couldn't survive without water, and dehydration was a terrible way to die. *Please.*

Liyana pulled the rope. She tried to pull steady and slow to avoid spilling. If she jerked the bucket up and spilled all the water, then she'd panic for no reason. But with each slow pull, the pain in her arm spiked until she felt dizzy. As the bucket got close to the top, she had to stop. She lowered her arm. It hurt so badly that her head swam. Gritting her teeth, she pulled the bucket up the rest of the way.

Wet sand.

It was full of wet sand.

She dug her fingers into it, and the sand clung to her skin. She made a fist, squeezing it, and then she flung it across the camp and screamed. Tears raged down her cheeks. She grabbed another clump and threw it. Continuing to scream, she hurled wet sand until the bucket was empty. She then fell to her knees and pummeled the sand that had piled up beside the well.

"I did everything right!" she screamed at it. "I worked. I trained. I did everything that was asked of me. I dedicated my life! I was pure! I was fit! I was worthy! *You* betrayed *me!* You . . ." Unable to find more words, she threw fistfuls of dry sand with her unhurt arm.

Her eyes were so blinded by tears and sand that she did not see the man walking toward her through the hazy air until he was only a few feet away. Hand raised with a fist full of sand, Liyana froze. She panted, her rib cage heaving. Her arm began to shake. She stared at the silhouette of the man—boy, really.

He came closer, and she saw he was beautiful: sculpted face, shadow-dark skin, haunting eyes. *He's not real,* she thought. He had to be a dream that her addled brain had produced.

Dropping her arm, she rose to her feet.

He didn't vanish.

He spoke. "I have been looking for you."

Chapter Five

Clamping his hands on her wrists, the boy twisted her arms to expose her tattoos. Liyana kicked him in the knee and sprang backward. She pulled out her sky serpent knife and held it in front of her. "Touch me again," she said, "and I will skewer you through the eye."

Clutching his knee, he winced. "I would prefer that you did not."

"Strangers do not touch me," she said. She had studiously kept this body pure. She would defend it with force if necessary.

Still favoring his knee, he executed a sweeping bow. "I am Korbyn. You are the vessel of Bayla, as your marks confirm. There, we are not strangers anymore."

She didn't lower the knife. He hadn't named his clan or his

ancestors, and Korbyn was a common name, often used by those who wished to hide their own name.

He sighed as if she were a child who had disappointed her teacher—it was an oddly old sigh from a boy who looked to be the same age as she was. "This is not a situation I have been in before. Would you like to offer me tea? I have traveled a long way to find you."

She didn't recall falling asleep, but this had the same insane logic of a dream. Handsome strangers didn't suddenly appear in an empty desert and request tea. "There's sand in the water. We can't have tea."

He peered into the dark shaft of the well. "You should have covered the well before the sandstorm," he said unhelpfully.

"Who are you truly?" she asked. There were a dozen more questions that went with it: Where had he come from? Why was he here? What did he want? "It's a hundred miles to the next well." She saw no horse. He carried no pack. He didn't have deposits of sand trapped in the folds of his clothes, the way he should have after a sandstorm. There was no sand plastered to his skin, like there was on her cheeks. In fact, he looked perfect, as if an artist had crafted an ideal boy with shining eyes, baby-soft black hair, and smiling lips.

He lowered the bucket into the well. It smacked the bottom.

For a moment he stared into the well. Around them, the wind paused, as if it held its breath. And then Korbyn relaxed. "That should do it," he said cheerfully. Yanking on the rope, he pulled the bucket up with careless ease. Water sloshed over the brim as he hefted the bucket over the lip of the well.

Liyana felt her mouth drop open. Her mother would have tapped her chin and told her not to catch flies. Or maybe her mother would have been stunned too. Talu couldn't have done that. "Who *are* you?"

"I am Korbyn." He unhooked the bucket from its rope and held it out to her. "Shall we?"

She didn't budge.

He heaved another long-suffering sigh. "As tricks go, that one was easy. The water was there. It was merely a matter of causing the sand to settle faster than usual. Now if you want a *real* trick . . . Have you heard about the time that the raven tricked the moon into sharing her light?"

Liyana knew the story. She'd told it to Jidali once. But she could only stare at Korbyn. He had to be a magician, but to be so powerful . . .

"He flattered her beauty and told her that she must see herself," Korbyn said. "He knew of a mirror, he said, where she could view her own beauty. He guided her to the sea. When the moon looked down at the rolling water, she saw her image broken on the waves. The raven complimented her shine and her color, but said it was a pity she wasn't round like the world. He said that if she gave him a sliver of her light, she would be fixed. So she did." He nodded at her, as if he wanted Liyana to finish the story for him.

Liyana swallowed. "But she still looked broken. So she gave him another sliver and then another until she was nothing but a crescent." His smile broadened, as if he were delighted with her. Encouraged, she continued. "And when she realized she'd been tricked, she struck a deal: The raven would return her light bit by bit until she was full if she would then share it again with him bit by bit. And so it continues, month after month, waxing and waning."

Korbyn beamed at her. "See, now *that* was a trick." Whistling, he strode across camp with the bucket in his hand. Precious water spilled out, darkening the sand around him. After a second of staring, she followed him.

Korbyn set the bucket down next to her tent. The torn side fluttered sadly in the wind. "Your fire pit is . . . ahh, here." He knelt beside a lump and proceeded to wipe away sand with his sleeve. He exposed her circle of rocks, as well as the remnants of her fire pit.

"What clan are you?" she asked.

He rolled back his sleeves for her to see the tattoos that decorated his arms. Black birds wound around his wrists and up to his shoulders.

"Raven Clan?" she asked.

Swirls twisted between the ravens in a pattern she knew very well, and she suddenly felt as if she couldn't breathe. She had the same swirls on her arms. She looked up into his eyes. "You're a vessel."

Shaking his head, he winked at her.

"You're a god?"

He laughed again, but she didn't feel as if he were laughing at her. It was the joyous, glad-to-be-alive sound of a child. It cascaded over him and shook his whole body. She thought of Jidali's laugh and how it would overcome him. You couldn't help but smile when Jidali laughed. When Korbyn laughed, the sheer joy in the sound made her feel dizzy.

Liyana sat down hard on the sand opposite Korbyn. She stared at him, and he, still amused, stared back. She thought she should be able to tell—divinity should beam out of his eyes. But he seemed human. "Truly? You are *the* Korbyn?"

Instead of answering, Korbyn laid one hand on the charred sticks, goat dung, and dried palm leaves from her last fire. He concentrated for a moment, with the same blank expression she'd seen on Talu's face when she was in a trance. Flames burst to life. He grinned at her as the fire licked his fingers. Smoke curled up.

She smelled a hint of burning skin. Korbyn's face contorted as if he were confused. Liyana lunged forward and shoved his hand off the fire. She smothered the flames on his palm with her sleeves. Once she was sure the fire was out, she released him.

He raised his hand and looked at the red, puckered skin.

SARAH BETH DURST

Blisters ran up and down his palm. "That hurts," he said, wonder in his voice.

Quickly Liyana grabbed the bucket and plunged his hand into it. "Keep it in there. I have aloe and bandages." She dove into her tent and then emerged with her supply pack.

"My attempt to impress you has failed," Korbyn noted.

Liyana lifted his hand out of the water. "We have to try to keep it clean." She squeezed the aloe leaf, and the precious white sap smeared onto his palm. Moving quickly, she wrapped white cloth bandage around his hand. "You have a high tolerance for pain."

"It's a novelty," he said. "I haven't felt pain for a century."

She knotted the bandage and then rocked back on her heels. She had no doubt about his identity now. No human would lack the instinct to yank his hand away from a fire.

He flexed his fingers. "Thank you. That was kind of you." He then looked at the bucket and grimaced. "We may want new water for the tea."

"Boiling fixes nearly any impurity." She dug the one small pot out of her pack, and she poured water in the pot and then set it over the fire. "You're in a vessel?" She was proud that her voice sounded so calm.

"I was summoned five nights ago, and I set out to find you."

"Me? But . . ." All calmness fled, and her voice squeaked. "Your clan! Your clan needs you!"

"All the clans need me," he said. "And I need you."

She understood the words he was saying, but the order of them made no sense. "You left your clan to find me?"

"Deities are missing. Five in total. They were summoned from the Dreaming, but their souls never filled their clans' vessels."

Liyana felt as if she had been dropped back inside the sand-storm. "Bayla . . ."

"I believe their souls were stolen. And I intend for us to steal them back."

Chapter Six
The Emperor

In the predawn, the emperor walked through the dead garden. Orange trees had once filled this place with a fragrance so heavy that it thickened the air. Now the trees were bare, and the branches looked like bones. A gardener had meticulously combed the dry, dusty earth, trying to create beauty from death. The emperor knelt next to an empty flower bed and ran his fingers over the spirals and swirls. He scooped up a handful of dirt. His people hadn't given up. Neither could he, no matter how impossible it seemed and no matter what his court said.

He heard them, even when they whispered, even when they didn't speak. *He's too young. Barely a man.* Their eyes accused him from every corner of the palace. His father had not been able to break the Great Drought, and he had been the finest emperor ever to grace the throne of the Crescent Empire. And now it was whispered that his son had a mad plan. . . .

He had dreamed of the lake again last night. He had walked through a valley framed by sheer, granite cliffs. Green had overflowed all around him. He had halted at the pebble shore of the lake. It had been a perfect oval, and the crystal blue water had been still. He had tossed a pebble into the water, and the smooth, glassy surface had broken into a million diamonds, each reflecting the sky.

Heels clicked on the marble stones that wound through the garden. The emperor let the dirt fall through his fingertips, and then he rose and turned to greet the guard. "Yes?"

The guard snapped his heels together and bowed. "Your Imperial Majesty. The court is assembled and awaits your decision."

Inwardly the emperor sighed. He wished he could tell the court to wait another hour, another day, another year. But he didn't have the luxury of emotions like that. The face he presented to the guard was as serene as the lake from his dreams. "Then I shall join them."

The guard bowed again.

Wiping the garden dirt off his hands, the emperor straightened his robes. "The gardener who tends this garden . . . See to it that his family receives extra water rations this month."

The guard's eyes widened ever so slightly, and the emperor had to suppress a smile. But he didn't explain himself, and the guard

SARAH BETH DURST

had had enough training not to ask any questions. Leaving the guard behind, the emperor strode out of the garden and into the palace.

The palace of the emperor of the Crescent Empire had marble pillars from the northern mountains and walls inlaid with mother-of-pearl shells from the western sea. Silk cascaded from the ceiling to mimic the wind, and the symbol of the empire— a crescent sun from a lucky eclipse—decorated everything from the exquisite chairs to the ornate mirrors to the jade vases that perched on blue glass pedestals. All in all, the emperor preferred the dead beauty of the garden. At least it didn't lie to him and claim that all was well.

Guards flanked him as he approached the massive double doors of the court. He nodded at them, and they threw open the doors before him. He didn't pause as he strode inside. All the men and women of the court—chancellors, judges, musicians, generals, princes, and princesses—ceased conversation and scurried to line the central corridor that led to the dais. Each bowed as he passed.

He climbed the marble steps to the throne. He'd composed a speech, filled it with arguments and eloquence. But looking out over his court, he felt tired. "Our salvation lies in the desert. I will lead the army across the border, and we will claim the sands and all the magic within," he said. "In my absence . . . try not to do anything stupid."

Chapter Seven

Korbyn peered into the pot. "It's boiling. Tea leaves?"

Mechanically Liyana fetched a wad of leaves from her pack. Trust Mother to think to pack tea leaves. Korbyn dropped them into the boiling water. She watched him use a stick to stir. "Bayla . . . She didn't . . ." Liyana licked her lips, swallowed, and finished in a rush. "I'm not unworthy?" Waiting for an answer, she didn't breathe.

He patted her knee. "You're lovely."

Air whooshed out of her lungs.

Korbyn frowned at her. "Your breathing is rapid. Are you well?"

She placed her hands on her knees and hung her head between them. Bayla hadn't rejected her! Or Jidali. Or Talu. Or her parents . . . Gulping air, she steadied herself. Her head quit spinning after a moment. When she looked up, Korbyn was pawing through her supply pack. "Cups?" he asked. "To drink the tea?" He abandoned his search before she could frame a reply. "Eh, no matter. Once it cools, we can sip directly from the pot." A grin lit up his face as he said, "I am having all sorts of new experiences this time around."

She thought of the string of delicacies that her clan had prepared for Bayla's arrival—fried goat cheese, sugared date pastries, sun-baked tubers with spices, and the finest array of meats from the clan's best-fed goats. "You should have been greeted with a feast and dancing."

He waved her words away. "Once we have succeeded, the desert will celebrate." Raising the pot to his lips, he took a sip. He winced and coughed. "Delicious!" He coughed again and then spit over his shoulder. Flashing her another bright smile, he said, "Do you know the story of the greatest lie that the raven ever told? The mountain was concerned that her beauty was fading—"

"Who stole the deities?" As soon as the question passed her lips, Liyana winced. Talu would be appalled if she'd heard Liyana interrupting a god. She bowed her head. "Forgive the interruption." She added the formal apology to be used for an elder whom one has wronged.

When he didn't reply, she dared to peek up at him. Again, he seemed far older than he looked. He was gazing across the oasis toward the desert mountains with an expression that she could not decipher. She followed his gaze. All traces of the sandstorm were gone. The sky was a bleached blue again, and sand swirled gently over the dunes. Each dune created a crescent shadow so that the desert looked like a sea of dark moons. "We will first need to find the other empty vessels in order to bring home all the missing gods."

He hadn't answered her question, but she nodded anyway. "How do we find them?"

"Horse Clan, Silk Clan, Scorpion Clan, and Falcon Clan." He pointed to different spots on the horizon with each clan name. She marveled at his surety—all clans were nomadic, but he pointed with precision.

Her own clan was out there too, en route to Yubay. If she and Korbyn walked quickly enough, perhaps they could catch them. She spent several glorious seconds imagining that reunion. "My family can help—"

"I am sorry," Korbyn said. She thought she heard true regret in his voice. "Your family is west, and we cannot afford the detour. Soon the other clans will conduct their summoning ceremonies. We must reach them all before any harm comes to their vessels. Not all vessels are as resourceful as you, and not all clans are as . . . forgiving as yours."

"Oh." Liyana studied the rip in the tent and fought to keep the lump of disappointment from clogging her throat. "Of course. I see."

SARAH BETH DURST

Putting the pot down, he wiped his mouth with his sleeve and then leaped to his feet. "In fact, we should begin!"

"Right now?" She looked around the oasis, her link to her family. But the sandstorm had erased the imprints from the tents. There was no trace that her family and clan had lived there for the last month. The desert had reclaimed its own. Any ghosts of her family were now only in her head. "Yes," she decided. "Right now."

Taking the pot, she drank her share of the tea and then cleaned the pot with palm leaves before stowing it in her pack. Korbyn balanced on one of the rocks. He was, she thought, like a four-year-old child and an ancient elder at the same time. As he experimented with shifting from the ball of his foot to his heel, she shook the sand out of her tent, rolled the tent up tight, and stuffed it into her pack.

"Ready?" he asked.

Liyana held up the two waterskins. "Can your magic keep these full?"

"No one can create something out of nothing, not even a god," Korbyn said. "Though once, the raven convinced the hawk that she had given birth to a lizard, even though she had no mate and had laid no egg. But that began with a lizard who did not want her child."

"These won't last us more than a day. Two, if we ration." She spoke her thoughts out loud as she frowned at the two waterskins. They weren't meant for extended treks.

"You won't feel thirst with me." His voice was intense, and she instinctively flinched. She hadn't meant her words to sound censorious of the god.

"It would set my mind at ease if you could be more specific." She thought that phrasing was diplomatic and was pleased with herself. Diplomacy wasn't normally a required skill for a vessel. In fact, Mother had threatened to tie Liyana's tongue in knots more than once.

"I crossed the sands to you by drawing moisture into the desert plants. I can do the same for two." He reached toward her face, and his fingers brushed her cheek. "No fear, Liyana. I won't let Bayla's vessel suffer."

She shivered at the touch of his fingers. He felt so human. His fingertips were warm and soft, and her skin remembered the trace of his touch after he lowered his hand. She kept expecting him to be ethereal, even though she, of all people, should know better.

"You can trust me," he said. "I want Bayla to return as much as you do."

"She's my goddess. What is she to you?" She didn't intend to sound disrespectful, but if she was to follow him, she had to know. He could be Bayla's enemy. He could be responsible for her disappearance. This could be part of an elaborate plot to destroy her clan. Liyana didn't know what transpired between the deities in the Dreaming, what alliances rose and fell.

"She's my love," Korbyn said. "Once her soul inhabits your

body, we will be together again." As Liyana stared at him, he lifted the waterskins out of her hands. "Allow me." He headed toward the well.

Belatedly she hefted the pack onto her back. Her wounded arm sent sharp stabs of pain up into her shoulder. Gritting her teeth, she followed her goddess's lover across the oasis and then into the desert.

*   *   *

The sun seared the desert. Liyana felt the heat rise through the soles of her feet, even through her beautiful shoes, and she felt the wind wick the moisture from her skin as it scoured her with sand. Over the distant dunes, the air waved and crinkled. She placed one foot in front of the other and tried not to think about how much her muscles still hurt from her endless dance or how much her arm throbbed from her wounds.

Korbyn seemed untouched by the heat. "Once, Bayla was the beloved of Sendar, the god of the Horse Clan, but he valued his horses more than her and lost her affection. He was irate when he learned that Bayla had chosen me to replace him, and he challenged me to three races. One, his choice of mounts. Two, my choice. And three, we would both choose our favorite."

Every time Liyana breathed, her lungs felt raw, scraped from the sand she had inhaled during the storm. She tried to focus on his words to distract herself. "You have horses in the Dreaming?" Talking felt like scratching her larynx with a fistful of needles.

"We have whatever we wish in the Dreaming. One's will determines one's surroundings . . . unless, of course, you encounter someone with a stronger will. Keleena of the Sparrow Clan is so indecisive that the land changes around her like the surface of the sea. You can grow a city around her without . . . But I was telling you about the three races."

On the horizon, the air wrinkled in the heat. Sand clung to her feet as she trudged with Korbyn up and down the red dunes. She flailed in the looser sand.

"First race, he chose horses. I lost dismally. Second race, we flew."

She yanked her feet out of the sand with each step. It felt as if the dunes wanted to pull her down into them, sweep her into their slopes, until she was a part of the sandscape. "You can fly?"

"I cannot fly here." He raised and lowered his arms as if to show her. His sleeves billowed. She thought of his totem animal, the raven, and she thought it was apt. He did move like a bird, fast and alert. "But in the Dreaming, there are no rules. It's a place of pure spirit."

She fell to one knee at the top of a dune. Struggling, she stood again and continued down the slope, jarring her knees painfully with each step. "Why would you ever want to leave?"

He grinned and raced down the slope past her. "For this! All this!" He stretched his arms wide as if to encompass the whole world, and then as she descended the dune, he caught her hand and pressed the top of her hand to his lips. "And this." Releasing her, he unwound the bandage from his burnt hand. "Even this."

She still felt his kiss tingling on her hand. Trying to ignore the sensation, she studied his burn. The blisters looked blotchy. "It needs more aloe." She swung her pack off her back, and pain shot down her arm from the gashes, making her breath hiss.

He waved her away. "I can fix it." His face became blank as he held his palm steady—a trance again. She marveled at how quickly he could enter a trance. Sweat beaded on his forehead and instantly dried. His hand shook, but he did not move. Slow at first and then faster, the skin smoothed, and the red faded. In a few minutes, his palm was smooth and perfect.

"You can heal," she said flatly.

He beamed at her. "I have many tricks."

She clenched her jaw. Of course he could heal. Even Talu had some basic skill with mending cuts and bruises. Liyana should have realized it sooner, but she hadn't been thinking straight ever since Korbyn had walked out of the swirling sand. In as polite a voice as she could manage, she asked, "Would it be possible for you to heal me?"

"My pleasure." He bowed.

Liyana rolled up her sleeve and unwound the bandages covering the claw marks. Red and oozing, the gashes were worse than before.

Korbyn flinched.

"Sand wolf," she explained.

His voice was gentle. "I am sorry."

"Sand wolves always come," she said. "It wasn't your fault." Granted, if he had arrived a day earlier, it wouldn't have happened—and her clan wouldn't have left, thinking her unworthy. She didn't say that out loud.

He took her hand in his left hand and then placed his right hand on her shoulder. He drew close to her. She didn't move. She knew from Talu that proximity helped the magic. Still, being healed by Korbyn was very different from being healed by Talu. His body pressed against her so closely that she could feel him inhale and exhale. His breathing slowed, deep and steady.

She felt the skin on her arm tingle, and then heat spread from her shoulder to her elbow to her fingers. As she watched, the dried blood dissolved, and a thick scab wove itself over the wounds. Fresh skin blossomed at the edges of the scab, and then it began to spread bit by bit. She thought of a weaver, adding row after row to a blanket. New smooth skin inched across her arm, shrinking the wounds. Watching her skin knit itself whole, she lost track of time. It felt as if the world had shrunk to just her and Korbyn. She breathed in time with him.

Then he released her. Her arm was perfect, as smooth as sand-scoured stone. She ran her fingers over her skin and marveled at it. No scabs. No scars. No trace of the gashes. She had no pain in her arms or in the rest of her, either. She felt wonderful throughout, as if she had drunk her fill from a crystal clear well.

Korbyn staggered backward. His chest heaved as if he'd run for miles.

"Are you all right?" Liyana asked, reaching toward him but stopping just short of touching him, remembering he was a god. He might not want a mortal's assistance.

He pitched forward. She caught him in her arms, sagging to her knees as his full weight sank against her. "Korbyn!" *Oh, sweet goddess!* Cradling him, she lowered him onto the sand. "Korbyn, are you all right? Korbyn!"

She checked his pulse. Still beating. He wasn't dead. Just . . . asleep? Unconscious? "Wake up!" she said. "Please, wake up!"

He didn't. But he continued to breathe, evenly and softly.

The sun beat down on them. Liyana checked his pulse again. His skin felt warm. "Oh, Bayla, what do I do?" She should get him into the shade. Working quickly, she pulled her tent out of her pack, and she unbent the poles. In a few minutes, she had pitched the tent. The rip fluttered in the wind.

"Korbyn?" She knelt next to him. "The tent is ready." She touched his shoulder. She felt the curve of his muscles and noticed how strong he was. She snatched her hand away.

Still he didn't wake.

"You'll sleep better in the shade," she said.

No response.

Gently she shook his shoulder. "You can't stay out here." She contemplated him for a moment. He looked so peaceful and so vulnerable and so beautiful. "Forgive this indignity." Grabbing him under the armpits, Liyana dragged him toward the tent. As she braced herself to hoist him inside, his eyes popped open.

"What are you doing?" he asked in an ordinary voice.

She released him so fast that she fell backward onto her rear. "You're all right!" Her heart beat so hard that it almost hurt. "I thought . . . You didn't . . ."

"Too much healing. Plus there was the well water and the fire. . . ." He made a face. "So much for my illusion of omnipotence. You're still impressed with me, right?"

"Yes, of course," she said automatically.

"Excellent." He crawled into the tent. "Then let's pretend this never happened."

Liyana crawled in behind him. There was very little space with two people plus the pack. Avoiding meeting his eyes, she squirmed past him. She tried to keep to the tarp wall, but her hip still brushed against his thigh. She instantly scooted against her pack.

Their breathing filled the silence. She was acutely aware he was only inches from her.

Inside the tent, the air was still, but at least they were shielded from the pounding sun. She unwrapped her headcloth and let her braids fall against her neck. She shook them out, and they sprinkled sand in the tent. She winced. "Forgive me."

He nodded graciously.

The silence thickened. Liyana had never been alone in a tent with a male who wasn't family. She couldn't help noticing how lean, muscled, and handsome he was. *Bayla will be pleased with him,* she thought.

"I should . . . um, fix the rip," she said. Twisting to face the pack, she accidentally elbowed him in the side. "Forgive me!"

He rubbed his ribs. "Of course."

Hands shaking, she pulled out the needle and thread. Mother had sensibly packed the thick sinewy thread, not the silk embroidery thread. Liyana threaded the needle and then pinched the two sides of the rift. She started at the top, making tight stitches, the way that Aunt Sabisa had taught her when she was deemed old enough to not stab herself too badly with the needle. She glanced over her shoulder and saw he was still watching her. She wondered what he thought when he looked at her, if he thought of her or Bayla. She broke the silence. "You didn't finish telling me about your race. Second race, you flew."

"We flew on birds, and I won easily. Sendar created a massive condor, large enough to accommodate his substantial girth. Even in the Dreaming, you see, he prefers as many muscles as possible. He likes to match his size to his ego. But I selected an ordinary-size raven and shrunk myself. His condor crashed from the weight, and I flew to the finish line with time to spare."

Behind her, she felt Korbyn shift, as if seeking a better position.

She tried to scoot her feet farther under her so he'd have more room, but that just caused her knee to bump against his shoulder. She flinched as if the touch had burned.

"He chose a horse for the third race, of course, and at the appointed time, he charged forward. He tore across the desert with sand billowing in his wake. Some say he created his own sandstorms. But when he reached the finish line, I was already there."

The wind teased the edges of the rip, trying to tug the tarp out of her hands. She held it tightly and speared the canvas with the needle. She tried to ignore the warmth of his body beside her. Once Bayla inhabited her body . . .

"You are supposed to be so intensely curious that you ask me how I managed to accomplish such a miraculous feat," Korbyn said.

Midstitch, she froze. "Please, forgive me."

He sighed. "You do not need to show me continuous deference. I'm not *your* god."

"You're my goddess's lover."

"True," he said.

She felt his eyes on her, and she wondered again if he were picturing her as Bayla. She wondered if he was evaluating her body. Or imagining it. She tried to focus on the stitches, but her fingers shook. She wondered if he planned to speak again. "Could you please tell me how you won?"

"Since you asked so nicely . . . I won the race by moving the finish line to me."

Looking over her shoulder at him, she tried to puzzle what he meant.

"Remember, this was in the Dreaming. I simply . . . bent the desert. Sendar believed he was racing straight to the finish line, but in truth, he completed a vast circle. I curved it as he ran until the finish line was at my feet. I never moved from the starting line."

"That's brilliant."

"I thought so. But I'm glad you agree. It will make this journey much more pleasant if you are impressed with my brilliance." He flashed her a smile.

She laughed. It felt good to laugh, as if her ribs were remembering some old game that they used to be fond of.

"Well, that's a surprise," he said.

"What is?"

"You can laugh."

"Of course I can laugh," she said. "Life simply hasn't been very amusing lately, with the exception of the lizard in my aunt's hair."

"Your aunt wears lizards in her hair?"

She told him about the lizard that had graced Aunt Sabisa's hair on the morning of the summoning ceremony and how she had stomped around like a human sandstorm. To her surprise, he laughed, filling the tent with untamed joy. They continued to trade stories and laugh until both of them sank into sleep.

* * *

Liyana snapped awake. She blinked once to prove to herself that her eyes were open. She was enveloped by darkness. She felt a warm body pressed against her side. Her cheek lay against the cool tarp of a tent wall. Usually she slept between her cousins, and for an instant she could not comprehend how she had rolled across them to reach the wall. But then she realized that the deep, steady breathing beside her was from a male.

Korbyn.

Like a sandstorm, memory swept through her, and she felt as choked as if she had swallowed sand. She forced herself to breathe evenly as she focused on a sliver of moonlight that gleamed through the door flap. She was aware of how close the man . . . boy . . . god . . . next to her was. She felt his warmth beside her, a sharp contrast to the chill of the tarp. She listened to him breathe. So close, she could smell his skin. He smelled of spices, like an expensive tea.

Still asleep, Korbyn cried out. She felt his body stiffen. His arm, splayed across her, tensed. She flattened against her side of the tent as he made a sound like an animal's cry. He flailed again, and his arm hit the opposite side of the tent. "Korbyn?" she whispered in the darkness. Louder: "Korbyn!"

The whimpered cry ceased. His voice was soft in the darkness. "You woke me."

"Forgive me," she said. "But you were dreaming."

"I am unused to dreams. In the Dreaming, there is no need for sleep, and therefore there are no dreams." His voice was conversational, even loud. Outside, the desert was silent except for the wind. "I suppose that is ironic, given the name. Tell me of your dreams, Liyana."

She thought of the jumble of images that cluttered her dreams. Often she saw Jidali shimmying up a date palm tree. Sometimes he fell. She dreamed about dancing, and she'd wake with her blankets tangled around her legs. Once, she dreamed of a sea of hip-high wheat that bowed in the breeze. "I dream about my family," Liyana said. "But if you mean bad dreams . . . in those, I dream I'm alone."

He didn't reply with details of his own dream. She wished she dared to ask. She wished she could see his face. If he were family, she would have comforted him. She listened to him breathe. Tentatively she said, "Stories say that sand wolves were born from bad dreams."

She heard him chuckle.

Emboldened, she continued, "Long ago, the rains didn't come to the hunting grounds of the Jackal Clan. Days were filled with thirst and hunger, and nights were filled with dreams of death. When the jackal god came to them, he filled the wells with water and brought the gazelle to the hunters. Days were filled with water and food, but nights were *still* filled with dreams of death—the memories of the time with no rain." She hesitated. She used to tell this story to Jidali when he woke from a nightmare, but Korbyn wasn't a child. He didn't stop her, though, and the silence expanded until she wanted to fill it. "One night, the jackal god bade his people to fall asleep, and then he gathered up their dreams and threw them into a storm. There, stirred by the wind, they mixed with the sand and became the sand wolves. And that is why we fear the sand wolves and why they continue to plague us—they are our nightmares and they want to return to us. But they cannot leave their wind to hurt us, just as your dreams cannot leave your mind to hurt you."

She fell silent. He didn't speak.

Searching for something to say, Liyana said, "My little brother loves that story."

"In the absence of truth, a story will do," Korbyn said.

"What is the truth?" she asked. She wished she could suck the words back in. It wasn't her place to ask to hear divine truths. She wondered what sort of secrets were in his mind—and what kind of horrors. He had seen generations of humans with their flaws and their failures. She wondered how she measured up against the thousands of lives that he had seen come and go.

"Once, there was a lizard who was obsessed with the truth . . . ," he said.

She knew this one, about a lizard who learned the value of a delicate lie and thus mastered the art of camouflage, but she let him tell it anyway. If he did not want to share his thoughts and secrets with her, that was his right.

But if he had a nightmare again, then god or not, she *would* wake him.

✳   ✳   ✳

At dawn Liyana rolled up the tent. She didn't speak of dreams or wolves, but she watched Korbyn as he stretched on top of a dune. He folded his body over, laid his palms in the sand, and balanced himself in a handstand. She checked over their supplies.

"Our food won't last more than two days," she commented. She shook the waterskins. Some water sloshed in one, but the other was empty. "Water won't last the day. That has to be the priority."

He flipped upright and executed a bow. "Your wish is my command."

She blinked. She hadn't meant that as an order. *Oh, goddess, have I offended him?* She thought of how familiar she'd acted with him last night, waking him from his sleep and swapping stories in the darkness. Had she overstepped then, too? Liyana dropped to her knees. "My continued lapses in discretion would be a source of vast embarrassment to my family and clan if they knew. Please pardon my behavior." She bowed her head and hoped that had been enough to cover the myriad of offenses she was certain she'd caused over the last day.

When he didn't answer, she raised her head. He looked amused. "There is a fine line between deference and sarcasm," he said. "You leaped over it."

Liyana winced. "I was never supposed to meet a deity! I don't know how you want me to behave." She noticed that he had packed the tent and was hefting the pack onto his shoulders. "At least let me carry that."

He refused, skipping backward as she reached toward the pack. "This body is as strong and healthy as yours."

"But you're a god!"

"I never asked for your deference, Liyana. So long as you do nothing to hinder our goal, you may behave however you wish. If you want to howl like a wolf, I won't stop you. If you want to cross the desert on all fours, please be my guest. If you want to pass the journey by telling bawdy stories . . ." He paused. "Do you know any bawdy stories?"

She couldn't help smiling. "I don't know you nearly well enough for those."

"Aha! So that means you do know some!" Carrying the pack, he began to walk across the sands. She scooped up the water-skins and followed. "So, what will it take to get to know me well enough? Do you want to hear about the first time I inhabited a vessel and how I failed to take into account the urgency of certain bodily needs?"

Liyana laughed. "Oh no."

"Oh yes. Almost all deities pee themselves at least once in the middle of performing a miracle." He strode across the dunes, and she matched his pace.

"Even Bayla?" she asked.

"She was summoning water from deep underground to create a new well. It is a difficult task. It's far easier to fill an existing well because the water is already present. Far more difficult to coax water into the bedrock of an area without it. At any rate, the task required fierce concentration over an extended length of time." He paused. "It is a blessing that you won't be able to tell Bayla that I told you this. She is far more concerned about her dignity than I am."

Her smile faded. "What is Bayla like?"

"Glorious! Also punctual."

Liyana nearly smiled again, but it was difficult when she couldn't help thinking of how Bayla should have come the night before last. She had not been punctual then.

"She values order and cultivates precision. Her section of the Dreaming has smooth, unblemished sand, and she does not tolerate imperfection."

"She sounds like my mother." Liyana tried to keep her voice even, as if this were an ordinary conversation, but she failed. She wondered what Mother would say if she saw her daughter trekking across the desert with Korbyn, and she felt an ache inside as sharp as the sand wolf's claws. *Mother must think I am dead.*

"Our clans often come to value our characteristics," Korbyn said. "In many ways, I am her opposite. I am imperfection personified. I am the rule-bender. I am the trickster. I am—"

"The raven," Liyana said.

"Yes."

"And proud of it?" It was a gentle tease, just enough to test the waters and see if he meant what he said about not needing deference. If so . . . Well, she had never been very good at deference. It would be a relief to abandon it.

"Justifiably," Korbyn said. "Do you know of the time when the raven—"

"So if she's so perfect and you're so imperfect, how did you fall in love?"

He weathered the interruption without blinking. "Bayla loves to laugh. And I can make her laugh." His voice was soft, as if he were filled with memories. Liyana wished she were filled with memories like that, ones that could fill her voice with warmth. As a vessel, that had never been possible. In a cheerful voice he asked, "Do you want to hear how I won her heart?"

"Of course," she said. She thought of Ger and Esti and the warmth in their eyes. She wasn't destined to ever experience that. She had another purpose, she reminded herself, and with each step across the sand, she walked closer to it.

She continued to walk with purpose as Korbyn launched into

an outrageous tale of how he'd impressed Bayla by rearranging her carefully laid out constellations in the sky above her portion of the Dreaming. Bayla had retaliated in kind until all the stars were woven together in a bright path across the sky, which they then walked upon.

Chapter Eight

In the mornings, as the sun slowly cooked the air, Liyana and Korbyn covered as many miles as they could. Once the desert reached what felt like fire pit temperatures, Liyana pitched the tent. She waited in the shade while Korbyn coaxed moisture from the nearby desert plants. He returned with full waterskins, as well as tubers that shouldn't have been ripe yet and clutches of lizard eggs that shouldn't have been laid yet. He then collapsed inside the tent while she took a turn outside, shredding the tubers and frying the eggs over a tiny fire. In the late afternoons, when the air didn't sear their lungs as badly, they continued on, trading stories as they walked. Liyana laughed so much that her ribs ached, and the dunes rang with the sound of Korbyn's laughter. They followed this routine for nine days, leaving the sand dunes

SARAH BETH DURST

and entering an area of caked earth pockmarked by patches of yellowed grasses and barrel-shaped cacti.

On the tenth day, Liyana saw the silhouette of date palm trees. They clustered in a grove of seven or eight with narrow trunks that curved up to crowns of leaves. "Real or a mirage?"

"Real," Korbyn said.

She squinted at the oasis, and the palm trees wavered and stretched. "How can you tell?" He couldn't have used magic. Even though he was a god, he had to be in a trance to work magic like any magician, and she didn't think he could enter a trance while he walked.

"I used my divine wisdom and superior intellect."

Liyana shielded her eyes and spotted a plume of sand. It billowed around three figures on horseback who were riding toward them. "Or you saw them." She pointed.

"Or I saw them," he agreed. Sloughing off the pack, Korbyn plopped down in the sand. "Let's eat lunch."

She halted. "Now? But we're so close!"

"Us walking will save them ten minutes of riding," Korbyn said. "Let them come to us. We can then ride into camp refreshed." He glugged water from the waterskin and then handed it to Liyana. Digging into the pack, he produced a flat cake composed of baked tuber. He bit into it. "Needs spices," he commented. "We can borrow some from Sendar's people. Oh, and I should warn you that Sendar's clan may or may not hate me, thanks to that whole incident with the race. Sendar's a sore loser."

Liyana choked down a bite of the baked tuber and then gave it back to Korbyn, who gobbled it up. "Have they had their summoning ceremony yet?" She wondered how this clan would react to their news. She wished she could have told hers. Instead they were bound for Yubay, not knowing their dreamwalk was doomed to fail.

"We will know soon enough," Korbyn said.

As they came, she saw that the riders were wrapped head to toe in blue. Thin slits in the cloth showed their eyes and mouths. Swords were strapped to their backs, and bows and arrows were affixed to their saddles. She wondered if they were hunters or warriors. She knew the Horse Clan had an ample supply of both. Their magnificent horses needed to be defended against thieves, especially during the annual fair. "What if they think we're horse thieves?" she asked.

"They'll cut off our hands, gouge out our eyes, and feed us to the vultures." He chomped on the tuber. "Or they'll feed us to the horses, if food is scarce enough."

"This doesn't worry you?" Liyana asked.

"I'd prefer not to lose my eyes."

She dropped down in the sand next to him and drank deeply from the waterskin. "With your divine wisdom and superior intellect, do you have a plan?"

He flashed her a smile. "I plan . . . to tell the truth." He spread both his hands, palms out, as if to show his innocence. "I know, it's a rash course of action, one that I personally have never attempted, but I believe it's worth a try."

"I hope they give you a chance." The riders had shifted into a canter. The horses thundered toward Korbyn and Liyana, kicking up sand under their hooves.

"As do I," he said softly.

Sand sprayed over Liyana and Korbyn as the riders reined in their horses a few feet away. One horse pawed the ground and snorted, as if it wanted to continue to run. The other two held as still as soldiers. None of the riders dismounted.

Korbyn held up his hand in greeting.

"You trespass on Horse Clan territory during the sacred time," the first said—it was a woman's voice, harsh and low. Liyana couldn't see the woman's face through the cloth. Only her eyes were visible.

The second, a man, added, "If you are in need of water and sustenance, we will share what we carry, but we cannot invite you to share the hospitality of our camp at this time."

The third didn't speak. He held a knife in his beefy hand.

Korbyn gestured at the tuber cakes and waterskins. "Please, we invite you to share our food and water. The tubers are not bad, albeit a bit bland."

"Your names and clan," the woman demanded.

"We have come to offer assistance to the Horse Clan," Korbyn said.

Liyana thought it was wise that Korbyn hadn't volunteered his identity, despite his resolution to tell the truth. The third rider had not loosened his grip on his knife.

"We do not need assistance from strangers," the woman said.

"Your clan chief will wish to speak with us," Korbyn said merrily. "At present our needs and interests coincide."

The third rider grunted, and his horse huffed as if echoing him.

"'At present' is an interesting word choice," the second rider said. "Are we to presume that your intentions are honest and peaceful 'at present'?"

The first rider shifted in her saddle. Her horse strained at the bridle as if the mare wanted to run again. "You cannot be considering—" she began.

"One man, one woman, no mounts," the second said, waving at them. "One supply pack. Two waterskins. And the nearest well is a week's journey."

"Nine days, actually," Korbyn volunteered.

Ignoring him, the second rider continued. "The chief asked for anything unusual, and I believe this qualifies."

"This is a mistake," the first rider growled.

"Your objection is noted," the second rider said.

Korbyn rose in a smooth movement. Belatedly Liyana scrambled to her feet. Her muscles, sore from the endless trek, protested. Korbyn noticed and reached out to steady her. "Could we ride with you?" he asked the riders. "It has been a long and tiring journey."

"Only if you give us your weapons," the first rider said.

Liyana was not giving up Jidali's knife. "I'll walk."

Korbyn raised both his eyebrows at her. "You surprise me," he said to her. "It has been a long time since I met anyone who surprised me." She wanted to ask if that was good or bad. If they'd been alone, she would have. Instead she began walking toward the oasis. Korbyn trudged along with her, and the three riders spread out on either side and behind them.

"If they touch their weapons on their way through camp," the second rider said to the third, "you have my permission to skewer them."

Through the mouth slit in the facecloth, Liyana saw the third rider's lips curve into a smile. His eyes remained as flat and expressionless as a diamond cobra's. She shivered and kept walking. She kept her hands by her sides, away from her knife.

*   *   *

The Horse Clan tents circled the date palm trees. Made of burgundy, black, and spotted hide, the tents were tall and round as opposed to low triangles—a visual reminder that this wasn't Liyana's clan. Men, women, and children were engaged in ordinary and familiar tasks: Clothes were being mended, bread was being kneaded, blankets were being woven, and animals were being cared for. Inside the circle of tents, the green heart of the oasis belonged to the horses. They grazed on the tufts of dried grasses and nibbled at the peeling bark of the trees. Seeking shade, foals leaned against their mothers. Under one tree, two stallions butted chests in a mock battle. From a distance, it looked idyllic. But as they passed the outer circle of tents, Liyana noticed that the horses' hides were as dull and patchy as worn blankets, and their ribs pressed against their flesh. Flies buzzed around the face of one chestnut mare, and pus leaked from her eyes. The horse troughs were empty.

"Sendar's herd used to be the jewel of the desert," Korbyn said in a soft voice.

Even more than her clan needed Bayla, these people needed their deity. Horses couldn't digest the brittle desert bushes that the goats ate in times of severe draught. "Who would take our gods away from us?" Liyana asked.

Again Korbyn didn't answer.

As they passed through the camp, Liyana scanned the faces, trying to spot a friendly expression. Most faces were covered in blue or white cloth, and those that weren't looked gaunt with prominent cheekbones and sunken cheeks—they mirrored their bony horses. Men and women dropped their tasks and followed. She heard whispers that rose to a steady locust-like hum.

The riders led them to an ornate tent covered in tassels. The hide walls were desert tan but decorated with images of hoofprints and swirls. The peak of the tent was higher than that of any of the other tents, and its girth was double. She guessed that this was the clan's council tent.

As they approached, the tent flap was tossed open, and the largest man that Liyana had ever seen emerged. He had to twist sideways to pass through the tent opening. Framed by the prevalent blue cloth, his long, horselike face tapered into a twisted beard that reminded Liyana of a horse's tail. He wore tan, leather robes with golden tassels. A fat sword hung from his beaded belt, and he held a horse whip in one hand. He scowled at them. "I am the chief of the Horse Clan. You trespass at a sacred time."

Korbyn bowed. "Please accept our apologies for this untimely intrusion, though once you hear why we have come, I think you will agree that it is, in fact, timely indeed."

The chief grunted in response.

"You are a man of few words, I see," Korbyn said.

His scowl deepened, and Liyana shrank back as if from a looming storm. She wondered if Korbyn could sense the chief's growing hostility. Perhaps this was part of his plan.

"Let me cut straight to the point," Korbyn said. "We need to speak with your vessel."

"He prepares for the summoning ceremony," the chief said, his voice a rumble.

"Ahh . . . in that case, please interrupt him," Korbyn said cheerfully. "What we need to discuss is directly relevant."

The chief flicked his arm, and the horse whip snaked out. It cracked in the sand at their feet. Liyana jumped. Korbyn didn't even flinch. Whinnying, the nearby horses shied away. Liyana thought of how he'd burned his hand. Perhaps he'd forgotten that he was in a mortal body. "You disrespect us," the chief said.

"He doesn't!" Liyana said. "Korbyn, tell him."

"As you wish," Korbyn said. All humor drained from his face, and when he addressed the chief again, his tone was serious. "Several of the desert deities, including Sendar, were summoned from the Dreaming but never arrived at their clans. Their souls have been, in essence, kidnapped."

"Lies," the clan chief said. "No one can kidnap a god."

"It's happened already," Korbyn said. To Liyana, he said, "Show them who you are."

Liyana pushed up her sleeves. "I'm the vessel of Bayla of the Goat Clan. We conducted the summoning ceremony. . . ." She felt a lump in her throat, and she swallowed hard. "She didn't come." Even knowing the truth, it was hard to say. She felt the weight of her failure all over again. She bowed her head. "Bayla was supposed to enter me, and she didn't."

"She couldn't," Korbyn said. "Like Sendar couldn't." He tapped his nose. "I can smell a lie. Your vessel isn't preparing for the ceremony. You have already completed it, and it failed. Hence the hostility in

SARAH BETH DURST

our greeting from your guards. Hence the lack of hospitality now."

Around them, murmurs rose into shouts.

The chief held up his hand.

Instant silence.

"Lies," the chief said. "Lies and tricks." He pointed at Korbyn with the whip. "Identify your name and clan."

Liyana inched closer to Korbyn. Like the tents surrounding the oasis, the Horse Clan encircled the two of them. She felt as if their stares were stones ready to be thrown. The pressure of Jidali's knife in her sash wasn't much comfort.

"I am a friend to all desert clans," Korbyn said.

The chief did not lower the whip. "You are Korbyn, trickster god of the Raven Clan, who has heaped countless humiliations on my god and stole his beloved Bayla through flattery and lies." He spat at Korbyn's feet.

Korbyn spread his hands in a show of innocence. "Your deity and I may have had our differences, but never at the cost of harm to any of our people."

"And you"—the chief pointed the whip at Liyana—"have joined the trickster to humiliate my people. We are not fooled. You are Bayla herself."

Liyana's mouth dropped open. "I . . ."

"I wish this were a trick," Korbyn said, "but for once, I am telling the truth. I can see how you would be confused. This honesty and nobility is new to me as well—"

"Seize them," the chief ordered.

Two men strode forward and caught Liyana's arms from behind. Two others grabbed Korbyn. Liyana yelped and struggled, but Korbyn held still. "For the good of your clan, I hope you will hear sense," Korbyn said. His voice was mild. "I believe that the souls of the lost deities have been captured in false vessels. They must be freed from their prisons and then transferred into true vessels. I can perform the summoning chant for the transfer, but the vessels must be there to dance. Liyana has agreed to accompany me on behalf of her clan. We hope that your vessel will too, as well as the vessels from the Silk Clan, the Scorpion Clan, and the Falcon Clan. Together, we can rescue your deities."

The chief glowered at Liyana. "You abandoned your clan to perpetuate this trick? I believed better of Sendar's beloved than to keep our god from us. You have fallen low."

"I'm not Sendar's beloved! I'm a vessel! And I didn't abandon anyone. My clan left me to die in the desert because Bayla never came." She pulled forward, straining against the hands that were clasped hard around her forearms. They squeezed, and tears sprang into her eyes.

"If you are human, then prove it." The chief strode toward Liyana.

For the first time, she heard worry in Korbyn's voice. "Let's not be hasty. Sendar would not want harm—"

The chief drew his sword.

Liyana's eyes fixed on the blade, but her mind couldn't understand what it meant. Surely he didn't intend to—

He plunged his sword into her stomach. "Heal yourself, goddess."

Chapter Nine

Liyana felt stillness for one endless moment. Everything seemed hushed. She saw faces twist and mouths stretch as if they were shouting, but she heard only the whoosh of wind. Her body felt light. She knew that two men held her arms, but she couldn't feel their grip. She looked down at her stomach. The sword hilt protruded. Red blossomed around it and spread through her sash, soaking the fabric.

The chief yanked the hilt, and the sword pulled out of her with a sucking sound that reverberated in her head—the only sound she heard. She felt as if all the air had been pulled out of her with the sword. She covered her stomach with her hands. Wetness poured over her fingers. She tried to hold the liquid back, but her wet fingers slid over one another.

Her stomach started to throb, a dull pulse of pain that intensified with each second. It spread like a fire eating the grasslands, overwhelming the feel of her arms and legs until the only sensation she felt was fire. She was burning inside and out. Hands lowered her down as she slumped into the sand. Blackness crawled into her eyes, and her vision narrowed to only the sand by her cheek.

And then she was cradled against a chest. She focused on a face. Korbyn.

She wanted to say she was sorry she'd failed to finish their quest. But her throat felt full of liquid. She coughed, and red spattered Korbyn. His face stilled, as if it had hardened into stone, while his eyes focused on her with a gaze as searing as the sun. Her vision contracted until all she saw was his eyes. And then even they were gone. She floated in a sea of darkness.

Colors came and went. Warmth. Coldness. Softness. Shooting, searing pain.

And then nothing.

Eventually she noticed cushions. Pillows were nestled all around her, and she was swaddled in blankets. She fluttered her eyes open, but she saw only shadows that swayed above her. She closed her eyes and drifted away again.

The next time she woke, she heard voices. They were hushed, and the words ran together like poured water. She listened to the trickle for a while, and it lulled her back to sleep.

She dreamed about Jidali.

"Liyana, am I going to die?" her little brother asked.

"Not for a long time," she said.

"But someday?"

"Why don't you ask Father about this?"

"He said to ask you."

She remembered this conversation. It wasn't a dream; it was a memory. She'd tried to change the topic. She'd tried to distract him with games. She'd even offered up a sugared date as a bribe. But in the end, she had told Jidali yes, and he'd cried.

The next day, Mother had let them shirk their chores. Liyana remembered that she had taken Jidali to visit Talu's mother, a woman so old that she had resembled a tortoise.

"You're seeking wisdom, little man?"

"I want to know about death," he'd said in his tiny, birdlike voice.

"Ah, and I look like I have seen death." She'd sounded amused.

"Everyone says not to be scared or sad because we go to the Dreaming and it doesn't hurt there and all my wishes can come true there."

The old woman nodded. "But you're still scared and sad."

He nodded, and a tear spilled out of one eye. He wiped it away with the back of his chubby fist. Liyana wanted to wrap her arms around him, but she stayed in the shadows. This visit was for him.

SARAH BETH DURST

"And I am supposed to tell you that they're right, and death is a time to celebrate a life well lived." The old woman beckoned him closer. "But I will tell you the truth: Death scares me. And it makes me sad. And it makes me angry. And this is the way it should be!"

Jidali's eyes widened.

"Oh yes, I have lived more than my fair share of a full life," she said. "Enough for two or three lives. But breathing every day . . . You are right to want to hold on to it, and you're right to mourn it when it ends."

The old woman had died before Liyana was named the clan's vessel. Liyana wondered what she would have said if she'd known that Liyana was destined to die young.

But I am not supposed to die this way! Liyana thought.

At the force of her thought, her eyes popped open.

Sunlight cut in slices through the tent, illuminating the red and gold pillows and blankets that surrounded her. Beside her, she saw a gold basin perched on a three-legged stool. A damp cloth was draped over its rim. Beyond it, she saw a fire pit with a silver tea urn. Everything in the tent reeked of wealth and opulence. She inhaled incense.

She should have woken in a healing tent. Or not woken at all.

She touched her stomach and felt soft cotton. She looked down at a burgundy blouse with silver embroidery. She didn't recognize the weave or cut. Someone had dressed her in clothes that weren't her own. Tentatively she lifted the hem to see her stomach.

No blood. No wound. But she had a scar.

She traced the lump of hard skin. She'd had no scars before this. It looked like a star just below her sternum. "Korbyn," she whispered. He had done this. And then what? What had happened to him? "Korbyn?"

Liyana pushed herself up, trying to sit. Her head swam, and she collapsed backward into the pile of pillows. A woman leaned over her, and Liyana bit back a shriek at how suddenly she'd appeared.

"Try again slowly," the woman said. She braced Liyana with a hand under her back. Liyana eased up to sitting, and the woman tucked pillows behind her to prop her up. Liyana stared at her, mentally flogging herself both for failing to notice the woman was there and for showing alarm. Already the woman had her at a disadvantage.

The woman had leathery skin, and her hair was streaked with white and silver. She wore a necklace of silver tassels that matched the chief's belt—this was the chieftess of the Horse Clan, Liyana guessed. The chieftess pressed a waterskin to Liyana's lips. "Drink. Sips only." She tilted the waterskin, and water poured between Liyana's lips. Liyana swallowed automatically. It tasted like silt, and it felt like a flame in her throat. She coughed, and pain shot through her body. She blacked out.

Liyana opened her eyes again. She was lying down, and the

chieftess sat cross-legged beside her. She had a crescent-shaped knife in her lap that she was polishing with a grayed rag. Liyana's eyes fixed on the blade.

"Where's Korbyn?" Liyana asked. Her voice sounded like a rasp, and the words raked over her throat. She licked her lips and swallowed, which caused her body to shudder.

"He speaks with the elders. Last I heard, he was being quite vivid in his description of what he planned to do to prove that my husband isn't a god. I do not know if the discussion has progressed any further."

Liyana wanted to see him with such an intensity that it felt like a pull on her skin. She struggled to push herself up. "I must—"

"You must drink some water," the chieftess said. She held out a waterskin. "If that stays inside you, we will try a thin broth. Your insides need to remember how to function." As Liyana reached for the waterskin, she felt as if her skull were being squeezed. She cried out. Leaning forward, the chieftess pressed her palm to Liyana's forehead and concentrated. After a moment, the pressure in Liyana's head lessened.

"You're the clan magician," Liyana said. She was about to ask if Korbyn had been right, that their summoning ceremony had failed, when the tent flap was lifted.

A young man poked his head inside. "Is Bayla's vessel awake yet?" His voice boomed through the tent as if he were accustomed to bellowing across the desert.

"You should be quiet when you enter a sickroom," the magician-chieftess said. "Didn't your mother teach you better manners?"

He hung his head. "Sorry, Mother."

"Come in, Fennik. She's awake."

Fennik trotted inside. Closer, Liyana saw the family resemblance: He had his mother's amber-flecked eyes and his father's wide shoulders. He squatted next to Liyana. As he squatted, his muscles compressed so that he looked spring-loaded. He was dressed as if for a traditional dance: an embroidered loincloth, several layers of gold necklaces, and black makeup in swirls over his cheeks and chest. His golden skin glistened as if he'd been rubbed with oil. His arms were bare, exposing the chiseled perfection of his arms as well as his tattoos. She knew those tattoos.

"You're Sendar's vessel," Liyana said.

The chieftess rose. "You two have much to discuss." She handed the crescent-shaped knife to her son and cryptically said, "The decision lies with you."

Liyana's eyes fixed on the blade. He shifted the hilt from hand to hand as if testing its weight. The chieftess swept out of the tent. With her exit came a breeze that rustled the tassels that hung from the ceiling of the tent. Bells tinkled, and Liyana thought of the bells that she'd left for her family.

"You believe the trickster?" Fennik asked.

"I danced through the night, and Bayla didn't come."

"And your clan?" He continued to toy with the knife. "Did they believe him?"

"My clan went to Yubay to dreamwalk again in hopes Bayla would choose a new vessel, and they left me behind so as not to anger her further." It hurt to think about it. But if anyone would understand, it was another vessel. His clan must have been bereft as well. "Korbyn came a day later."

"My clan would never reject me," Fennik said, his confidence absolute.

His words felt like a kick. She focused again on the knife. He continued to switch it from hand to hand. She couldn't tell if it was habit or preparation. "Bayla didn't reject me. She was taken. She must have been. I *am* worthy."

"So you say."

Liyana glared at him. She wished she were fast enough to snatch that knife out of his hands. "You must at least believe that I'm not Bayla."

After a brief hesitation, he nodded. "My father deeply regrets the pain that he caused you."

She noticed his father wasn't here extending an apology. "I do wonder what he would have done if I *had* been Bayla. I cannot imagine that my goddess would have taken kindly to being stabbed through the stomach."

"He was prepared to die for his god."

"That's not dying for your god; that's dying for your stupidity."

Knife clenched in his hand, Fennik rose. "You do not take my family's hospitality and then call my father stupid."

"I don't call this 'hospitality.'" She raised her shirt to show her scar. "If you plan to stab me again, there's your target. Is that why Korbyn isn't here? So he can't save me twice?" She felt fury mix with her fear, and she grabbed onto the fury and let it fuel her. "We did not have to come here. Korbyn and I could have skipped your clan and rescued Bayla and left your god to rot in whatever false vessel he's trapped in. But instead of a 'thank-you,' I'm greeted with a knife in my stomach, separated from my companion, and stuck in a tent with an oiled-up muscle boy who has a 'decision' to make that may or may not involve another knife. I did nothing to you or your clan! Whatever issue you have with Korbyn and Bayla has nothing to do with me. All I want is my goddess to be where she belongs so that my little brother will not have to die before he has truly lived!" She was shouting, and she noticed that she had risen to sitting. Her whole body trembled. Liyana sank back into the pillows. "Ow. I still hurt. And I will scar. Bayla won't be pleased about that. I have been so careful to keep this body unblemished for her. She won't like that it's been used as a pincushion. Later, if there is a later, *you* can justify it to her."

She heard applause from the entrance to the tent. Korbyn walked inside, clapping. "I should have waited and let you speak with the elders. That was masterful."

Liyana couldn't help the smile that blossomed over her face. "You're all right! Are you all right?" She tried to rise again, but her arms shook so badly that she collapsed backward.

Ignoring Fennik and his knife, Korbyn knelt beside Liyana. "You were the one who was stabbed and yet you ask about me. Again you surprise me."

"I know how I am. You're the unknown. You healed me, didn't you? Have you recovered?" Healing her sand wolf gashes had knocked him out for hours. This had to have been far more serious. She studied his face and saw his eyes were sunken with deep lines as if he hadn't slept.

"After three days, yes, I am well."

Three days! She shot up to sitting. Her head spun. She cried in pain, and Korbyn helped her lie down. She felt his arms around her, warm and comforting.

"You would heal faster if you would lie still," Fennik commented.

She ignored him. "Three days?"

"I expressed my displeasure at the chief's actions," Korbyn said mildly.

"You what?"

"He attacked my father and his guards," Fennik said, glaring at Korbyn. "Broke my father's ribs, sliced one guard's leg, and nearly cracked the skull of another. Other clan members joined in until the trickster god was subdued."

"Korbyn!" Liyana said. "Did they hurt you?"

Korbyn stretched and twisted to demonstrate his fitness. "Afterwards, it took a while to heal you, the chief, his guards, and myself. In apology, the chief has offered us horses to help speed our journey and compensate for the lost time, though the damage may already be done."

She lay against the pillows with the words "three days" reverberating inside her. She didn't know what that time loss would mean to the other vessels . . . or to Bayla.

"My father's actions were necessary," Fennik said.

Korbyn barely looked at him. "Who's golden boy?" he asked Liyana.

"He's Fennik, the vessel of Sendar and the son of our esteemed hosts." She wished she had her sky serpent knife to bat that blade out of his hands. Her scar was *not* necessary. Nor was the loss of three days. She glared at him as if it were his fault.

In response to her introduction, Fennik inclined his head. He waited for a similar show of respect in return, but Korbyn did not oblige him. Instead he sniffed and then asked Liyana, "What do you think of him? Will he make a decent traveling companion?" Doubt infused his voice.

Outrage blossomed on Fennik's face.

Liyana shrugged and then winced from the movement. "He seems strong. You never know when we might need to lift something heavy."

"True," Korbyn said seriously. "There are many rocks in the desert. If memory serves, the hills of the Scorpion Clan are particularly rocky."

Fennik growled. "You mock me."

Korbyn's face was innocent, like Jidali's after he sneaked a cookie from Aunt Sabisa. "I would never mock such an illustrious personage," Korbyn said.

Liyana felt a twinge of guilt. This couldn't have been easy for Fennik either. After all, he had suffered a failed summoning ceremony as well. "I am sorry, Fennik. It isn't your fault that your father stabbed me."

"He acted in the best interests of the clan," Fennik said stiffly. "In his place, I would have done the same. And I am still prepared to do so, should the need arise."

All her sympathy for him evaporated.

Faster than her eyes could track, Korbyn's fist darted out. It slammed into Fennik's solar plexus as his other hand snatched the knife away from him. With a roar, Fennik lunged for him. Korbyn dodged. Skipping across the blankets and pillows, he evaded Fennik's fists. Liyana struggled to sit, searching around her for anything to use as a weapon.

After another failed lunge, Fennik halted. Still holding the knife, Korbyn waited. Liyana felt a wave of tiredness wash over her. "Enough," she said. "Either you believe us or you don't. Either you come or you don't. Just decide so I can sleep." This was the decision that the chieftess had meant, she realized. "Also, I want my knife back."

"You heard the lady," Korbyn said. She heard amusement in his voice, but she noticed that his eyes tracked Fennik's movements. He was ready to spring if necessary.

"Exactly who is in charge here?" Fennik asked.

"Does it matter?" Korbyn asked. "She's correct. You have the opportunity to save your god. It is up to you whether or not you take it."

Fennik's eyes narrowed. "Is it?"

"No," Liyana said. Her eyes flicked to Korbyn for confirmation.

Korbyn sighed. "Bayla would be upset with me if I allowed Sendar's clan to die because of the stubborn stupidity of a father and son. You will be coming with us."

* * *

The Horse Clan supplied them with eight horses: one for each of them as well as the other vessels they hoped to find, plus two spare horses so they could rotate mounts. To Liyana's shock, she saw that several large water containers had been loaded onto the horses. She remembered the silty taste of the water and knew their well had to be low. To donate this much water was an extraordinary gesture. The clan also loaded them with food pouches, grain for the horses, pots and pans, a larger tent (in place of Liyana's travel tent), and six different kinds of bows for Fennik to use.

"Do you really need six?" Korbyn asked as the bows were strapped to a horse.

"Different game requires different tools," Fennik said. "You wouldn't ask me to use a mallet for the same task that needs a knife, would you?"

"They're bows," Korbyn said. "You fit an arrow; you release it."

Fennik shook his head as if Korbyn were an object of pity.

Liyana skirted the edge of their miniherd. She'd ridden once or twice, a treat from the clan's hunters before she had become a vessel. She wasn't convinced she could ride for miles on end without falling off and humiliating herself in front of the god and the horse warrior. She wished Korbyn would abandon this plan to ride so she could keep her feet firmly in the sand. And she wished it were still only her and Korbyn.

Fennik leaped onto his horse's back without touching the stirrups. He waved his hand to his clan, and they cheered. He was decked out as the departing hero with sky blue robes of the finest weave and a headcloth with gold tassels.

Beside him, Korbyn slid up into his saddle with such grace that it looked as though he'd merely stepped onto a ladder. He didn't preen; he merely waited. Fennik continued to play to the crowd, prancing his horse in front of Korbyn and Liyana. Taking a deep breath, Liyana grabbed the saddle with both hands and put her foot into the stirrup. She pulled her body up, and pain from her scar shot through her torso. She let go.

"Allow me," a voice said behind her. She was tossed gently and easily into the saddle. She looked down to see the chief beside her. Instinctively she shied back. Responding to her, the horse sidestepped away.

Coming up beside her husband, the chieftess pressed a pouch into Liyana's hand. "Herbs for the pain. Mix a few with your water each time you stop. It won't eliminate the hurt altogether, but it should allow you to keep riding. There are more in the packs."

"We picked a horse with a smooth gait for you," the chief said. "According to our traditions, you may name her."

Liyana managed a polite nod. She couldn't bring herself to voice the words "thank you." Her scar ached. She watched the chief and chieftess say good-bye to Fennik. Bending down, he embraced each of them. They pressed their foreheads together and talked softly. Each parent kissed him multiple times on his cheeks.

Liyana wished she'd had that kind of good-bye with her parents. She missed her family with an ache that matched the pain from her wound.

At last his parents stepped away.

"Do not return to us," his father said. "Either succeed in your quest and give your body to Sendar, or do not return at all."

Liyana saw a flash of an emotion in Fennik's eyes—surprise

perhaps, or hurt—but he recovered quickly. "I will not fail!" Fennik said. Raising his hands to wave at his people one more time, he shifted in the saddle. The horse surged forward. Sand kicked up behind him. He galloped south in a plume of sand and dust.

Korbyn squeezed his knees around the barrel of his horse, and the horse trotted forward. Liyana kicked her heels into hers. After three kicks, the horse lurched into a walk. She followed Korbyn and Fennik, and the cheers of the Horse Clan faded behind them.

Chapter Ten
The Emperor

All the farms in the west had withered. Mounted on a roan war-horse, the emperor rode at the front of the army caravan and forced himself to look at each dry field, the shriveled rows of dust and the twisted sickly trees. He rode past abandoned farmhouses and some that looked abandoned but weren't. Men, women, and children clustered in the doorways and watched the army march by. Their faces wore the pinched, hollow look that he'd come to recognize as the look of his people, and their hungry eyes devoured the caravan.

At the first few farms, he'd quietly had his soldiers shuttle food to the families. But after a while . . . He needed the supplies for the army. Just as quietly, he'd had his soldiers stop.

Still his people drank in the sight of the army, consuming it with their empty eyes.

"You give them hope," General Xevi said. His two best generals flanked him. General Xevi, an older man who had counseled the emperor's father, rode on his right. General Akkon, an even older man who had known the emperor's grandfather, was on his left.

"False hope," General Akkon said.

"Hope is a powerful tool if it is not abused," General Xevi said.

The criticism was there, unspoken. "You think this is madness," the emperor said.

"It is not my place to cast such judgments," General Xevi said.

The emperor's mouth quirked. It was almost a smile, though it didn't warm him. "Of course it is. I trust you to advise me, and that includes speaking up if you believe that I am acting like a nightmare-addled lunatic."

"To base so much on a dream and a myth—"

"And the claims of a madman," General Akkon added.

"The magician is not mad," the emperor said, "though I admit he has his moments of . . ." He cast about for the proper euphemism, and words failed him. The magician was indeed flawed. "You did not speak your concerns before."

"The court is filled with fools," General Xevi said, "but they are powerful fools. You needed the full confidence of the military when you stood before them."

"And do I have the full confidence of the military?" the emperor asked. He did not let either his voice or his face betray the way his insides clenched.

For a moment, General Xevi did not answer. They rode past another farmstead. The wooden door swung open and shut in the wind, as if in rhythm with the footfalls and hoofbeats of the army. Torn curtains fluttered in the windows. But no family came outside.

"You have our hope," General Xevi said.

The emperor nodded. It was enough. "I will not abuse it." He twisted in his saddle. Dust rose in clouds from the road, and his army stretched into the distance. "Send a scouting party ahead. Secretly, if you can, so as not to admit any doubt. Send them to the desert mountains. . . . And let us see if they find false hope or true."

Chapter Eleven

Liyana laid her cheek against the horse's neck and wished she didn't hurt so much. With every step the horse took, she felt a throb of pain from her scar, and she had fresh bruises and blisters on her thighs from the saddle. She'd named her horse Misery. Misery collected dust on her hide that mixed with horse sweat. This dust clung to Liyana's skin—clogging her pores, filling her nose, itching her eyes. Trailing after Korbyn and Fennik, she listened to them argue about what route to take.

"Five days," Fennik promised. He was pushing for a route that would take them north of the salt flats. He claimed he could hunt there, plus there would be occasional springs of water between the rocks.

Korbyn shook his head. "We cross the salt flats. Three days."

"They're a wasteland," Fennik objected. "Zero animals. Zero plants. I need fresh meat for optimum strength." He flexed his arm muscles.

"We have supplies," Korbyn said. "What we don't have is time. We must reach the Silk, Scorpion, and Falcon Clans before their ceremonies fail. We cross the salt flats." He kneed his horse and trotted ahead of them, effectively ending the discussion.

To Liyana, Fennik said, "I always pictured the trickster god as more jovial."

Liyana didn't reply. Since Fennik had joined them, neither Liyana nor Korbyn had talked much. Instead Fennik had regaled them with tales of breeding horses, training horses, and selling horses. At first Liyana had tried to interject stories of her own clan, but Fennik hadn't been interested in listening and Korbyn had seemed preoccupied. As her sores from riding all day worsened, it became easier to stay quiet. She missed the conversations with Korbyn, though, and she caught herself watching him as they rode. He wasn't sleeping well—she'd woken him from nightmares twice last night, squeezing his shoulder so he'd wake without alerting Fennik.

Fennik babbled as cheerfully as if she had encouraged him. "My clan tells the tale of when the trickster god attempted to trick Sendar into trading his favorite horse for a scorpion. The scorpion recognized Sendar's strength of character and refused to act against him. He stung the trickster instead." Fennik laughed, a booming sound that seemed to roll across the desert.

On the crest of the next sand dune, Korbyn waited for them. Catching up, Liyana and Fennik reined in alongside him. The other horses, guided by Fennik, slowed as well.

Stretched out before them were the salt flats. Heat waved over the white surface. Liyana felt her eyes water from the glare of the sun on the bright white. She shielded her eyes. Despite the name, the salt flats were not flat. The crumbling flats were split by cracks, the work of salt worms.

Liyana had never seen a salt worm, though she'd heard stories, of course. In most of the desert, they lived so far below the surface that they might as well be myth. But here . . . they tunneled vast networks just below the crusted earth, excreting both salt and the fine threads that the Silk Clan collected for their famous cloth. They also left in their wake a chopped, treacherous terrain. Liyana pointed to one of the broken areas. "What do we do about the salt worms?"

Korbyn shrugged. "We avoid them." He dismounted and offered water to the horses. Then he redistributed the packs while Fennik checked the hooves and fetlocks of each horse.

"Stories say that some worms can grow up to fifteen feet long," Liyana said. She ran a curry comb over Misery's hide. The horse heaved a sigh when Liyana didn't remove the saddle. She wanted the most placid horse possible for this terrain. "Large enough to swallow a man whole."

"Stories can lie," Korbyn said as he mounted a different horse.

This one, a sorrel mare, whickered at him, clearly pleased to be exchanging the water containers for a rider. "Your precious Sendar ordered the scorpion to sting me while I slept. He's not as noble of character as you'd like to believe." Without waiting for a response, Korbyn kneed his horse, and the mare lurched forward, descending the sand dune. Over his shoulder, Korbyn added, "And the worms can grow *much* longer than fifteen feet."

*   *   *

The sun beat down on Liyana's back until she felt as if every drop of moisture had been pounded out of her. She unhooked her waterskin from the saddle and drank. As much as she loved the desert, she hated the salt flats. Fennik was right that they were a wasteland. Utterly colorless, they stretched in every direction. Even the stone mountains looked pale, like clouds low on the horizon. Cracks left behind by the worms laced the flats and slowed Liyana, Korbyn, and Fennik—they couldn't risk a horse stumbling.

After a few hours, they rested the horses. Fennik slid off the back of his horse and poured water into a dish. The water sloshed over the rim and was instantly sucked into the hard ground.

Korbyn jumped off his horse and caught Fennik by the wrist before Fennik could fill the next dish. "The worms are drawn to moisture," Korbyn said. "Do. Not. Spill." He released Fennik's wrist before the horse boy could wrest it away.

Carefully Fennik filled dishes halfway for the other horses. A few drops stained the salt as the horses nuzzled against the dishes, and Liyana held her breath as she watched for worms. As soon as the horses finished, they moved on quickly.

They rode for two days without seeing any salt worms. "I think I'll kiss the sand," Liyana said on the dawn of the third day, the day they were to leave the salt flats. "And forswear all salt in my food forevermore."

"Imagine that it's sugar," Korbyn said. "You're riding across candy."

"Salt can never be sugar," Fennik said.

"We should talk about the definition of the word 'imagine.'"

Before Fennik could reply, one of the spare horses caught her hoof on a crack in the salt. Her tired leg kept moving even though her hoof had stopped, and she pitched forward. With a yell, Fennik launched himself off the back of his horse to catch the falling horse's reins. Startled, his horse reared, which frightened the other horses. One of the other horses tried to bolt, crashed into a nearby horse, and fell onto her side. She scrambled upright.

Liyana struggled to cling to her reins as Misery sidestepped and snorted. She didn't buck or try to run, thankfully. Soon Liyana was able to loosen her grip on the reins and look over at the others. Fennik was soothing the startled horse, murmuring to her and stroking her neck, while Korbyn rounded up the others.

Beneath the horse who had fallen, Liyana spotted a dark patch. Worse, the patch spread outward, and the darkness stained the salt.

The horse had held a water container, and it had cracked on impact. The precious liquid flowed freely down the horse's flank. "Water!" Liyana cried. She slid off Misery and ran to the horse. The two boys were instantly beside her, pulling the container off and trying to plug the holes. Fissures zigzagged over it.

At their feet, the liquid was swallowed up by the salt flats.

"Leave it," Korbyn commanded. He backed away from the container. "Lead the horses away." He scooped up three sets of reins and began to pull the horses away from the water stain.

"My clan sacrificed to give us that water! Saving it is—" Fennik began to argue.

Beneath Liyana's feet, she felt the earth tremble. She heard a rumble. She yanked on Misery's reins. Eyes wide, the mare flexed her knees and refused to budge. Salt pellets rattled and then were tossed into the air as if bounced from below. Misery rolled her eyes and snorted. Her body shook but her knees stayed locked. Liyana stroked her neck and pleaded, "Come on. Just a step and then another. You can do it. Please!"

Beside her, Korbyn shouted at the other horses. Fennik slapped the flanks of another, and yanked on the reins of two more. Several bolted.

"She won't move!" Liyana yelled. She braced herself and pulled the reins. Misery rolled her eyes back in her head again, exposing only the whites of her eyes.

As the shaking increased, Liyana fell to her knees. The reins slipped out of her fingers. Feet spread to keep his balance, Fennik unhooked one of his bows and arrows. He aimed it at the ground. All but three of the horses had fled.

The worms burst through the crust of the salt flat. Chunks of salt flew into the air and then rained down. Salty dust instantly blanketed them. At Liyana's feet, finger-size worms crowded their writhing bodies over the damp earth. Dog-size worms followed them, squeezing their bodies through the cracks. Fennik fired arrows into their oozing flesh.

As the ground continued to quake, Liyana scrambled backward, and Misery reared, finally breaking her paralysis. A four-foot worm with a body as thick as a child's burst out of the ground directly in front of them. Misery slammed her hooves down on the worm's soft body. It squished under her hooves but continued to writhe. Its mouth opened and shut to show multiple rows of rock-hard teeth.

Another worm shot out of the ground beneath Misery and clamped its mouth onto one of the horse's legs. "No!" Liyana shouted.

The mare whinnied and shuddered, and then fell to the ground as the worm sucked. Other worms converged on the horse, spreading over Misery's torso. They latched on and sucked.

Liyana yanked Jidali's knife out of her sash and hacked at the worms that covered Misery. Gray pus poured out of the bulbous bodies, but still more worms surged out of the earth to replace the ones she had chopped away.

Liyana felt a sharp pain in her leg. She looked down to see that a worm the size of her arm had latched onto her calf. She sliced through its body, and the worm fell away.

One of the two remaining horses broke through the worms and ran. But the other horse fell and succumbed, collapsing beside Misery. *Too many!* Liyana thought as she tried to wade through the oozing bodies. "Korbyn, use magic!" she yelled. He couldn't hear her over the screams of dying horses and the crunch of the salt earth as it was torn up by the worms. She waded through the worms toward him. She grabbed his arm.

Startled, he met her eyes.

"Use your magic," she said. "I'll guard you."

He hesitated for a fraction of a second, and then he lowered his knife. Closing his eyes, he steadied his breathing. She sliced at the worms that crawled toward them.

The ground shook harder than before, and Liyana was knocked backward. She landed hard on her tailbone, and the air whooshed out of her lungs. In front of her, in the midst of the writhing worms, the ground exploded, and a massive worm—larger than she'd ever imagined—burst out of the ground. Its mouth gaped wide. It looked as if it could swallow the sun.

"Fennik!" she yelled as she scrambled to her feet. Bracing herself, she held the sky serpent knife in front of her. The worm swung its head from side to side as if sniffing the air. Arrows hit its body, plunging deep into the mucus coat that covered the bulbous segments.

"Run!" Fennik yelled.

Liyana didn't. She turned to Korbyn, who was deep in a trance, and sliced away a worm that had latched onto his back. He stood still as stone, his eyes closed, his breathing even. She stomped and stabbed at the smaller worms that ringed them as the giant worm towered over them.

"Coward!" Fennik shouted at Korbyn. "Fight them!"

"Help me guard him!" she yelled.

But Fennik continued to shoot the worms near the dead horses.

The giant worm flexed in the air, and then slowly, miraculously, it sank back into the ground. The smaller worms retreated as well. The ground shook again as the worms sped away, cracking the salt flat as they fled.

In seconds, all was quiet.

Korbyn collapsed.

*　　*　　*

Liyana lifted the supply packs off the two dead horses. She tried not to look at Misery. Tears openly poured down Fennik's cheeks as he cut away the saddles and bridles. Wordlessly Liyana and Fennik carried their remaining supplies several hundred yards away from the torn salt earth. Liyana set up the tent, and they placed the unconscious god inside.

While Fennik went to search for surviving horses, Liyana examined the bite marks that covered Korbyn's body. He'd been torn all over, despite her best efforts.

Trying to be gentle, she pulled the fabric of his clothes away from the wounds. Some of them oozed blood. Some were coated in mucus and pus from the worms that she'd sliced away. She wondered if she dare use water to wash them out. She wondered if she dare *not* use water to wash them out.

Fennik crawled into the tent. "How is he?"

"Bad," Liyana said. She didn't look at Fennik. "He can't heal himself if he's not conscious." She dug the healing herbs out of her pack.

"He drove the worms away, didn't he?"

That was so obvious she didn't bother to reply. She located cloths and bandages, and she pressed a clean cloth to a wound on his calf to slow the bleeding.

Fennik tucked a wadded robe underneath Korbyn's leg. "We need to keep the blood from seeping into the ground. It's moisture too."

She'd rather keep the blood inside Korbyn's body entirely, never mind where it went afterward. She felt as if her heart was beating uncomfortably hard inside her rib cage. Liyana tied a bandage around his arm. Her hands shook.

"How can I help?" Fennik asked.

Liyana bit her lip. If he'd helped when she'd asked before . . . She refused to meet his eyes. If she did, she thought she might lose her self-control, and that wouldn't help Korbyn. "More bandages," she said.

He fetched more.

She wrapped his wounds as best she could, using damp cloths to clean the worst bites, and then smothering the dampness in dry cloths. Fennik took extra wads of cloths outside to care for the horses. He returned after a while.

"How many horses did you find?" she asked. She still couldn't bring herself to look at him.

"Two," Fennik said. "One is unridable. The other has only superficial wounds and will live, with care. But there's no sign of the four that ran across the flats."

She nodded. He didn't have to say that that was bad. Wounded and without water, those horses wouldn't last long. "What about our water supplies?"

He hesitated. "A day's worth left, if we ration."

Korbyn had slept for three days with the Horse Clan. She didn't know how long he'd be out after this level of magic. He'd once said summoning water where none existed was immensely difficult. "We could strap him to the good horse and walk to the Silk Clan."

"In the sun and walking . . . the water wouldn't last a day." Fennik slumped down beside her. "I said we shouldn't cross the salt flats. He thinks he's invincible."

"Does it feel good to be proven right?" Liyana blinked back the tears that sprang into her eyes. She couldn't afford to lose the moisture. "Korbyn had said three days to cross the flats. So we have to be close to the Silk Clan. Take the last horse and whatever water you need and find help."

"You cannot ask me to leave you alone—"

"I won't be alone," Liyana said. "He'll wake. And I'm not asking."

"Come with me," Fennik said. "If we leave all the supplies except for the water, the horse can carry us both. We can make it to the Silk Clan and send help back for Korbyn."

She shook her head. The idea of leaving him felt as repugnant as the flesh of the salt worms. She'd failed to protect him against the worms; she didn't intend to fail him again.

"He'll be all right," Fennik said. "As soon as he wakes, he'll heal himself."

She focused on Korbyn's face. It was twisted in pain. Every second Fennik wasted arguing was a second longer until they had help. Without thinking, she wrapped her hand around Korbyn's hand. "You'll be faster if you ride alone," she told Fennik.

"But you—"

"Stop!" For the first time since the worms, Liyana looked him directly in the eyes. "Stop arguing. Stop needing to be right. Stop trying to prove you're better than he is. Take the horse and find help."

Fennik fell silent for a moment. "Bayla chose him over Sendar too."

"I'm not Bayla and you're not Sendar. And if he dies, then neither of us ever will be. Go!" Liyana bent over Korbyn.

She heard Fennik leave the tent. She heard him murmur to the horses, and then the sound of a horse being saddled. And then he rode away over the hard salt.

Alone, she listened to Korbyn's harsh and fast breathing.

She felt his forehead for signs of a fever. His skin was slippery with sweat. *Don't you die on me,* she thought at him. Fingers shaking, she checked her stock of medicinal leaves. She'd used up half her supply already, and the remaining stash was a pathetic handful of dried weeds. She'd have to be more sparing in the future, if there was a future. Liyana banished that thought.

After a while, she ducked out of the tent to tend to the last horse. She was a roan mare, though it was difficult to tell beneath the salt, dried blood, and pus. Liyana remembered that Fennik had named her Plum after her fondness for date plums. Gently Liyana peeled back the bandages Fennik had applied to check on the wounds. Most seemed clean, and none oozed. She secured the bandages again. Plum was in better shape than Korbyn. Patting the horse's neck, Liyana looked out across the salt flats. She saw no one and nothing. All was still.

Carefully she offered the horse a few sips of water. She drained the dish gratefully and whinnied for more. Liyana poured her a handful of horse-meal pellets instead.

Returning to the tent, she checked her own wounds, and then lay down beside Korbyn. She closed her eyes but her muscles stayed tense, waiting to feel the earth shake again. Eventually she slept.

She woke to the sound of a horse whickering. Poking her head out the tent flap, she asked, "Plum, what is it?" In the distance, she spotted a cloud of salt dust. In its center was a horse, walking toward them. "Fennik!" She waved. But as the horse drew closer, she saw it wasn't the same horse—this horse was black and white, and it had no rider. Korbyn had named this horse Windfire.

The horse swayed as she walked, but she didn't slow. She trudged toward them step by painful step. After nearly an hour, Windfire reached them, and her legs folded underneath her. Plum nuzzled the other mare's neck.

"Good to see you," Liyana said as she lifted off the saddle and the supply packs. She poured the horse-meal pellets and (very carefully) a small amount of water, and then she examined Windfire's wounds. She saw only superficial cuts, which had ceased bleeding and dried in the hot air. The horse should recover—*assuming we don't all die,* Liyana thought.

She spent the rest of the day alternating between Korbyn and the horses. She tried not to think about how little water remained or to count the hours since Fennik had left. She listened to Korbyn's shallow breathing, and she tried not to think at all. As night fell, Liyana remained outside the tent with the horses and watched the stars spread across the sky. She located the goat constellation (Bayla's stars) above the forbidden mountains and then the raven constellation near the eastern horizon.

"Beautiful, aren't they?" a voice said behind her.

She twisted around to see Korbyn emerge from the tent. He plopped down beside her and proceeded to strip off his bandages. The skin underneath was healed. Liyana touched the smooth skin, and then all of a sudden her cheeks were wet.

Kneeling, he cupped her face in his hands and caught her tears in his palms. "Don't bring back our writhing friends," he said gently.

She stared into his eyes and gulped hard once, twice, until she no longer felt as if she were splintering. He was alive! Her skin shivered where he touched it. "Whatever you did worked," she said evenly. "They left."

"I summoned water elsewhere." He studied her. "Let me fix you."

She wanted to object—he'd only just recovered—but before she could frame a reply, he'd rolled up her sleeves. Concentrating, he focused on her. In a few minutes, the bite sealed shut. He repeated this for the other bite marks. Everywhere he touched tingled, and it took all her strength not to scream, *You're alive!* She told herself that it was relief on behalf of her goddess. When he finished, she touched her healed skin and then his. His skin felt warm and smooth, and her fingers lingered.

He was watching her fingers. "Surface wounds are simpler than a knife through internal organs." His voice sounded rough, and she met his eyes. They stared at each other in silence for a moment. He then looked away. "What happened to the other horses? I only see two sets of bones."

The worms had stripped the two fallen horses bare. *Poor Misery,* Liyana thought. "They ran off. Only this one, Windfire, has returned so far." She was pleased that her voice sounded normal. Her ribs felt tight, as if they'd been knit closely together, squeezing her lungs.

"I'll call them to us," he said. He dropped into another trance. Liyana watched him silently. He was so perfectly beautiful. She breathed with him, evenly and deeply, and she wished she dared reach over and touch him again—just to reassure herself that he was alive. After a few minutes, he broke the trance and reported, "Only located three. One is in bad shape but close. Two others are on their way." His voice light, Korbyn asked, "And where is our favorite warrior boy? Out searching for the horses?"

Liyana scanned the starlit flats. The moon bathed the white earth in a soft blue. She thought she saw shadows stir. "He took the healthiest horse and rode for help."

She heard Korbyn's breath catch in his throat.

"We didn't know when you'd wake," Liyana explained, "and we don't have much water left. It was the sensible option."

Korbyn shot toward the tent and quickly began to collapse it. "We need to catch him," he said. "You pack. I'll heal the horses."

She began to pack up their camp. "Why do we need to catch him? What's wrong?"

Laying his hands on Windfire, he focused on the horse's wounds. As he worked and as she packed, she heard the clip-clop of hooves on the hardened salt. One by one, the other three horses trotted and limped to them, and one by one, he healed them.

When he finished, he lay down in the sand. She let him rest, either unconscious or asleep. Only a few minutes later, he opened his eyes and lurched to his feet. "Ready?"

Liyana reached toward him to steady him, but he turned toward Windfire and checked the saddle. "You need more rest," she said. "Why can't we wait until dawn?"

"The Silk Clan . . . does not like strangers." He mounted Windfire, and she climbed onto another horse. She stroked her mare's neck as the horse protested. Korbyn held the lead ropes of the other horses.

With the stars above, they rode over the salt flats.

Chapter Twelve

Flute music, carried by the hot breezes that swept over the cracked land, drifted across the salt flats. Riding on Gray Luck—a gray mare she'd renamed because she had lived despite a worm bite inches from her jugular—Liyana listened to the plaintive melody. It was echoed by a second flute and then a third. The notes swooped and soared as they spiraled up toward the stars.

"Beautiful," Liyana said.

Korbyn didn't respond. Instead he coaxed Windfire into a trot. Salt dust rose in a cloud under the hooves of Korbyn's horse. The other three horses plodded after him.

"What do we do if Fennik is in trouble?" Liyana called after him.

"Try to get him out of it."

She glared at his back. "Your plan seems vague."

He shrugged as if unconcerned.

"You could have warned us that the Silk Clan is dangerous," she said. "You seem to think you're doing this alone. You're not."

"I noticed that." He waved his hand at her and the injured horses as if she were also a wounded animal that he had to shepherd across the desert.

Her voice low so that only Gray Luck could hear, she muttered, "I didn't realize pigheadedness was a raven trait." Following in the cloud of salt dust, she trailed him to the Silk Clan's camp.

Clustered on the border of the salt flats, each tent was swathed in white cloth that reflected the light of the stars, the moon, and the torches until it seemed to glow. Beyond them, far in the distance, were the black silhouettes of the stone hills, cutting into the starscape.

Drums had joined the flute music. The soft rhythm rolled beneath the interwoven melodies. And then the voice started: a crystal clear voice that soared above the flutes and drums. A wordless melody, it was sweeter and clearer than any birdcall.

"She's the vessel," Korbyn said.

"How do you know?" Liyana asked.

"Oyri always chooses a vessel who can sing," he said.

Liyana listened as the singer's voice cascaded over several octaves. She thought of water running from a cup. Her voice was as beautiful as water. Liyana felt the notes seep into her skin, and she swayed in the saddle to the music. Her feet itched to dance to the drumbeat.

Ahead, the camp was still. No one came forward to intercept them. The outer circle of tents looked empty, as if they were waiting like shadows on the cusp of dawn, expectant and motionless. She thought that everyone must be with the musicians, obscured from view in the center of camp.

"Someday I'd like to see you dance." His voice was so soft that she nearly missed his words. She wondered if he meant her or Bayla in her body. She felt herself shiver, and she told herself she merely felt the night wind worm through her clothes.

For an instant, she imagined dancing for him, feeling his eyes on her. . . . *He must mean Bayla*, she thought. She changed the subject, keeping her voice as light as she could, as if she were merely curious. "Did Bayla choose me because I can dance?"

"Are you asking 'why me?' If so, I cannot answer that for Bayla."

"So how did you choose your vessel?" She tried to imagine another's soul looking out of his eyes, and she couldn't. Those eyes were Korbyn's.

His face was in shadows, but she thought she saw a flash of sadness. He didn't answer her question. "I do know you are not merely a dancer, Liyana. Only a few per generation can be vessels— and many of them become magicians instead." He lowered his voice. They had reached the tents. Still no one approached them, and the music swelled louder. "Only someone whose soul came from the Dreaming instead of being born within his or her body can be a vessel or become a magician."

"I have a reincarnated soul?"

"You do."

"Whose?"

"Yours."

Before Liyana could ask more, an elderly woman shuffled toward them. She held a torch in one hand, and the orange glow encircled her. Black soot stained the deep blue sky. Her skin was as dark as smudged charcoal, and in contrast, the whites of her eyes seemed to blaze in the torchlight. Wrinkles creased her face, swallowing her features, so that her cheeks resembled the inside of a fist.

Quietly to Liyana, Korbyn said, "I swear I will be more careful than I was with Sendar's people. Even after burning my hand, I forgot there is true danger here. But I will not forget again, and I will not permit you to be harmed."

Her breath caught in her throat at the vehemence in his voice, and she reminded herself that he had to preserve her for Bayla's sake. Like the dancing, this wasn't about Liyana.

Korbyn halted and dismounted. Holding the reins, he genuflected before the old woman. "We come with peace in our minds and song in our hearts." Quickly Liyana dismounted and knelt beside him. She wondered if she should repeat his words as well. She opted for silence.

"I am Ilia, First Magician of the Silk Clan." The woman closed her hand into a fist and thumped her chest with such force that she staggered back a step.

Korbyn continued to kneel. "It is said that Oyri of the Silk Clan once tamed one of the great salt worms to create the finest silk threads just for her. It lived beneath her feet wherever she walked, and when she wished to weave, it would spew threads from the earth in such quantities that it created new hills."

"It is said, yes," Ilia agreed.

"But do you know *how* Oyri tamed the great salt worm? She asked her friend the raven to create a river of water far beneath the ground that would follow her wherever she walked, leading the great salt worm to her."

"We do not know this tale."

"I am the raven," Korbyn said.

"You claim friendship with Oyri?"

He bowed over his knee. "I am so honored."

Ilia raised her arm. Her hand trembled, and the loose flesh on her arm shook. Then it stilled as her fingers splayed open—a clear signal. Suddenly and silently a dozen warriors stepped out from between the tents. Bows and spears were trained on Liyana and Korbyn. Liyana didn't dare breathe. Her muscles felt locked in place. Korbyn's pretty promise of safety would evaporate if they were both riddled with arrows. The magician Ilia lowered her hand, and the warriors lowered their bows and spears in perfect synchronization.

Retreating, the warriors disappeared into the shadows between the tents. Liyana felt prickles run up and down her spine. She knew the warriors were still there. "Fennik?" she whispered.

Korbyn shook his head nearly imperceptibly—either to say he didn't know or not to ask. Or he could have meant that he suspected the worst. Fennik could have met these same guards and not fared as well.

"You may leave your horses here," Ilia said. "My boys will tend to them." She snapped her fingers, and two young men appeared from nearby tents. They scurried to the horses and unsaddled and brushed them.

"We thank you for your kindness," Korbyn said. He bowed again.

Watching strangers curry the horses, Liyana wound her fingers in Gray Luck's mane. The horse raised her head from the trough and nipped her shoulder with soft, wet lips. Liyana patted the horse's neck and wondered if she would ever see the animals or gear again. She wondered if Fennik's horse was here, hidden within other shadows. She saw hoof marks in the sand, but she lacked a tracker's skill to distinguish them.

"Come," Ilia said.

The old magician did not wait to see if her guests followed. Briskly she hobbled deeper into the heart of the camp. Korbyn trailed her. As they turned a corner, the torchlight stretched their shadows on the tent walls around them. Reluctantly leaving Gray

Luck and the other horses, Liyana hurried after the god and the magician.

As they neared the center of camp, the music crescendoed. Other voices had joined in, but the soloist's soared above them. She trilled impossible notes like some glorious bird.

"Oyri will be pleased with her," Korbyn said.

"She is the finest singer we have had for generations," Ilia said. "Even the winds quiet to listen to her."

"May I ask for what she sings?"

"Judgment," Ilia said.

The magician led them to an open circle. In the center, tied to a stake, was Fennik. He was shirtless, and his arms were bound behind him and twisted so that his tattoos were exposed to the starry sky. He was on his bare knees on the hard, salt ground. A silver dish lay below him. Sweat dripped from his face to his chin and then fell onto the dish with a ping. Gagged, he could not speak when his saw them, but his eyes widened and he strained against his bindings.

Around the stake were the drummers and other singers. Opposite them, in a throne draped with white silk, sat the soloist. She had straight, white hair, the same color as the salt, but her face was as soft as a child's. She was tiny and thin, half the size of Ilia, and she looked fragile perched on the large throne. She didn't look at Liyana and Korbyn. Others did, faltering in their drumbeats and losing their melodies as they stared. Soon only the soloist sang.

"May I ask what his crime is?" Korbyn sounded casual.

At his voice, the singing ceased.

The girl, the vessel, tilted her head toward Korbyn and Liyana. Liyana saw that her eyes were covered in a white haze, and she did not focus on anyone's face. She seemed to stare at the air between the tents and the stars. "He came to us with no talk of friendship and no words of peace. He demanded obedience to his will," the girl said. Her speaking voice was as beautiful as her singing voice. The words fell as if in a melody. "But ignorance alone would not condemn him. This man . . . this boy . . . this *vessel* abandoned his clan! Do you claim knowledge of this traitor?"

Ilia spoke. "This stranger claims to be the raven, the god Korbyn. His companion is yet unnamed."

"He is not alone?" the girl asked. "Speak, companion, so I may know you."

All eyes turned to Liyana, except for the girl's. She continued to focus on nothing. Shrinking back, Liyana looked at Korbyn for help. His face was unreadable. "I am Liyana, vessel of the Goat Clan." She heard murmurs around her. She added, "But I did not abandon my clan, and neither did Fennik!"

"A person who would abandon her people surely would not hesitate to lie to save herself." Unwinding herself from the silk on her throne, the girl rose. Instantly two men flanked her side. Cupping her elbows with their hands, they guided her across the circle, past Fennik, and stopped in front of Liyana and Korbyn.

Her milky eyes still did not fix on them. *She's blind*, Liyana thought. She had never heard of a blind vessel. "You, trickster god, know all about lies. What lies did you tell these vessels to convince them to leave their clans?"

"Shockingly, none," Korbyn said. He sounded vaguely surprised at himself.

She drew herself tall, her petite frame stiffening. "I am Pia, vessel to Oyri. Are you here to tell *me* your lies?" The power in her voice sent her words soaring across the camp.

Liyana noticed that the warriors had surrounded them again. Several had raised their bows. "My clan left me," she said. "Bayla didn't come. We do not lie!" She inched closer to Korbyn until her arm brushed against his. His hand found hers. She wondered if he was reassuring her or himself. His face remained calm.

"Five deities have been captured and imprisoned in false vessels," Korbyn said. "We need five vessels to save them: Goat, Horse, Silk, Scorpion, and Falcon. We seek your help in the rescue of your goddess."

"We do not believe my goddess needs rescuing," Pia said. "She is Oyri. She is our strength and our light and our song." She spread her arms wide and sang the final words.

Liyana heard Korbyn sigh. "For the first time in my existence, I tell the truth, and I am greeted with lack of belief. This is the universe laughing at me."

"I believed you from the start," Liyana said, continuing to hold his hand.

He looked at her, and he smiled. "Yes, you did." His smile was like Pia's song, beautiful and pure. It lit up his whole face, erasing the shadows that had deepened ever since they had entered the Silk Clan's camp—truly, ever since they'd entered the Horse Clan's camp. For an instant, she couldn't breathe. She was lost in that smile.

As if her words had given him strength, Korbyn raised his voice, and she heard his old cheerfulness. "I am indeed attempting the greatest trick of my career, but the trick is not on you. It is on the thief who is stealing the heart of the desert."

"We do not believe that is—" Pia began.

Enough, Liyana thought. She'd told the truth. Korbyn had told the truth. While they wasted time, Bayla remained trapped. Liyana interrupted Pia. "What you believe doesn't matter. You can prove him right or wrong. Summon your goddess. If she does not come, then join us. If she does come, then punish us as you see fit."

The Silk Clan was silent.

Softly Korbyn said, "You truly trust me."

She met his glorious eyes. "Yes, I do."

The moment hung in the air, and he laughed, the sound full of joy. She hadn't heard that laugh in days. She began to smile as if his laugh were bubbling inside of her. "Go ahead," Korbyn said to Pia. "Summon Oyri."

"Very well," Pia said. "I shall."

Guards closed in on Liyana and Korbyn, and suddenly Liyana wished she hadn't spoken. She lost sight of Pia through the wall of guards.

Ilia pulled a strip of white cloth from her pocket, and she tied it over Korbyn's mouth. He didn't protest. Liyana flinched as Ilia raised a cloth to her mouth. "Is this necessary?" she asked.

"You have submitted to judgment," Ilia said. "This must be."

Korbyn squeezed her fingers as if to reassure her, and then he released her hand and held out his arms so that the guards could bind his wrists with rope.

I trust him, she reminded herself. *The Silk Clan goddess will not come.*

Opening her mouth, Liyana let Ilia gag her. Mirroring Korbyn, she held out her arms so that her hands could be tied as well. She met Korbyn's eyes. His eyes were warm on hers, as warm as an embrace, as if he saw only her.

They were led to Fennik. Hands on their shoulders pushed them down to their knees. She knelt on the hard salt-sand between Fennik and Korbyn. Fennik's eyes were wild, and she could smell his sweat. On her other side, though, Korbyn seemed calm.

She thought of the accusations of the Horse Clan and the Silk Clan. *He may be known as the trickster,* she thought, *but his tricks helped the desert clans.* She knew a story about him, one of Jidali's favorites, that said he was responsible for giving the clans fire. Once, long ago, only gods could start fires. Each clan treasured their fire, carrying it from camp to camp with greatest care. If the fire was lost before the clan's deity returned, the result was disaster. This happened to the Raven Clan—a sandstorm wiped out their fire. So, on his next visit to the desert, the raven stole a chunk of flint from the mountains of the sky serpents and gave it to his clan so they would always be able to make fire for themselves. He then stole flint for each of the other clans. The sky serpents were furious that every clan now had a piece of their mountains, and they guarded their territory even more jealously against intruders. But the raven's trick was done, and he never returned to face their wrath.

She wondered how much truth there was in the stories. Staring into his eyes, she decided she didn't care. Oyri, goddess of the Silk Clan, would not come. She had to believe that for Bayla's sake, if not her own.

Drums started across the circle. Surprised, Liyana tore her gaze away from Korbyn. She'd expected a delay. Pia must have people to say farewell to. Parents. Siblings. Friends. A teacher. But instead she spoke to no one. Alone in the center of the sand, Pia affixed silver bells to her ankles. She was barefoot, and her skirt was composed of strips of silk that fluttered around her like feathers. Her arms were bare to expose her tattoos. She reached up toward the night sky. "Begin!" Pia cried.

Ilia began to chant. In the circle, Pia twirled and leaped. As she danced, she sang a soaring tune that repeated the summoning words. She looked and sounded like a wild bird.

She's magnificent, Liyana thought—and a tendril of fear crept into her heart. Pia was what a vessel should be. It did not matter that she was blind. She flowed and soared with effortless beauty. Every movement was perfect, and she danced with transcendent grace. She was the wind itself. As the drums beat louder, Pia leaped higher and spun faster. Her white hair whipped around her, and the silk skirt swirled and flowed. Her silver bells rang out, echoing across the desert.

Liyana thought of her bells, the ones she had left behind for her family. She'd worn those bells with such pride. She had believed that she'd molded herself into the ideal vessel. But now, seeing Pia . . . This was what she should have been. Maybe Bayla *had* deemed Liyana unfit.

Barely breathing, Liyana waited for the moment when the goddess would take Pia's body. Pia danced faster and faster, and her voice cascaded from impossibly high notes. With each moment, Liyana became more convinced that this would be the moment.

Suddenly Pia fluttered her arms down to her side like a bird settling her wings. She raised her head, and the drums stilled. Ilia fell silent.

"Untie our guests," Pia said. Her voice was crystal clear. The clan was silent. "I will accompany them and henceforth be dead to you." Her final words fell like stones into water, and ripple-like, their effect spread through the clan. The men, women, and children of the Silk Clan bowed low with their fists over their hearts, and then one after another, they turned their backs on the center of the circle.

Alone, Pia swept into a tent. Liyana noticed that she raised her arms only once, to feel for the tent flap. Otherwise she moved with a smooth surety that no one and nothing would be in her way.

Liyana felt a blade slice through the ropes. Fingers untied the gag. She spat the cloth out into her hands, and she felt as if her insides were churning. Korbyn was right! She'd been right to trust him! Their deities truly were trapped. Oh, she'd believed it before in her heart, but now . . .

Beside her, Fennik's ropes were cut, and he fell forward into the salty sand. She knelt by his side. "Fennik? Can you hear me? Are you all right?" She kept her voice low. Backs still turned, the men and women spoke only in hushed murmurs.

Fennik raised his head and crowed, "She was glorious!"

Shushing him, Liyana examined his wrists. The ropes had bitten into his skin. Fresh blood oozed at her touch. "You'll need bandages until Korbyn can heal you. What did you say to them?"

"Only the truth," he said. "But that girl—she commands! Did you hear her voice, how they obey? We have no one like her in the Horse Clan. No wonder her clan so reveres her."

She helped him stand, and she turned to Korbyn. She wanted to ask how soon they could leave. Each day they delayed, Bayla was imprisoned longer. But Korbyn had crossed the circle to speak to Ilia. "We were right to trust him," Liyana said, "but he needs to start trusting us, too. This should not have happened."

"He's a god," Fennik said. "They aren't used to needing humans."

"They need our bodies," Liyana said. "If he'd share information, we could help. We can do more than get ourselves tied to stakes." Whatever Korbyn believed, they were not like the injured horses. Perhaps it was sacrilege to think so, but they could be partners . . . *if* he shared what he knew.

"This was not my fault."

"Exactly."

With Korbyn, Ilia crossed to them. "Judgment has been made," she declared. "You will share our vessel's fate. May the blessings of the divine Oyri be upon you in your quest."

Craning his neck, Fennik strained to see the tent that Pia had disappeared into. "Can we speak to the vessel?" He sounded like an eager puppy.

Korbyn leveled a look at Fennik and said to Ilia, "We honor your judgment and thank you for the blessings."

Ilia clapped her hands. Two men and one woman scurried forward. "Lead them to tents and see to their needs," she ordered the three servants. To Fennik, she said, "No one may speak to the vessel within our hearing. She is now dead to us."

"Our quest is urgent," Liyana said. "If we could—"

"You will accept our hospitality," Ilia said.

Liyana looked to Korbyn. She didn't want to waste time with

"hospitality." They still had two more clans to reach—and that was before the true rescue mission could begin. She didn't know how far they would have to journey for that. "But—" Liyana began.

After tossing a smile at her, Korbyn was escorted away by one of the men, and Fennik by the other. The smile was clearly meant to reassure her, and Liyana tried to feel reassured. She told herself that it was unreasonable to expect to leave instantly. They had to wait until dawn's light to travel. And the horses had to recover from their ordeal. But still, after seeing the summoning ceremony fail . . .

Silently the woman led Liyana in the opposite direction. Liyana looked back over her shoulder as Korbyn disappeared around the corner of a tent. The Silk Clan had begun to disperse, vanishing into the shadows of the tents as if swallowed. She felt her anxiousness curl up like a creature inside her stomach. At the very least she wished she could have talked to Korbyn. She had many, many questions for him, and god or not, he couldn't avoid answering them forever.

Opening a tent flap, the woman waited for Liyana. "Thank you," Liyana said as she entered. Without a word and without meeting her eyes, her escort inclined her head and left Liyana alone.

Inside the tent was a bed of silk. A basin with a thin layer of salt-choked water was in one corner. Layers of cloth lay around it to absorb any stray drops. Liyana washed herself as best she could, and she crawled between the skeins of silk. The silence was absolute, and she lay for a long time waiting for dawn and wishing she could hear Korbyn breathing beside her. Eventually she slept.

*　*　*

At dawn she woke. Her dreams had chased her through the night, images of Pia dancing and of sand wolves attacking. She wondered what Korbyn had dreamed about and if he'd had nightmares without her there to wake him. Sitting up, she noticed that a tray with several pieces of flatbread and a strip of dried goat meat waited for her by the tent flap. There was also a cup of precious, drinkable water.

She drained the cup instantly. Eating the food, she listened for sounds of the camp waking. If she had been with the Goat Clan, she would have heard chickens, goats, and children clamoring to be fed. People would have been shouting morning greetings at one another as they bustled to complete tasks before the sun scorched the air. By contrast, the Silk Clan was disturbingly quiet. Liyana emerged from her tent to find the camp empty.

As she wound her way through the tents, she saw and heard no one. She found the troughs where they'd left the horses—the troughs were dry and the horses were gone. Her heart began to hammer harder. It felt as though everyone had sneaked away in the night. "Hello?" she called. "Is anyone here?"

A child peeked around a tent flap. She had dark, wide eyes and concave cheeks. She was so thin that her shoulder bones poked against her robe.

Liyana waved at her, and the girl gasped and retreated. "Wait, I don't mean any harm!" Liyana called after her. But the girl was gone.

She saw no one else.

Alone, she crossed the camp.

On the outskirts of camp, she heard voices. She recognized Fennik's voice and then the melodious cascade of Pia's voice. A horse stamped its hoof. Picking up her pace, Liyana jogged to the edge of camp.

On the sands, Fennik was coaching Pia on how to mount. Korbyn was with the other horses, securing their saddles. He waved when he saw her. "Good morning, sunshine."

"Did I oversleep? I didn't sleep well." She scanned the area. None of Pia's people were nearby. Even Ilia and the guards were absent. "Where is everyone?"

"We aren't enough?" Korbyn asked, mock-hurt.

"The camp feels deserted."

He lowered his voice and switched to serious. "She declared herself dead. They do not wish to risk hearing her speak."

"But . . . she leaves to save them. And where are her supplies?" Fennik's clan had loaded them with supplies, water, and horses. Liyana's parents had left her the pack, and her brother had braved the wrath of the clan to sneak her the sky serpent knife. But she saw no new supplies from the Silk Clan.

"The dead do not need supplies," Korbyn said. And then in a merrier voice he said, "Or perhaps I am wrong, and they simply don't want to watch this."

Liyana watched Fennik lift Pia into the air. She swung onto the horse with a fluid grace and sat in the saddle. Pia smiled, a look like the gentle wind that swept over the horse and Fennik at once. Fennik smiled back goofily, though he must have known Pia couldn't see him, and then he laid the reins in her hands as if gifting her with a glorious present. Pia held the reins lightly as if they were an accessory, not a tool.

"Oh my," Liyana said. "She is going to be a problem."

"She compensates for her blindness."

Liyana shook her head. "That's not the issue, and you know it." She watched Fennik guide Pia through the basics. Liyana could have used such a lesson. "She's too used to being the princess. Mark my words. She'll slow us down."

Laughing, Pia slid off the side of the horse. Fennik caught her, a bundle of fluttering silk that landed softly in his arms. Clearly, he had forgiven her for having him tied to a stake.

"How soon can we leave?" Liyana asked, her voice still low.

Given how ritual-driven these people seemed to be, there had to be an elaborate farewell ceremony, even for the "dead."

"We can leave now," Pia said in her clear singsong bird voice.

Liyana winced.

"The princess has excellent hearing," Korbyn commented.

"But your clan—" Liyana said to her.

"I will see them in the Dreaming."

With Fennik's assistance, Pia mounted a new horse, the more placid mare, Plum. Still no one came to say good-bye to her. No one was willing to break tradition to give her a single embrace. Liyana was grateful for her own clan—at least she knew they cared about her before they left her to die.

Liyana mounted Gray Luck and urged her horse into a walk. Guiding the other two horses, Korbyn rode after her on his favorite mount. Ahead, Fennik kept close to Pia as she started across the sands.

Because Pia couldn't, Liyana looked back at the Silk Clan as they rode away. Emerging from every tent, silent men, women, and children watched them leave.

*　　*　　*

Leaving the salt flats behind them, they rode west across the cracked earth toward the rocky hills, the territory of the Scorpion Clan. Liyana and Korbyn led. Behind them, Fennik regaled Pia with horse tales in a voice not quite loud enough for Liyana to hear. Every few moments, Pia's laugh would ring out like a bell or Fennik's chuckle would boom.

"Once again, vessels surprise me," Korbyn said.

"How so?" Liyana asked.

"Based on initial impressions, I was not aware that either of them had a sense of humor."

"Believing you have a sense of humor and actually having one are two different things," Liyana pointed out.

"Indeed," he said. He winced as Fennik let out a loud cackle. "At least they are enjoying themselves."

Liyana studied Korbyn for a moment. Worn by travel, he looked very different from the boy who had walked out of a sandstorm, unrumpled and untouched by the gritty air. Now his soft hair was matted and his cheeks were sunken in. Dark shadows highlighted his eyes. "Are you?"

"Not so much," he admitted.

At midday they halted. Pia slid off her horse and promptly crumpled to the ground. She tried to rise, but her legs buckled under her again. Fennik leaped from his horse to assist her. He offered her water, lifting the waterskin to her lips so that she could drink more easily. "She needs healing," Fennik said.

Pia moaned. "I do not wish to slow us."

"You need to heal her," Fennik said. "She's a new rider. Her flesh is tender." He patted Pia's hand. "Continue to be brave," he said to her. "All will be well."

Korbyn sighed, but he dropped into a trance to heal her blisters and sores.

Massaging her own sores, Liyana pitched the tent. Once she had it ready, she laid her hand on Korbyn's shoulder. After a moment, he opened his eyes. "The Silk Clan did not replenish our supplies. We need water for the horses," she said gently. He heaved a sigh as he lurched onto his feet.

"Come inside and rest," Fennik said to Pia.

He led her toward the tent while she favored him and the world with her beautiful smile.

Staying outside, Liyana checked the horses' hooves. She left their hides matted with caked-on dirt and dust—it would protect them from the worst of the sun, plus Fennik preferred to curry them himself, or at least he did when he wasn't doting on Pia.

Liyana kicked a barrel cactus and wondered why Pia's frailty bothered her so much. The cactus broke at its stem. Carrying it into the shade of the tent, Liyana sliced it open with her sky serpent blade and scraped the insides out. She held a clump over her mouth and squeezed. Liquid dribbled onto her tongue. It tasted sweet.

"Fennik and Pia, are you thirsty?" She thrust the remainder of the scrapings into the tent. She listened as he offered it all to Pia. She refused, insisting he share. Liyana prevented herself from rolling her eyes at them by checking on Korbyn.

He was squatting next to a half-dead plant, and he was deep in a trance. His face looked too thin, as if he'd aged a year over the past week. *This is why it bothers me,* she thought. Pia's needs on top of their survival needs were exhausting him. Keeping an eye on him, she started a cooking fire with a chunk of flint. She patted the dried cactus innards into cakes and baked them while she waited for Korbyn to finish. At last his eyes rolled back. She lunged forward past the fire and caught him before he slumped into it.

In front of him, the plant was covered with berries.

She dragged him by the armpits into the tent and laid him next to Pia, who was sleeping curled up like a cat with her head on Fennik's thigh. Without a word, Liyana went back outside to pick the berries before the sun withered them. She then rescued the cactus cakes from the fire.

Tasks complete, she sat alone in the sand, looking out across the desert. Heat waved over the desiccated soil. The forbidden mountains rippled in the distance. She wished Korbyn were awake to sit with her. She would have told him a story to make him laugh. Gray Luck nipped her shoulder, and Liyana shared her portion of the berries with her favorite mare. She was beginning to hate the rest times. There were two vessels left to find, and Korbyn still would not share any details about their final destination. The lost deities could be on the other side of the sands. She was acutely aware of the vastness of the desert around them, and with every delay, the distances seemed to stretch. But she could think of no alternative or anything she could do to lessen the shadows under Korbyn's eyes.

Late in the afternoon, after Korbyn and Pia woke, they continued on. But only a few hours later, they had to stop to camp for the night. Again Korbyn placed himself in a trance—he healed Pia's new blisters, he sealed a wound in one of the horse's hooves, he summoned water from the roots of nearby plants, and he flushed out desert rats from the rocks for Fennik to shoot. He finished after the moon was high, and then he collapsed. Liyana lay next to him in the tent, listening for the sound of his nightmares and waking him as needed. He woke three times. She didn't ask what he had dreamed.

The next day was more of the same.

While Fennik catered to Pia, Liyana continued to watch Korbyn. His eyes began to look like hollowed-out rocks, and he shuffled when he walked. *He's getting worse,* she thought. God or not, he had limits. He could only focus his magic on one task at a time, and there were simply too many tasks that needed to be done. As their only magician, he had no time to recuperate between trances, and with each additional task, they lost travel time. She found herself wanting to take him into her arms, like a mother with a child, and stroke his hair and say, "Stop. Stop before you hurt yourself." But she didn't.

On the fifth day, Liyana squatted beside Korbyn as he prepared to summon more water for the horses from a seemingly dead plant. "I was wrong," she said. "Pia isn't the problem."

He nodded as if satisfied with her. "As I told you—"

"The problem is you."

"Excuse me?"

"You told me that only people with reincarnated souls could become vessels," Liyana said. "And you said 'or magicians.'" She touched one of the brittle branches of the desert bush. It didn't snap. Its inner core was still alive.

"I may have said that. I say a lot of things."

She tried to imagine leaves bursting out on these branches—and what it would feel like to make that happen. "So can a vessel become a magician?"

Behind them, Pia gasped. "You cannot! Vessels do not work magic!"

"Can't or don't?" Liyana countered.

"Banish such thoughts from your head!" Pia said. "We must preserve these bodies and protect them from unnecessary harm. Working magic is too dangerous!"

"Starvation and dehydration are also dangerous," Liyana said, eyes still on Korbyn. "You know you need the help."

"Training a vessel—it's forbidden," Korbyn said.

"Like the mountains of the sky serpent were when you stole flint for the clans? What's more important: tradition or success?" Liyana asked him. "You want the deities back. So do I."

Pia's voice rose to a squeak. "Fennik, tell her no! Expediency does not triumph over right. She risks too much!"

Korbyn studied Liyana's face as if he were trying to read her thoughts. "It has never been done."

She leaned closer to him, so close that she could feel his breath. "Once, the raven and the horse had three races. . . . You bent reality to win. And that was merely a race. This involves the fate of your beloved and five entire clans."

His lips twitched and then broadened into his bright smile. His smile washed over her, and she realized how much she had missed it these last five days. "Very well," he said.

Chapter Thirteen

Overhead, the stars filled the bruise-black sky. Liyana breathed deeply. The night air crinkled inside her lungs instead of scorching her throat.

"You can still change your mind," Korbyn said behind her. He was close enough that she inhaled his scent. "Magic is forbidden to vessels because it is dangerous. If you try to reach too far . . ."

She realized that this was the first time they'd been alone since the other vessels had joined them. Behind them, Pia and Fennik slept cocooned in their sleeping rolls. The horses dozed in a semicircle around the tent. "I don't need to work miracles," Liyana said. "Just teach me enough to help."

"Magic isn't about miracles," Korbyn said. "All we do is speed up or slow down what happens naturally." He pointed to a shriveled bush a few feet in front of them. His arm brushed against hers, and her skin tingled. "For example, this plant is capable of blooming. We can induce it to bloom faster. But we can't cause it to sprout wings and fly."

Causing a plant to bloom *was* a miracle. Talu couldn't cause a bush to bloom. She could improve its health, thicken its roots, and mend a few leaves, but not cause it to defy the seasons. Liyana wondered what Talu would say if she saw Liyana alone in the night desert learning magic from their goddess's lover. "How do I begin?"

"Sit." Korbyn pointed to the hard ground next to a shriveled bush.

Liyana sat cross-legged. She patted her thighs to wake up her sore muscles. Korbyn joined her on the ground, his knees almost touching hers. He didn't look at her, and Liyana wondered what he was thinking. She wished he'd tell her a story, like he used to when it was just the two of them. It had been easy to talk to him then. She tried to think of words to say.

"Your soul fills your body." He paused. Wind whistled across the dry earth. A desert owl cried out. "You can nod to show you're engaged in the lesson."

"I assumed that was an introduction."

"I am attempting to be pedagogical," he said. "I have never taught anyone before."

"The stories say that deities were the ones who taught the first magicians. In fact, Talu said that Bayla instructed Talu's many-times-great-grandmother—"

"I was busy at the time."

"Doing what?"

"Creating a mountain range."

She tried to picture a mountain bursting out of the ground. Staring at this boy-man-god, she wondered what it would feel like to change the shape of the world. "Truly?"

"We needed a valley. It took a very, very long time. Several lifetimes, in fact." Reaching out, he put his hand on her chin and turned her head so that she faced the bush instead of him. He released her, and she had to fight the urge to look at him again. "Your soul fills your body. So to work magic outside your body, you must expand your soul. In other words, if you want to cause this bush to bloom, you need to make it a part of you, at least temporarily. Once you've done that, then you can use magic to influence it."

She nodded, though she had a thousand questions.

"You may ask, 'Where does the extra soul come from?' After all, your soul is a fixed size—it fits your body perfectly. So how can it expand? The answer is that the 'extra soul' is magic drawn directly from the Dreaming." He smiled broadly as if he were pleased with himself for explaining the matter so clearly and concisely.

"But how—"

He tapped her forehead with his finger. "By concentrating.

You've seen me in a trance. I am connecting to the magic of the Dreaming with my mind. You can learn to do it too. Only reincarnated souls and deities can."

Sorting through the questions in her mind, Liyana opened her mouth to let them flood out. She hoped that these were questions he'd answer.

"Your soul will be lost." Pia knelt in the opening of the tent, holding the flap open with one hand. Her milky eyes seemed to encompass them both. "Your body will wither and die without it, and your clan will perish."

"She isn't wrong," Korbyn said in a cheerful voice. "A body without a soul cannot survive. You must maintain your connection to your body throughout the process, or you risk losing yourself."

"It is wrong to take such a risk," Pia said. "If the gods thought it an acceptable risk, it would not be forbidden." Her voice was earnest and sweet. She had a hint of melody when she spoke that made one want to listen to her.

Liyana felt fear curl inside her gut, but she kept her voice confident. "The gods never anticipated any vessel, much less multiple vessels, needing to make this kind of journey. If they had known, they may have made an exception."

Pia smacked the side of the tent with her palm. "Fennik! I need you."

Bursting out of the tent, Fennik grabbed Pia's shoulders. "Are you all right?"

"I am fine," Pia said. "But this"—she waved her hand toward Liyana, Korbyn, the bush, and the desert beyond—"is unnatural. We cannot allow this to continue."

Fennik looked from her to Liyana to Korbyn and back again as if they'd suddenly crowded around him. "I . . . She . . ."

"Fennik!" Pia's voice sounded as though he had slaughtered a kitten for dinner. She clung to him. "You said you agreed with me! If we embrace unnecessary risk for the sake of expediency—"

"If we keep arguing, none of us will have strength for the ride tomorrow," Liyana pointed out. "You don't want to be the one to slow the rescue of your goddess, do you?"

Fennik awkwardly patted Pia's arm. "If the gods wished us to know magic, we would have been taught it. But . . . we are four days from the hills. Even if we find the Scorpion Clan quickly, we still need the Falcon Clan."

Pia let out a gasp like a tiny wounded animal. Without another word, she vanished into the tent. Muttering a curse, Fennik ducked into the tent after her.

"Korbyn is a god, and he wishes it!" Liyana called after them.

"Thank you for noticing," Korbyn said. He flashed a smile at her, and she felt the warmth of his smile pour over her. "Shall we begin? Close your eyes and look inside. Follow the course of your breath. Feel the pulse of your blood as it throbs through your veins. Feel the limits of your skin. Truly inhabit your body. Only then will you avoid the fate that Pia fears."

Three hours later, Korbyn called an end to the lesson.

Liyana crawled inside the tent without looking back at the leafless bush. She curled into her sleeping roll and was asleep before Korbyn even settled into his.

She resumed the lesson at dawn, sitting cross-legged on the sand while Fennik packed up camp and Pia combed her soft, white hair.

Approaching her, Korbyn said, "You must be anchored to your body when you work magic. You cannot waver." He shoved her shoulder.

Liyana toppled to the side. She caught herself with the heel of her hand. "Ow." She glared at him.

"Keep concentrating," Korbyn said. Whistling, he strode over to the horses.

She continued to practice as they rode. She focused on her calf and thigh muscles as they jolted and shifted with Gray Luck's stride. She felt the wind as it blew grit against her face cloth. She felt the fabric of her clothes move across her skin. She counted her breaths. Every time they halted to water the horses, she listened to her heartbeat.

"We could spend a year on simply this," Korbyn told her that night. "Unfortunately, we don't have a year. So let's skip ahead."

Across the campfire, Pia looked horrified, an elegant expression on her doll-like face. "If she dies, so dies the hope of her clan. I will not allow you to endanger an entire clan with this recklessness."

"Pia . . . ," Liyana began.

"I will sing so that you cannot focus," Pia warned. "If you cannot focus, then you cannot work magic." Filling her lungs, Pia shrieked. Liyana covered her ears as Pia's scream-song reverberated inside her bones. Crescendoing, Pia's voice rose an octave higher. It felt sharp enough to slice the sky. She stopped and smiled at them. It was not a sweet smile.

Liyana rubbed her ears. The notes still echoed inside her skull. "How exactly do I focus with that?"

"You outlast her," Korbyn said with a shrug. "She'll lose her voice eventually."

"I have trained for my entire life," Pia said. "It will be some time before my voice runs out. I can last all night if I must."

Korbyn sighed and then stilled. Watching him, Liyana saw the moment that he entered a magician's trance. Only a second later, Pia crumpled.

"Pia!" Fennik cried. Lunging forward, he caught her. Her body draped gracefully over his arms.

"Shh," Korbyn said. "She's asleep."

"You did this?" Fennik asked. Liyana thought she heard a tendril of fear in his voice.

Korbyn smiled cheerfully at him and then turned to Liyana. "I want you to imagine a lake in a valley. Once you picture it correctly"—he tapped her heart—"you will feel it here."

As Fennik carried Pia into the tent, Liyana concentrated.

After four more days of travel, Liyana had pictured her lake in the valley so many times that she could see it in perfect detail. Her lake was framed by sheer, granite cliffs, and it opened onto a valley that was filled with a lush spread of green grasses, thick groves of trees, and cascades of wildflowers. The lake itself was a perfect oval, and its clear, blue water reflected the cloudless sky above. It lapped at a pebble shore. Each pebble was a different shade of quartz that sparkled in the sun like a precious jewel.

So far, though, she had yet to draw out any magic from the lake. She hadn't caused a single plant to bloom or a drop of water to surface through the rocky ground.

Liyana was not impressed with herself.

On the plus side, though, Pia had quit objecting to the lessons, thanks to Liyana's lack of success. And Fennik had added a dollop of much needed humor when he had claimed he had enjoyed the evening quiet while Liyana practiced because it helped him calm his thoughts. In unison, Liyana and Korbyn had commented, "I didn't realize you had thoughts." They'd burst into laughter, while Fennik fumed for the next hour.

But that was the only time she'd laughed.

Liyana felt the passage of time as if her heartbeat were count-ing away her chances to reach Bayla. She couldn't explain why she felt such urgency, but it pulsed through her veins. She was acutely aware that once they collected two more vessels, the demands of that many mouths would slow them even further, and she didn't know how far they had left to ride after that. So she continued to try—and continued to fail.

Once they entered the hills, she had to quit practicing as they rode. Thousands of loose rocks were scattered over the terrain, and riding required everyone's full concentration. No one wanted a hoof to slip on a rock, even if Korbyn could heal a lame horse.

By late morning, the sun beat down on the rocks, and they had to stop. Korbyn caused a trickle of water to well up in a dry streambed. Liyana and Fennik soaked cloths in the water and then squeezed it into their waterskins. The horses licked the wet rocks.

In the shadows of the rocks, Liyana resumed her practice while the others rested until the horses were ready to proceed. As she moved to mount, Fennik stopped her. "The terrain is worsening. We must walk the horses."

Leading Gray Luck, Liyana walked beside Korbyn. The pace, as they picked their way over the rocks, felt far, far too slow. She chafed at their new speed.

"Can you tell if they've had their ceremony?" Liyana asked.

"I could tell if they'd succeeded," Korbyn said. "You could too, once you learn. Once you can draw magic from the lake, you will be able to feel every rock, bird, and soul around you. Divine souls feel . . ."

"Divine?" she supplied.

"I was going to go with 'glorious' or 'amazing,' but 'divine' will do."

"So either they haven't tried yet . . . or we're late."

Korbyn halted and held up his hand. Behind him, Liyana patted Gray Luck's neck and slowed the horse to a standstill. Holding the reins of the other horses, Fennik stopped them as well. He put his other hand on Pia's shoulder to signal to her to stop.

"What is it?" Pia asked, her crystal clear voice ringing over the stones. "Have we found the Scorpion Clan?"

An arrow thudded into the ground at Korbyn's horse's hooves.

"Yes, we have," Korbyn said calmly.

Shouts echoed on all sides as warriors sprang from behind rocks. The horses reared and shied, and Liyana fought to control Gray Luck. Fennik pulled down hard on Pia's horse's reins as she clung to her horse's neck. Snorting and huffing, Gray Luck walked backward in a circle, and Liyana saw an array of arrows and spears trained on them. Attempting to keep her voice light, she said, "I've already been stabbed. Fennik was tied to a stake. I think it's someone else's turn. Pia, would you like to volunteer?"

"I beg your pardon," Pia said.

Fennik shielded Pia by guiding his horse in front of her. "Do not even joke about her being injured." Eyes on the warriors, he leaned to reach for one of his bows.

All around them, the warriors tensed. Some crouched, spears ready. Liyana saw bowstrings drawn. "Fennik," Korbyn said. Listening for once, Fennik halted.

For an instant, no one moved. No one even breathed.

And then Pia began to sing. Raising her chin, she let the notes pour out of her mouth. Her melody cascaded over the rocks and echoed through the hills.

"Is that her answer to everything?" Liyana asked under her breath.

"You have to admit it's effective," Korbyn said. Around them, the warriors lowered their weapons. Pia continued to sing. Wordless, the song was a soothing melody that was at once as sad as a farewell and as uplifting as a child's laugh.

"You know, I think I like her," Korbyn said.

"You're just happy you don't have to heal anyone," Liyana said.

"True." Raising his voice to be heard over Pia's song, Korbyn called to the warriors, "I am Korbyn of the Raven Clan! These are my companions! We bring word of your goddess! We must speak with your vessel!"

One of the men laughed. "Good luck with that."

Liyana felt as though her innards had curdled. *Oh, goddess, we're too late.*

"It is vital!" Fennik said. "We must speak with her immediately!"

"You can try," said the man who had laughed. "Pretty sure she's still drunk."

Soiled clothes and empty jugs were strewn over the camp. Tents were pitched askew on boulders. Liyana picked her way through the debris. Behind her, Fennik had chosen the expedient solution of scooping Pia into his arms and carrying her. Left on the outskirts of camp, the horses grazed on the scant, tough grasses—they could not navigate through the rubble.

"There are no bodies. No blood. I don't understand this," Fennik said. "It looks as if they were attacked, but I don't see any wounded."

Korbyn marched in front of them with zero regard for where he stepped. As Liyana hopped over another shattered pot only to land on a soggy shirt that reeked of urine, she thought that he might have the right approach.

Pia clung to Fennik's neck. "Are we in danger?"

"We are late," Korbyn said.

Liyana felt her stomach clench. Men and women perched and sprawled on the rocks. Some looked listless. Others celebrated. And others clutched jugs and waterskins as if they held all the liquid that remained in the world. Perhaps, for this clan, they did.

"The waste here . . . I do not understand it," Fennik said, frowning at the jugs. "They cannot be immune to the drought, can they?"

An old woman lurched out of a tent. She wore a headdress of

bones and feathers that dangled down to her ankles. The bones clacked together as she moved. "You!" She leveled a crooked finger at Korbyn. "Bah! You again, pretty talker. You can change your face, but you can't change your soul."

Korbyn swept forward in a bow. "Runa, you are just as beautiful as you always were."

"Humph. None for you today. Runa has standards, she does!" With that, Runa lurched back into her tent. The door flap smacked her on her wide rear.

"You can't know her, can you?" Liyana asked. Once he was summoned, he'd come straight to Liyana from his clan. The old woman must have mistaken Korbyn for someone else.

"She was younger then. Same sunny personality."

Fennik frowned at him. "Impossible. She would need to be . . ."

"One hundred sixteen years old, yes," Korbyn said. "Mathematics are not your forte, are they? She always excelled at convincing magicians and deities to heal any ailments." A smile danced on his lips. "It was fun being convinced."

Pia sniffed. "Spare us the details of your lascivious youth."

Liyana quit walking. "You didn't! What about Bayla?"

He shrugged. "She was with Sendar. I was pining." Eagerly he began climbing the slope toward the woman's tent.

"Korbyn, we have a mission!" Liyana called after him.

"She's the chieftess," Korbyn said.

He swung the tent flap open. Liquid splashed him full in his face, and he staggered back. Liyana gasped. To waste liquid, be it water or liquor . . . An image of the wide-eyed child from the Silk Clan flashed through her mind.

Spitting, Korbyn wiped his face. "I'm honored I rate the quality refreshment, but you'll wish you hadn't wasted it."

Runa stuck her head out of the tent. "Eh, I'll lick it off you." Cackling, she pointed at Liyana, Fennik, and Pia. "Oh, look at their faces! Don't worry, children. My husband would have his testicles for trophies if we revisited old times." She wagged her finger at Korbyn. "You watch yourself, my boy."

Korbyn laughed, and his laughter echoed off the rocks. A few of the Scorpion Clan warriors stared at him. Others, sprawled by their tents, laughed with him.

"You always were a force to be reckoned with," Korbyn said.

"You'd better believe it," Runa said. "I hear you want our vessel. Go take her. We're done with her." She waved her hand toward the northern side of camp. "Fair warning, though—she'll be less happy to see you than I am." Smiling, Runa spat in Korbyn's face.

Wiping his cheek and neck with his sleeve, Korbyn trotted down the slope back to them. "Believe it or not, I deserved that," he said cheerfully.

Pia looked disgusted. "Water is life."

"I think there are a few stories you haven't told," Liyana said. It seemed the safest thing to say. Korbyn whistled as he crossed through camp, aiming for the north corner. She shoved the image of Korbyn and that woman into the back of her brain. She had no right to feel . . . whatever it was she felt, even on behalf of Bayla.

Men and women were sprawled between the tents. A few whispered and pointed at them as they passed. Some laughed. Liyana tried to ignore them.

Korbyn climbed the rocks toward a lone tent perched precariously on a boulder. Liyana, Fennik, and Pia followed him. He held the tent flap up, and they all entered.

Inside was a young woman. Her telltale vessel tattoos were visible. She wore a sleeveless tunic that was stained with grease and blood. Near her was a heap of shredded silk and silver bells—her ceremonial dress, destroyed. Her hair flopped over half her face. Several thin braids were stuck to her forehead and cheeks. She snored loudly.

"This is she?" Fennik said.

"Is that her snore or a pig's?" Pia asked, wrinkling her nose. "And what is that odor?" Liyana guessed it was the dried vomit in the corner, but it could have been the girl herself. Or both.

Korbyn nudged the girl's leg with his toe. "Good morning!"

Groaning, the girl opened one eye. "Outta my tent." She leveled a finger at each of them. "Don't like you. Or you. Or you."

"That's okay," Korbyn said cheerfully. "We probably won't like you either."

"She cannot be the vessel," Fennik said.

Oh, goddess, it was going to take hours to coax this girl into sobriety, much less convince her to come with them. Liyana wanted to scream. Every day they encountered more delays! She thought of her family, facing day after day, believing that Bayla would never come, believing they were doomed. And this girl, this drunk, pathetic girl, was keeping Liyana from saving them.

"Set me down, Fennik," Pia said. "I want to go to her." Fennik lowered her to the ground, and Pia felt her way across the room. She knelt next to the girl, and she patted her hand. "We'll find your goddess. Everything will be okay."

The girl bit Pia's hand.

Yelping, Pia snatched her hand back and cradled it to her chest. Fennik rushed to her and wrapped his arms around Pia's shoulders.

The girl giggled.

"What's your name?" Korbyn asked.

"Raan. Raan, Raan, Raan. Rrrrrrr-aaaaaaa-nnnnnnn, ra-ra-ra-ra . . ." She swirled her fingers in the air as if she were conducting music. "Na-na-na-na . . ."

"Sober her up faster," Liyana said to Korbyn. "We can't talk to her like this." Liyana had once seen one of the herder boys in this state. It had taken him hours to be coherent. Aunt Sabisa had dumped a pitcher of precious water on his head.

Korbyn knelt next to her. "Don't bite. I bite back."

Giggling, the girl Raan gnashed her teeth together.

Laying his hand on her shoulder, Korbyn concentrated. Over the course of a minute, the girl's face flushed and then paled into a sickly green and then settled in the normal range. Liyana noticed she had nice brown eyes, now that they weren't dilated. In fact, she was beautiful, if you discounted the disheveled hair and stained clothes.

"Do you feel better, Raan?" Pia asked solicitously.

Raan scowled at them. "What did you do?" She searched through the piles of blankets that had been tossed around her tent. "Aha!" She displayed a waterskin as if it were a trophy.

Korbyn intercepted it and tossed it across the tent. "You're done celebrating."

"But it's a new era! We are free!" Scrambling across the tent, she fetched the waterskin, took off the cap, and lifted it to her lips. Crossing the tent in three strides, Korbyn covered the opening with his hand. "Aw, don't let it go to waste," Raan said. "Once the drink is gone, it's gone. This is the last of it. Can't make more without a miracle." She seemed to find this amusing. "Come on. Half the clan is celebrating with me."

"And the other half?" Pia asked, distaste clear in her voice.

Raan shrugged. "Drowning their sorrows. They didn't like me much anyway."

"I cannot imagine why not," Liyana muttered. She crossed her arms. All the time to journey here, and this was what had waited for them. This girl would be a greater drain on Korbyn than Pia was. At least Pia tried.

Raan pointed at her. "I heard that. Who are you people and what are you doing in my tent? Did Runa tell you where to find me? I shouldn't have punched her."

"You *punched* your chieftess?" Pia's voice rose an octave.

"You're a judgmental little thing, aren't you?" Raan said. "Do I enter your tent without an invitation and ruin *your* party? If you must know, she blamed me for the failure of her barbaric ceremony. And while I am thrilled it failed—"

Pia clenched her delicate hands into tiny fists. "You disgust—"

"Enough," Korbyn said.

"She celebrates the demise of her clan!" Pia said.

"I rejoice that the goddess wants us to find another way to live," Raan said.

Korbyn stepped between Pia and Raan. He laid his hand on Pia's shoulder, as if to prevent her from charging bull-like at the larger girl. "We need her, and she needs us, whether she knows it or not."

"I don't need anyone," Raan said. "That's the whole beauty of being free." She spun in a circle with her arms raised in the air, and she kicked at the clothes and blankets at her feet.

"You are *not* free," Pia said. "You have responsibilities to your clan. You must die so that your people can live. Like the rest of us."

Raan quit dancing and stared at them.

Pia rolled up her sleeves to display her tattoos. "Fennik, Liyana, show her."

Flexing his biceps, Fennik showed his tattoos.

"Our goddess chose not to come," Raan said. "She granted me life!"

Liyana didn't move. By the tent flap, she watched the others argue with Raan, trying to convince her that this was the correct course, explaining their mission and their reasons, and resorting to guilt (from Pia) and threats (from Fennik) and reason (from Korbyn). Raan refused to believe them. When Korbyn poured her waterskin out, Raan pummeled his chest. She then shouted obscenities until Pia covered her ears with her hands and screeched as loud as a whistle.

Liyana backed out of the tent. She let the flap fall down, muffling the sound only slightly. Men and woman clustered at the foot of the boulder, listening to the drama and taking bets on the outcome. She walked past them. A few men whistled at her. A few women laughed. A few children ran up to her and tugged on her sleeves. As before, she ignored them all.

She marched directly to Runa's tent and barged inside.

Runa was dunking her fingers into a bowl of honey and then licking them, slurping as she sucked at her knob-like knuckles. "Excuse me, child?"

"You aren't as drunk as you were pretending," Liyana said. "I've seen drunk before. You wanted to throw liquor at Korbyn because it was fun. I've wanted to throw things at him too. He can be infuriating." She thought of how closemouthed he was about their final destination. "But this isn't about him. Or me. Or Raan. It's about whether our clans survive. Our deities have been kidnapped, and Korbyn says we need the deities' vessels in order to rescue them. He won't want to leave until Raan joins us."

Runa blinked at her. "Let me guess. Raan is refusing."

"You forced her to submit to the ceremony, didn't you?"

"It required three of our warriors to ensure her presence." Runa dug her fingers back in the honey and scraped the bowl with her nails. "We had to threaten her cousin's life before she would dance. But she danced while I filled the words with magic and sent them to the Dreaming. Yet still Maara didn't come. Perhaps . . . you speak the truth."

"You need to force her again," Liyana said. "You must exile her. She has a strong self-preservation instinct. She'll know the only way to survive is to come with us."

"And when the time comes for her to give up her body for our goddess?"

Liyana hesitated. "We outnumber her."

Runa chuckled. "Your friends are in her tent trying to convince her, aren't they? But you, you are here. You are a determined one. And clever."

"The needs of the many outweigh the desire of one." Liyana felt as if Talu were here, whispering words in her ear. "She can't be allowed to kill your entire clan simply to hoard a few more years of her own."

"Ah, the certainty of youth," Runa said. "You care a lot about a clan that is not your own. I wonder. . . . Is this out of a sense of what is right or out of a fear that you may be wrong?"

Liyana thought of Jidali. Of Mother and Father. Of her cousins. She wasn't wrong. "Will you do it for your people?" she asked. "Or if not for your people, then for Korbyn, for whatever he was to you and whatever you felt for him."

Runa didn't answer. She dunked her fingers into the honey again.

Liyana waited, wishing she could scream like Pia. She hated the taste of the air inside Runa's tent. It was thick and smelled overly sweet. She felt as if the smell were pouring down her throat and permeating her skin. It made her skin itch, and she longed to run outside and let the desert wind scour her clean.

"Yes, I will," Runa said at last. "But I will regret it, as will those who love you. And perhaps even Korbyn himself."

*   *   *

Liyana fidgeted, and her horse shuffled beneath her. Up the hill, Runa was breaking the news to Raan, and Raan was not taking it well. Her reaction echoed through the camp.

Raan rattled off a string of expletives that caused Pia to wince. "You were wise to interfere, Liyana," Pia said. "She will realize that this is the right course of action."

More shouting, and then a crash. Raan had begun to throw pots and pans. "I am not certain she will realize that anytime soon," Korbyn commented.

Liyana wondered how long they could afford to wait. She thought again of Jidali and how her clan must feel with despair pressing down on them.

"Do you think she'll try to flee?" Pia asked.

"She won't be allowed to jeopardize our mission," Fennik said. "I'll guard her myself."

"But how will you prevent it?" Pia asked. "We cannot harm a vessel. Her deity needs her body to be pristine."

"No, she doesn't," Liyana said.

Pia began to object.

"Her goddess only needs her alive and able to dance," Liyana said. "If Raan tries to run . . . we blind her. She can't run away if she can't see where she runs."

Pia paled.

"You are . . ." Korbyn paused, clearly searching for the appropriate adjective.

"Mother called me practical," Liyana said. "Fennik, I am sick of delays. Will you fetch her? Carry her if you have to. And if she protests, we can tie her to a horse."

"She isn't going to like us very much," Pia noted.

"I won't let my family suffer because she wants to throw a temper tantrum," Liyana said. She noticed Korbyn was staring at her. She refused to meet his eyes. She didn't want to see what he thought of what she was saying. "We are leaving, whether she likes it or not. Fennik?"

Fennik strode toward the tent. A few minutes later, he emerged with a sullen Raan. His hand was clamped around her arm, and he was nearly dragging her.

Runa watched from on top of a rock. From where she stood, Liyana couldn't read her expression. But she did notice that the clan's warriors fanned out on either side of her. The rest of the clan huddled by their tents, watching and whispering. When Raan tried to run back toward Runa, the chieftess signaled to the warriors. Standing on the rocks all around the camp, the warriors raised their bows and spears.

Scooping Raan up as if she were Pia, Fennik lifted the Scorpion Clan's vessel onto a horse. She kicked him once before she sank into the saddle.

"Fennik, tie her to the saddle," Liyana said.

Raan shot her a glare. "Don't. I will ride."

No one spoke again as they rode out of the hills.

Slumped in her saddle, Raan refused to meet any of their eyes, which suited Liyana fine. *One more vessel,* Liyana thought. She wished she could urge her horse into a gallop and race across the desert to Bayla, wherever she was. *Just one more.* She hoped that the final vessel cooperated easily.

As the sun set and shadows stretched around them, they

pressed on. By unspoken agreement, they wanted as many miles between them and the hills before they camped. On unfamiliar ground, Raan would be less likely to make an escape.

As the stars speckled the sky, they selected a stretch of baked clay punctuated by rocks and cacti to be their camp. Pia commenced her nightly ritual of brushing her white hair. Fennik tended the horses while Korbyn put himself in a trance to summon water and food. After drinking away their supplies in the wake of the failed ceremony, the Scorpion Clan had had little to spare.

Liyana pitched the tent and started the fire. All the while, she kept her eyes on Raan. The others, she noticed, did the same.

Huddled by the tent flap, Raan was glaring at Korbyn as he caused a bush to sprout leaves. "It sickens me," Raan said. "Killing people so they can play at being human."

Pia clucked her tongue but didn't quit brushing her hair. "Without the gods, we'd perish. We need them to revitalize our clans—to fill our wells, bring life to our herds, and instill health in our children."

"Or we could simply move somewhere we don't *need* gods," Raan said. "Move to where there's water. And fertile land. Leave the desert."

Pia dropped her brush.

Liyana heard the words but they sounded foreign. Leave the desert? But they were the desert people! She couldn't imagine not feeling the sand beneath her feet or the wind tangling her hair or the heat searing her lungs. It was a part of how she breathed. Outside the desert . . . she'd shrivel like a ripe date in the sun.

Fennik had quit currying the horses. "If we leave, we lose ourselves."

"Better than losing our lives," Raan said.

"We'd lose our way of life!" Fennik said.

Raan snorted. "Oh, and that would be such a loss. Half my clan poisons themselves with alcohol. The other half works themselves to death trying to squeeze life out of dry rocks. We can't heal our own sick. We can't save our babies. I lost two sisters because my mother's milk wouldn't come. She didn't have enough water to make milk. Yet her brother was drunk every night. He drank away my sisters' lives. And you want to preserve this? Haven't you ever wondered if there could be more out there? If life could be better?"

"I have all I could wish for," Pia said. She resumed brushing her hair.

"This is a pointless conversation," Liyana said. She tossed a handful of dried horse manure and then a clump of dried leaves onto the fire. The leaves crackled and fizzed. "Fennik's right. We *are* the desert." She wiped her hands clean and crossed to Korbyn. Dropping down next to him, she closed her eyes.

Picturing her lake, she inhaled. She felt the water fill her like the sweetest air in her lungs. She reached out toward the desert—her desert, her beautiful home that she would never leave because it was as much a part of her as her body and how dare Raan even consider leaving! How dare Runa even suggest that their choice was wrong! Liyana had spoken the truth—she *was* the desert! She was the sand. She was the sun overhead. She was the hot wind. She was the cracked earth and the rocks, the barren hills and the stone mountains. She was the brittle bush that held its strength coiled tight inside, waiting for the moment to unfurl its leaves. She was the snake that hunted for a desert mouse in the cooling evening air.

As if from a distance, Korbyn's voice drifted toward her. She sensed him, a shimmer that spiked inside flesh, and she touched the other vessels, smooth swirls of energy within their bodies. She could tell the difference between mortal and divine souls, as Korbyn had claimed. "A snake hunts near us," Korbyn said.

"I feel him," Liyana said.

"Draw him closer."

She felt the snake slither over the sand. It hitched its body sideways. Its tongue tasted the air. *This way,* she coaxed it. She felt the snake slither, felt the sand on the scales of her belly. She inched across the desert, closer, closer.

"Now think of the shape of your body and the feel of your own skin," Korbyn said. "Reshape yourself inside your body, and release the excess magic." She remembered the length of her arms and the curve of her legs. She felt sweat clinging to her back and prickling her armpits. She poured herself back inside her own skin. She imagined the excess magic flowing away from her, and she felt it dissipate.

Opening her eyes, she wiped her forehead with her sleeve. "Did it work?"

"You tell me." He pointed.

Fennik raised his bow and aimed an arrow at the sand. The horses rolled their eyes and stamped their feet. Pia stroked the neck of the closest horse, cooing to it.

"I felt the magic," Liyana said, awed. "I summoned it."

The cobra reared.

Fennik released the arrow. It pinned the snake to the sand. He stared at it. So did Liyana, Raan, and Korbyn.

Raan found her voice first. "You . . . But you're a vessel."

"She finally did it," Pia said. "Sacrilege." But the word lacked heat.

"Tasty sacrilege," Korbyn said, picking up the snake.

Liyana collapsed backward in the sand and smiled up at the stars.

✻   ✻   ✻

At dawn Liyana used magic to locate tubers buried beneath the earth. She dug them up and had them shredded and fried before Korbyn finished summoning water. She also located a second snake, the mate to the prior night's dinner. She failed to coax it into moving—she wasn't strong enough to overcome its natural instinct to lie on a rock to soak in the early sun—but she was able to direct Fennik to it, increasing their food supply.

"Nicely done," Korbyn said, handing her a full waterskin.

Liyana felt as though he'd handed her the moon.

"Keep the heads away from Raan," Korbyn told Fennik. "We don't need her getting any clever ideas about poison."

"Unlike some, I don't kill to get what I want," Raan said.

Stiffly Pia swept toward the horses. She did not feel her way as she normally did, and Raan was forced to scoot backward. "Korbyn's vessel was a sacrifice," Pia said.

"Convincing someone that murder is justified doesn't make it any less murder."

Fennik hefted a saddle onto a horse. "In my clan, such talk would have gotten you punished a long time ago." He cinched the saddle around the horse's stomach.

"Ooh, the big, strong warrior is afraid of the truth."

He strapped his bows onto the horse. One bow, two, three. He handled them as if he wanted to use them on Raan. "I don't fear words. Or death. Only failure. That, I fear. But your fear . . . your fear will condemn your clan. Don't you have anyone you care about other than yourself? What about your parents? Brothers or sisters? Cousins? Friends? What about the children in your clan? The babies? The not-yet-born?"

"She had sisters," Pia said. "She said she had sisters who died as babies."

Raan leaped to her feet. "I *am* thinking of them! You have no idea—"

"Enough," Korbyn said. He sounded colder than Liyana had ever heard him sound. "I never expected to have to babysit humans. We've already lost more time than I'd planned."

"What *is* your plan?" Raan asked. "Where are the deities? Who has them? How are they trapped? Can they be rescued? You could be leading us to our deaths while our clans wait and wither—"

Korbyn laid his hand on her shoulder, and Raan slumped to the ground. He then picked her up with more care than Liyana thought she would have, and he placed her in a saddle. He looped the reins around her so that she wouldn't slide off while she slept.

Pia smiled brightly at them, the sky, and the desert in general. "The day has become so much more pleasant!" By feel, she located the horse that Fennik had saddled for her, and she mounted without assistance for the first time.

As they rode away from their campsite, Korbyn kept his horse beside the sleeping Raan. Liyana matched his pace. Once Fennik and Pia pulled into the lead, Liyana said, "Raan did raise valid questions in her rant."

Korbyn nodded gravely. He then leaned and checked the strap that secured Raan to her mare. "To answer her: You follow me because I am charming. And yes, I do know where we are going."

"You could share that information with us," Liyana said.

He rode for a while without answering. She waited and watched the sand swirl in the wind as if twirled by an invisible finger. Finally he said, "Not yet."

"You should trust us. We want what you want."

He looked pointedly at Raan.

"She's asleep," Liyana said.

"Have I ever told you the story of how the parrot once cheated the raven? Once, the raven was a bird with jewel-colored feathers brilliant enough to dazzle the sun itself. The parrot, a drab, brown bird at the time, was jealous. . . ."

Jerking upright, Raan slammed her heels into Plum. The horse jolted forward, and Raan urged her into a gallop. She raced across the desert.

"She's the parrot," Korbyn said.

Fennik yanked his horse's head in her direction, preparing to chase after her.

Korbyn stopped him. "Let her run," he said. "It may make her feel better."

Liyana watched the sand billow in the wake of Raan's horse. She hoped that Raan didn't allow Plum to overheat. "She's heading toward her clan." Without water for herself and her horse, she'd never make it.

"Poor Raan," Pia said. "So much rage to so little effect."

"What happened to the parrot?" Liyana asked.

"He plucked the raven, and then, fearing punishment, fled the desert to live in the rain forest. But once there, he discovered that he was no more beautiful than any other bird or flower. So every night, he flies above the forest canopy and pines for the desert he left."

They watched the shadow of dust recede. "She will have to run very far to reach a rain forest," Fennik commented. He dismounted and tended to the horses.

Setting up the tent, they rested in its shade. Liyana used her magic to corral several scorpions. Once she sliced off their tails, she added their bodies to their food supply. She buried the stingers.

Soon Korbyn pointed to a cloud on the horizon. "She's returning." Together, they watched her fight with the horse's reins as a determined Plum bore down on their camp. Pia shared her tuber cake, and they each nibbled it as they waited for Raan and Plum to cross the sand. When the cake was gone, Fennik stretched out to full length and propped his legs up on a rock. Liyana rested her chin on her knees.

"You used magic on the horse," Liyana said.

"I might have . . . influenced her," Korbyn conceded.

"Clever."

"Delighted you noticed."

As she got closer, Raan shouted a string of obscenities at them. Pia gasped with each one. Fennik looked disgusted.

"Impressive vocabulary," Korbyn said. "I feel as though I should take notes."

"I think she's making them up," Liyana said. "Half of them are not anatomically possible."

"And the rest is . . . ill-advised," Pia said.

Continuing to curse them out, Raan dismounted. Liyana packed up camp while Fennik fussed over Plum. Once the mare had recovered enough, they rode on without a word to Raan.

Her second escape attempt came that night. She didn't take a horse, and Fennik caught her before she'd made it a hundred yards. He carried her kicking back to the camp and deposited her inside the tent.

"Are you trying to make a point?" Liyana asked. "If so, we get it. You don't want to be with us. Well, we don't want to be with you either, but we aren't about to condemn your entire clan because of your personality flaws."

"My clan could find another way to survive," Raan said.

"They won't, though," Liyana said. "None of our people will leave the desert."

"You don't know that. If you"—she glared at Korbyn—"hadn't given them false hope, maybe they would. If I return, they'll know hope is gone, and they'll find another way. Maybe a better way!"

"There is no other way!" Liyana said. Her fists clenched, and she had to fight the urge to shake Raan. "We can't survive the Great Drought without the deities!"

"If we leave the desert, we could escape it! We wouldn't need the deities!" Raan said. "Why should we follow them? Why follow *him*?" She pointed at Korbyn.

He smiled coldly. "Because you don't have a choice." He then walked away from them. They watched his silhouette fade into the blackness of the desert night.

In a panic-filled voice, Pia asked, "Did he leave us?"

"He'll return," Liyana said. "I don't think he has a choice either."

Chapter Fourteen
The Emperor

Golden grasses snapped beneath the emperor's feet. Holding his horse's reins, he surveyed the plain. Already his soldiers spread throughout the grasses. With expert precision, they sliced the stalks to store for later—he'd been told they made adequate horse feed, though humans could not consume them. Other soldiers scurried behind, establishing rows in which to erect the tents.

Beyond the plain, the land sloped up into a ridge that ran north-south. A few twisty black trees crowned the peak of the nearest hill. Leaving his horse, he strode toward it. His guard followed him.

He nodded to soldiers as they passed, and they paused to bow to him. He heard voices, cheerful, around him. The mood was light—the march was, for now, finished—and they'd camp here until they had collected enough supplies to proceed. He kept his face pleasant to maintain the mood around him, but was grateful when he'd passed the last of the working men and women. His stomach was a hard knot inside him, and his heart thudded fast within his chest. He climbed the hill, and then he stood on top of the ridge.

He was here, the border of the Crescent Empire, the border of the desert.

The emperor gazed across the sands.

Brittle plants pockmarked the sand, bumps of brown and deep green in a spread of tan. Groves of leafless trees huddled in spots closer to the border. But beyond . . . the desert spread and stretched. He felt his hands begin to sweat as he absorbed the enormity of it all.

Far in the distance, the mountains seemed to crack the sky. He fixed his eyes on them. The lake was there. He could feel it deep inside with the kind of certainty that he normally reserved for proven facts. In the middle of this barren wasteland was his people's best hope for survival.

His two best generals climbed onto the hilltop beside him.

"Hostile," General Akkon observed.

"It is a wonder that anyone survives such an environment," General Xevi agreed.

"And it is the source of that wonder that will save us," the emperor said.

The two generals studied the desert and the outline of the

mountains with him. "The desert people will not take kindly to our invasion of their land," General Xevi said.

"Hence the army," the emperor said dryly.

"They are rumored to be a highly superstitious people," the general continued, as if the emperor hadn't spoken. "To them, those are the forbidden mountains."

The emperor knew this far better than the general did. But the general never spoke without purpose so the emperor allowed him his speech.

"You must be prepared for resistance," General Xevi said.

"You think I am not?" the emperor said. "Again, I did bring an army."

"I think you are young," General Xevi said bluntly. "And the scouting party has not returned."

The emperor switched his gaze from the mountains to his two generals. "We have not yet crossed the border. Do you believe that we should turn back? Turn away from the only hope, faint as you may believe it to be, that we have seen for the past three years? Return without the miracle our people need?"

"I believe that your miracle will come with blood," General Xevi said. "And you must be ready to both spill it and have it be spilled."

The emperor kept his face impassive, as always. "You believe I am not."

General Akkon snorted. "You are not."

The emperor studied the desert again. "I will be," he said.

Chapter Fifteen

Five days later, shortly after dawn, they rode into the camp of the Falcon Clan.

Liyana breathed in the stench of rotted meat. Three falcons tore apart a carcass in front of a tent. The birds didn't budge when Liyana and the others rode past.

Unlike the birds, the people of the Falcon Clan did notice them. Drawn from their tasks and their tents, the men, women, and children of the Falcon Clan emerged to stare at Liyana and the others. Liyana blinked, surprised to find tears in her eyes, as a boy about Jidali's age ran past them. He clutched a leather ball in his arms. A mother called to the boy with the ball, and he ran to her. He peeked out at them with frightened eyes. His clothes hung loosely on his body.

All the people had feathers in their hair and sewn into their clothes. Most of the men and women wore thick, leather wraps around their wrists, shielding against sharp talons. The birds themselves were everywhere, perched on the tents and on twisted branches that had been driven deep into the sand.

Korbyn dismounted first and called out a greeting. Liyana, Fennik, Pia, and Raan followed suit. Fennik loosened the saddles and curried away the worst of the sweat and sand. More people drew closer to stare at the new arrivals.

"I don't like this," Raan said softly.

Liyana tried to smile at the boy with the ball. His mother hid him behind her skirt. Liyana noticed that he was one of only a few children. Surely, the clan had others. "At least they aren't pointing arrows at us."

"Something's wrong here," Raan said.

"What do you mean?" Pia asked, her voice as high as a mouse's squeak.

Korbyn pressed his lips into a thin line. "We must be certain before we leave."

"But we just arrived!" Pia objected.

Liyana studied the faces around them. Their eyes were hostile, their cheeks sunken, and their shoulders hunched. She wondered what they were thinking, if they saw them as more mouths to feed.

"We must speak with your vessel!" Fennik called to them.

As if his words were a knife to flint, the men and women of

the Falcon Clan burst into whispers. Several of them ran toward the center of camp—presumably to spread word of their arrival and their request. At the sudden activity, one falcon shrieked a cry. It fanned its wings, but it was tethered to its perch.

"We have at least piqued their curiosity," Korbyn murmured.

Liyana patted Gray Luck's neck. The mare shifted from hoof to hoof as if she could sense the unease that permeated the air. These people were clearly uncomfortable with strangers.

Shuffling through the crowd, a man approached them. He bowed low. "We would be honored if you would share tea with our chief and chieftess."

"See, that did not sound hostile," Pia said softly.

Raan snorted.

"I'll stay with the horses," Fennik volunteered.

"Wise idea," Korbyn said, and Liyana saw Fennik's eyes widen at this compliment. She realized this was the first time that Korbyn had ever complimented Fennik. Perhaps Korbyn had finally quit seeing Sendar in Fennik.

Under her breath Raan added, "You might want to keep them ready."

Liyana checked Gray Luck's bridle, and then she patted her again before handing the reins to Fennik. She joined Korbyn, Raan, and Pia, and followed their guide across the camp.

When they reached the chief and chieftess's tent, their guide halted. Korbyn strode inside without pause. The vessels followed.

Inside the tent, three people were seated around the cooking fire—an ancient man with a necklace of bird skulls and a man and woman who wore feather headdresses and ornate multi-colored robes. A silver kettle warmed over the fire. The man with the skulls fetched a tray of silver cups. He laid them on a carpet and then poured tea in each.

"Welcome to our clan," the chieftess said. She was a soft-spoken woman with thick coils of black and gray hair wound tightly against her scalp. Her headdress consisted of three rows of falcon feathers that dangled over her cheeks. "Share the water of life with us, steeped in the food of health." Ceremonially she raised a cup of tea to her lips and sipped.

Korbyn sat cross-legged in front of her. "We thank you for your hospitality and bring greetings from across the desert, as well as from the Dreaming." He selected a cup and sipped the tea. Liyana watched the ancient man's eyes widen at the mention of the Dreaming. She guessed that that was not part of this clan's traditional greeting. "I am Korbyn, god of the Raven Clan. My companions are Liyana, vessel of Bayla of the Goat Clan; Pia, vessel of Oyri of the Silk Clan; and Raan, vessel of Maara of the Scorpion Clan. Our companion, Fennik, vessel of Sendar of the Horse Clan, tends to our mounts."

The chieftess's hands shook. She laid her teacup on the tray, and she folded her hands in her lap as if to disguise the way they trembled. Liyana noticed that the old man's eyes had widened so much that he resembled a horse about to bolt.

"Why have you come to us?" the chief asked.

"Five of the desert deities have been stolen from the Dreaming," Korbyn said. His voice was even, and his face was expressionless. Liyana had an urge to hold his hand as if he needed comforting. She stayed behind him and didn't speak. "We seek to return them to their rightful clans. Your god, Somayo, was one of them, and so we have come to ask your vessel to join us."

The chief rose to his feet. Without speaking, he left the tent. The man with the bird skull necklace covered his face with his hands. The chieftess blanched but did not move.

Liyana felt a sick knot form in the base of her stomach. *Please, no.*

"How . . . how long ago was it?" Raan asked. Her voice was hushed.

The chieftess lowered her eyes and stared into the teacups. "Two nights ago."

Oh, goddess, two nights! If she'd learned magic faster, if Pia's tribe had believed them faster, if Raan hadn't wasted time with her escapes, if Fennik's father hadn't stabbed Liyana . . .

"We didn't know." The old man's voice was low and husky. "I should have. . . ."

"I do not understand," Pia said.

Raan laid her hands on Pia's shoulders and hauled her back toward the tent flap. "We'll explain outside, princess. Liyana, help here?"

"I'm not a princess," Pia said. She dug her feet into the carpets and resisted. Liyana grabbed her other arm, and together she and Raan propelled Pia out of the tent. "Ow, ow, ow! But the vessel!"

Outside, Liyana whispered in her ear, "They killed him."

Pia gasped.

"Keep your face calm," Raan ordered in her other ear. "We need to get out of here before it occurs to these people to blame us."

"But we didn't——" Pia began.

"It's what people do, princess," Raan said. She plastered a smile on her face and waved at the people who had gathered around the tent. Liyana did the same. "Better get Korbyn before they decide that any god will suffice."

Pia gasped again. "They wouldn't!"

"Return to Fennik," Liyana said. "If Korbyn and I aren't with you in three minutes, ride the horses through camp past this tent." Releasing Pia, she walked back inside.

Inside, the chieftess was openly crying. Korbyn held her hands, trying to comfort her. The old man looked as if he'd been punched in the gut. He huddled on a cushion, holding his knees to his chest and looking at the roof of the tent with wild eyes. Liyana wondered if he was the vessel's magician—or if he had been his executioner.

Liyana took a deep breath, marched across the tent, and pried the chieftess's fingers off of Korbyn's hands. "My clan is in Yubay," she told the chieftess. "I recommend you join them there.

Together, you can pool your resources until we rescue the deities." She wondered what Korbyn had been telling her and hoped she hadn't contradicted it. She decided she didn't care. With Korbyn, she backed out of the tent.

Outside, men and women milled between the tents, filling the spaces. Their stares felt like arrows. Pulling Korbyn by the elbow, Liyana strode in the direction of the horses.

A woman with a baby in her arms rushed toward them. "Please, help my baby. She's sick!" She thrust the baby at Korbyn. Korbyn stumbled as he caught the child.

As if the woman had ignited a spark inside the crowd, others pressed forward. "The well is nearly dry," one man said. "A few more months, that's all we need."

"The birds . . . The eggs won't hatch right. Please . . . If you help them . . ."

"I broke my leg. Can't work."

"My husband is ill. . . ."

"Can't find our usual prey. Hunting has gone bad. The drought . . ."

They clustered closer. The mother of the baby was pushed toward the back of the crowd, and in Korbyn's arms, the baby began to cry soft mewling sounds like a hurt kitten. A few began to push and shout as requests switched to demands. Liyana tried to force her way through.

She heard hoofbeats. "Get ready," she told Korbyn.

The crowd broke apart as the horses thundered through. Fennik grabbed Liyana's waist and yanked her up in front of him. Clutching the horse's neck, she shot a look behind them to see Korbyn swing himself onto one of the other riderless horses. With a tight grip on the reins, Raan led Pia's horse as Pia clung to her mare's neck. They pounded through camp and burst out the other side. Men and women chased after them.

Several miles away, at Fennik's signal, they slowed, and then stopped. Fennik dismounted and began to care for the horses. All the horses had foam around their mouths. Sweat glistened on their sand-coated hides, and their sides heaved. Dismounting also, Pia soothed them, cooing to them as she stroked their necks.

The baby whimpered.

"You have a baby!" Pia cried.

"Her mother said she was sick," Korbyn said. He held the baby away from his body as if he were afraid that the baby would bite.

"You have to help it," Pia said.

"Did you think I planned to leave it for the sand wolves?" Korbyn said. "Of course I'll help it." He slid off his horse. A dried-out cactus crunched under his feet.

"You should have given it back," Liyana said. She tried not to look at it, tried not to care, but at the baby's cries, she felt herself twist inside. She thought of the babies in her clan, of the ones who needed Bayla.

The baby cried louder. Her face squished and reddened.

Pia scooped the baby out of Korbyn's arms. "Let me." Pacing

in a circle, she sang a lullaby. The baby quieted and then began to utter a string of nonsense syllables, as if she were singing with Pia.

Korbyn lowered himself to the ground. "Give it to me."

"We don't have time for this," Liyana said. But she didn't say it with any conviction. If Korbyn didn't heal this baby, no one would. The baby's god wasn't coming.

Still crooning, Pia lowered the baby into Korbyn's arms. Immediately the child wailed louder than before. Pia scooped her up again and sat close to Korbyn. "Will this work?" Singing, she calmed the baby. Her tiny, pudgy fingers wrapped around Pia's white hair.

As Korbyn focused on the child, Liyana sidled closer to Fennik and Raan. The three of them watched the camp. A plume of sand advanced from it. "He'll collapse after he heals," Liyana said. "He always does. It's his worst trick."

Both of them looked grim. "We are fortunate that the Falcon Clan does not have horses, but even on foot, they'll catch up," Fennik said.

"Loan me one of your bows," Raan said.

"We cannot shoot unarmed people," Fennik said. The sand cloud obscured the number of people, but it had to be more than a dozen. It could have been a hundred. It could have been the entire clan. "Plus I do not have enough arrows."

Liyana rubbed her forehead, trying to think. She kept feeling the stones that her clan had thrown at her. If Jidali hadn't inter-vened, this could have been her fate, and her clan could have condemned themselves. This baby could have been her cousin.

Fennik checked on Korbyn. "He isn't finished yet."

The plume of sand drew closer. It spread out wide, blanket-ing a stretch of the desert. Liyana heard shouting roll across the desert toward them.

"They're coming," Raan said. "A lot of them."

"Five minutes, and we interrupt him," Liyana said. *If he isn't finished healing the baby by then . . .*

Fennik tightened the saddles on the horses, who pawed the ground and snorted. Closer, Liyana recognized the magician and the chieftess at the head of the horde. At least a hundred men and women fanned out behind them.

"I don't think we have five minutes," Raan said.

Liyana knelt beside Pia and Korbyn, but she couldn't speak. She kept picturing Jidali as a baby. It wasn't this child's fault that his god hadn't come.

Singing the words in the same lullaby tune, Pia said, "Leave me here, and I will deliver the baby to her mother when she comes."

"You can't risk it," Liyana said. "Your clan needs you."

Pia broke off singing. "I cannot leave a baby alone and merely hope they find her!" Hearing Pia's agitation, the baby scrunched her face into a knot and screamed. Her cheeks flushed red.

Korbyn's eyes snapped open. And then he toppled over.

Using one of Raan's choicest swears, Liyana shook him. "Korbyn, wake up! You need to ride!" She and Fennik hauled him to his feet and with Raan's help, they hoisted him onto a horse.

Fennik secured him on and called to Pia, "You need to mount now!"

"I'll take the baby back," Raan said. She lifted the child out of Pia's arms. Immediately, the baby began to wail, reaching for Pia. Raan bounced the baby on her hip with a practiced ease. The baby fussed but then settled against her.

The Falcon Clan was close. The chieftess shouted to them. Liyana could nearly distinguish words in the yell. Fennik scooped up Pia and tossed her onto a horse. "Raan has the baby?" Pia said. "I don't hear crying. . . ."

"I'll escape north after I deliver the child," Raan said. "Be there so I don't die of dehydration."

Liyana began, "How can we trust—"

Raan flashed Liyana a smile. "You don't have a choice. Or rather, you do: me or Pia. And which of us has more practice escaping?"

There was zero time left to discuss it. Liyana swung herself onto a horse, and they galloped away, leaving Raan to greet the doomed clan.

❉   ❉   ❉

SARAH BETH DURST

Just north of the Falcon Clan, Liyana climbed the branches of a tamar tree. She squinted at the sands beyond and saw no one. The camp was a smudge in the distance. Below her, Korbyn, Fennik, and Pia camped in the tree's wide shadow, obscured from view by the spread of drooping limbs. The ancient tree covered nearly thirty feet of desert with limbs that reached the ground and then stretched vine-like a hundred feet in every direction. In the heat of the day, its broad leaves had curled into tight rolls, but the branches still sheltered Liyana and the others from the endless hot wind.

So far they'd waited half a day.

Liyana climbed down the tree, negotiating her way through the tangle of branches. She dropped to the ground next to their tent. "She isn't going to come," Liyana said. "We should have left the baby."

At the base of the tree, Pia cried, "Are you heartless? It was a baby!"

"I didn't say leave it to die," Liyana said. "The clan was five minutes away. If we'd left it on bright cloth, they would have seen it, rescued it, and taken it happily home. Raan used that baby to flee."

"She'll rejoin us," Pia said. "She has to. She won't let her clan die."

Another hour passed. And another.

Korbyn lit a fire, a small fire with little smoke, on the opposite side of the tamar tree. He set the various rodents, insects, and other food they had to cook.

Fennik oiled his bows. He also worked on fashioning new arrow points from rocks he'd collected. Liyana tried to practice her magic on the tamar tree. She wondered if her family had attempted their dreamwalks. Without Bayla, they couldn't have chosen a new vessel. She wondered if they felt despair. She thought about her mother and father, Jidali, Aunt Sabisa, her cousins . . . She thought of Talu and wondered what she had done when the dreamwalks failed. Eventually Liyana gave up on her practice, and she crawled into the shade of the tent. Korbyn lay there with his eyes closed and his arms crossed over his chest. She pulled her knees up to her chin and looked out the tent flap, through the drooping branches, toward the Falcon Clan. "What should we do?" she asked Korbyn.

Eyes still closed, he said, "I could have been sleeping."

"You weren't," she said.

"How did you know?" He opened his eyes.

"You have a little purr to your voice when you sleep."

"I don't purr."

"Don't worry," she said. "It's a divine purr."

His mouth quirked a little, but the faint smile faded too quickly. "This shouldn't be my responsibility," he said without looking at her. "I'm not leadership material. I'm a trickster god. Little tricks. Not this!"

Liyana was silent, considering how to reply. She thought of Jidali crying "Why me?" when he was asked again to card the goats. And she thought of herself after she'd been chosen in the dreamwalk. "Why is it you?"

"I was with Bayla on the day she was summoned," he said. "Her soul was drawn east, though your clan was west." *East*, she thought. At last there was a direction. "No one believed me. It happened again. . . . The Scorpion Clan, the Horse Clan, Silk, Falcon. All drawn east. Still no one believed me, for who would believe a trickster god? I did this to myself. I made myself untrustworthy, and here is the price I pay."

"Surely they must believe you now," Liyana said.

"Most don't watch the world," Korbyn said. "You can't affect the world of the living from within the Dreaming, and it hurts to see your clan suffer and be unable to help."

"How did you avoid the fate of the others?"

He snorted. "Side effect of being a trickster god. Trust no one. When I was summoned east, I suspected a trick. I did not leave until I was certain that it was my clan who called."

You're trusting me now, she thought, but she didn't say it out loud. This was the most truth he'd spoken to her in weeks. "Who's in the east who would do this?"

He didn't answer. Instead he watched the sky above the tamar tree. Above, two sky serpents danced. Their glass scales caught the sunlight and reflected it like a thousand jewels as their bodies twisted and intertwined. Their eyes burned like minisuns as their bodies etched through the blue.

Quietly Liyana said, "You don't know. You don't know who took the other deities or why they were taken, or even if others have been taken since. *That's* why you never answer questions. You have no idea how to rescue them. Just like you don't know what to do if Raan doesn't come."

"You know, I used to be a very good liar."

"I'm sure you still are." She patted his hand. "You just don't want to lie to me."

"Oh, I don't?" He looked amused.

"You don't," she said, her hand still on his. "Because you don't want to do this alone."

He stared at her, and then he covered her hand with his.

Fennik raced to the edge of the tamar tree. "I see her!"

Jumping up and down, Pia clapped like a child. "I knew it!"

Liyana chased after him. Korbyn followed closely behind. They stayed just within the branches as a figure walked toward them.

Fennik rode out to meet her, leading a second horse. In moments, both rejoined them. Raan slid to the ground and collapsed onto her knees.

"I knew you'd return," Pia crowed.

Raan covered her face with her hands. Her sleeves rode up her arms, and Liyana glimpsed bandages. Kneeling beside her, Liyana pushed Raan's sleeves back. Raan lowered her hands but didn't resist. The bandages were wrapped all the way up her arms, over her tattoos. Hesitating, Liyana unwound the bandages.

Underneath, the skin was red and raw in between new black markings of soaring falcons. Liyana looked at Raan. Raan's eyes were wet. "I didn't plan to return," Raan said.

The falcons obscured the scorpion images. Recoiling, Liyana wrapped her own arms around her stomach as if that would protect her own clan's tattoos.

"They were supposed to take me in and help me return to my clan. Then my clan would quit waiting for a miracle and find a way to save themselves. But instead . . ." Raan stared at her arms, and her arms shook. "This isn't . . . I can't . . ." Her voice rose higher. She looked at Liyana, and then at Pia and Fennik. Lastly she looked at Korbyn. "You must fix this!"

Liyana had never heard a story of a clan stealing another's vessel. A vessel was a clan's future. To force Raan . . . Such a thing should have been inconceivable.

Korbyn knelt and held the girl's wrists. He studied the wounds. "I can help the pain. I can't change the marks."

Raan yanked her hands away from him. With fumbling fingers, she reached into her robe and pulled out a small waterskin on a cord. She yanked out the stopper and poured yellowish liquid onto her arms. She hissed as the drops hit, and Liyana smelled alcohol.

Fennik nodded approvingly. "That will ward off infection."

"Raan . . . ," Liyana began. She didn't know what to say, how to comfort her. She knew Raan hadn't wanted to be a vessel, but to have her destiny stolen from her . . . To have her clan condemned by another . . .

Raan lurched to her feet and stumbled over the roots of the tamar tree.

"What is she—" Pia began to follow the sounds of Raan's passage.

Liyana put a hand on Pia's shoulder to stop her. "Let her mourn in peace," Liyana said softly.

Raan dropped to the ground beside Fennik's fire. She pressed her alcohol-dampened arms directly onto the embers. Flame shot into the air and blanketed her skin. Raan screamed.

Fennik lunged forward and crossed to her in three strides. He wrapped his arms around her waist and yanked her away from the fire. Her arms continued to burn. Fennik smothered the flames with the cloth of his robe. Raan kept screaming.

Korbyn seized her shoulders and dropped into a trance while Fennik held her still.

"What's happening?" Pia cried.

Liyana clapped her hand over Pia's mouth to keep her quiet. "He's healing her," Liyana whispered. "Shh."

A few minutes passed, and then Korbyn released her and stumbled backward. He sank to the ground and dropped his face in his hands.

Raan curled against Fennik's chest, whimpering. Liyana took her hand off of Pia's mouth. "It's over," Liyana said.

"What happened?" Pia asked.

Slowly, Raan held out of her arms. All the tattoos were now a swirl of red scars. Even the ones that marked her as a vessel were obliterated. She took a great, shaking breath in.

"She burned them away, the markings, all of them," Liyana said.

"But . . . her clan!"

"The Falcon Clan had already taken them from her."

"She'll need new tattoos," Pia said.

Raan wrapped her arms tightly around her. She stood and backed away from them. Her gaze darted across the desert. Liyana knew she was thinking about running, but there was no place to run to. Certainly not back to the Falcon Clan. "Only when you're ready," Liyana said as soothingly as she could. "For now . . . we should ride."

A few minutes later, the camp was packed, and they were each mounted on a horse. They had three hours before sunset. "Which way?" Fennik asked.

Everyone looked at Korbyn.

But it was Liyana who answered. "East," she said.

Chapter Sixteen
The Emperor

The emperor signaled to his guards. At his feet, a man knelt, and the emperor knew the man was dying. He'd smelled the stink of infected wounds before, and he recognized the signs in the man's mottled, red hands, bloated to stiffness.

"You have done well," the emperor told him gently. "Your empire thanks you."

The man shook his head. "They came from the sky. Blinding, like the sun. At the top of the mountains. We tried to fight them. As hard as we hacked, we couldn't damage them. But their scales cut like swords, and they sliced us like we were wheat in a field. Three of us lived. Of them . . . I am all that is left. Your Imperial Majesty, forgive my failure."

Escorted by the emperor's guards, the doctor and his assistants entered the tent. The four men wore the traditional blue face-cloths obscuring all but their eyes. The emperor held up a hand to halt them. He had to ask one more question. One more question wouldn't change this man's fate, but it could mean everything for the empire. "Did you see it?"

"Oh yes."

"Describe it."

"A green valley. Sheer cliffs. And a perfect oval lake. Most beautiful sight I have ever seen."

The emperor nodded to the doctors, who rushed forward. One had a stretcher. The man collapsed onto it, and he and the smell of dying were whisked out of the emperor's command tent in a swirl of blue robes.

The emperor wanted to sink down into the cushions and bury his face in his hands. But he was not alone, so instead he walked in a measured pace behind his desk and studied his collection of sculptures. Each was carved of diamond from the northern mountains of his empire. He picked up the falcon. It fit in the palm of his hand. The feathers caught and twisted the candlelight, sparkling like a thousand stars. Calmer, he placed it back on the shelf.

At least he knew the lake was real. He tried to console himself with that. Before, he had not been certain, and instead of engaging an entire army to discover whether he was chasing a myth, only one group of soldiers had suffered. But still he felt each death as if it were a knife to his gut.

He let none of his emotions show on his face. "Summon the magician."

The emperor paced in a circle around his tent. The silk carpets whispered beneath his sandaled feet. The heat in the tent pressed against his skin. He paused to drink water from a silver pitcher. He couldn't question himself, not now, especially not now. He should be glad to have confirmation. None of this was a waste, and they could proceed.

The magician entered and bowed low until his forehead nearly touched the carpets. The emperor let him stay in the bow for a few seconds longer than was strictly protocol. He'd learned it was best to start these conversations with a reminder of their roles. The magician often forgot, and that was something the emperor couldn't permit to happen. His generals barely tolerated the man. If they ever felt that he received undue favor or carried greater influence than they . . . Emphasizing the difference and distance between the emperor and the magician helped keep the magician alive. Not that the emperor could explain that to him.

He had no one to whom he could explain any of his actions. His parents had had each other. He remembered how they used to stroll through the gardens, heads close together, deep in conversation. As a child, he'd trailed after them, playing in the flowerbeds and watching the birds with their jewel-like feathers. He wondered what his parents would have said about his actions here.

Would they have been proud? Or would they too have believed he risked too much?

"Rise," the emperor said. "I have my confirmation. I am satisfied. But it seems the sky serpents pose a greater threat than we anticipated."

The magician threw himself prone on the carpets. "Forgive me, Your Imperial Majesty. I *did* warn you, but—"

Every time the man groveled, the emperor had to resist the urge to kick him. He was certain that the man did not do it out of any real respect or remorse. It was merely a way to preserve his skin. The emperor wondered if the magician had ever respected anyone. "Get up."

The magician scrambled to his feet.

"You warned me, and I took a calculated risk," the emperor said. "It was my decision, and the responsibility and the burden are mine. Absolve yourself of guilt. So long as you share your knowledge, you do not need to concern yourself with how that knowledge is applied." He paused. "I do hope you have shared all relevant knowledge?"

"Yes, of course!"

The emperor let the silence stretch. He'd learned that technique from his father—it often induced people to fill the silence with words they hadn't meant to say. But this time, it didn't. *Unfortunate,* he thought. He had hoped the desert man would cough up further helpful secrets. Perhaps there were none. "Very well. Once we have sufficient supplies, we will enter the desert. You will speak to any clans we encounter, explain our purpose, and solicit their cooperation."

"They will not listen," the magician objected. "I know my people."

"It must be tried," the emperor said. "If there is a chance that we can have the lake without bloodshed, then we must attempt it."

"With all due respect, your Imperial Majesty, the desert people are not yours," the magician said. "You don't need to concern yourself with their fate."

The emperor smiled. "And that, my good man, is why you are not emperor."

"They will fight us."

His smile faded in the face of that truth. "If they do, they will not win."

Chapter Seventeen

Sandstorm coming," Korbyn said.

Liyana scanned the horizon and saw—oh yes, there it was, a smudge of tan that blotted out a patch of blue sky. All of them dismounted. Liyana and Raan pitched the tent while Korbyn unsaddled the horses. He tossed the supply packs into the tent. Without guidance Pia crawled inside and pushed the packs so they'd brace the walls. Fennik hammered stakes into the ground around the tent and secured the horses' reins to them. He wrapped cloth around the horses' heads to protect their eyes from the sand. It couldn't protect the horses from the sand wolves, but it would at least prevent the horses from panicking and drawing the wolves. All was completed with practiced ease well before the sandstorm arrived.

As Fennik and Raan joined Pia inside the tent, Korbyn plopped down cross-legged in the sand. Pausing at the tent flap, Liyana asked, "Aren't you coming in?"

"You need another magic lesson." He patted the sand next to him.

Liyana checked the sandstorm. The wall of sand advanced across the desert, blackening the sky above it. The wind had already picked up, tossing grains of sand and debris into the air. Behind them, the horses stomped their hooves and sniffed the air.

She sat and waited for him to explain.

"You are going to push the wind," Korbyn said. "It's already moving, so this is far easier than starting a sandstorm from scratch. You are simply going to encourage it to blow around us."

"And you?"

"I'll keep the sand wolves from eating you when you fail."

She scowled at him. "I won't fail."

"Good for you, goat girl." He grinned at her. "Go on and impress me."

Liyana regarded the mass of writhing black clouds. "It's said that once, the god of the Tortoise Clan spent an entire century inside a sandstorm. The weathering of the sand and wind is what gave the tortoise its distinctive shell pattern."

"Oh yes, we teased him about that for days."

She studied him, trying to determine if he was serious or not. "If I make a mistake, will we be stuck in a sandstorm for a century?"

"I hope not," he said cheerfully.

She drew her sky serpent knife out of her sash. "This seems to work on the wolves. It sliced through the one that attacked me before I met you." She handed him the blade.

Korbyn examined it. "Beautifully made." She watched his fingers caress the carved handle. The bone had been worn down to fit smoothly in one's hand. The blade was lashed to the handle with goat sinew in an elaborate array of knots.

"It's been in my family for generations," Liyana said. "Don't lose it."

"Your lack of trust wounds me." He slashed the air with it. "I assume there's a story about how a sky serpent scale came to be the blade in your knife?"

"It's a family story," Liyana said. She watched him cut designs in the air, and her fingers itched to take the knife back. She didn't know what had possessed her to share it with him. It had never been wielded by anyone outside the family before. She felt as if he were holding a piece of herself.

"You can tell me. I'm like family."

She snorted like Raan. "You are nothing like family."

He mimed a stab to the heart with the hand that did not hold the knife. "After all we have been through together . . . you wound my heart."

"Tell me one of your family secrets, and I'll tell you mine." She didn't know what possessed her to offer that bargain. She simply . . . wanted him to share something of his as he held her knife.

"I don't have a family," Korbyn said. "Gods were never born. We simply . . . are."

She rolled her eyes at him. "Tell me a secret of the gods."

He leaned close to her. She felt his breath on her neck, warm and soft. She shivered as if his breath touched all of her skin. In a mock whisper he said, "Sendar has horribly bad breath."

She heard Pia giggle from within the tent.

Also in a mock whisper Liyana said, "Tell me one of *your* secrets."

"You want to play confession?" Korbyn's eyes glittered, and a smile played over his lips. She felt as if she were playing with a flame. She didn't back away.

"One thing," Liyana said, "and I'll tell you about the knife."

Korbyn was quiet for a while. Liyana watched the sandstorm build in front of them, a wall of blackness. Not far away now, it obliterated the line between land and sky. "I can't dance," Korbyn said at last.

Liyana laughed.

"Bayla doesn't know," he said mournfully. "So far I have hid my inadequacy by always serving as audience. But she loves to dance. One day she'll discover my secret and flee from me in horror."

Liyana patted his knee. "I'll teach you. Before you're reunited with Bayla, you'll be a master of dance. She'll never need to know about this horrible flaw in your character."

"I accept your offer," Korbyn said solemnly. "Now, the knife?"

"My great-great-great-great-grandmother was in love with the chief's son. But he said that he would only marry her if she was the bravest woman in the clan. She asked how she could prove her bravery, and he said that she had to walk into the forbidden mountains and return with proof that she had been there."

Liyana heard a gasp, and then Pia stuck her head out of the tent to hear better. "She did that? But no one has ever entered the forbidden mountains!"

"According to the chief's son, she did it, and he married the bravest woman in the clan. But according to my mother and my mother's mother and my mother's mother's mother . . . she stole it off a sky serpent only a few miles from home while the serpent was distracted with . . . um, mating."

Korbyn roared with laughter.

"I think that still qualifies as the bravest," Pia said, after consideration.

After he wiped the tears from his eyes, Korbyn pointed at the storm. "Almost here. Concentrate on the feel of your body. Think of the lake." Behind them, Pia retreated into the tent, and the flap was sealed shut.

Liyana rested her palms on her knees and straightened her back. She tried not to think about how exposed they were outside the tent. Around them, the horses snorted and stamped their feet as the wind tossed sand. Liyana breathed. In and out. In and out.

Keeping herself firmly tethered to her body, she imagined her lake.

In her mind, she saw her lake. But the surface bubbled and frothed as if the wind stirred it, too. The cliffs roared with the sound of the sandstorm. She plunged into the churning waters, and she felt the magic fill her.

"You are the desert," Korbyn said in her ear. The piece of her still in her body heard his words and felt his breath on her neck. "You are the wind."

She poured herself into the air around their tent and felt her soul overflow. She rushed over the sands to meet the oncoming storm, and she slammed into it.

Wind crashed into her, and she felt as if she were splintering. Sand swirled around her and into her, and she was caught and twisted. The world spun with her, blackening as the sand blotted out the sun. She heard howls within the wind.

"Liyana!"

She heard her name from far away, as if the speaker were at the base of a well. She tried to draw closer to it, but she was whipped in circles. She felt herself rip from the center and shred within the storm.

"Do not lose yourself! Remember you!"

She was wind. She was desert.

She ran with the wolves.

She felt her own jaws made of rock and her own flesh made of sand. Her wolf body shed sand, dissolving and reforming as the storm spiraled. She howled and felt sand pour down her throat. She swallowed the sand as if it were air. She breathed sand.

"Liyana!"

The name sounded like mere syllables. She was more than a name. Releasing her wolf form, she spun into a cyclone of wind and sand. Faster and faster. She felt herself race over the desert floor.

She felt hands on her shoulders, her human shoulders, and for an instant she was yanked back fully into her body. She lost the feel of the wind inside her, and instead she felt the sand pelt her skin, stinging where it hit, but then her spirit stretched. She was more than a body! She was pure spirit merged with the storm—

Liyana felt warmth, a soft pressure, on her lips. She was aware of hands on the nape of her neck and fingers entwined in her hair. She breathed in and tasted Korbyn's sweet breath. She kissed Korbyn as he kissed her.

He released her. "Change of plans!" he shouted over the storm. He pressed the handle of the sky serpent blade into her hands. "I'll turn the storm. You watch for wolves."

Lips tingling, Liyana clutched the knife. Beside her, Korbyn faced the storm. After a moment, she felt the wind spin faster and faster. *It's working!* she thought. Korbyn's cyclone tightened around their tent, and the wind stilled within it—their tent was in the eye of Korbyn's storm. The true storm raged around them, but within Korbyn's wall of wind and sand, the air did not move. She lowered the knife.

Through the furious circle of wind, Liyana saw shapes move, blurs at first but then more distinct. She caught a glimpse of a muzzle and then a thigh. She stared hard at the dark swirl of sand. The silhouette of a wolf appeared. It vanished into the storm.

Suddenly a wolf burst through the wall of wind and sand. It leaped at Korbyn. Springing toward it, Liyana sliced with the sky serpent blade. It hit the wolf's torso, and the wolf dissolved into a spray of sand that spattered her and Korbyn.

His concentration broke, and his cyclone collapsed.

Wind and sand knocked Liyana backward against the tent. She clung to the tarp and to her knife. Wolves howled around her. She saw their shapes as shadows rushing in circles around them. Sand stung her eyes.

She tried to yell, "Korbyn!" but sand poured into her mouth. She coughed and gasped for air. She felt arms wrap around her and yank her down. Her cheek was pressed against Korbyn's chest. Sand pounded at her back, and the howls shook her bones. One of the horses screamed.

He needed to drive the wind away. But to do that, he had to quit protecting her and let her protect him. Into his ear she shouted, "Forget me! Stop the storm!" She broke away from him.

Eyes shut against the blinding sand, she held her knife ready and listened.

She heard a howl, and she sliced at the sand. She felt the blade hit. She struck again. And again. And again, as the wolves lunged for them.

An eternity later, she felt wind, clear wind, push from behind her, pushing the sand away. Korbyn's wind intensified, blowing harder and faster. The howls receded.

Slowly, eventually the wind stilled.

Behind her, Korbyn collapsed.

Liyana was coated in sand. Her eyelids were caked with grit, and her eyes burned. She tried to wipe her eyes with her sleeve, but she only smeared more sand onto her face. With shaking hands she tucked the knife back into her sash, and then she collapsed beside Korbyn.

*　*　*

After the sandstorm, no one objected to Liyana's magic lessons. The wolves had come too close for anyone's comfort, and everyone knew it was sheer luck that the horses had survived. At every stop, Liyana practiced.

Occasionally Raan joined her, though she lacked the concentration to picture the lake for more than a few minutes. She wasn't able to pull magic from it at all. Liyana, on the other hand, continued to improve. When at last she caused a desert bush to burst into bloom, all of them, including Pia, cheered. Liyana bowed before she collapsed in the sand.

An hour later she opened her eyes. "Ready for lesson two?" Korbyn asked.

Shaking the sand out of her hair, she sat up. "Your turn. I promised you dance lessons." She got to her feet and held out her hand toward him.

He shot a look toward Fennik, Pia, and Raan, who were watching from the other side of the fire. "With an audience? How will I continue to impress with my omnipotent divinity once everyone has seen my feet fumble?"

"Think of them as musicians, not an audience," Liyana said. "And no one is all that impressed anyway. Fennik, I'll need a steady drumbeat."

Unable to suppress his grin, Fennik fetched a pot and hit it with the heel of his hand.

"Keep it even. Like a heartbeat." Liyana hauled Korbyn to his feet. "First step is to feel the music inside as if it's your heartbeat. *Bum-ba, bum-ba, bum-ba.*" She placed her hand over his heart, and she put his hand on her heart. For an instant she couldn't move, feeling the warmth of his hand.

His eyes were fixed on hers. "I feel it." She wondered if he meant the drums, her heartbeat, or her.

"Good." She looked away and was able to breathe again. "Step with the beat. Shift your weight. Little movements for now, just your heels, until you have the rhythm." Her hand on his heart, she shifted from side to side. His hand on her heart, he swayed with her.

Stepping back, she dropped her hand. He did the same.

She swallowed, and her throat felt dry. She told herself this was no different than teaching Jidali to dance. "Raan, can you keep this beat?" Liyana clapped out a staccato rhythm. Raan mimicked it. It was syncopated with Fennik's drum. "Pia?"

Pia sang a melody as light as air. It danced over the tent and up toward the sky. Liyana felt her feet itch. She wanted to twirl and leap. She hadn't danced in so long!

"This will be a disaster," Korbyn warned.

"Listen only to the drum," she said. "That's your center, your source, your . . . Think of it as your lake. You're connected to it. Everything else is simply layers on top of it."

"*Bum-ba, bum-ba, bum-ba,*" he said. "Got it."

She smiled. "Not yet you don't. Run with me." Grabbing his hand, she pulled him after her. Her feet hit the sand in rhythm with the drum. He fell into step beside her, and she ran with him until the beat faded under the sound of the night wind. Pivoting, she ran back toward the camp. The wind was cool in her face. It caressed her neck and tossed her hair. His footfalls matched hers.

By the fire, Liyana caught Korbyn's free hand. She swung in a circle with him. "Feel the beat! *Bum-ba, bum-ba, bum-ba.*" She released him. He continued to move with the beat. She raised her arms to match Pia's soaring melody, and she let the music take her. Her feet danced to Raan's syncopated rhythm while Korbyn stamped out the central heartbeat. Letting go of her thoughts, she spun around him.

Korbyn turned with her, and she felt his eyes on her. She orbited around him, the moon to his sun. As the melody dipped, she twirled closer. She lifted her hands, palms forward. He lifted his, and they pressed their hands together. Palm to palm they danced.

As the song rose above the desert, Liyana felt as if the wind were dancing with them. Sand churned under their feet. She tilted her head backward as Korbyn cradled her back in his hands. He spun her in a circle, and she saw the stars spin above them. He raised her up, and their faces were only inches apart. Slowing, they swayed to the heartbeat-like drum. His eyes were like the night sky, deep and endless and full of stars.

He slowed, still swaying. So did she.

The melody ceased.

She realized that the drums had stopped as well, though she didn't know when. She and Korbyn were swaying to their own rhythm. Liyana stopped. She couldn't read his expression, but his eyes were fixed on hers as if nothing else in the world existed. Both of them breathed fast.

Releasing him, she broke away. His hand reached toward her

SARAH BETH DURST

and then fell back. "You're ready for Bayla," she said. Her voice sounded thin to her ears.

She didn't look at any of the others as she ducked into the tent. Curling up in her sleeping roll, she pretended to be asleep when they all came in for the night.

Chapter Eighteen

We are leaving the desert," Pia announced.

Liyana pulled on the reins, and Gray Luck slowed. In the distance, she saw the silhouette of hills—the eastern border of the desert. Black trees with bare branches marked the peaks. On the other side of those hills was the Crescent Empire. "She's right," Liyana said.

"Different birds," Pia explained.

Liyana heard them, unseen to one another, calling in low caws and piercing trills. They hid in the thorned bushes and dried grasses that pockmarked the land, and they perched on the twisted trees that grew out of boulder-filled hollows. The branches of the trees were so knotted that they looked like misshapen fingers folded into fists.

"You want us to leave the desert?" Fennik asked, scandalized.

Raan rode past Fennik. "And where exactly did you think we were going? The fair?" She sounded so pleased that Liyana expected her to break out in a whistle.

"Why would anyone in the Crescent Empire want our gods?" Fennik asked. "The empire has always left the desert alone and vice versa."

Liyana had imagined a lone madman or a rogue clan. She'd never thought about an enemy from beyond the sands. She'd never met anyone from outside the desert. She didn't know any of their stories.

"Horse boy does have a point," Raan said. "Why mess with our sand? They already have fertile fields, rivers full of fish, cities of surpassing wealth . . ." The note of longing in her voice was clear. *We'll have to watch her again*, Liyana thought. She felt a sinking in her stomach as she remembered Raan's lack of tattoos.

"Besides, don't they have their own gods?" Pia asked.

All of them looked at Korbyn.

"Fennik, keep your bows accessible." He urged his horse forward. Liyana followed, her horse stomping on the bushes. Branches crackled under Gray Luck's hooves.

By afternoon they reached the border hills. Miniscule, white flowers coated the slopes, and lichen painted the rocks in orange, green, and white. Liyana spotted rodents scurrying between the rocks. As they rode uphill, she thought about setting snares for them, and she wondered if there was larger game in the hills, perhaps gazelles or wild goat.

Korbyn crested the hill. Immediately he yanked his horse's head around and trotted down the slope. "Down," he ordered, and they followed him.

At the base, Fennik said, "Tell us. What did you see?"

Korbyn swore, borrowing some of Raan's favorite words as he dismounted. His horse plunged his snout into the nearest bush and began stripping the leaves off it. On foot Korbyn trotted back to the hill without answering Fennik.

"Go on," Pia said. "I'll stay with the horses." She patted hers on the neck. Leaving her, Liyana, Raan, and Fennik crept up the slope behind Korbyn. All of them poked their heads over the ridge.

Beyond was a broad plain of golden grasses.

It was filled with tents.

Hundreds of dark green tents lined the plain like crops. Around them, horses grazed—not sleek desert horses but large, muscled horses. Men and women in white uniforms paced between the tents.

Liyana tried to count the number of tents and gave up after the fifth row of twenty. The encampment was larger than a clan. In fact, it was larger than five clans.

"You didn't expect this," Fennik said to Korbyn.

Raan snorted. "He's been making it all up as he goes along."

Liyana flinched as Korbyn shot her a look. Not meeting his eyes, she studied the encampment again. Deep within the rows, a banner emblazoned with a crescent sun waved over a large, golden tent. At this distance, the white-clad soldiers who circled the gold tent looked like moon moths around a candle flame.

"You can quit glaring at her. She didn't give up your precious 'secret,'" Raan said. "It's been obvious that you're winging it."

Fennik drew back from the edge. "Can we have this argument down the hill?"

Silently they retreated down the hill and rejoined Pia and the horses. Liyana still felt exposed. She watched the top of the hill and wondered if there were patrols that watched the border. If so, how often did they pass there?

"Please, tell me," Pia said.

"It's an army," Fennik said. "Korbyn either deliberately neglected to tell us, or—"

"Does it matter?" Liyana interrupted. "I'd say we have a lot more important issues than what Korbyn knew or didn't know, and did or didn't tell us."

Pia clutched her horse's reins as if she were on the verge of fainting. "Army?" she squeaked.

"Crescent Empire," Korbyn said.

"See, he knows something!" Fennik said.

"Don't be too impressed," Raan said dryly. "They had flags, you know. Also, that *is* the Crescent Empire's land, so it's a good bet that it's their army. I doubt they'd let another army wander through."

"But . . . Why? What do they want?" Pia's voice trembled.

"Looks like they want the desert," Raan said. "It would hardly make sense for them to invade themselves. But I can't imagine why. We don't have anything they need."

Liyana shook her head. "'Why' doesn't matter, at least to us. Our job is to rescue our gods. Once they walk the world, they can handle the army."

"We don't even know if they have our gods," Fennik said. He looked pointedly at Korbyn. Korbyn's gaze was fixed on the ridge. Liyana wasn't convinced he was even listening to them.

"Our gods were summoned east, and there's an army east," Liyana said. "I have trouble believing that's a coincidence." Somewhere in that encampment, Bayla waited for Korbyn.

"Fine," Fennik said. "But we don't know where they're being held. Or how. Our gods could be trapped in anything. Or anyone."

Pia gasped. "Oyri, in another?"

Gaze still fixed on the border, Korbyn spoke. "Once, there was a god who mistakenly entered his vessel's companion. This was in the time before vessels were marked with tattoos. The results were disastrous—inside the wrong body, the deity couldn't work magic. And so, the god drank poison, killing the body and freeing his soul to return to the Dreaming, where at least he would not have to watch the suffering his mistake had caused. One hundred years later, he returned to a decimated clan and built it back to a sustainable size. But he was never the same after that. Every time he returned to the Dreaming, he hid in a cave of his own making so the souls of the clan he failed would not find him. And ever after, vessels have been marked with tattoos so his mistake will not be repeated by another."

Raan's hands were clenched into fists. "That is a hideous story."

"If it's true, it means you can summon your goddess without tattoos," Liyana pointed out. "All you have to do is dance while a magician chants."

Raan turned away from her.

"First, though, we need to free the deities so they can be summoned," Fennik said.

"Will we . . . will we have to kill anyone to free my goddess?" Pia's voice quivered.

Still watching Raan, Liyana shook her head and answered for Korbyn. "No. If they were in a person, they'd have killed themselves already." Raan blanched at that, but Liyana continued. "Whatever trap they're in, it has to be something they *can't* destroy. We will have to destroy it for them."

"Then how do we—" Pia began.

"I thought it was obvious that I'm winging it." Korbyn smiled, and the smile lit up his entire face.

"Ooh, big powerful deity has a plan," Raan said.

"As a matter of fact, yes, I do." Korbyn swept his hand to

indicate the horses. "Fennik and I are horse traders. We have come to view their horses and show them ours in the hopes of establishing trade between the Horse Clan and the Crescent Empire. Once within the encampment, Fennik distracts them with fancy talk about horse fetlocks while I determine the location of the captive deities."

All of them were silent. Liyana stroked Gray Luck's neck.

"That's the entire plan?" Pia asked.

"Simple plans are the best," Korbyn said.

"Think of another plan," Liyana ordered. "You could be caught."

"I'll be tricky." Korbyn wiggled his fingers at them. "Trickster god, remember?"

"And what are we supposed to do while you are being 'tricky'?" Raan asked. "Twiddle our thumbs and hope for the best?"

For once, Liyana was in complete agreement with Raan. He couldn't expect her to sit idly by and wait for him to be captured, or worse. She put her hand on his arm. "If they're kidnapping gods, you can't just wander in!"

"I won't wander; I'll ride," Korbyn said. "You three need to find a grove of trees. Stay hidden. Stay safe. Liyana is skilled enough to take care of your food and water needs. Once I know the situation, Fennik or I will return for you." He patted her hand.

Abruptly she realized she was clinging to him. Releasing him, she backed away. She felt as if she heard roaring in her ears. "A million things could go wrong. Please, Korbyn."

"Have a little faith." He grinned at his word play.

"Your body is mortal with mortal limitations," Pia said.

Liyana reached out again. Her fingertips brushed his cheek. "Korbyn, you think you need to save the entire desert by yourself. You keep forgetting you're not alone."

His grin faded. "My problem is that I can't forget that."

Liyana's breath caught in her throat as he held her gaze.

"She must be rescued," Korbyn said gently.

*　*　*

In the light of dawn, the encampment seemed to spread endlessly in all directions. Liyana wondered if this was what the sea looked like—each tent a wave crest, all poised to roll over her beloved desert. She watched Korbyn and Fennik lead the horses down the slope. They slowly picked their way around the rocks and bushes. At the base, they allowed the horses to graze for several minutes before they waded forward into the tall, golden grasses.

Liyana felt as if she were the one exposed out there on the plain. Every muscle felt like a knot, and her heart thudded inside her chest. She watched Korbyn and wished she could see his face. "Keep him safe," she whispered, though she knew no one would hear her prayer.

The slow speed had been Korbyn's idea—he'd said it would present them as harmless. Fennik had agreed, and they'd spent the bulk of the night meticulously planning their approach as if it were an elaborate performance. But watching their show was torture.

As they reached the halfway point, a trio of guards cantered toward them. Crisp white, their uniforms reflected the sun. Brimmed hats shielded their faces from the sun and from view. Scarlet scarves covered their necks. "Please," Liyana whispered, again to no one.

Liyana saw Fennik sweep his arms open to gesture at the horses. She imagined she could hear him say the words that they'd rehearsed last night. The guards didn't unsheathe their swords— she would have seen the metal flash in the sun—but they were too far away for her to tell if their hands were on their hilts.

"Lovely to see the boys working together, isn't it?" Raan said behind her.

Liyana jumped. Absorbed in the show on the plains, she hadn't heard the other girl approach. "I should have insisted on going."

"You're needed to babysit me in case I decide to avoid my 'fate' by crossing the border."

The bitterness in Raan's voice felt like a slap. Liyana didn't know what to say—Raan wasn't wrong, though none of them had voiced that concern out loud. Side by side, in silence, they watched the figures of Korbyn, Fennik, and the guards on the plain.

Softly Raan asked, "If I find a way to save the clans *and* our lives, will you do it?"

"And save the deities?" Liyana asked.

"I can't promise that," Raan said.

"Then I can't promise either."

Raan was silent. Escorted by the guards, Korbyn and Fennik led the horses toward the encampment. At last Raan said, "Pia sent me to tell you that we're low on food."

Scooting back from the edge, Liyana joined Raan for the trek to the tent. They'd picked a grove of leafless trees about a mile from the hills as their camp. It was mostly obscured from view by the thick tangle of branches. If they huddled inside the tent with all of their supplies, chances were that a patrol on the ridge wouldn't see them. Or at least that was the hope.

Pia popped out of the tent to greet them.

"You know, it might not have been us," Raan said. "You should stay in the tent until you're sure it's safe." She squatted next to the tent and took a gulp from her waterskin. "Getting low on water, too." She waved the waterskin at Liyana.

"You shuffle your toes when you walk," Pia said. "Liyana lengthens her stride every few steps. I am always careful. If they catch us, it will be because they know where to look." She scooted inside the tent, again out of view from the hills.

"I can't summon water like Korbyn," Liyana said, joining Pia in the tent. Without the boys the tent felt empty, and without the horses the camp felt deserted. She missed the comforting stamp of hooves, and she wished Gray Luck were here. She hadn't realized how used to the horse's presence she'd become. "Get ready for lots of tubers."

"Let me know how I can help," Raan said as she crawled into the tent. She stretched out and then put her arms behind her head. Both Liyana and Pia sat at the edges. "I know it's not the same as your special time with Korbyn. . . ."

Liyana felt herself stiffen. "Excuse me?"

Raan waved her hand. "You two. Always swapping stories. Laughing about something. At night you comfort away his nightmares. A person begins to feel like she's intruding."

"He is the beloved of my goddess. I don't like what you're suggesting." She'd never said a word about what had happened in the sandstorm, and she was certain that no one else knew. Mostly certain. Her eyes slid to the tent flap. It felt stifling inside the tent.

"You must remember that," Pia said, her voice as placid as always. "You can't afford to care too much about anyone or anything. None of us can."

Propping herself up on her elbow, Raan looked at Pia. "Is that how you do it, how you're okay with your clan offering you up on a platter for your goddess?"

"This life is ephemeral," Pia said. "I cannot afford any attachments because they will be severed. My clan knows this." Folding her hands in her lap, she smiled serenely.

Raan blinked at her. "That is the saddest thing I've ever heard."

"It isn't true for me," Liyana said firmly. "I'm very attached to my family."

"Even though they left you to die?" Raan asked.

SARAH BETH DURST

She felt the hilt of the sky serpent knife tucked into her sash. Even far away, her family had saved her life multiple times over. "Yes."

"You're both crazy," Raan said.

"Everyone I love will be reunited in the Dreaming," Liyana said. She thought of Jidali, growing old without her. He would have a lifetime of stories to tell her when they were reunited.

"Except for Korbyn," Pia said intently.

"Once his vessel dies, he'll return there as well," Liyana said. She shouldn't need to tell Pia that. Everyone knew gods could only exist in the real world while their vessel lived.

"But he'll be reunited with Bayla, not with you."

"I know that," Liyana said.

"Good," Pia said, her perfect doll face serene. "Remember it." As Liyana stared at her, Pia fetched her brush and began to pull it through her soft, white hair. She hummed softly as she brushed, clearly done with the conversation, content that she'd made her point.

"I'm going to find water," Liyana said. She stalked out of the tent.

Only when she was a hundred yards away did she feel her chest begin to loosen. *Unfair accusations,* Liyana thought. *Untrue!* She dropped into the sand beside a clump of cacti. She breathed in and out, trying to tame the swirl in her mind.

She focused on her heartbeat, which rattled in her rib cage as if it wanted to escape. With practiced ease, she imagined her lake and pulled out magic, inhaling as she felt the magic fill her. Korbyn had taught her the simplest way to summon water: Draw it into a plant that would naturally draw water, and then extract the moisture by hand. Full of magic, she flowed into the cacti before her. She plunged deep into the earth with its roots. Whispering to it, she coaxed it to suck the water up, up. *Thirsty, so thirsty,* she thought at it. She felt the moisture seep faster into its roots.

Last time she had done this, Korbyn had been beside her. She had laughed with him and shared stories. She thought of how it had felt to dance with him, the warmth of his hands and the nearness of his breath. She remembered the way his eyes had poured into hers as if there were nothing else in the world . . . and how a smile would spring to his face . . . and the way his laugh would cascade out of him . . . But even when his laugh filled her, she always, always knew he belonged with Bayla! Every action she'd taken was designed to unite him and Bayla.

Thinking of him, she let herself flow across the dried grasses and over the hills. She felt the thousands of souls in the empire's encampment like a distant hum. Which one was Korbyn's? Was he all right?

Forgetting the cacti, she pushed her awareness into the encampment. Each of the humans felt like candle flames, their souls flickering inside them. A deity would feel . . . more like sparks, as if it were barely contained rather than burning contentedly. She sensed the horses tethered to stakes. If she reached further, then perhaps . . . She stretched the magic thinner and thinner.

She felt herself fragment as her thoughts flew apart.

Her body! She didn't feel it!

Racing over the desert, she tried to imagine the shape of her skin and the feel of her breath in her lungs. She pictured her soul pouring into her body, shaping back into herself.

She inhaled deeply, and then she collapsed, unconscious.

She woke with her cheek pressed into the sand. She didn't know how long she'd lain there. Her rib cage hurt. Her fingers felt numb. How long could a body function without a soul in it? Seconds? Minutes? It hurt to breathe. The sun beat down on her.

Eventually she pushed herself upright. Hands shaking, she took out the sky serpent knife and sawed the cacti off at their bases. She tipped them over so that no liquid would ooze out the cuts, and then she wrapped them in a scarf to carry back to the tent. She got to her feet, and her knees wobbled.

She sank onto her knees in the scalding sand. *Sweet Bayla, what have I done?* Korbyn would have been so furious with her. This time he hadn't been here to kiss her into alertness. Liyana tried again, straightening slowly. She wobbled as she walked forward, feeling like a newborn foal. Concentrating on each step, she clutched the cacti to her chest, determined not to drop them. The thorns pressed against the cloth but didn't pierce her skin. By the time she reached the tent, she felt the ache of every muscle and bone.

Pia rushed out to greet her. "You were gone for hours!"

Liyana handed her the scarf full of cacti. "You were right. I care too much." She crawled into the tent and slept without dreams.

*　*　*

Two days passed with no word from Korbyn or Fennik.

At dawn on the third day, Liyana shot out of the tent, thinking she had heard hoofbeats from the ridge. But the ridge was empty. A knot of brambles blew across the slope.

"Go fetch more water," Raan said behind her.

"We have water," Liyana said.

"You are driving us crazy with your worrying."

Pia chimed in. "Occupy yourself. The hours will fly faster. Korbyn and Fennik's mission will take time. First they must determine where the deities are. Next they must ascertain how they are being held. And last they need to know what will free our gods and goddesses from the false vessels. It will take time." She sounded like a teacher, talking in a calm voice to an agitated child. "Fetch us enough water so that we may bathe."

"Very well," Liyana said curtly.

She stalked across the desert and didn't stop until she found a massive clump of cacti. Filling these broad leaves would keep her occupied for several hours. Dropping onto the dirt, Liyana began.

Leaf by leaf Liyana filled the cacti until their skin felt taut with water and the sun was at its zenith. Sweat trickled down the back of her neck and dried in seconds. She gathered up the cacti to begin the trudge back to camp. She wanted the first bath. She thought she had a few flakes of soap left from her family's pack. After that, though, she'd need to find a new task to distract her from the fear that made her feel as if her lungs had shrunk and her stomach had hardened into rock.

She wished she hadn't let Korbyn convince her to stay. It had seemed sensible at the time. Fennik was essential for the ruse of horse traders, and Korbyn was ideal for reconnaissance. Bringing Liyana, Raan, and Pia would have been an unnecessary risk. But still . . .

A hundred yards from camp, Liyana heard a melody soar into the sky. *Pia!* But what was she thinking? Someone would hear her! Picking up her pace, Liyana hurried toward the camp—and then she stopped as the melody swelled louder.

Pia isn't stupid, Liyana thought. *She's warning me.*

Liyana ducked behind a group of boulders. She tried to calm her breathing. Slowly, breath by breath, she dropped into a trance. She pictured the lake, filled herself with magic, and then stretched her awareness toward the tent, careful not to overreach.

She felt the plants and the rocks, the wind and the heat. She felt the birds and the snakes and the scorpions . . . and the people. Six of them were by the grove of trees. All human.

Abruptly Liyana stuffed her soul back inside her body and released the excess magic. She was panting and dizzy from the effort of working a second magic so close on the heels of summoning water. Laying her forehead against the rocks, she caught her breath.

She had to help them! But how? Her magic wasn't strong enough to do anything useful. Still clutching the cacti, Liyana listened as Pia's song cut off.

Unable to wait any longer, she emerged and jogged toward the grove. She didn't see anyone as she got closer. The camp was all still there—the fire pit with the still-smoldering embers, the packs with all their supplies, the hollowed-out cacti—but Pia and Raan were gone. The open tent flap billowed in the breeze. The sand around the tent was covered in footprints. From the way the sand was churned, Liyana guessed that one of them had fought. Maybe both. She didn't see blood, and her chest loosened a little.

Please, let them be alive.

Dumping the cacti on the ground, Liyana ran toward the hill. She clambered up it. Staying low, she peeked over the ridge.

Down on the plain of golden grasses, she spotted them: four white-clad soldiers with the two desert girls. From this distance, they looked as tiny and fragile as dolls. She wished she could reach out and pluck them away to safety. *What good is magic if you can't save anyone?* she thought. She should have stayed at the tent.

Maybe she could have helped. Most likely she would have been caught too, but was being left behind truly better?

She watched them cross through the field toward the encampment. Pia had said that they wouldn't be found unless the soldiers knew where to look. Korbyn and Fennik must have been caught.

Feeling sick, she sank back behind the hill and put her face in her hands. *I failed them*, Liyana thought. *I failed everyone.* All her companions were gone now, and she was alone, just as she had been all those weeks ago when her clan had walked away without her. She might as well have stayed in that oasis for all the good she had done.

Eventually Liyana returned to the tent. She crawled inside and curled into a ball. She thought of Jidali and her parents and Aunt Sabisa and Talu and all her cousins; of Runa, the magician of the Scorpion Clan; of Ilia of the Silk Clan; and of the Falcon Clan and their despair. She knew what that despair felt like now.

But she'd come so far! She'd crossed the desert. She'd survived two sandstorms. She'd caused a bush to bloom and water to fill cacti. She'd taught a god to dance. She could not simply declare defeat!

Forcing herself to sit up, Liyana pulled her pack closer. She searched through it until she found her ceremonial dress. She fingered the soft panels and let the fabric rub against her skin, which was worn from wind, sand, and sun. Quickly, before she could change her mind, she changed into the dress. She let the soft cloth fall around her like gentle rain. Using Pia's brush, she combed her hair, braided it, and wound it onto her head. She tucked Jidali's sky serpent knife into her sash, and she slung her waterskin over her shoulder.

Trickery had failed. Hiding hadn't protected them. So she was going to try the direct approach. After all, what more did she have to lose?

Liyana crossed the last stretch of desert as the sun painted the west with splashes of rose and ocher. She climbed the hill without slowing. Her skirt swished around her legs. The dying sun prickled the back of her neck. She tried not to think about what was happening to Korbyn or to the others, or what had been done to Korbyn and Fennik to cause them to give up the location of their camp. She tried not to think how ill-conceived her plan was or how little chance it had to succeed. She stood on the crest of the hill and looked down at the empire's army.

Her mouth felt dry. She licked her lips, and she took a sip of water. There were soldiers, white-clad specks between the tents. She saw guards on horseback riding back and forth on the perimeter. It would only be minutes before one of them spotted her, silhouetted against the dying sun. Legs trembling, she walked down toward the plain.

She strode into the tall, golden grasses. She let her arms sway by her sides, and she felt the tops of the dry grasses tickle her palms. This was the world beyond the desert. The air tasted the same, but she felt as if her whole body was screaming at her to turn and run.

                                      SARAH BETH DURST

She glanced behind her. Far away, above the sunset, she saw a sky serpent. He caught every color of the sunset in his glass-like scales. She wondered if these invaders saw how beautiful her desert was.

She had crossed halfway to the encampment before one of the soldiers thundered toward her. She stopped and waited for him. He had a bow aimed at her. "You trespass on the lands of the Crescent Empire!" he called.

"I am Liyana, the vessel of the goddess Bayla of the Goat Clan." Liyana raised her arms so that her sleeves fell back to expose her tattoos. "I demand an audience with your emperor."

Chapter Nineteen
The Emperor

The emperor pored over a stack of judgments. He couldn't second-guess his judges, not without hearing the testimony for himself, but he needed them to know that he *could* overrule them if he chose. It was the best he could do at this distance from the palace.

Trust your people, his father had often said. An emperor isn't one person; an emperor is all people, the embodiment of the empire. *Rule with them, not over them.*

He did trust them, at least most of them, on occasion and with supervision.

He added the flourish of his signature to a parchment, and then he massaged the back of his neck with one hand. Later, once they were within the desert, he wouldn't have the leisure to attend to matters from the capital. He'd have to trust his people—just like they were trusting him now.

Suppressing a sigh, he picked up the next judgment, yet another petty land squabble. The number of cases had drastically increased due to the drought. Everyone was scrambling to hold as much land as possible, as if that would grant them security while their empire's future shriveled around them.

"Your Imperial Majesty?"

The emperor raised his head. A soldier saluted him. He hadn't knocked, a military habit that the emperor hadn't tried to break. If a matter were important enough to bring to his attention, then it was important enough to skip the pleasantries.

"Our perimeter guards have apprehended a desert person," the soldier said.

The emperor set down the judgments and straightened, aware he resembled a dog who had spotted a hare. The army often caught stray desert men near the border, but they rarely brought the matter to his attention. "And?"

"She demands an audience with you."

"A bold demand," the emperor commented.

"She was armed with only this." The soldier laid a knife on the emperor's desk. "A family heirloom, she claimed, and her gift to you."

The emperor examined it. The blade was as clear as glass but felt harder than steel. He tested it on his desk, and it scored the wood as if the desk were sea foam, not the heart of an oak. He was certain that the blade was made from the scale of one of the glass sky serpents. His pulse raced, but he kept his voice as calm as a still lake. "Beautiful." His scout had said that the serpent's scales had cut like swords. The existence of this knife proved that the desert people had ways to defeat the sky serpents—yet another reason he needed them as part of his empire.

"She came to us in formal dress, unlike the other nomads we've encountered. She claims to be something called a 'vessel,' presumably a position of authority within her clan."

A vessel, here. "Well. That *is* unusual." He doubted that the soldier knew how much of an understatement that was. According to the magician, vessels never left their clans. Ever. They were treated like jewels—or prisoners. For a vessel to be here without her clan . . . Such a thing should be unheard of. "You were correct to come to me. I will see her."

The soldier bowed. "Yes, sir."

The emperor returned to reviewing the judgments, but he could not focus his attention on them. According to the magician, from the moment a vessel was "chosen," he or she lost all control over his or her own life. Vessels were not allowed their own thoughts, their own choices, or their own futures. They sacrificed their lives to their clans long before their true sacrifice. He'd always been curious to meet one, and now he was flat-out intrigued. At the least, this should provide a welcome distraction while the army finished acquiring supplies.

Five soldiers marched into his tent. All of them halted, saluted, and then rotated to reveal a young woman. She was beautiful, as vessels were purported to be, with skin that looked like burnt cinnamon and features as perfect as a sculpture. Coiled in elaborate braids, her black hair shimmered in the light of the candles. Her dress flaunted every color in the sunset. Her hands had been tied in front of her, but she held her delicate chin high and her shoulders back as if she hadn't even noticed the ropes. She met his gaze evenly with black eyes that were as clear and piercing as a sword. He'd imagined a subservient sacrifice. Instead she was a desert princess.

"Untie her," the emperor ordered, his eyes not leaving hers. "Asking to speak with me is not a crime."

The soldiers obeyed.

She held still while they cut the ropes, and her eyes stayed on the emperor's. His soldiers removed the ropes and retreated, though not far. He approved of their caution. Even assassins could dress well. In fact, some of the finest assassins he knew were lovely.

"You have your audience," the emperor said.

She raised her arms, and the sleeves fell back to reveal swirled tattoos on her arms. "I am Liyana, the vessel of Bayla of the Goat Clan, and I have come to tell you a story."

Only a lifetime of habit kept the surprise from registering on his face. Keeping his expression carefully neutral, he gestured for her to proceed.

"Once, there was only sea. The moon loved the sea, for the moon was vain and her reflection was like a beautiful jewel on the water, but the sun wearied of the endless waves. All day he looked down on the same blue. So one day he burned hotter and hotter, and he dried the ocean. That night, the moon was horrified to see mountains and plains instead of her beloved sea. So she flooded the land. The next day the sun scorched the world again, and the next night the moon summoned the tides and covered it with water. This continued until at last there was only one creature left alive. It was a turtle, and she called to the sun and moon and begged for mercy—"

"You crossed a desert to speak to me about a turtle?" Most of his people considered stories fit only for children at bedtime. Certainly they'd never brave a desert crossing to tell their emperor a story. He had to fight to keep the excitement out of his voice and off his face.

"I speak of the turtle who was our mother," Liyana said.

"I have heard many creation myths from the regions of my empire," the emperor said, and he was pleased that his voice conveyed only mild interest. He was aware that his soldiers were listening. They knew it was a story that had led their emperor here—a story of magic that could save his people. But this woman couldn't know that. "Fetch us water and dates," the emperor ordered a soldier. The soldier bowed and exited.

The vessel continued. "She proposed a bargain: The moon

could have an ocean if the sun could have an island. But when the sun created the island, he shone with such intensity that he scorched the center of it. In this barren desert, the turtle laid her egg. It hatched, and the desert people were born."

"I had not heard this tale," the emperor said. He continued to control his voice, as if this were only of passing amusement to him. In truth, he collected stories like past emperors collected rare jewels or exotic animals. This was the best way she could have chosen to capture his attention, but he wouldn't let her know that. Accepting a golden dish of dates, he held it out to Liyana. She didn't touch it. He ate one, and then poured water into two gold chalices. "You have a point in telling me, I presume?"

"The desert people exist to ensure that the moon remembers her promise to never flood again. If you threaten us, you threaten the whole of the world. You don't want to do that. You want to leave and return to your green fields and blue lakes. Leave us to our sand. There's nothing for you to gain here and much for you to lose."

Chapter Twenty

L iyana presented the same smooth face that she'd shown her clan on the day of her summoning ceremony, and she hoped the emperor couldn't hear the way her heart galloped inside her chest.

"You'd like us to leave because of a turtle's bargain with celestial bodies." The emperor sounded amused. He was younger than she'd expected, at most only a few years older than she was, but he had a presence that filled the tent. He held himself with a power and stillness that reminded her of carved stone.

"I ask you to leave because we belong to the desert, not to your green lands," Liyana said. "We have no wish to join your empire."

The emperor plucked another date from the tray and held it up as if contemplating its color in the candlelight. He let the silence stretch. Liyana kept herself still and silent as well. She knew this was a tactic—Mother wielded silence as a weapon too. Finally he asked, "How do you know that is why we are here?"

She chose a date from the platter to show she was not afraid. "You have an army camped at our border," she said. "I assume they are not here simply to enjoy the heat."

His mouth twitched.

She wondered if she had almost made him smile. "Of course I would be delighted if there were another explanation." Feigning casualness, she bit into the date.

"It is my hope that your clans will join my empire without bloodshed."

The sugar tasted sour in her mouth. She swallowed, forcing it down, as she tried not to imagine this vast army overwhelming her clan. "When the people of the turtle were born, many of them died in the harsh desert—these were the first deaths in this new world. Unfortunately, there was no place for the dead souls to go, so they wandered through the sky. This annoyed the stars, who loved their quiet and solitude. And so, one of the stars sacrificed himself and fell. He hit the desert with such force that he ripped a hole in the world. Flocking to this hole, the souls left our world—and discovered, or some say created, the Dreaming."

"You may leave us," the emperor said to the guards.

One of the soldiers looked as if he wished to object.

"If she assassinates me, you have full leave to declare war on the desert clans and exterminate every man, woman, and child you find."

Liyana felt as if water, cold from a deep well, had been poured into her veins.

The soldiers bowed and filed out of the tent.

"Continue," he said.

She clasped her hands together to hide their shaking. "The souls were happy in the Dreaming, but when they looked back at their desert home, they saw suffering. So they created the gods out of the magic of the Dreaming, and they sent the gods' souls to walk among their people and help them live in their waterless world. Because of this, because of our deities, we of the desert are strong and free. And so we will remain."

He fingered the sky serpent knife on his desk. She ached to take it back, take back her link with her family. "Tell me why you are truly here," the emperor said.

She thought of Bayla and the Goat Clan, of Pia and Fennik and their deities and clans . . . and especially of Korbyn. "The empire has never shown an interest in our desert before. Tell me why *you* are here."

His eyes widened, the first crack in his perfect, sculpted face. He placed the knife down, folded his hands, and leaned back as if to contemplate her from a distance. "You do realize that you are addressing the emperor of the Crescent Empire."

"And you are addressing a free woman of the desert. You

are not my emperor. Therefore I am your equal." She felt like a rabbit blustering before a wolf. Everything about this man, or boy, radiated power. He sat at a wooden desk, a luxury that Liyana had never seen. It looked as if it weighed as much as a horse. Behind him were wooden shelves graced by glass sculptures. Each sculpture was a masterwork of perfect details: a fox with fur tufts on his ears, a falcon with outstretched wings, a cat poised midhunt. . . . Each one was more beautiful than the next. Only an emperor could have such impractical extravagance around him. She waited for his response, expecting to be savaged like a rabbit by a wolf.

"Very well then," he said. "I should consider you a visiting dignitary?"

Liyana's knees felt weak with relief, but she locked them and held herself straight and strong. "Use whatever terminology you wish."

"Hostile visiting dignitary?"

"Cautious visiting dignitary," Liyana said. "I am not here as an enemy, unless that is what you are." She took a deep breath and asked, "Are you?"

To her shock, the emperor smiled. It transformed him from a stone sculpture into a flesh-and-blood human being. She was stunned for a moment by how handsome he was, the perfect beauty of his face. "You are refreshingly blunt," he said.

"My mother would agree with you on that."

"I do not wish to be your enemy or the enemy of your people. Indeed the empire has much to offer your people. And I believe you have much to offer us." He twirled Jidali's sky serpent knife between his fingers. She watched the glass-like blade catch the candlelight. "Mulaf, as always, your timing is impeccable."

Liyana turned to see a man with a thick beard and sunken eyes enter the tent accompanied by a trio of guards. The man wore the robes of a desert clansman, though she didn't recognize the patterns embroidered on the blue silk panels. He bowed to the emperor while his eyes swept over Liyana. She took a step backward. His gaze felt like a lick of fire.

"She is Liyana, the vessel of Bayla of the Goat Clan," the emperor said. "This is Mulaf, chief magician to the Crescent Empire. Mulaf, this woman is a visiting dignitary and my personal guest. Show her to a tent and then return to me. We have much to discuss."

In contrast to the expressionless emperor, Mulaf was awash with emotions. His face twisted and stretched. His eyes narrowed then widened. At last he said, "I would be honored to escort her, Your Imperial Majesty. Please, accompany me."

The trio of guards closed around her, and she was swept out of the tent flap without any chance to protest. Outside, other soldiers sealed into a line, effectively blocking her return. She looked back at the golden tent. She hadn't asked about Pia and Raan, or Korbyn and Fennik, for fear that would endanger them further. Had that been a mistake? She ran through her mind what she'd said. Had she chosen the right words? Had she done any good at all? He'd seemed . . . interested in what she had to say. He'd listened to her stories. She wasn't certain a clan chief would have done as much, and he was the emperor of a vast land. He had even let her speak with him alone, though she didn't doubt that the guards had lurked mere inches beyond the tarp. But if she had expected a miracle . . . He wasn't about to withdraw his army, and she had not found the stolen deities.

Now what? She hadn't planned beyond speaking with the emperor.

With the guards, Mulaf escorted Liyana through the encampment. She noticed that all the tents were identical—green, triangular, and plain. There were no names or stories woven into the tarps. She saw no smoke from cooking fires within. All the fires were outside and tended by soldiers. She saw no children.

Liyana had expected the emperor's people to look different from the sun-worn desert people, but she hadn't expected them to be so different from one another. One had a narrow, pale face with a nose as pointed as an arrow. Another was dark skinned and wore a full beard. A third sported tattooed dots over his cheeks. All of them, though, bore the serious look of men and women with weapons. All of them, also, looked too thin. She saw pinched cheeks, bony shoulder blades, and uniforms that hung loosely on gaunt bodies. Everyone had a task, whether it was repairing a boot or fixing a meal or patrolling between the tents, but everyone paused to watch her pass—or perhaps they watched Mulaf.

She studied him as he shepherded her through the encampment. His beard was riddled with white, but he moved like a jackrabbit with a startled leap to his step. His eyes darted fast in all directions. She noticed he didn't greet anyone, and no one greeted him.

"I didn't know the empire had magicians," Liyana said.

His smile was tight-lipped. "I have been blessed with good fortune."

He led her to a nondescript tent, and the guards positioned themselves on either side of the tent flap. Mulaf ushered her inside. Inside, the furnishings were minimal. A few unhandsome blankets had been tossed around the floor as rugs. A cot with a thin pillow was set up on one side. A washbasin stood on a stand in a corner next to a pot. It all smelled faintly of urine. She wondered if she was a prisoner.

He dropped to sit cross-legged on one of the blankets. "Come. Sit. I apologize for not offering you tea." He smiled broadly at her in what she was certain he meant to be a reassuring manner, and he patted the blanket next to him.

Liyana lowered herself onto a blanket several yards away from Mulaf. She wished she had her sky serpent knife.

"Tell me, my dear child . . . Liyana, is it? How did you escape your clan?" he asked. His eyes were as bright as a desert rat's, and he leaned forward eagerly.

She stuck to the truth, or at least part of it. "My goddess didn't come, so my clan exiled me."

He clucked his tongue. "What a shock that must have been."

"Yes, it was."

He bounced to his feet and paced in a circle around her. "Bayla of the Goat Clan did not come. What a pity. What a tragedy." Without warning he dropped to a squat in front of her. There was something about him that made her think of a bird fluttering with a broken wing. Instinctively she pulled her knees toward her chest and shrank away. "You are a lucky girl, you know." He reached out and stroked her cheek with a fingernail. "You have an opportunity that no other vessel has ever had. You can make your own life in the empire. You can change your fate!"

She wanted to bolt out of the tent. The tarp walls felt as if they were pressing inward. She inched backward, away from Mulaf. "When did you escape *your* clan?"

He laughed like a hyena. "Years ago, my dear. Would you believe that I am over one hundred years old? I am from the Cat Clan. I was once their magician." Popping to his feet, he paced again.

She'd heard of the Cat Clan. One hundred years ago, the clan had become extinct. An abnormal number of disasters had befallen them, one after another. They had been hunted by sand wolves, attacked by sky serpents, caught in quicksand. Stories about the Cat Clan were whispered late at night when the camp's fire burned high enough to stroke the stars. If he were truly from the Cat Clan, then it was no wonder he saw the empire as a sanctuary. "It must be difficult for you to live with people who aren't the turtle's children." She tried for a note of polite sympathy while she calculated the distance to the tent flap—she could reach it in three strides.

He snorted. "Turtle. Another lie told by the parasites. Oh yes, the desert people are the special chosen ones. Chosen to be prey for the parasites!" He squatted again in front of her. His face was too close. "You don't believe me. I can see it in your eyes. But you will, once you have tasted the freedom that the empire has to offer."

She shrank back. "When will I be able to speak with the emperor again?"

"The emperor will grant you sanctuary, I can assure you," Mulaf said. "In time you will understand that you are safe here."

"Am I?" She breathed the scent of his breath, sour as rancid goat's milk.

"Oh yes, Bayla's vessel. You never need to fear your goddess again."

She forced herself to sit still while everything inside her shrieked. *He knows!* She wanted to leap at him and force the truth out of him. *Tell me what you've done to her!* But in the heart of the empire's army, she didn't dare move.

The magician rose to his feet. "Welcome to the Crescent Empire, Liyana."

Chapter Twenty-One

A lone, Liyana huddled in the center of the tent. *Sweet Bayla, what have I done?* She'd walked willingly into a cage, as stupidly as a goat to slaughter. She wrapped her arms around her knees as waves of terror crashed over her.

She didn't know how much time had passed while she had been trapped inside her own fear, but minutes or hours later, a soldier shoved the tent flap open and strode inside. He wore the white uniform with a red scarf, but his shoulders were decorated with swirls of gold. His face had the same pinched look as the others she'd seen, but he was older, so the flesh hung on his cheeks like loose cloth. Based on his age and the gold on his shoulder, she guessed he was an officer, perhaps even a high-ranking one. He bowed. "The emperor requests that you join him for dinner."

She tried not to look as surprised as she felt. Standing, she smoothed her skirt. "I'd be delighted." He led the way out of the tent, and she followed.

She couldn't imagine why the emperor had requested her. Had he connected her with Pia and Raan? Or Korbyn and Fennik? If so, why honor her with dinner? Reaching the emperor's golden tent, the officer raised the flap. As the guards watched her, she was shepherded inside and then, again to her shock, was left alone with the emperor.

Surrounded by embroidered pillows, the emperor sat on a gilded chair. "Please, join me," he said. He indicated a second chair across a table.

She sat, feeling like a bird on an awkward perch. She was far more used to pillows or, lately, sand. The table between them was inlaid with a mosaic of smooth stones. It depicted a river running through green farmland. It was an utterly impractical item for a tent. "You are usually a stationary people?" she asked. She gestured at the table, as well as the massive wood desk and the shelves with the glass sculptures.

"Indeed," the emperor said. "Our land feeds us where we live—or did until the Great Drought began."

"I hadn't known the drought touched the empire too. I . . . am sorry to hear it." Liyana wondered if Raan had seen the gaunt faces of the soldiers and realized what they meant. She'd wanted so badly for the empire to be the answer.

"My empire and your desert . . . We are all one land. The Great Drought affects us all." He leaned forward. "But together, we can survive it. We are here to offer . . . cooperation. The desert people cannot survive alone."

"We are not alone," Liyana said. "With our deities, we will survive it." Raan had been so hopeful when they had neared the border. The truth must have crushed her.

"And you would have given your body to your deity to ensure that?"

She wondered what the magician had told him and whether the emperor believed she had escaped and wanted sanctuary. She chose a cautious answer. "I was chosen to do so."

"A shame," he said.

In that one word, she heard the condemnation of her people's choices, their stories, and their way of life. It was worse than Raan's condemnation. This stranger with his silk robes and jeweled fingers dared pass judgment on her people, when her people had survived the harsh desert for a thousand years. "My clan deserves to live, and I was honored to grant them that life."

"The empire can grant them life if they join us."

"How can it if it can't feed its own people?" she countered.

Abruptly he rose. She thought for a moment that she had gone too far and angered him. She waited for him to summon his guards, but instead he paced the breadth of the tent. At last he halted directly before her. Light from a lantern flickered over his face. "I have dreamed of an oval lake in a lush, green valley. Granite cliffs surround it, and it laps at a pebble shore. This lake holds the answers."

Liyana felt as though her ribs had pierced her lungs. He'd described her lake, the one she pictured when she worked magic, in perfect detail.

Before she could formulate a response, servants entered the tent carrying an array of trays. One carried a silver platter of fluffed breads. Another held a bowl of fruit on his head. A third brought a tray of steaming spiced meats. The servants placed their bowls and platters on the mosaic table, bowed, and retreated.

The emperor sank into his chair. She thought she saw tiredness around his eyes. He focused on the feast before them, but she suspected that he wasn't seeing it. She wondered what thoughts were churning in his mind and how the emperor of the Crescent Empire could have dreamed of a lake she'd imagined.

"Tell me about the Dreaming," the emperor said, eyes on her. All trace of exhaustion vanished. He seemed intent on her response.

"Once, the raven and the horse had a race. . . ." She told him the story of Korbyn and Sendar, and how Korbyn had bent the desert in the Dreaming in order to win. "The Dreaming is a place of pure magic."

He nodded as if the story had pleased him. "And the lake is made of that same magic, spilling into our world through the rift made by the star. Your magicians and your deities draw their power from that lake."

"I . . . I have heard that magicians imagine a lake to symbolize the source of magic." She didn't want to admit that she had done so herself in defiance of tradition. "But I don't believe that it exists." She had simply imagined it. Korbyn hadn't even described it. Certainly not the granite cliffs or the pebble shore . . . "Stories are sometimes just stories."

"Nothing is 'just' a story," the emperor said. He reminded her of an ember, quietly burning but with the potential inside to explode into a wildfire that would chase across the grasslands and destroy all life. "The lake is real."

"I don't believe—"

"There is a man, one of my soldiers, who has seen it. But the lake is guarded by glass sky serpents." He pulled Jidali's knife out of a pocket in his silk robes. "Your people know about the sky serpents. Tell me what you know. Tell me how to defeat them!"

"I know of no one who has defeated them," Liyana said. "And the sky serpents guard the mountains, not a lake."

"Tell me of the sky serpents and the mountains."

"Once, the sky serpents preyed on the people of the desert. Arrows could not pierce their scales. Swords could not slice their skin. The serpents attacked men, women, and children, and they left death in their wake. Seeing the destruction and fearing for their clans, the gods bargained with the sky serpents. The sky serpents would not harm any of the desert people, and in return no human would ever set foot in the mountains—"

He leaned forward, his hands clasped in front of him, his face alive with excitement. "You have never wondered what lies within those mountains? If there are peaks, there must be valleys! And if there are valleys . . . one of them could hold the lake."

"We call them the forbidden mountains for a reason. Break the promise with the sky serpents, and they'll attack. That knife . . . My ancestor didn't defeat a sky serpent. No one ever has!"

"No one has ever directed an army such as this to the task." The emperor spread his arms to indicate the whole encampment.

"You can't! You'll be killed! And the sky serpents will turn on all of us!" There would be no defense. Her people would be slaughtered.

"We have no choice but to try. My people are dying. We need the magic of the lake so that we can survive." He clasped her hands. She'd expected his hands to feel as cool as gold, but his hands were warm as they enveloped hers. "I cannot allow my people to die. You of all people should understand that, vessel of the Goat Clan."

She stared at their hands, entwined. The crazy thing was that she *did* understand. She even admired him for it—after all, his plan to march into the desert mountains to find magic was not so different from her plan to march into an army encampment to find her goddess. Both were mad, and both were necessary.

"There must be another way," she said. "Pray to your gods! Ask them to join you as ours do."

Releasing her hands, he withdrew. "Let me tell you a story of my people. Once, there were only gods on our world, and each of them was an artist. The sculptor shaped the dirt to create the mountains, valleys, and plains. The weaver wove roots under the ground and grew the plants, trees, and flowers. The singer created the birds. The dancer created the animals. And the painter filled the world with light and shadow. When the gods finished, they looked at the world and said to one another, 'But there is no one to enjoy this beauty.' And so they worked together—sculptor, weaver, singer, dancer, painter—to create people to live in their world. When they finished, they were pleased. They said to one another, 'Let us find a new world to fill,' and so they departed, leaving us this world to enjoy."

He fell silent as the servants filed into the tent and filled two chalices with water that smelled like fruit. The emperor waved them away from the untouched food. Bowing, they exited.

Liyana tried to imagine such horrible emptiness. Facing the world knowing that you were alone . . . "Your gods left you?"

"They left us the gift of a world," he corrected.

"But that's not enough," Liyana said. "You can't fix a drought alone."

"With the magic of the lake, I believe we can."

Liyana could only stare at the emperor, this handsome boy-king filled with such light in the glory of his impossible dream. "People will die," she said flatly. "Yours. Mine. The clans will never allow you to violate the peace of the forbidden mountains."

He took her hands again. "That is why I need your help."

"Me?" Her voice squeaked.

"Once we cross the desert border, we will begin to encounter the clans," the emperor said. "Someone must explain our cause to them—prevent misunderstandings and encourage cooperation. You have met Mulaf. He is ill suited to such a task. But you, a vessel, one of the desert's own precious jewels . . ."

"I . . ." She pulled her hands away from his.

"Think on it tonight," the emperor said. "I will not force a free woman of the desert. But through your words and actions, you could save many lives." He handed her a chalice of fruit-water. "Drink. Eat. You may answer me in the morning. We will speak of it no more now."

She took the chalice.

*   *   *

Liyana's dreams that night were filled with armies and sky serpents and an emperor with shining eyes who toasted her health with a gold chalice. She woke before dawn and discovered that her water pitcher had been refilled, and that a sapphire-blue robe, the same style as the emperor's, had been left for her. She hesitated—her ceremonial dress was creased, but she did not want to lose it. On the other hand, she did not want to offend. Hoping her clan would forgive her, she dressed in the robe. The fine fabric felt like a whisper on her skin, but she felt as if she wore a nightshirt.

She noticed a strip of gold silk that had fluttered to the floor. She retrieved it and tied it in the desert style, like a sash around her waist. She wondered if it had been the emperor who had ordered a sash to be provided or if the magician had shown her this kindness. She found herself hoping it was the emperor.

Sitting on her thin cot, she held the sky serpent knife in her hand. Last night, between sharing stories and eating the meats and breads and rich, pungent soups, the emperor had given her back her brother's knife.

It would have been far easier to hate him if he hadn't done that.

She thought of his black eyes, so intense and so sincere. She couldn't hate him. But she couldn't help him either. He was chasing the moon, and he would never succeed. He'd only end up causing the deaths of his people and hers.

Tucking the knife into her sash, Liyana rose. She didn't know for certain that the guards would let her leave the tent. She was a "visiting dignitary," but that could be a polite way to say "foreign prisoner." It was time to test this freedom that Mulaf claimed she had and find Korbyn and the others. She opened the tent flap.

"All the talk is of the desert princess who dines with the emperor," a voice said behind her. "I knew it was you."

She spun around, and the flap fell shut behind her. Lounging in the shadows was the trickster god. He wore a soldier's uniform, and he was smiling at her. "Korbyn?"

In three strides he crossed to her. He wrapped his arms around her waist, scooped her into the air, and swung her in a half circle. "You are as infuriating, stubborn, and single-minded as a goat," he whispered in her ear. "You were supposed to stay safe!" He set her down. As she opened her mouth to protest that comparison, he kissed her.

Her eyes flew wide as his lips pressed against hers. His hands cradled her back, and hers wrapped around his neck. She felt as if the outside world had faded away, and the universe had shrunk to just her and Korbyn.

And then it was over.

He pulled away. "I . . . Liyana . . ."

"Please, don't," she whispered, aware of the guards on the other side of the tent flap. She didn't want to hear an apology or an explanation or any words at all. She turned away, unable to look at him. She still felt a tingling on her lips and the taste of his sweet breath. Abruptly, to shatter the choking silence, she said, "Pia and Raan were captured."

"Then we must free them," he said. "I know where the prisoner tents are. Fennik was a prisoner for about a day . . . which probably accounts for Pia and Raan's capture. Fennik is not skilled at deceit." As if her change in subject had energized him, Korbyn strode past her toward the back of the tent and lifted up the base of the tarp—it had been slit with a knife, presumably his. "If anyone stops us, I'm under orders to take you to the doctor," he said. "You feel ill and need immediate attention. If you can arrange to vomit on their shoes, so much the better. I found an abandoned medical tent, complete with uniforms. You'll be safe there. And later we can use the uniforms to seek out the false vessels."

He held out his hand for her to take. His eyes were beseeching.

She thought of how his hand had felt on her back. She had fit into his arms so perfectly. "I can't." She shouldn't touch him again. She shouldn't be near him. He belonged to Bayla, and Liyana . . . She had a different fate. "My absence will be noticed. Rescue the others first, and then come back for me."

"You can't ask me to leave you here." All trace of light cheer had been swept from his face and voice. She felt his eyes on her, and she knew he was seeing her, not the future Bayla. She wondered when that had begun, when he had started to see her for herself. She should have tried harder to stop it.

"The emperor won't hurt me," Liyana said. "He needs me." She summarized her conversations with the emperor, as well as her encounter with the magician Mulaf. "I'll be safe, at least until I say no. And I have a chance to learn more about our deities. I am certain the magician knows where they are."

"Liyana . . ." He paused and then appeared to change what he had planned to say. She risked looking at him and was caught in his eyes. She felt as if her ribs squeezed her lungs. It hurt to breathe. "These people are dangerous." He looked at her as if she was all that mattered in the world.

"Just go, Korbyn. It would be better if you went."

"I will return for you," Korbyn promised.

He disappeared through the slit in the tarp, and she sank to her knees and put her face in her hands. She shouldn't have danced with him. She shouldn't have told him stories. Or laughed with him. She should never have noticed the way a smile would sneak over his face when he was delighted or the way a laugh would consume his whole body. She sucked in air and tried to calm herself. Once Bayla was here, he would forget her vessel, and everything would be as it should be.

Forcing herself to sit still, Liyana focused on her breathing. She tried to erase all other thoughts from her mind. She had a purpose: rescue Bayla. Once she achieved that purpose, every problem she had would be solved.

A soldier entered the tent. She was a copper-skinned woman with gold markings on the shoulders of her uniform and with intricate tattoos on her neck. "The emperor requests your presence." She offered no other explanation.

Without hesitation, Liyana rose to her feet and followed.

*   *   *

Liyana studied the emperor. He had asked her to wait while he completed a task. Bent over a stack of parchments, he scribbled notes on a scroll. His lips were pursed in concentration, and his forehead was furrowed as if he wore the worries of his people—which he did. *We are not so different,* she thought. She was startled by the thought, and she turned it over in her mind, poking at it. He'd become emperor so young. He may not have chosen his fate any more than she had chosen hers.

"I have a little brother," Liyana said into the silence.

The emperor raised his head.

"His name is Jidali, and he believes that I placed the moon in the sky just for him so that he won't have to fear the dark. He has a laugh that shakes his entire body so that even his toes laugh with him. He thinks that bugs are the world's best toy, and he can transform anything into a toy sword. What about you? There must be someone, a reason you are doing all of this. Who do you want to save?"

Looking down, the emperor resumed reviewing his papers. "Every man, woman, and child in the empire are my reasons."

She knelt in front of his desk so that her face was even with his papers. He had to look at her. "Who do you think of when you have doubts? You must have doubts. The lake may not exist. And even if it does and you are able to reach it . . . you might not be able to end the drought. After all, our deities have access to the lake's magic, and none of them has ended the drought.

How can you have faith in your ability to succeed where gods have failed?"

"I think of my parents," the emperor said, his face blank. "I think of my mother and my father, who gave their lives to the empire. I can do no less than they did."

"How did they die?" she asked.

He was silent, and she wished she hadn't asked. She thought of her mother and father, of their faces as they had said they'd remain with her. . . . His hands clenched and unclenched, betraying his expressionless face. Noticing them, he stretched them flat on the parchments. When he spoke, his voice was as hard and lifeless as stone. "Once, in the kingdom of Gracin, there was a famine. The fields would not yield crops, and the skies would not yield rain. Children starved, and the elderly died. It was as if the land had forsaken them. And so the king, who was beloved by his people, took up a plow as if he were an ox and pulled it across field after field. He poured his blood in the furrows and commanded his people to spread his flesh across the land. From his body and blood grew plants so high they pierced the clouds. Red rain fell, then turned to clear water—and the people of Gracin were saved."

She watched him flex his hands. He had clenched them into fists again.

"Gracin is in the northeast corner of our empire. One year into the Great Drought, my mother and father paid it a visit." His voice was empty. She felt an ache inside her, hearing it, and she wanted to cover her ears, as if that could change whatever horror made his voice flatten. "There was a ritual that harks back to this myth of the King of the Fields. Wine for blood. Cakes for flesh. My father agreed to participate. But several traditionalists believed this was not enough. They killed my mother to reach my father."

She rose to her feet. She wanted to reach toward him, to fill that horrible emptiness, to find a way to heal . . . But she didn't. And he wasn't finished.

"He could have defended himself. He chose not to. He was outnumbered, death was inevitable, and the myth required a willing sacrifice. And so, he lowered his sword." He swept his hand out as if it were a sword, and a jar tipped over. Ink spilled onto the parchment. It stained his fingers, but he did not stop it. "But the myth failed, and the people of Gracin continued to starve with the rest of us."

"If it failed, why do you . . ." She trailed off. She shouldn't ask. His parents, murdered by his people. Liyana could not imagine how it must have felt to hear that news.

His mouth quirked, but the smile did not light up his eyes. He straightened the ink jar and wiped his fingers on a silken handkerchief. His movements were precise but jerky. "Why do I chase a myth when a myth killed my father to no purpose? Fair question." He rose from his desk and turned his back. Hands clasped behind him, he faced the sculptures that lined his shelves. Liyana watched him, the tightness of his hands and the stiffness of his shoulders betraying him. This was a man who felt deeply and had learned to hide it. "Because he lowered his sword. When all hope was lost, he tried the impossible. And now that all hope is lost for my people, I can do no less than he."

She was silent. Raan would have argued with him. Pia might have agreed. But Liyana couldn't think of any words that felt right. Standing beside him, she faced the sculptures too. She noticed that all of them were desert totems: falcon, tortoise, raven. . . . He must have chosen them to inspire him as he invaded her home. She spotted her clan's totem on the lowest shelf, and she knelt to see it better. Every detail was perfect, from the tuft under the goat's chin to the curve of its hooves.

He knelt beside her and lifted the goat statue from its shelf. He placed it in her hands. She held it up, and it flickered in the rays of sunlight that crept into the tent.

"Some in the empire believe that your deities do not exist," the emperor said. "Yet you were willing to die for your goddess. You and I, we are not so different."

She looked at him, surprised to hear him echo her earlier thought. He was close beside her. She could see the rise and fall of his breath in his chest. Only a few inches closer, and she thought she'd hear his heartbeat. "We are not so different," she repeated.

He held her gaze. "Help me save my people, Liyana."

"At the cost of my people's freedom?"

"Do you and your people value freedom more than your lives?" he asked. His eyes were as endless as the night sky. Intense, they nearly blazed. "You cannot survive without the empire."

He said it with such surety that her breath caught in her throat. *He knows,* she thought. Her hands began to shake, and she held tight to the glass statue, her clan's totem animal, Bayla's totem. . . . *Oh, sweet goddess.*

There was one sculpture for every clan.

One for every deity.

Vessels of glass.

"The desert people would have the full rights of every citizen of the empire—access to all of our resources," the emperor said. "In exchange, we ask only a fair contribution to our economy, obedience to our laws, participation in mutually beneficial trade, and assistance in matters of concern to our combined people."

She peered into the depths of the statue. It looked to be hollow. Inside, colors caught the light and swirled. Turning the statue in her hand, she thought the colors spun more than they should have, as if they spun on their own. She saw markings on the base that matched her tattoos. She bet each statue had similar markings, transforming each of them into false vessels.

"Of course, we would not interfere with your culture or traditions."

Liyana clutched the statue to her chest. "Except to imprison our gods."

"Except to free you!" He placed his hands on her shoulders so that she could not turn away. "Don't you want to save yourself, as well as your people, Liyana? If you had another option, a way to have both, wouldn't you at least consider it? You could return to your clan. You could see your brother again, see him grow up!"

She closed her eyes, trying to grasp an inner calmness that was slipping away with the emperor's proximity. Opening her eyes and looking directly into his, she said, "I am my people's King of the Fields."

"You aren't anymore," he said quietly. "You are free." Releasing her shoulders, he folded his hands around hers—around Bayla's statue, the false vessel—and they held Liyana's goddess together.

She heard the flap open, and a man's voice cut across the tent. "Your Imperial Majesty." She tried to pull back, but the emperor continued to hold her hands. "An urgent matter has arisen in the east camp," the soldier said.

"I must attend to this," the emperor said to Liyana, "but I will return and ask you one more time. Join me. Be my ambassador. Save your people and mine."

Liyana blinked. "You're leaving me with her?" she blurted out before she had thought. She bit her lip and wished she could recall the words. She didn't want to be forced to relinquish Bayla.

"You cannot break the statue," he said. "Besides, I know my

SARAH BETH DURST

stories. Even if your goddess were free, you could not summon her without a magician. The chant must be infused with magic." He rose. "Hold your goddess in your hands, Liyana. Think about your life. Think about your future."

He swept out of the tent, and Liyana was alone with the trapped deities.

Her hands shook. "My goddess," she whispered. Could Bayla hear her? She looked at the statue of a raven, Korbyn's intended prison. She shouldn't have kissed him. She'd stolen that kiss from her goddess. It was not right.

And no matter what the emperor said or what pretty promises he made, it was not right for her to sacrifice her clan's freedom to save her own life.

She wasn't supposed to have a life anymore. She had said good-bye to her family, to everything she knew and loved. She was not supposed to see them again or sleep in their tent or see the stars with them or share a meal with them or . . . All the moments she had had since the ceremony were stolen, just like Bayla had been stolen from the Dreaming. She had to fix it and restore everything to the way it was supposed to be.

This was her chance.

Steeling herself, she brought the statue down hard on the corner of the desk. She expected it to shatter into a thousand pieces. Instead, it only dented the wood. She bashed it again and again. It didn't chip.

It's not glass, she realized.

She held it up, turning it so that it caught the light. "Diamond," she said out loud. This was why the deities hadn't broken out themselves. There was no natural process to speed or slow. Magic could not break diamond.

Liyana drew the sky serpent knife out of her sash. Knives couldn't slice a sky serpent scale. Arrows couldn't pierce it. She laid the blade against the statue. Taking a deep breath, she pressed down.

In her hands, the statue cracked.

Quickly she concentrated and pictured her lake. Pulling on the magic, she chanted the words that Talu had spoken so long ago. "Bayla, Bayla, Bayla. *Ebuci o nanda wadi,* Bayla, Bayla, Bayla. *Ebuci o yenda,* Bayla, Bayla, Bayla. *Vessa oenda nasa we.*" She sent the summoning words wrapped in magic into the fractured statue as she carried it to the center of the tent. She laid the shards down on the silk cloths. She thought of magic and of emperors and of kisses.

And she danced.

Chapter Twenty-Two
The Emperor

The emperor surveyed the expanse between the encampment and the border hills. Brittle grasses filled the slope. On the other side of that rise was the desert. "Tell me about the prisoners who escaped," he said.

"Two women," one of his lieutenants said. Several other lieutenants stood silently at attention. "One of them was blind. The other needed to be subdued. They claimed to be from the Silk Clan and Scorpion Clan—"

Hairs on the back of the emperor's neck prickled. Mulaf had stolen the deities from both of those clans. They slept in their diamond statues inside the emperor's tent. "Did either of them have tattoos on their arms?"

"I do not know. Your Imperial Majesty, please accept my

apologies. Interrogation of a blind woman and her companion was not a priority." Fist over his heart, he bowed low.

"I should have been informed of their capture immediately," the emperor said. The prisoners had been taken only a few hours before Liyana walked into his camp. He didn't believe in coincidences. "Why was this not brought to my attention?"

The lieutenant fell to his knees. "Forgive—"

"Stand," the emperor said crisply. "Answer my question."

"We often apprehend desert men who stray too close to the border," he said, rising. His head hung low like a dog who had been struck. "We did not think it warranted Your Imperial Majesty's attention—"

"You were mistaken."

The lieutenant cringed and began to babble. "Until their escape, there did not seem to be anything unusual . . ."

The emperor breathed deeply and pictured the lake as the soldier continued to rattle through excuses. As always, the lake calmed him. "Demote this man. Devote resources to recapturing these women. Alive. Bring them directly to me when you have found them."

Another lieutenant saluted. "Yes, Your Imperial Majesty."

The emperor strode back toward his tent. Everything inside him shouted to run, but his people could not see their emperor afraid. Compromising, he lengthened his stride. It had been a strategic move to leave Liyana alone. She valued her independence, and he wanted to demonstrate that he would not seek to control or force her, or her clans. He pushed open the tent flap and halted.

She lay alone in the center of the tent. Beautiful and peaceful, she could have been asleep. "Summon a doctor," he ordered his guards. He felt his heart beat painfully in his chest. In two strides he was beside her. He knelt and pressed his fingers to the pulse in her neck.

She moaned. Alive.

"Stay back, Your Imperial Majesty," one of his guards said. "We don't know the cause."

The goat statue lay beside her. Its neck was severed. She must have used the sky serpent blade. This was his fault. He'd returned it to her. "Summon the magician as well."

One of the guards bowed and exited.

He stroked her forehead. Breaking the false vessel should not have hurt her. If she had conducted the ceremony . . . But how could she have without a magician? And why would she have? He had offered her freedom! Life on the desert was bleak and cruel. He'd offered all her people an escape. She could have led them to a better life.

He felt her pulse again. Faint but there.

A doctor burst into the tent. He wore an ill-fitting uniform. A protective surgical cloth obscured his face. All that the emperor could see was his eyes, but those eyes quickly assessed the situation. Without a word the doctor knelt next to Liyana and began examining her. She was breathing shallowly. Every few seconds she twitched and moaned.

The emperor paced around them. He picked up the broken statue and turned it over and over in his hands. Spasming, Liyana screamed, and the emperor hurled the statue against the wall of the tent. It smacked against the tarp and tumbled down. In a calm voice he said, "This was an unnecessary waste of a life."

"She still lives," the doctor said. "But I must take her to my tent. I have supplies and equipment there that may be of use." He waved a hand. Three doctor's assistants, also dressed in blue uniforms with the traditional face coverings, scurried forward with a stretcher. They loaded Liyana onto it.

"Accompany them," he ordered the nearest soldier. "Ask her name when she wakes. If she answers 'Liyana,' return her to me. If she answers 'Bayla,' kill her immediately."

She was carried out of the tent, and he turned away to face his shelves of statues. He touched his cheek. It was damp. Absently he rubbed his tears between his fingers and thumb. Funny that he should mourn the loss of one desert woman while he prepared his army to invade. In the end, though, eliminating the deities would free the desert people. They would see that their best course was to join the empire. In the end they would be grateful.

"Alert my generals," the emperor said. His eyes were clear. "We move out at dawn."

Chapter Twenty-Three

Liyana felt as if she had swallowed the desert. Sand poured into her body and flowed through her veins. It pressed against her from the inside out until she felt as if her skin might break. She tried to scream. But sand filled her throat.

She knew it wasn't possible. She wasn't in a sandstorm, and there was no sand inside the emperor's tent. It had to be magic. Mulaf! He must be trying to stop her from saving Bayla.

As if she were working magic, she concentrated on her body. She felt her breath fill her rib cage, and she felt her pulse throb through her arteries. She focused on the shape of her skin, the curve of her legs, the length of her arms. Limb by limb she forced out the sand.

The sand changed to water and swept through her body, filling her lungs until she forgot how to breathe. She fought back. *There is no water*, she thought. *There is only me. Breathe!* She inhaled and exhaled. She felt how each breath came in through her mouth and flowed down her throat and filled her lungs. She imagined the air dispersing within her, displacing the water. One breath at a time.

Slowly she regained the feel of her body again.

The third assault was air. It whirled inside her, as if it wanted to rip her away. She clung to herself with her memories: how it felt to dance, how it felt to ride for hours, how it felt to sleep protected between bodies, how it felt to kiss Korbyn.

She heard a voice. It echoed as if the speaker were within a vast cavern, and each word were a stalactite plummeting from the ceiling to the floor. *You. Must. Cease.*

Liyana tried to speak, but her voice wouldn't obey her. *No!* she thought at the voice. *I will not fail my clan!* She would protect this body. It belonged to Bayla, and she would not let it be torn by imaginary wind, or wrecked by water and sand.

Howling, the voice battered her with all the ferocity of a storm. With sheer volume it threatened to overwhelm all other senses, but Liyana was entrenched in her skin.

She tried to open her eyes to see who spoke to her. Her eyelids felt like heavy metal plates, fused shut with fire. She concentrated, bringing all her awareness and determination to bear on her eyes.

Slowly her eyes opened.

She saw Korbyn. He wore a new, ill-fitting uniform, and a blue cloth obscured most of his face, but she'd know his eyes anywhere. Beyond him she saw shelves of labeled jars, stacks of bandages, and a row of cots. She was no longer in the emperor's tent. She lay on a table. Beside her was a tray of silvery knives, as well as more bandages.

"Is she awake?" Pia's voice. Anxious.

Korbyn's eyes bored into hers. Liyana tried again to speak, but her vocal chords wouldn't respond. She took a deliberate breath. "Still unconscious," Korbyn said. He cupped her cheek in his hand, shielding her eyes from view.

Liyana closed her eyes. Immediately she was assailed by wind again. This time it screamed through her, erasing all external sound.

Stop! Liyana thought at the wind. *Please, stop!*

Let me free, the voice said. Strangely, it felt as if the voice were coming from inside of her, not from someone in the tent. *Let me live!*

A terrible thought bloomed in Liyana's head. It wasn't possible. Two souls couldn't be in one body. . . . *I am Liyana, vessel for Bayla of the Goat Clan,* Liyana said. *Are you . . . Are you Bayla?*

All trace of wind vanished.

Silence, then a whisper: *This is not possible.*

Oh, my goddess. Cringing, Liyana lowered her mental voice to a whisper. *Forgive me.* She'd been fighting against . . . The thought of it made her stomach churn.

Leave this body, you insignificant speck of sand!

About to apologize again, Liyana hesitated. *I am not insignificant,* her mental voice whispered. Vessels were cherished by their deities. Their sacrifice was honored.

Bayla did not seem to hear her. *I will wreak revenge on he who dared confine me!* Liyana felt a cyclone build inside her—sand, water, and wind. *You have played your last trick, Korbyn!*

She felt pressure in her arms as if her muscles wanted to raise themselves. She knew, though she couldn't explain how she knew, that the goddess intended to wrap her hands around Korbyn's throat. Liyana arched her back, fighting to keep her hands pinned down. Her fingers curled, digging into the table.

You say you are my vessel yet you will not relinquish control of this body. Bayla's voice felt like a lick of fire.

Korbyn is not to blame, Liyana said. *He came to save you!*

And this is his rescue? A jail of flesh instead of a jail of stone? Bayla's voice was so loud inside Liyana's skull that it hurt. *I will show you what happens to those who cross a goddess.* Suddenly the pressure inside her vanished as if the goddess had left.

Alone in her head, Liyana drew a full breath. She imagined the air spreading through her body, and her arms and legs trembled. "Korbyn," she said.

"Bayla," Korbyn breathed into her ear. She felt the tickle of his breath. "Do not move. We are in danger." She felt his hands on her shoulders, holding her down on the table. She lay still.

SARAH BETH DURST

"I'm not Bayla. I'm Liyana." Opening her eyes, she saw his face close to hers. He was bent over her, and behind him she saw a white-clad guard. Quickly she shut her eyes again.

She wasn't quick enough. The guard pulled Korbyn away from her. "Speak your name," he ordered. She felt hard coldness on the hollow of her throat.

She opened her eyes again. A sword tip touched her throat. "Liyana," she croaked. She pressed her back against the table as if she could sink away from the blade.

The guard raised the sword . . . and then returned it to his scabbard. Scowling at her, he grunted. "The emperor wished her to return."

Korbyn shielded her. "She isn't well enough to move—"

"Carry her," the guard said.

"I can walk," Liyana said. She pushed herself up to sitting—and the wind slammed through her again. She collapsed backward as the world snapped into darkness. This time it felt much worse. Instead of merely Bayla's soul, she felt the magic of the lake flood into her, and she instantly expanded to feel the tent, the sand, the camp, the plains, the desert, as if she were them and they were her. . . .

No! she cried. She focused on her body, rejecting the magic and huddling within the confines of her skin. *I can't let you hurt Korbyn. Or endanger my friends.*

Bayla's voice increased to a howl. *I was tricked and trapped and—*

And you will be free! Liyana promised. *But you must let me help first! You don't know the situation—*

Wind and sand battered her insides. She felt as if her blood were churning in her veins. *I am your goddess,* Bayla said. *You belong to me!*

I am a free woman of the desert, and I belong to no one, Liyana said. *I will give you this body of my own free will as soon as it's safe to do so.*

Inside, the storm quieted. She felt the goddess's presence inside like a swirl of wind, stirring the sand in all directions, but she was not raging. *You will then leave if I cooperate?* Bayla asked.

Of course! You are my goddess! Liyana said.

She felt warmth circle inside her, and there was silence, blissful silence. Her chest loosened, and she inhaled and opened her eyes. She was in a medical tent. She remembered that Korbyn had mentioned he'd found an unused medical tent. Korbyn peered down at her. So did the emperor's guard and three people with blue facecloths.

"Liyana?" It was Pia's voice. She was one of the people in blue. "You—"

The person next to her squeezed Pia's shoulder, and Pia cut off what she was about to say. "It is a good thing that she is Liyana." It was Raan. "Otherwise she'd be dead from our friend here, per the emperor's orders." Raan fixed her eyes on Liyana—the only part of her visible—clearly delivering a hint.

"I *am* Liyana."

For now, Bayla said within her.

She let Korbyn and the other assistant—Fennik, she guessed—help her from the table onto the stretcher. As they hefted her up, Pia and Raan flanked her, keeping the stretcher steady. The guard led them out of the tent. With their footsteps masking her voice, Liyana whispered to Pia and Raan, "The deities are trapped in diamond statues in the emperor's tent. We can free them with the sky serpent knife."

"But . . . it failed," Pia said. "You're here."

"Bayla's here too, inside me," Liyana said. "I don't know why I'm not gone."

Raan's eyes were wide. "You didn't die." She began to tremble. "We . . . we don't have to die?"

Before Liyana could respond, their guard hefted a corner of the stretcher, picking up their pace and ending the opportunity for conversation. As she was carried through camp, she tried to think of what she'd say to the emperor. She wondered what he'd think of what had happened, if he knew what she'd done. *He must know,* she thought. Otherwise the guard would not have been ready with his sword.

Who must know what? Bayla asked.

The emperor of the Crescent Empire, Liyana said. She pictured the emperor ordering her death—Bayla's death—and then she thought of him telling the story of his parents, trying so hard to hide his pain. She wanted to tell him that she was still alive, though she didn't know why it mattered to her that he knew. Perhaps because he'd treated her honorably? Or because he'd listened to her stories and shared his?

Liyana felt a burst of surprise—not her own emotion. It felt like bubbles in her abdomen. *This is not the desert?* Bayla asked. *I was taken from the desert? Who would dare?*

Gleaming in the sun, the emperor's golden tent rose before them. Lying on the stretcher, Liyana saw the banner of the crescent sun as the guards escorted them inside. Korbyn and Fennik lowered her stretcher onto the floor. Liyana sat up. She steadied herself with both hands on the floor, then rose to her feet. "Your Imperial Majesty—" she began.

The man behind the desk was not the emperor. A statue in each hand, Mulaf the magician froze as he stared at her. "Bayla," he breathed. She saw crates around him lined with velvet. Several of the statues were already nestled in the crates. One crate was sealed shut.

Liyana shook her head. "Still Liyana."

"But . . . the broken statue."

"It failed. Where is the emperor?" Liyana asked.

You lied to him, Bayla said. Liyana felt her outrage like an ember of fire in her fist. *Vessels should be pure of heart and mind—*

I believe he is the one who trapped you, Liyana said.

Fury flamed inside her so fast and hot that she gasped in air. As she swayed, Korbyn grabbed her shoulders. He steadied her. His hands felt warm through the fabric of the robe.

"So now you understand that you are free," Mulaf said. He placed the statues back on the shelf, and he scurried to Liyana's side. He clasped her hands to his heart. "You will be an example to the others. They will flock to your side!" He kissed her hands. "This is a wonderful moment."

Liyana felt Bayla raging inside her, and she managed a weak smile.

I want him to suffer! Bayla howled.

Can you use magic against him? Liyana asked.

You control the body so you control the magic . . . but perhaps I can feed you the power. In an instant Bayla was gone, and then she returned with a roar that filled Liyana's ears. Mulaf was speaking, but Liyana couldn't hear the words. She watched his mouth move as a flood of magic flowed into her. Her soul stretched to encompass Mulaf—but she was still not in a trance. According to Korbyn's lessons, all magicians and deities had to be in a trance to access magic, but with Bayla feeding her power, Liyana remained alert and aware. Awed by this, she experimented with a step forward. She could walk, and the magic stayed stretched around Mulaf.

Kill, Bayla said.

Liyana smiled at the magician. "Sleep."

He toppled over.

She reached further with the magic, and the guard slumped to the ground. Liyana had expected a wave of exhaustion when she finished. But it didn't come. Yanking the sky serpent blade out of her sash, she ran to the statues. She found the silk worm, shattered it, and thrust the pieces to Pia, who clutched them to her heart.

Entering a trance, Korbyn chanted Pia's words, softly so the guards outside would not hear. Pia began to dance. "Mine next," Fennik said.

Liyana scanned the shelves for the horse statue. . . . She didn't see it. She searched the open crates. No horse. Beside her, Fennik yanked off the cover of the sealed crate. The metal nails bent and screeched. He pawed through it and then held the horse statue aloft.

She severed its head.

"Liyana . . . thank you." Fennik cradled the pieces. "I cannot express—"

"Then don't," Liyana said. "Just dance."

He pulled down his facecloth, smiled broadly, and then kissed her cheek. With a wink he replaced the facecloth.

As Korbyn chanted the words for Sendar, Fennik joined Pia in the dance, leaping and twirling. Silent, drumless, they kept each other's time. Liyana's eyes slid to Raan, who was staring at the dancers with a stricken expression in her eyes.

Korbyn whispered urgently to Liyana, "Break the other statues!"

Liyana scanned the shelves. She could see no difference between the diamond statues with deities and those without. The emperor could have caught more than the five she knew of. "I don't know which ones have deities—"

"Break them all. At least then they can never be used." He resumed chanting for Oyri and Sendar. Pia and Fennik were dancing faster, their feet beating a tattoo on the silk-covered sand.

Liyana turned her knife on the statues that littered the shelves. Systematically she sliced and shattered them. She halted at the scorpion. Coiled diamond, the arachnid looked as if it was mid-strike. She held it in her hand and turned—

Raan was beside her, only inches away. "Swear to me you didn't die. Swear you are Liyana."

"I am Liyana, but I don't know why I lived," Liyana said. Raan was shaking, and her eyes were as wide as a wild horse's. "I can't promise you anything."

"The Great Drought . . . It's here too, isn't it?"

Liyana nodded.

"Then there isn't an escape," Raan said. "There is no other life for our people."

Liyana wanted to embrace her, but Raan may not have welcomed it. She thought about saying that she was sorry. The words caught in her throat. She didn't think Raan would have believed her anyway.

Tears poured from Raan's eyes and were caught in the face-cloth. "Break the statue. Korbyn, say my words. Use your magic. Call my goddess."

Liyana sliced the scorpion statue. She held out the shards.

Raan stared at the shards for a long moment. "If you lived

through this, I can live through it." She took the shards. Liyana watched her walk shakily to the center of the tent. Around her, Pia and Fennik silently swirled and leaped on the silk carpets. Korbyn chanted. Imitating the other two vessels, Raan danced. She held the shards of the scorpion statue so tightly that the edges sliced her fingers. Red stained the diamond.

Liyana turned to the crates. She picked up the falcon statue.

Across the tent, Mulaf woke. He leveled a shaking finger at Liyana. "You're her! Bayla! Murderer!" His voice rang out. "Guards!"

The three other vessels collapsed.

Six guards burst through the tent flap, and Liyana dropped the falcon statue. She raised her sky serpent blade in front of her. Quickly Korbyn pointed to the magician. "He attacked my assistants with his magic! Arrest him!"

Swords raised, the guards advanced on Mulaf.

The magician continued to point at Liyana. "Kill Bayla! Before she destroys us all!"

Liyana backed away. "You escorted me from this tent to mine after I met the emperor. You told me about the Cat Clan. You said I was safe and free. How could I remember this if I was Bayla?"

Eyes wide, Mulaf lowered his arm. "But . . . your power . . . You used magic. I felt it!" He didn't resist as the guards surrounded him. Two of them clamped their hands on his arms.

Another guard knelt next to Pia and felt her pulse. "This one's dead," he reported. He stood and wiped his palm on his uniform, as if to wipe away the feel of death.

Liyana rushed to Pia's side. Shaking, she felt for her pulse as well. She couldn't find it on Pia's wrist. She felt for the pulse on her neck. Nothing. She lay her head against Pia's chest. "She isn't breathing!"

"That's normal," Korbyn said. Fennik also lay still and silent. But Raan writhed on the floor and moaned. "This"—he knelt beside Raan—"is not."

Pia's eyes popped open. "I live," she said. It was Pia's voice but it wasn't. "But it's dark! I cannot see!" She clawed at her face and yanked away the facecloth.

"Shh," Liyana whispered in her ear. She replaced the facecloth and glanced at Mulaf. His eyes were on Raan. "Pretend you're Pia, the vessel. We're in danger. Say as little as possible." Sweet goddess, it had happened so fast. Like that, Pia was gone.

Fennik sat up. He looked around.

Korbyn bolted to his side. He made a show of checking Fennik's vitals, but Liyana guessed he was whispering in Fennik's ear as well. Sendar's ear.

She knew she should feel joyful for them, but instead all she felt was an ache. Pia and Fennik! She helped Pia—Oyri—to her feet. Several of the guards had left Mulaf's side and had trained their swords on Liyana and Korbyn.

Sendar held himself still, and Liyana knew he was in a trance.

Outside, a horse trumpeted. And then other horses whinnied and cried. Liyana heard shouts and the stamp of hooves.

"Check outside," one of the guards ordered.

The soldier nearest to the door obeyed. He returned only a minute later. "It's the horses, sir! They're stampeding!" He darted out again.

Sendar opened his eyes.

Clever boy, Bayla thought.

Mulaf's eyes widened. He looked at the doctor and his assistants as if the force of his gaze could help him see through the facecloths. In another second he would connect them with the broken statues. Liyana glanced at Korbyn. She didn't know if he had a plan. *We need to leave now,* Liyana thought.

We need a larger distraction, Bayla thought. *Horses aren't frightening enough.*

"Are there worms beneath us?" Liyana whispered to Oyri. Often the great worms burrowed below the bedrock, following water deep within the earth, surfacing only in the salt flats to spin their thread.

Oyri nodded. "Far, far beneath, but yes." Stilling, she concentrated.

Mulaf flapped his arms like an agitated bird. "You must stop them!"

On the ground, Raan moaned and twitched.

Liyana saw Mulaf close his eyes, preparing for a trance. She picked up the falcon statue and threw it at him. It hit his stomach. He flinched, his concentration broken, and a guard pressed a blade to Liyana's throat. "He was about to use magic!" she said. "You can't trust him!"

"Tie them all up and gag them, including the magician," one of the guards ordered. "We will sort this out after the crisis is over." He pointed to three of the guards. "You and you and you, help outside." The three soldiers rushed out. Only three remained.

"Ready yourself," Oyri said softly.

The floor began to shake. Liyana fell to her knees.

Across the tent, Mulaf fell against one of the guards. He grabbed for the guard's sword hilt and tried to yank it free. A second guard rushed to stop him. Sendar leaped on the third guard. He slammed his fist into the soldier's chin.

Korbyn hefted Raan over his shoulders as the ground began to crack beneath her. "Liyana, watch out!" he yelled.

In the center of the tent, the earth split apart. A giant silk worm burst through the floor and reared above them. Oyri grabbed Liyana's arm. "Guide me to the tail!"

Liyana yanked her away from the worm's gaping maw. "Here! Back here!" The bulbous tail lashed in front of them. It swept into the emperor's desk, knocking it onto its side with a massive crash.

"Help me jump on it!" Oyri ordered Liyana. She tightened her grip on Liyana's arm.

Liyana balked. "You can't mean—"

Jump, vessel, Bayla ordered.

Pulling Oyri with her, Liyana threw herself onto the worm's tail. Oyri wrapped her arms around it. Liyana dug her fingers into the wet silk strands that coated the worm's body. As Oyri and Liyana clung to it, the worm thrashed, tearing the tent further. The tarp fell, covering Mulaf and the guards. "Do not let go!" Oyri shouted.

The worm arced in the air. It flipped its body upward, and Liyana screamed. She closed her eyes, and the worm slammed into the earth. Rocks and dirt flew around them as the worm dove into the tunnel it had made.

Liyana felt rocks and dirt pummel her back. She clung tight and buried her face in the wet silk. Her body hit the wall of the tunnel, and she nearly lost her grip. She squeezed tighter. The tunnel felt hot around her, and she smelled the worm's sickly sweet sweat. It clogged her throat.

I will feed you magic, Bayla said. *Guide the worm!*

Liyana felt the magic pour into her, and she expanded in a rush. Suddenly, without entering a trance, she was the worm, tunneling through the earth, aware of the two bodies clinging to her flesh. *Water,* Liyana thought at the worm. She pictured water beyond the army encampment, near the grove of trees where she and Pia and Raan had pitched their tent.

The worm raced for it.

With a crash the worm burst out of the earth. All of a sudden Liyana felt the sun on her face. She couldn't open her eyes—dirt flew all around her. Chunks of earth rained everywhere.

"Release now!" Oyri shouted.

Liyana let go.

She fell to the ground, and the wind rushed out of her lungs as she impacted. When she opened her eyes, the worm was gone.

Chapter Twenty-Four

The dust settled.

Liyana wiped the dirt out of her eyes with a filthy sleeve. She pushed herself to sitting. *You have bruised my body,* Bayla said.

"Are we safe?" Oyri demanded. She walked in a circle, arms outstretched. She stumbled over the cracked earth that the worm had left, and she fell to her knees. Her facecloth was gone, and the blue uniform was torn and streaked with dirt.

Liyana scanned the hilltop. So far, no soldiers, but that could change. She thought of the emperor and wondered if he was caught in the chaos. She wished she could have explained—but no, he wouldn't have understood anyway. He'd given the order to kill Bayla. Her mind, deep beyond where Bayla could hear her, whispered, *But not me. He did not wish to kill me.* She pushed aside thoughts of him. "We're too visible. We need to hide in the tent." Wincing from her new bruises, she hobbled over to Oyri and helped her stand.

On the walk to the tent, Oyri stumbled three times, even with Liyana escorting her. Liyana hadn't realized how proficient Pia had been at compensating for her blindness. Pia had never taken a false step. She had walked with the confidence of a sighted person. By contrast, Oyri shuffled and stumbled like a baby goat learning to walk.

Pushing Oyri's head down so she'd duck, Liyana guided her into the tent. Their packs were still inside, as was the withered pile of cacti that Liyana had gathered before entering the encampment. Oyri flailed her arms to feel around her, and she hit the packs. She recoiled. "I demand to know why my vessel is blind. I should be flawless!"

"Pia was flawless," Liyana said. "You should honor her sacrifice." Unable to watch the goddess flounder in Pia's body, she checked outside the tent. Still no soldiers, but no Korbyn, Raan, or Fennik either. *Sendar,* she reminded herself. He was Sendar. Fennik was gone.

"Get back here!" Oyri screeched. "I require immediate answers. You must tell me where I am, who you are, and how I came to be here."

Tell her the traitor's name was Mulaf, and we will kill him, Bayla said.

Liyana ducked quickly inside. "Shh, you'll draw the soldiers. You and several other deities were captured by the Crescent Empire. . . ." Quickly she summarized everything that had occurred for both Oyri's and Bayla's benefit. As she talked, she felt Bayla churn inside her. "The emperor will march on the desert soon."

We will mount an attack on the encampment! Bayla shouted within.

"I must warn my clan!" Oyri cried.

Destroy Mulaf, and cut the viper off at the head! Bayla swirled like a sandstorm inside Liyana.

"My people must hide from this scourge!"

Give me the body, and I will wreak such havoc—

"Quiet, both of you!" Liyana held up her hands. She thought she heard noises from outside the camp. Inside her, Bayla continued to rage, scattering Liyana's own thoughts. *Please, stop, I need to listen!*

Bayla fell silent, though Liyana felt her continue to churn.

Listening, Liyana heard hoofbeats hitting the sand. She crawled out of the tent and peeked through the trees. Five horses trotted down the hill. Three had the lithe bodies of desert horses, while the other two were stocky empire horses. Squinting in the sun, Liyana tried to see the riders. There were two . . . no, three. One horse held two figures. The others were riderless.

"Who is it?" Oyri called out to her.

"Shh," Liyana said. She watched as they came down the slope. Sand billowed around the horses' hooves. She saw the blue of their robes. Behind her, Oyri exited the tent loudly, thrashing her arms to feel her way.

It is them, Bayla said. *Only Sendar rides like that.*

Relief poured through her like sweet, clean water. "It's them," she repeated to Oyri.

"Who's 'them'?" Oyri asked.

Liyana stepped out of the shelter of the grove and waved her arms in the air. She saw one of the riders wave back. In a few minutes the riders and horses reached their camp. Liyana ran toward them. Behind her, Oyri tried to follow. She clung to the trunk of one of the trees. "This is intolerable. I should not have to ask. Tell me who it is!"

"Korbyn, Sendar, and . . ." Liyana saw that Raan was still unconscious. Korbyn had her draped across the horse's neck in front of him. Liyana sprinted the last few yards.

Korbyn slid off the horse with Raan. Liyana caught the girl's arm, slowing her descent.

"Is she—" Liyana began.

"I don't know." Together, she and Korbyn carried Raan into the tent and laid her inside. Liyana tucked a blanket under her head.

"Are they chasing us?" she asked.

"Not yet. But they'll notice our absence soon enough, and they'll be after us, especially without Sendar there to agitate the horses." Liyana heard Sendar outside the tent, walking the horses in a circle around the grove to cool them. "We can't stay here long." Korbyn caught her chin and peered into her eyes. "Bayla . . . Is she truly . . ."

Tell him yes.

"Yes, she's inside me."

"This shouldn't be possible," Korbyn said. "Is she . . . well?"

Kiss him, Bayla said.

Liyana flinched. *What?*

It will prove I'm here.

His hand was still on her chin, and his face was inches from hers. Leaning forward, Liyana kissed him, and then she sprang back.

He touched his lips. "Was that you or Bayla?"

"I . . . I don't know." Liyana could still taste his lips on hers and knew that Bayla had not forced her to move. She had done it herself.

Liyana felt Bayla shift inside her. *Of course, it is me! Why would he doubt?* This time the swirling felt deeper, as if a chasm widened within. Recoiling, Liyana didn't answer.

"How is this possible?" Korbyn asked again.

The swirl intensified, shifting from confusion to anger. Bayla's anger whipped inside Liyana. *Tell him I blame him.*

"She blames you."

Korbyn's mouth twitched. "Now I believe she is within you." His fingertips brushed her cheek. "Bayla? Beloved?"

Flailing, Raan groaned. Liyana swiftly turned away from his touch. She felt Raan's forehead and then her pulse. Her heartbeat was erratic. "What's wrong with her?" Liyana asked.

She's fighting her goddess, Bayla said, *as you fought me.*

"I don't know," Korbyn said, his eyes still on Liyana. Or Bayla. Liyana felt her insides twist. He should be looking at Bayla. She shouldn't still be here.

"Bayla thinks she's fighting Maara," Liyana said. "Like I fought Bayla." She met his beautiful, deep eyes. "You must know I didn't intend for this to happen."

The tent billowed and shook as Oyri negotiated her way through the tent flap. Korbyn reached out a hand to steady her, and the second his hand touched her, Oyri leaped backward as if she'd felt a snake. "It's Korbyn," he said. "Be at ease."

Oyri let him guide her into the tent. She settled herself between the packs, pulling them around her as if they were a protective wall. "I must heal myself."

"I have tried," Korbyn said. "It is not possible."

"You tried? When?" Liyana asked. She'd never overhead Korbyn and Pia discuss this. She couldn't imagine Pia asking him to try. Across the tent, Oyri pawed at her face, as if she could feel the scope of her blindness.

"Several nights," Korbyn said, "while she slept . . . until she woke one night and asked me not to try again. She said if she gained her vision, then she would lose her way." His mouth quirked, but Liyana felt her heart squeeze. She could picture Pia saying that.

"Ridiculous sentiment," Oyri said. She rubbed her eyes hard and then harder. "And I may succeed where you failed."

He laid his hands on her wrists and gently lowered her fingers away from her face. "Still you must wait to try. The healing will exhaust you, and we cannot afford to have two of us incapacitated. We must ride as soon as Sendar says the horses are ready."

"I will not proceed without vision," Oyri said. "It is insupportable that I should have a deficient vessel. How she could have hidden this in the dreamwalk—"

In a mild voice Korbyn said, "Your 'deficient' vessel crossed a desert that has killed seasoned warriors." He met Liyana's eyes. At least she was not the only one who had valued Pia. She suddenly felt less alone. She was aware of his closeness inside the tent. For an instant Oyri and her tirade melted away.

Liyana broke eye contact as she felt Bayla churn inside her. *Exactly where does my darling boy propose we ride to?* Bayla asked. *The enemy is here!*

"Bayla wants to know where we're going," Liyana said. She shifted away from Korbyn. The air was thick and hot inside the tent, and she tried to breathe deeply.

"To unite the clans," Korbyn said.

"The Scorpion Clan joins with no one," Oyri declared.

Waste of time, Bayla said. *You will never achieve full cooperation.* She continued to expound on the futility of Korbyn's plan and the lack of cohesion of the clans. *The isolationism has been increasing. Oyri is but one example—*

Korbyn's mouth twisted into an almost smile. "She's ranting, isn't she?"

"Yes," Liyana said.

His smile broadened.

Bayla broke off midsentence. *I do not rant.*

"Bayla, Oyri . . . The army must be stopped," Korbyn said. "If they reach the mountains, they'll bring disaster to the entire desert."

Stop them here! Bayla said. *Vessel, repeat my words. Better to fight now before the invaders soil our sands with—*

"She says to stop them here," Liyana said.

"It is a very large army," Korbyn said mildly. Bayla began to protest again, but before Liyana could speak, Korbyn looked beyond her. "Are the horses ready?" he asked.

Liyana turned her head and saw Fennik—Sendar—in the entranceway. She stared at him and tried to convince her brain that this was not her friend, even though it was his body. Sendar's eyes roved over her. "Bayla?" he breathed.

Tell him he still smells of horses, and I do not forgive him for the humiliation he—

"She's angry with you," Liyana said.

Sendar looked pained but did not address her. "The horses will be ready shortly. Give them ten minutes to rest, and then we can—and should—move out." Though he had the same voice, he did not speak like Fennik. His words rolled as smooth as pebbles. Liyana noticed that his stance was different as well. He held his shoulders farther back, and his body was stiff and still. Fennik had been always in motion. His fingers used to braid together or run through his hair. His expressions, too—Liyana was reminded of a puppet whose each facial tick was deliberate and pronounced. Sendar moved and spoke with intent.

Raan's eyes popped open. "If someone does not pour whisky down my throat right now, I will be kicking every man in the balls and scalping every woman."

Sendar roared with laughter and slapped his knee. "Maara, it is good to see you."

Liyana suddenly felt as if the tent were too tight and the air had vanished. She pushed past Oyri and Sendar, and ran out into the desert. She stopped at the crater that the salt worm had created, and she knelt, face in her hands.

You mourn her, Bayla said quietly.

She didn't want to die. Liyana felt an ache twisting inside her. Perhaps she understood Raan better than she'd ever thought she did. She wished she'd had a chance to tell her.

But she was a vessel. This was her fate.

I honor you, Bayla. You are my goddess, and you have my love. But for the space of a moment . . . do not speak to me.

I feel your hostility—

Liyana screamed and threw a clump of dried dirt into the salt worm's tunnel. It smacked into the wall and fragmented. She threw another and another.

She heard footsteps behind her. "This is a familiar sight," Korbyn said.

Liyana placed her face in her hands again, and she felt his hands on her shoulders. She sank down into the dirt. He cradled her against his chest.

He comforts you, Bayla said.

Silence, or I will not speak for you ever again.

Bayla faded into the back of her mind. Liyana felt a hint of her anger, like a whiff from a distant cooking pot. "Why me, and why not them?" she asked Korbyn.

He didn't answer. He just held her.

Cheek pressed against his chest, she looked across the desert. It was pockmarked with dry bushes and thick-as-leather cacti. The forbidden mountains loomed in the distance. Their journey wasn't over. "What do we do now?"

He pressed his lips to the top of her head. "I don't know." She didn't think he was talking about Maara or even the invading army.

Sendar emerged from the tent. She didn't look up to see his expression, so like Fennik and yet not. "We don't stay here," he said with Fennik's voice. Raising her head, Liyana watched him adjust the saddles. Behind him, Maara stepped out of the tent and stretched. She turned her body, examining herself, and made pleased noises.

And then she collapsed into the sand.

All of them rushed to her side. Pushing Sendar aside, Liyana threw herself onto her knees next to Raan and cradled her head.

Bayla observed, *She still fights.*

"Keep fighting," Liyana whispered to her. "You can survive this. Stay in your body."

Inside, Bayla reared like a sandstorm, and Liyana felt herself blown backward. The world went black and silent, and she kept falling back, back, back. Liyana forced her mind into her body, flooding her arms and legs and fingers and chest and feet.

Subdued again, Bayla was silent. At last she said, *You seem to have forgotten your role, vessel. You promised me this body.*

Liyana blinked open her eyes to see Korbyn only a few inches away. He cradled her in his arms. "Still me," Liyana said. Guilt washed through her—it shouldn't still be her. Bayla was right. Liyana had promised to leave. But if there was no harm in staying a little while longer . . .

A look of relief flashed across his face.

Korbyn? Bayla's voice was tinged with pain and confusion.

"Bayla, is she—" Korbyn began.

"Inside," Liyana said. "Angry. Confused." She thought of what Talu would say if she knew Liyana remained. She wouldn't understand why Liyana delayed. Of course Liyana intended to leave as soon as it was truly necessary. She got to her feet and checked on Raan. She was unconscious again. Liyana felt her pulse—stronger than it had been. "We'll tie her to one of the horses, a calm mare preferably, and someone will ride beside her."

"And what about me? How do you expect me to ride?" Oyri

demanded. "Will you tie me to a saddle like a sack as well? It is insupportable that I must rely—"

Liyana cut her off. "Pia learned to ride. Fennik . . . Sendar, would you please choose their horses and help them mount?"

Sendar looked at Korbyn quizzically. "You allow the mortal to give orders?"

Korbyn shrugged. "She gives good orders."

He cares for you, Bayla said. *More than for me? I will see you suffer for this outrage.*

Liyana felt a wave of fear crash through her, and she knew Bayla must feel her reaction too. She'd never thought she would fear her goddess. *Any harm to me is harm to your future body.*

Then I will break you from the inside out, Bayla vowed.

Sendar prepared the horses while Korbyn packed the tent. Leading Oyri and Raan and the supply horses, they rode out. Liyana tried hard not to think at all.

✶   ✶   ✶

Once the border hills were distant silhouettes, the deities and Liyana halted and set up camp under the light of the moon. Liyana and Korbyn pitched the tent and started a fire while Sendar tended to the horses. He cooed to their mounts as if they were kittens. As he curried them, Liyana and Korbyn helped Oyri off her horse and into the tent, and then they slid Raan off her horse.

No one spoke.

Korbyn laid Raan next to the fire, and Liyana checked her pulse. Strong again. She wondered if that was a good sign or not. Adding more fuel to the fire, Liyana turned away.

"She's awake," Korbyn said. He pointed at Raan. Or Maara.

Liyana knelt in front of her. "Are you . . ." Her throat closed, and she couldn't complete the question. *Please, please,* she silently begged.

Acidly, Bayla asked, *Who precisely are you praying to?*

Liyana stopped.

"Raan." Her voice was a croak. "You?"

"Still Liyana," she said. Relief poured through her and made her head swim. She felt her cheeks stretch from her smile, though she hadn't realized she was smiling. Her eyes felt hot. She blinked hard, holding back the hot tears. She didn't know why she felt such relief—the fact that she and Raan remained was unnatural, and she should have abhorred it.

"I should have practiced more," Raan said. "Never could get the sense of my full self. And now . . . Liyana, I can't feel my arms or legs."

Liyana suddenly understood. She met Korbyn's eyes. "It's the magic, isn't it? All your training. That's why I can hold my body. And Raan . . . She's only partially trained."

I knew this was his fault! Bayla said. She swirled fast and furious. Liyana tried to keep her breathing even, but her head whirred and her heart thudded.

Coming out of the tent, Oyri stumbled toward them. "You taught them magic?"

Of all the arrogant, ignorant . . . , Bayla raged.

"Vessels should never be taught magic!" Oyri said.

Raan coughed, and her body spasmed. "Because that makes us harder to kill? Do you feel any remorse for murdering Pia? She was the purest person I have ever met, and you displaced her!"

Joining them by the fire, Sendar glanced at Raan. "She's not Maara," he observed.

Oyri spat into the sand. "It's Korbyn's fault. He taught them magic."

Korbyn rose to his feet. "Did you know? Any of you, did you know that training a vessel could save him or her?" He turned to Liyana, and he knelt on one knee. "I swear to you. I did not deliberately keep this knowledge from the desert people. If I had known . . ."

Bayla churned. *If you had known, what would you have done? Saved your vessel? I doubt that. You know as well as I do that we have responsibilities, and we need bodies to perform them.*

Taking a breath, Liyana repeated Bayla's words.

"If we can fulfill our responsibilities *without* causing death . . . ," Korbyn began.

Sendar waved his hand at Liyana. "You aren't revolted by this creature? A mortal is keeping her goddess caged inside of her. You should hate her for this crime, especially since the victim is your purported love." Sendar lifted Liyana's chin and stared into her eyes as if he could see Bayla within them. "Bayla, I love you enough to set you free, if there were but a way."

Liyana felt Bayla's emotions roil inside her—betrayal, pain, anger, all directed at Korbyn. *I gave you my heart, and this is how you repay me. Loyalty to a sheep.*

Just because he doesn't want me to die doesn't mean he doesn't love you, Liyana thought at Bayla. *It only means that he has a good heart.*

The raven has no heart, Bayla said.

"Of course I love Bayla," Korbyn said. "I simply do not see why Liyana should have to die if both souls can inhabit one body."

"I think it's her fault," Raan whispered. "Maara. She won't let me move."

"Focus on your body," Liyana said. She clasped Raan's hand. "You don't lack for willpower, Raan. You're strong. You can do this."

"You're the strong one." Raan closed her eyes as she winced. "It hurts. Why does my goddess hurt me?" She started to whimper.

I could hurt you, Bayla whispered.

Liyana froze. She felt as if her blood had chilled. Bayla churned inside her. "Our stories claim you choose vessels because of your great love for us. So why do you do this?" Liyana asked. She looked up at Korbyn and at Sendar, but her words were for Bayla. "You're supposed to love us! To help us! If we don't have to die, why kill us? Mulaf believes deities are parasites. Please, tell me he isn't right!"

Korbyn looked ill. His hands shook, and he turned away from her.

"Bayla, fight this human," Sendar said. "She poisons the very air with her words."

Raan coughed again. "You are the poison." She then closed her eyes, and her head lolled to the side. Her body twitched. After a moment she lay still, unconscious again.

"Raan!" Liyana shook her.

"I have had enough of this sacrilege," Sendar said. "At dawn we split ways. I will lead my clan to intercept the army at the foot of the forbidden mountains. You will join us there. United, our clans will eliminate this scourge."

"If this is a ploy to seize power—" Korbyn began.

Sendar scowled, his face tinting purple. "I am best able to lead!"

"Debatable," Korbyn said. He held up a hand to forestall further argument. "We will fight *alongside* you." He turned to Oyri. "And will the Silk Clan fight with us?"

"The Silk Clan does not need—" Oyri began.

"But you do," Liyana pointed out. "You need help to rejoin your clan, and the clans need your help against the empire."

Oyri opened her mouth and shut it.

"That is the price of my assistance," Sendar said. "I will guide you to your clan if you will fight with us against the intruders."

At last Oyri nodded.

"Still it won't be enough," Korbyn said. He began to pace. "We must contact as many other clans as we can. For clans who have their deities, use magic to reach them. For those without, send runners. Liyana, Bayla, and I will bring our clans, the Scorpion Clan, and the clans in the southern desert."

You have until then to vacate this body, Bayla said. *I will not face my clan trapped within you!* She produced another sandstorm that knocked Liyana backward.

This time Liyana did not lose consciousness. She clung on as Bayla battered her from within. *You're my goddess! Why do you do this to me?*

I want to breathe, to see, to feel, to eat, to sleep, to dance! With each word, the storm inside whipped faster. *I want to walk the sands, embrace my lover, fight with my people! I want to live as was promised to me!*

Softly, in a near whisper, Liyana said, *But I don't want to die.* She felt as if the words were ripped out of her gut.

Immediately the wind died. Bayla fell silent.

Liyana felt a hand on her arm. She focused on Korbyn's face. "Liyana?" he asked tentatively. "Bayla?"

"Liyana," she said. And she turned away so she would not have to see whether he was pleased or disappointed.

Chapter Twenty-Five

At dawn Sendar cared for the horses: curried them, trimmed them, and examined every inch of their flesh for abrasions and sprains. Thinking of Fennik, Liyana wondered if Sendar cared for his people that much. She scolded herself for criticizing a deity. But it was difficult not to, now that she had met Sendar, Maara, and Oyri.

Oyri hadn't stopped talking since she'd woken at dawn. "I shall require a bath when we reach our destination, Sendar. Do your horse people know how to prepare a proper bath? I have sand on my skin, and it is terribly abrasive."

Liyana wished she could tune her out. Instead she returned to Raan's side. Earlier she'd woken as Maara but then she'd lapsed into unconsciousness again. "Raan, can you hear me? Are you still there?"

She heard footsteps behind her. She twisted around and saw the horse god studying her with narrowed eyes. "We should take Maara with us," Sendar said to Oyri. Fennik's jocular voice was chilled when Sendar spoke.

Oyri nodded. "Indeed. I do not trust that their motives are properly aligned."

Liyana felt a hand grip her wrist. She looked down to see Raan's eyes open, beseeching her. "She comes with us," Liyana said. Raan's grip loosened.

Oyri continued as if Liyana hadn't spoken. "While Maara and I have had our differences, I believe it is the duty—"

Inform Oyri that Maara will accompany us, Bayla said.

Liyana repeated Bayla's words and then asked silently, *Truly?* She felt hope flutter inside her. Perhaps Bayla was not unsympathetic to Raan . . . or to Liyana.

Oyri echoed her thought. "Truly, Bayla? What if this human of yours contributes to her downfall? Would you wish another to suffer your fate?

Repeat my words: I do not believe it is in the best interests of the Scorpion Clan to be beholden to the Silk Clan. Liyana repeated Bayla's words. *And, Oyri, if you ever think of expanding to the Goat Clan, I will personally render you deaf as well as blind.*

Oyri gasped. "I would never!"

Once, the salt worms roved the desert freely. . . .

"Once, the salt worms roved the desert freely," Liyana

began. She knew this story. She continued without prompting. "Everywhere the worms tunneled, they tainted the sand with salt. Living things withered, and the desert was laced with trails of death. Maara of the Scorpion Clan saw them approach the hills, and she sent her scorpions to sting the salt worms until they fled. Some burrowed deep below the rocks, never to rise again. Others retreated to the plains, creating the salt flats, never to leave again."

You know your tales, Bayla said, sounding pleased. *It would please Oyri greatly to cause the Scorpion Clan to leave their hills and beg for mercy from the Silk Clan.* Liyana repeated that out loud.

Sendar raised both eyebrows at Oyri. "Is this true?"

Oyri opened her mouth and then shut it like a fish.

"Maara stays with us," Korbyn said firmly. "And you would do well to remember that the clans are one people. Perhaps your blindness will open your eyes to that."

"Let us ride, Sendar. I can no longer abide our present company." Oyri held up her arms like a child, and Sendar lifted her onto one of the horses.

Sendar mounted his own horse. He held the reins of Oyri's horse. "You will see that your horses are well cared for." It was a command, not a question. He was leaving them with the three desert horses and taking the two empire horses—either out of kindness or a certainty that they could not care for the nondesert horses. Regardless, Liyana was grateful that Gray Luck was one of the horses he was leaving. "Remember: We must intercept the army before they enter the mountains. Do not be late."

"As I recall, I wasn't the one who was slow to the finish line," Korbyn said.

The two deities rode away without a farewell. Sand plumed in their wake and then wavered in the heat. Liyana and Korbyn watched them until they shrank to specks in the distance. "There is a reason why most deities are loners," Korbyn said.

"Everyone will put aside their differences to face the invaders," Liyana said. She pictured the emperor, a most polite invader.

How sweetly optimistic, Bayla said.

Practical, Liyana corrected. *For all our differences, there is one thing the clans have in common: the desert. We'll fight for it if we have to.*

I think that may be the first thing you have said that I agree with, vessel.

Liyana and Korbyn secured the unconscious Raan to a horse. Taking her reins, Liyana climbed onto Gray Luck. Korbyn led the extra horse. They rode west.

At midday they camped.

While Korbyn located food, Liyana sat beside a clump of cacti, intending to fill the leaves with water. She began to breathe evenly, trying to calm her thoughts so she could picture the lake.

Oh, let me, Bayla said.

Power flooded into Liyana. She gasped and reached out to the cacti. Instantly it plumped with water. She then reached out further, and every cacti within a hundred yards of the tent filled with water.

That was a lot of magic, she said as mildly as she could manage.

Indeed, Bayla said and then fell silent.

The goddess stayed silent as Liyana collected the cacti and extracted their moisture, filling their waterskins and setting a pot with tea leaves to boil. Korbyn returned with several desert rats. As they fell into the comfortable rhythm of preparing food, Liyana relaxed. It almost felt like it used to, just her and Korbyn. She watched him out of the corner of her eye as he cooked dinner. After a few minutes, she noticed that he was sneaking glances at her as well. She wondered who he was looking for, her or Bayla. He offered her a strip of meat. Their fingers touched briefly as she took the meat. They stared at each other.

Ask Korbyn if he remembers our first meal together.

Liyana asked him.

"Of course I do," he said, looking back at the fire. "She dared me."

I do not like to be spoken of in the third person, Bayla said. *I am here.*

Liyana repeated this. Still stirring the fire, Korbyn said, "You told me you would poison me for stealing Sendar's horses, and you dared me to eat with you."

"You stole horses?" Liyana asked.

"Only a few," Korbyn said. "I wanted to teach them to fly."

He said it as if that were a sensible reason. "Did it work?" Liyana asked.

Clearly not, Bayla said. *Do you see any horses flying across the desert?*

"Almost," Korbyn said with the trace of a smile. "All right, no, it didn't. Even with hollow bones and a significantly reduced mass, the required wingspan was impractical. But I did create a flying rodent."

I always hated your bats, Bayla said, and Liyana felt a wave of fondness roll over her.

"Bayla had . . ." Korbyn looked at her and corrected himself. "*You* had prepared a meal with dozens of sauces and flatbreads for dipping. There was spiced wine. And you had made baked chocolate for dessert. You said that if I ate with you, I would worship you and be in thrall to your every whim. I replied that there was no magic that could enslave a man's mind."

And I said, "Yes, there is."

Before Liyana could repeat Bayla's words, Korbyn said, "And you said, 'Yes, there is. There are women.'"

I poisoned you with love.

"Per your request, I returned the horses in the morning," Korbyn said. He reached toward her, and his fingers brushed Liyana's cheek. "Bayla . . ."

Liyana turned her face away. It felt hard to breathe. Her heart was a fist inside her rib cage. She felt her hand tremble. Liyana wasn't causing it to move.

Why do you value this ephemeral human? Bayla asked. *We could be together!* Liyana's hand reached toward Korbyn.

Clamping down on her wrist, Liyana thought at Bayla, *You will be together in the Dreaming for all eternity. Please . . .* A shudder wracked her body as Bayla tried to force her hand to move again.

Sarah Beth Durst

"In my nightmares I search and cannot find you," Korbyn said, cupping her face in his hands. His eyes searched hers. Feeling his touch on her cheeks, Liyana remembered all the nightmares she had calmed over their journey. *I'm keeping him from her,* she thought, deep where Bayla couldn't hear. She felt her insides twist with guilt.

Raan moaned. Her eyelids fluttered open. Both Liyana and Korbyn peered at her. Raan smiled broadly. "She weakens!"

Maara.

Liyana recoiled. "It isn't necessary to sound so gleeful about it."

"Her presence is an unnatural offense," Maara said. "One soul per body. And we take priority—our magic will save an entire clan."

"Bayla has worked magic with Liyana," Korbyn said. He gestured to the cacti.

Maara fixed her eyes on Liyana with an expression that said she thought Liyana was worse than a venomous snake. "You're still here. Bayla, the key is to disorient her so badly that she cannot focus. Then push the areas where she's weakest."

Liyana felt chilled. "You're torturing your vessel."

Korbyn squeezed Liyana's hand. "Bayla." He stared into Liyana's eyes. "Please. If you love me . . . do not harm Liyana. We will find a way to be together."

Bayla was silent for a long while. At last she said to Liyana, *You do not kiss him again.*

Liyana started. *I wouldn't . . . I mean, I . . .* She stared at Korbyn's lips and remembered how safe and warm she had felt in his arms—how right it had felt and how wrong it was. *Never again,* she promised her goddess.

✳   ✳   ✳

By midday the next day Maara had lost control to Raan. Liyana and Korbyn carried Raan into the tent. She'd woken as herself while they rode but had been unable to move. They laid her down onto the blankets.

"I still cannot feel my legs," Raan said.

"What can you feel?" Liyana asked.

"Hands, but not so much fingers. It's tough to turn my head."

"How about your lungs? Any trouble breathing?"

"I can feel myself breathe, but not deeply," Raan said. Tears leaked out of her eyes. Liyana wiped her cheeks for her. "I think I am slipping away, Liyana. I can feel her, nesting in my body. She has more control, doesn't she?"

"Can you hear her?" Liyana asked. "Does she talk to you?"

"She's never spoken to me. I didn't think . . . I never thought my goddess would hate me. Why does she hate me? Is it so wrong to want to live?"

Korbyn knelt next to her. "Concentrate on your breathing. Let's see if we can regain some control. Inhale, and feel the air expand your lungs."

As Korbyn worked with Raan, Liyana slipped out of the tent.

SARAH BETH DURST

She needed to fetch both food and water so Korbyn wouldn't have to. She scanned the desert around them. Away from the border, the land was desolate. Still, a few stubborn plants gripped the dry earth.

Maara does not hate Raan, Bayla said quietly. *I do not hate you.*

Liyana did not know how to reply to that. She wasn't certain she believed her. Locating a tuber plant, she sat beside it. She touched the brittle stalklike leaves. *I'm ready for the magic.*

She waited while Bayla's presence receded. Since Liyana didn't need to be in a trance while Bayla fetched the magic, her thoughts drifted to Korbyn. He didn't want her dead—he'd made that clear—but she wished she knew what he was thinking when he looked at her, and who he saw.

The power flooded into her. She shut off her thoughts and worries, and focused instead on the tasks at hand. Fattening, the tuber ripened. She shifted her awareness to the next tuber. It plumped. And another. She then dug the ripe tubers out of the sand and carted them back to the tent. Silently she poked her head in. Korbyn was deep in concentration, and Raan lay still, either sleeping or unconscious again. Liyana entered and stretched out beside her.

Raan's eyes opened.

"Maara or Raan?" Liyana asked.

"Korbyn helps the vessel. Why?"

Maara. Sitting up, Liyana wrapped her arms around her knees.

She studied Raan's face, trying to see a hint of her friend within. "The vessel's name is Raan. And why don't you ask her? She says you haven't spoken to her."

"She is a body," Maara said.

"She's a person," Liyana said. She spoke softly so she wouldn't disturb Korbyn, though she wanted to shout. A thought occurred to her. "I think . . . perhaps you are afraid of discovering that." Inside, she felt Bayla listening. "If you admit she deserves to stay in her body, then you have to admit that all those deaths of all those vessels in all the generations before were unnecessary."

"I act for the good of my clan," Maara said.

"I am proof—"

"You are an abomination!" Maara sat up, and Liyana scooted backward. She hadn't imagined that the goddess had so much control over the body already.

Korbyn's eyes snapped open. He sagged and then caught himself. Leaving Maara, Liyana helped him lie back on the blankets. He clutched her arm, but she hastily withdrew as if his touch burned. "Are you all right?" she asked. "What were you doing?"

"Contacting the deity of the Dog Clan," he said.

"You can do that?" Liyana asked.

"It is similar to the summoning chant," Korbyn said. "I fill words with magic and send them across the desert. It is an awkward way to converse but sufficient for emergencies."

"And did he reply?" Maara asked.

"He's in his vessel with his clan, but he refuses to join us. Once again my reputation precedes me. He believes it's a trick."

Stubborn idiot, Bayla said. *We do not have time for this. The clans need to mobilize now! Let me send words to the imbecile.* Her tone left no question as to what kind of words they would be. *Vessel, you will aid me.* Liyana repeated Bayla's offer.

Korbyn shook his head. "They won't trust you either. Apologies for tarnishing your good name, my love." He smiled wanly at her, and Liyana knew he was smiling at Bayla. She tried not to feel a pang at the word "love."

"They would trust me," Maara said. "But I cannot use magic while the vessel remains. For though I control the limbs, she retains primacy." She slapped her thighs hard enough to bruise them.

"Yet another reason you should talk to Raan," Liyana said.

"Yet another reason she should vacate this body," Maara said.

Liyana felt Bayla sigh. *Tell Maara she needs to work with her vessel.* Stumbling over the words, Liyana repeated this. She didn't dare ask what this meant for herself.

Maara narrowed her eyes. "Was that truly Bayla?"

Does she want me to share about the time the scorpion became besotted with the butterfly? Liyana repeated this as well. *Once, in the days when death was new—*

"Very well," Maara interrupted. "I will speak with the vessel." She closed her eyes.

The tent fell silent.

Liyana wanted to talk to Bayla. She searched for the words and failed. She glanced at Korbyn, wishing he would speak and break the silence. She tried to remember the last thing he'd said to her, not Bayla. She wished she could hear him laugh again. "Your clan will be happy to see you," Liyana ventured. It wasn't much of a conversation starter, but at least it was something.

Korbyn shrugged. "Perhaps. They were fond of this vessel."

"Oh." Liyana lowered her eyes and watched Maara, who lay silently in her blankets with her eyes closed. "But you didn't know."

"That doesn't make it right," Korbyn said.

After waiting another half hour, they tied the unresponsive Maara to a horse and continued on. There were still several more days of travel ahead of them before they would reach the oasis where Liyana had first met Korbyn. From there it would be several more days to Yubay—if her clan was even there.

Would you like to see where they are? Bayla asked softly. *If you wish, I will feed you the magic.*

For a moment Liyana was robbed of a reply. She never expected such a kind offer from Bayla.

They are my clan as well.

After a moment Liyana felt the magic fill her. She let her awareness spill outward. She felt Gray Luck moving in a steady stride beneath her. She felt the sand and the wind and the heat. She felt the plants scattered across the sand, and the insects that hid in their centers. She touched the birds of prey and the rodents. She brushed past the sky serpents as they soared above. She shied away from the sandstorms with their howling hearts. Fueled by the goddess's magic, she reached much further than ever before. All the while, the tether to her body continued to stretch.

As she spread, she became aware of the people: their souls pulsing all over the desert, grouped in areas where she also felt water. She touched the oasis where her family had camped and where she had left the silver bells—and she touched the souls of hundreds of people. Her clan!

Retreating back to her body, she felt Gray Luck still plodding along beneath her, and the sun battering her skin again. *That was the oasis where I was left behind. Only my clan uses that oasis.* She'd see them soon!

You were left behind? There was shock in Bayla's voice.

You didn't come. Liyana tried not to let the pain of the memory seep into her thought. Her clan had done what they'd believed was best. *They thought you'd rejected me and that you'd forgive them if they exiled me.*

I would never—

How were they to know? You didn't come. She tried not to sound as if she blamed Bayla.

She felt Bayla churn inside her. *The traitor Mulaf must be stopped.*

I want the same, Liyana said.

You are suggesting a truce between us.

Yes.

Bayla was silent. At last she said, *Tell me about our clan. It has been many years since I was one of you.*

As they rode, Liyana told stories about her childhood, about Jidali and Aunt Sabisa, about her cousins and her parents, about Talu and the chief and chieftess, about the master weaver, about the goatkeepers and the herds. Bayla continued to prod her for more and more, and so Liyana fed her memory after memory.

When she was midstory about the time she and Jidali had raced the weaver's boys up the date palm trees, Raan woke with a jerk. She sat bolt upright, and the startled mare reared back. Raan was tossed forward into the horse's neck. Korbyn slid off his horse and grabbed the reins of Raan's horse. He steadied her.

Sitting upright with ease, Raan dusted the horsehairs off her robes—or more accurately, Maara did. Raan hadn't had much physical control in days. This had to be Maara. "I hate horses," Maara commented.

"Did you speak to your vessel?" Korbyn asked.

Maara sighed. "She is alarmingly like me." The goddess did not meet Liyana's eyes. Instead she focused on her horse's ears. "Tonight she and I will attempt to reach the other clans together."

At dusk they pitched the tent and tended to the horses. Once all was set, Maara lay down inside the tent, and Liyana and Korbyn joined her.

"You two aren't going to stare at me the whole time, are you?" Maara asked. "Because that might make it difficult to focus."

Maara, you should allow the vessel to have primary control of the body while you draw power from the lake. Channel it to the vessel. Surprisingly, this allows you to draw more power with less fatigue since you do not have to hold the body simultaneously.

It does? Liyana asked. She knew she was more powerful with Bayla, but for Bayla to be more powerful with her . . .

Bayla's voice was so soft that Liyana could barely sense it. *It has been my observation that we are more effective together than not. Quit wallowing in self-satisfaction, and repeat my instructions.*

Liyana obeyed, and Maara closed her eyes. Her back arched and then spasmed, and then her eyes popped open. "Oh, oh, I can feel my legs! And my fingers and toes!" Raan.

Liyana squeezed her hand. "Welcome back, Raan."

Raan smiled at both of them. "Walk me through what I'm supposed to do."

"Maara will fill you with magic," Liyana said, "and you use that to spread yourself. You don't even need to enter a trance! You're going to love it. It's a tremendous feeling."

Raan rolled her eyes. "Korbyn, explain it, please. Clearly."

Korbyn talked her through what she should envision. She'd be expanding her consciousness exactly as Liyana had done to locate the Goat Clan.

"You can do it," Liyana said. "Just make sure you maintain

awareness of your body." She tucked blankets around Raan and propped up her head so she'd be comfortable. "Do you want to eat first? Cactus? Baked rat? Tuber cakes?"

"As mouthwateringly tempting as all that sounds, no," Raan said. "I want to get this over with. I'm not supposed to be mentally wandering the desert. It's unnatural."

"You sound like Pia," Liyana said. She meant to say it lightly, but she couldn't say Pia's name without her voice cracking. Oyri never had the chance to speak with Pia and know how amazing her vessel truly was.

"Let's do this," Raan said. She closed her eyes.

Liyana watched Raan's chest rise and fall in a slow, even rhythm. Korbyn leaned back and rested his eyes. Liyana supposed he had the right idea. There was nothing for them to do but wait. *Bayla?*

Yes, vessel?

I told you about me and my clan. What about you?

There was a pause. *I do not know what you mean.*

Tell me about yourself.

She felt Bayla's reaction: startled at first and then a rush of pleasure. *I have so many memories,* the goddess mused.

Pick your favorite.

Bayla told her of the time she saved a chief and chieftess's son over a thousand years ago. One week before he should have been born, his heart quit. It had not formed properly. And so Bayla used magic to finish its growth, but because his body had died, there was no soul in his tiny, unborn body. So she reached into the Dreaming and retrieved a soul for him. With his reincarnated soul, he became the very first magician.

She followed this with another tale of divine heroism, and then another.

Korbyn said he makes you laugh, Liyana said. *Tell me about a time that you laughed.*

Once, Korbyn masqueraded as a donkey. He attended an assembly of the deities with an ass's head on his shoulders. Such a gathering is a rare, solemn event. We create a vast amphitheatre in the Dreaming made of stone steps with cascades of desert flowers and the music of hundreds of birds. Speeches traditionally wax poetic. Every time one of us said something he considered untrue or arrogant, he brayed. I laughed until my sides hurt. It also became one of the most productive gatherings we have ever had.

Raan's eyes popped open. "I lost her."

"Raan?" Liyana asked.

She sat up. Liyana felt her heart constrict. *She's not Raan.*

"I lost her," Maara repeated.

Chapter Twenty-Six

Maara buried her face in her hands.

Liyana couldn't move. She felt as if her blood had frozen in her body. She tried to speak, but her vocal cords wouldn't respond. She licked her lips and tried again. "She's gone?"

"Believe me, it was not my intent, and if you suggest—"

"Liyana suggested nothing," Korbyn said. He placed his hands on Maara's shoulders. "I am to blame for not preparing her better. She had never successfully touched the lake. I thought if we removed that element . . ."

"She spread across the desert, and she didn't stop. I felt her . . . dissolve."

Liyana crossed her legs and closed her eyes. *Feed me magic, Bayla. I am going to find her.*

You could lose yourself as well.

I didn't before. Besides, then you'd get what you want, right? Everybody wins. Feed me as much magic as you can. Please.

As you wish.

The magic roared inside her like a wall of water crashing over her and filling her mind and her body with its sweet touch. She anchored herself inside her body and then she let the magic stretch her.

Tethered to her body, she skimmed over the desert. She knew what she had felt earlier in the day, so she was looking for anything different. A whisper maybe. A wind that blew in the wrong direction. She didn't know what a lost soul would feel like—or worse, lost pieces of a soul.

She headed southwest toward the Dog Clan. In the distance, she felt an oasis. She aimed for it. Closer, she could feel that it was filled with the souls of people. She spread herself throughout the clan.

Listening, she heard a voice, the familiar tone of Raan's voice. She wrapped herself around it. Now that she knew the feel of Raan's soul, she spotted its pieces more easily. She gathered them together like pulling droplets of water out of the earth. The pieces adhered to each other. Soon there was a swirling vortex.

Come back with me, Liyana thought at the swirl that was Raan.

She felt sorrow oozing from the stray bits of thought.

Maara understands now, Liyana told her. *You can return to your body.*

Softly Bayla said, *I don't know if she can. Her grasp on her body was already failing. She has lost the feel of it.*

You have to try, Liyana thought at Raan.

She's whole now, Bayla said. Her voice was gentle. *You have helped her. Now it's time to let her go to the Dreaming.*

No! Come back with me, Raan. I'll guide you. You can do this. I won't give up on you.

The swirl that was Raan spun faster, knitting tighter together. Raan then sped across the desert, leaving behind the oasis. Liyana sped after her toward the mountains.

Raan, no! Liyana said.

Let her go, Bayla said. *She feels the pull of the Dreaming.*

But she doesn't want to die!

If you follow her, you will be pulled in too, Bayla said. *Your hold on yourself already weakens.*

Liyana slowed. She felt her link to her body. It vibrated like a silk thread pulled taut. She was spread too thin, too far. Soon the magic would fail like it had when she'd stretched herself to see the empire's encampment. *I can't give up!*

Once, there was a fish who learned how to walk on land. He crawled out of the ocean and onto the beach. He explored the meadows and the forests. After many, many days and nights of walking, he crossed the plains and entered the desert. A raven stopped him at the border and said, "You appear lost, little fish with legs." And the fish replied, "Oh no, I am home." And so the first lizard entered the desert.

What is your point? Liyana asked. Raan's soul was flowing faster toward the mountains. She could sense her as if she were a bird against the backdrop of the sunset.

Raan has moved on. Let her go.

Liyana felt Bayla's soul fold around her. Pulled, she retreated into her body. The excess magic fell away as Liyana huddled within her own skin. She curled into a ball and cried. After a little while, she felt Korbyn curl himself against her and wrap his arms tight around her.

Bayla was silent.

*   *   *

None of them spoke much as they journeyed on.

With three of them capable of magic, they did not need to stop for longer than it took to rest themselves and the horses. The miles flew by.

After only two days of travel, Liyana saw the silhouette of the oasis, black against the bleached blue sky. Soon she saw the outline of tents. She increased her horse's speed to a trot and then to a canter. Sand bloomed under Gray Luck's hooves. The others followed.

As she got closer, she saw people between the familiar outline of tents. She felt her mouth go dry, and she drank in the view. Goats bleated. She saw children run to the edge of camp and point. By the time she was close enough to see faces, men and women had joined the children.

"Mother! Father!"

Liyana dismounted before Gray Luck halted. She landed on her knees, and then she scrambled to her feet and ran toward her parents. She ripped off her head cloth so they could see her face.

"Liyana!" Jidali shoved through the adults and ran across the sand. She dropped to the ground in front of him, and her little brother leaped into her arms. "Is it you? Is it really, really you?"

"It's me," Liyana said.

Jidali hugged her hard.

She heard a moan sweep through the clan like the wind. A few wailed. Others turned away. *Vessel, perhaps you should tell them that I am here as well,* Bayla suggested.

"Not just me, though," Liyana said. "Bayla is inside me."

Talu elbowed and pushed to the front. She fell to her knees in front of Liyana and touched her face. "My goddess? How . . . how is this possible?"

"I have a story to tell you, to tell all of you," Liyana said. She rose to her feet. "But first, this is Korbyn, god of the Raven Clan, and this . . . this is Maara, goddess of the Scorpion Clan."

Chieftess Ratha approached. "We bid you welcome to the Goat Clan. Join us for the sharing of tea." She signaled to several boys in the group. "We will tend to your mounts." Ger and two other boys ran up to claim their horses.

Wordlessly Father embraced her. She buried her face in his shoulder and breathed him in. She felt as if she were inhaling every memory of her childhood.

SARAH BETH DURST

"Good to see you found our pack," Mother said.

Jidali tugged on her sleeve. "Did you use my knife?"

"Your knife saved our goddess," Liyana said. She took his hand, and he squeezed with all the strength in his small fingers. "Come, I'll tell you everything."

Jidali skipped next to her. "We found your bells! We buried them under the largest palm tree for your funeral. I got to say the burial prayer. I didn't miss any words!"

"Um, that's wonderful, Jidali."

Several people wanted to touch her as she passed, as if to reassure themselves that she was not a dream. A few bowed. Others kept their distance, as if she were dangerous. The master weaver blocked her children with her broad skirts.

Liyana was swept toward the council tent. Blankets were laid outside in the shade of the tent walls, and tea was served. Korbyn and Maara sat on either side of her, and Jidali positioned himself by her feet and would not move.

Fanning out around her, the clan quieted.

All of a sudden she could not think of what to say. Squeezing her hand, Korbyn smiled encouragingly. For once, she was certain that he was seeing her, not Bayla.

Begin with this, Bayla said. *On the day she was to die . . .*

"On the day she was to die," Liyana said, "a vessel woke to see the sun. . . ."

Chapter Twenty-Seven

With Bayla, Liyana filled the well. Korbyn caused the dates to ripen. Maara drew various rodents, snakes, and birds to the camp for meat. After feasting with the clan, Korbyn and Maara were led to guest tents, and Liyana was given her old sleeping roll in her family's tent. She collapsed into her blankets and was asleep instantly.

She woke to the smell of flatbread cooking on the family fire pit, and for an instant she thought she'd dreamed it all. *I missed that bread,* Bayla said.

Liyana sat up.

"Ooh, you're awake!" Aunt Sabisa bustled toward her. "You have been using your hair as a nest for rodents and birds." She whipped out a metal-toothed comb.

Liyana shrank back. "Isn't that the goats' comb?"

"You have goat's hair." Aunt Sabisa stabbed it into the thick of Liyana's hair and yanked. "Hold still. Bayla will thank me for this."

Please thank her for me, Bayla said, amused.

Relaying the message, Liyana winced as Aunt Sabisa tugged on a clump of hair. "Are Korbyn and Maara awake?"

"Both went into the chief and chieftess's tent an hour ago."

Liyana stood up with the brush dangling from a clump of hair. "I should join them!"

"Sit down, Liyana, I'm not finished. You do not need to join them. You talked enough yesterday. Let them speak their fill."

Out of habit Liyana obeyed. She felt Bayla's amusement bubble inside her. *Clearly,* Liyana said, *you have never tried disobeying Aunt Sabisa.*

"Is it true what you said last night?" Aunt Sabisa asked. "She is inside of you?" She wiggled the brush through a thick snarl.

"Yes, of course," Liyana said. "I wouldn't lie to you."

"Except for the time you sneaked a slice of my pie."

"I was six."

"And the time you borrowed my finest scarf without asking."

"Four years old."

"And when you let the goats out of the pen."

"Maybe a bit more recently," Liyana said, "but in fairness, it was an accident."

"And then there was the incident with the chickens. . . ."

Bayla's laughter felt like a spring of bubbles. *You are beginning to lose credibility with me.* Liyana realized she had never heard her goddess laugh.

"I have never lied about anything important," Liyana said, smiling.

Aunt Sabisa laid down the brush. "Then do not lie to me now. Am I dying?"

Liyana could only gape at her. "You . . . you look well. Have you been sick?"

"I have pains." She held up her hand, and she demonstrated closing her fingers to her thumb. Her hand shook, and the thumb barely grazed her other fingertips. "I suspect it is age, but I worry it is more."

Look inside her, Bayla said. Liyana felt a tendril of magic flow into her. She held Aunt Sabisa's shoulders and let her awareness wash over her aunt.

What do I look for? Liyana asked.

Anything that is not your aunt. You will know it when you see it.

Liyana swept through Aunt Sabisa's body. Blood flowed through the veins. Some veins had thick walls. One had lumps. But the stream still continued through. Her lungs had flecks inside, like soot from the fire. Liyana snaked down her intestines.

Suddenly Liyana flinched at the touch of coldness from within Aunt Sabisa. A spiderlike spread of cold flesh clung to the insides of her intestines. *What is it?*

Death, eating her.

Liyana shrank back from it. *How do I get rid of it?* She circled around the spiderlike lump and saw that little tentacles stretched over the whole surface of the intestines. Minuscule bits circulated in her bloodstream.

It is not in its nature to vanish, Bayla said. *Magic can only encourage what nature allows. I am deeply sorry, Liyana.*

But there must be something! She's your clan! First, Pia and Fennik. Then Raan. And now Aunt Sabisa. What was the point of having deities and knowing magic if you were still helpless when it mattered? For a moment, that question filled Liyana, and she couldn't breathe.

We might be able to slow its growth, Bayla said, her voice gentle in Liyana's head, *but we'll have to repeat the treatment daily. It is an expenditure of time and effort we can ill afford now.*

Aunt Sabisa kissed her on the forehead. "It is good to know. You know how I like to plan ahead. Your mother has laid out appropriate clothes for you. You'd do best to wear them."

"Aunt Sabisa . . ." She hadn't said anything!

"Goddess or not, I know my Liyana. Your eyes give you away every time. You care too much, my dear. And now you shoulder the weight of the world." She shook her head. "Bayla, take care of our girl. She is a gift to all of us."

Before Liyana could think what to say, Aunt Sabisa swept out of the tent.

Remarkable woman, Bayla said.

Liyana did not reply. Feeling numb, she dressed in the clothes that Mother had left: a paneled skirt and an embroidered blouse. She had the blouse halfway over her head when she realized that these were Mother's wedding clothes, the finest she owned. Gingerly she removed her arms from the sleeves. She laid the blouse back on the blanket and looked for her own clothes.

"Put it on," Mother said from the front of the tent.

Liyana jumped and scooped up the blouse. "But I'll ruin them. These aren't for travel."

"You may change before you mount. But today, as they prepare to leave, to fight, even to die, the clan will see you as they should. They need that."

Your mother is wise, Bayla said. *You would be wise to heed her.*

Liyana put on the blouse. Mother arranged her hair so that it fell around her in waves. "No braids, I think. We'll let them see your full glory. You are not a child anymore, and they must realize that if you are to lead us to battle."

"Me? But Korbyn—"

"The trickster is not ours, and he must return to his own clan to lead them."

She hadn't thought about that, but Mother was right. He'd delivered her to her clan, and he had to gather his. She felt cold at the thought of proceeding without Korbyn. "But . . ."

"Bayla, speak to her," Mother said.

You must be as a goddess, Bayla said. *The clan must see me in you.*

Whatever reaction Liyana showed in her face must have been enough to satisfy Mother. Mother nodded and said, "Eat the flatbread and then walk the camp. Do not pack. Do not dirty your hands or your dress. Approve or disapprove of what you see. But be seen."

Mother left. Liyana helped herself to the flatbread that cooled by the fire. It was Aunt Andra's recipe with roasted dates. Each bite melted in her mouth and triggered a hundred memories of birthdays and anniversaries and other celebrations for which Aunt Andra had made her special bread. Liyana savored the flatbread, but it sat as a lump in her stomach.

I will help you, Bayla said. Her swirling thoughts wrapped around Liyana like a blanket. With the goddess whispering to her, Liyana walked out of the tent to face her clan.

Bayla coached her, and on behalf of the goddess Liyana greeted men, women, and children whom she had known for her entire life. As Bayla fed her words, Liyana added her knowledge of each person. Eventually the starry-eyed looks of her people drove her back to her family tent. She found Korbyn and Maara there.

Maara was deep in a trance.

"She's contacting other clans with deities," Korbyn said. "I have asked your chief to send out runners to nearby clans without deities. Word is spreading."

"What about your clan?" Liyana asked.

"After the midday sun has passed, I'll leave," he said.

Liyana felt a pang, but she nodded. She had no right to ask him to stay. "You'll rejoin us?"

"That *is* the point," Korbyn said, not unkindly.

She searched for something else to say. "Do you need help?"

"With my own clan? They'll be intrigued by the idea of the clans stopping a massive army." His tone was light, but she thought he looked worried.

"You don't think we can do it?" Liyana asked. She had been so caught up with Bayla and then Raan and then her clan. . . . She hadn't stopped to think about the impossibility of their efforts. Even with the united strength of all the clans, the empire's army would still vastly outnumber them.

He hesitated before he answered. "I think we will need to be tricky."

The empire does not have deities, Bayla said. *We will even the numbers.*

"If they were to attack with full strength . . . it would be ten to one, not in our favor," Korbyn said. "We have to hope that they will not. If they underestimate us, we may have a chance." He did not sound certain.

Liyana paced through the tent. She touched the tarp walls, walked between her family's sleeping rolls, and picked up and then put down her father's favorite teapot. Being here didn't reassure her. She'd thought it would have. But soon all of this would be packed, and they would be on their way to face terrible odds. She thought of Pia and wondered if she was right about how ephemeral they all were.

"Done," Maara said, opening her eyes. "It is time for me to rejoin my own clan." She stood and stretched. "I will see you soon, Bayla. And Liyana."

Liyana nodded.

Without any further discussion or any emotional farewell, Maara left the tent, and Korbyn and Liyana were alone. Or nearly alone.

"I have never liked good-byes," Korbyn said. He leaned forward, and Liyana quickly turned her head. His lips brushed her cheek. She couldn't bring herself to meet his eyes. Her chest felt tight, and it was hard to breathe. "Take care of each other," he said.

Liyana nodded again.

She listened as Korbyn left the tent. Outside were the sounds of the clan packing the tents and preparing the goats for travel. Orders were shouted, and people whistled and laughed and chattered as if this were a trip to the fair.

He is mine, Bayla reminded her. *This body may be yours. But Korbyn is mine.*

Chapter Twenty-Eight
The Emperor

The emperor drank water from his canteen as he surveyed the array of clan tents. He didn't taste the water. The view was as bad as his scouts had reported. At least thirty clans had staked out sites, with more joining them every day.

He had marched his army across this wasteland without seeing one desert person. But here, a short march away from the mountains, he found them waiting for him, blocking his way to the mountains. He had no doubt that if he tried to bypass them, they would adjust accordingly. Their presence here was not an unfortunate coincidence. They were here to stop him.

He wondered if Liyana was with them, or if Bayla was.

"I had hoped to avoid any deaths," the emperor said.

General Xevi grunted. "Your Imperial Majesty has inherited your father's optimism. It is an admirable trait."

"But not a realistic one, you believe." He had hoped that during the journey, his generals would learn to trust him. The emperor caught himself before he sighed. Around them, soldiers were watching him for his reaction. He smoothed his face to project unconcerned interest.

General Akkon nodded his agreement.

"We outnumber them ten to one," General Xevi said. "As you ordered, we have allowed their scouts to return unharmed. By now they must know the size of our force."

The emperor heard the disapproval in his voice and ignored it. He had hoped the sheer size of his army would cause the clans to disperse. But instead the clans had pitched their camps as if this were a joyous festival. "Gentlemen, your recommendations," the emperor said.

"Cavalry," General Akkon said.

He was a man of few words. General Xevi was not. "Indeed. It will show our intent and our power. We hold the remainder of the army in reserve to emphasize our superiority, and we trounce the savages with one elite force."

"The 'savages' could win," the emperor pointed out.

"Extremely unlikely," General Xevi said. "We have superiority of armament and training. If they had chosen their battle in an area of topographical variation, then I would say they'd have the geographical advantage due to their familiarity. But a flat plain? Their choice of location reveals their inexperience with battle tactics."

"They have resources beyond sheer numbers," the emperor said.

General Akkon grunted. "Bedtime stories."

"Might I remind you of the horses, as well as the worm that terrorized our finest?" His pet magician had not captured all the deities. The ones who still remained in the Dreaming would not be a problem, but a few had reached their clans successfully. Add in the ones who escaped. . . .

"Luck," General Akkon said. "A localized abnormality."

"Look at these people," General Xevi said. He waved his hand at the clans. His jeweled rings flashed in the glaring sun. "They are barely above animals, scratching their lives out of the sand. If they had access to special powers, they would have built cities! We would be facing an advanced culture with civilized tools and weaponry. As it is we are facing the equivalent of our ancestors. Let us show them what the modern man can do."

"One strike with one elite force," General Akkon said.

"Yes!" General Xevi said. "Shatter their naive belief in their own power. Teach them what it means to stand in the way of the Crescent Empire."

The emperor thought about Liyana and pictured her as he'd first seen her, walking into his tent as if she owned it. He hadn't seen her escape, but he'd heard about it. She had ridden on the back of that monster, the salt worm. She must have been magnificent. He wished he could have seen it. After the chaos had died down, he had not ordered pursuit. Looking at the gathering of clans, he wondered if that had been an error.

Mulaf had seemed so certain that it was Liyana, not Bayla. But Mulaf was not available now to lend his expertise. He had been unconscious ever since they entered the desert. The doctors had hopes for his recovery—they reported moments of alertness and said he often twitched unlike any coma victim they had ever seen—but they could not identify the cause of his ailment. In his moments of clarity, he was said to be in good spirits, even giddy. Regardless, the man was useless in the moment in which the emperor needed him. The emperor had no one of the desert to mediate. Still he had to try.

"We will parlay," the emperor said.

"They will not listen," General Akkon said.

General Xevi nodded vigorously and opened his mouth to expand on that sentiment.

The emperor interrupted him. "Slaughtering them is a poor welcome to the empire for our future citizens. Send messengers to issue invitations. Invite one representative from each clan."

He returned to his tent to prepare his speech for the representatives, but he imagined saying each phrase to Liyana.

❋　❋　❋

One by one the messengers filed into the emperor's tent. Each held a folded parchment. Each handed the parchment to the emperor, bowed, and retreated without ever meeting the emperor's eyes. A few sported bruises and broken noses. One limped. None spoke.

The emperor accepted each parchment and thanked each messenger for his service. He then opened it, read the single line printed or scrawled on it, and laid it in a pile. Finishing, he bowed his head.

"Your Imperial Majesty?" General Xevi ventured. "What is the response?"

He swept the parchments off his desk with a swat of his hand and stood up so fast that he tipped over his chair. It crashed backward, and the gilded edges cracked. He stalked to the back of the tent and stared at the broken diamond statues that Liyana had left behind. Liyana had destroyed nearly all of them, even those without deities inside them. Resourceful woman. And stubborn. Like her clans. He'd kept the broken statues to ensure that he did not forget that. He couldn't underestimate her or the clans.

He heard the elderly generals bend to scoop the parchments off the floor. Each was stamped or marked with the symbol of a clan: wolf, silk, horse, raven, scorpion, wind, sun, snake, tortoise . . . Each held one sentence: *You will not enter the mountains.*

"We must proceed with the aim to minimize casualties," the emperor said. These were Liyana's people, not his enemies.

General Akkon grunted. "Cavalry. Or fifth squadron."

Turning to face them, the emperor shook his head. "You misunderstand me. The only way to minimize casualties is to ensure that we win the war, not merely one battle. We must convince them of the impossibility of opposing us now and in future generations. This victory must be swift, decisive, and thorough."

"Merciful brutality," General Xevi said. "Your father would have approved."

He thought again of Liyana and wondered what she would say. "I am not doing this for him," the emperor said. "Spread the word. We attack at dawn."

Chapter Twenty-Nine

Liyana woke before dawn. She burst out of her tent and scanned the horizon. Black shadows, the tents of the emperor's army, still filled the eastern view. Gray blue, the predecessor of the dawn, tinted the east. She saw a flash of distorted stars overhead—a sky serpent twisting in the sky. Ever since the clans and the army had pitched their tents at the foot of the forbidden mountains, the sky serpents had circled overhead. Liyana hoped that they would convince the emperor to retreat. But still he sent his messengers and made his demands.

Her heart raced, and she didn't know why. *Bayla. There's something wrong. Something woke us. I don't know what it is.*

Bayla was silent for a moment, and then she said, *I do not see the emperor's guards.*

Guards typically paced the perimeter of the emperor's camp. Liyana had gotten used to seeing them, a distant audience, as the clans went about the business of establishing their base. She had also become used to the sounds of the large camps as they drifted across the desert—their horses, their cooks, their hunting dogs, their endless practice drills. It was never quiet. Until now.

Liyana accepted the magic from Bayla as easily as catching a ball, and she flowed across the desert to the emperor's encampment. She expected to touch the souls of the sleeping soldiers. . . . But she felt no one. *Bayla, they're gone!*

An army that size cannot vanish. Check further out.

Keeping herself tethered to her body, Liyana sped beyond the camp. She swept the distant horizon, and she circled the clans' tents. And then she found them: fanned out on either side of the clans' tents. The army had split into two forces. Each soldier was shoulder to shoulder with another. Row after row of them marched toward the clans' tents as if to squeeze the desert people between them.

Pulling back, Liyana sucked in air to shout, "Attack! Coming from the north and south!" She ran through the camp, sounding the alarm.

Around her, the men, women, and children from her clan poured out of the tents. As per the plan, young children were shuttled by older children to the center tent. Also in the center was the clan's precious water supply. Circling the children were those too elderly or infirm to be nimble. They armed themselves with spears and stakes, long-reach weapons that would slow anyone who broke through the outer defenses. All the able-bodied men and women rushed to the edge of camp. Liyana knew this was repeated in other clans with minor variations. For example, in Korbyn's clan, the children laid traps around their tents, and the elders of Maara's clan dipped every weapon in scorpion poison.

Half the clans clustered to the north of camp, and half to the south. Readying their weapons, they waited for the armies to appear. Liyana pushed through the warriors, looking for Korbyn. His clan had dispersed and was distributing a variety of "surprises," including throwing knives dipped in snake venom and ropes made of tough-as-wire silk that could trip horses. Everyone had a knife, sword, or bow—though as prepared as they all looked, Liyana knew that most had never used a weapon on a person.

She found Korbyn on the north side. Moving forward, the army stirred a cloud of sand. Each soldier was clad in armor, and each held a weapon with practiced ease. Softly she said to him, "If the soldiers reach us . . ."

Korbyn nodded. "We won't let them."

He reached out and took her hand, and together they retreated to Korbyn's tent. The others deities were already waiting for them—eleven total, including Sendar and Maara. As Liyana and Korbyn entered, they all positioned themselves in a circle on blankets.

"Since Liyana does not need to be in a trance to work magic, she will coordinate our efforts," Korbyn informed the others.

A few deities whispered to one another.

Sendar scowled. "I will not obey a—"

Do not prove yourself to be a horse's ass, Sendar, Bayla said. *Out of respect for me, you will cooperate.* Liyana repeated her words, and Sendar fell quiet. Other objections were similarly quashed, primarily by Bayla.

Korbyn squeezed Liyana's hand. "Be clever, and be quick."

Around her, the deities closed their eyes and fell into trances. Liyana felt Bayla disappear for a moment and then return with the familiar flood of magic. Using it, Liyana expanded throughout the tent. Beside her were the souls of the deities. Each flickered like a ball of lightning. She spread further, blanketing the camps of the clans, and then she crossed the desert to touch the frontlines of the two halves of the emperor's army.

Circling around the deities, Liyana whispered in the ears of four of them, "Water. Summon water to the surface twenty feet in front of the armies. Create sinkholes and quicksand. Oyri, draw your worms to the water." The chosen deities pulled the water up from the bedrock. It weakened the sand. Patches of quicksand blossomed in the path of the emperor's soldiers. Liyana flitted from patch to patch, widening them.

She ordered four of the deities to stir the winds, and she directed them toward the frontlines. Sandstorms whipped toward the soldiers. Wolves howled within the storms. Guided by Liyana, the deities blocked the storms from touching the desert people and channeled them through the ranks of the emperor's army.

Maara called the scorpions from the surrounding desert, and the Snake Clan deity summoned the snakes. Numbering in the thousands, they scurried over the desert floor and swarmed the feet and ankles of the soldiers.

From deep below the ground, massive worms moved through the rocks, churning up the earth beneath the feet of the army. The sand shook and tossed rocks as the worms attacked the water. Some burst through the surface. Liyana heard the desert people cheer, and she heard the soldiers scream.

Leaving the deities, Liyana bolted out of the tent. She looked across the camp to see her people side by side, watching. They had not moved. Across the desert, the army was lost in a writhing mass of sand.

"Retreat," Liyana whispered at the army, knowing that even if she had shouted, the emperor couldn't have heard her over the sounds of dying. "Please."

She sent her consciousness out again.

At last she sensed the bulk of the army pulling away. She ducked back into the tent. "Hold the line. Do not let the water seep farther. Keep the scorpions and the snakes here." She guided each deity, drawing a ring around the clans' camp.

Breaking his concentration, Sendar began to object. "We could defeat—"

"Do not chase them," Liyana ordered. "Keep the sandstorms high. But hold them." Controlled destruction would be more impressive and terrifying than chaotic annihilation, but there wasn't time to explain that to Sendar.

As the deities continued to pour more magic into the battle, the empire's soldiers ran from their ring of death.

Sendar opened his mouth again, and Liyana clapped her hand over it. "Silence, or I will silence you." As magic swirled inside her, Liyana meant every word. She felt Bayla's surprise, and she ignored it, keeping her eyes boring into Sendar's until he backed down.

As Sendar sank back into his trance, she threw her magic toward the armies to corral the winds. "So long as the emperor does not attempt to pass," she said to all the deities, "we will not harm them." It was the same bargain that the sky serpents had made long ago with the people of the turtle. Liyana bet that the emperor would understand her message.

*　*　*

All the clans celebrated.

Not a single warrior had been harmed, and not a single soldier from the empire had crossed the deities' defenses. As the celebrations stretched into the night, Liyana walked through the camps. She heard men and women swapping stories, and children chased each other in games as if they were at a fair. Everyone was outside under the stars. In several places, people were dancing. She heard music from various sections of the camps: flutes and drums and voices. People flowed from clan to clan, blurring the invisible boundaries between the camps until they felt like a single clan.

She wished she felt like joining them. But as the deities recovered, she'd used the quicksand pits to bury the empire's dead, and then she'd let the water disperse back into the bedrock. Without the moisture, the earth hardened above the bodies, and the wind swept the sand clean. Spread across the desert, she had felt it all happen. So many lives, ended.

She walked to the edge of the camp beyond the singing and the laughter, and she looked across the expanse to the emperor's camp. She didn't see the guards, but she saw movement between the tents. She imagined that they were dealing with their wounded— and with their fear.

"It isn't over," Korbyn said behind her.

Liyana jumped and then nodded. He was right. Though many had died, the empire's army still vastly outnumbered them. "They won't underestimate us again."

Maara was with him. "Did you see the size of that army? That was stamp-on-us-like-we-were-bugs size. Hardly underestimating us."

"The magician was not in the battle," Korbyn said.

Liyana nodded.

"One magician?" Maara snorted. "Most likely he stayed out of it because he knew *we* were here. Come, you two, celebrate with us." Swaying, she spread her arms wide.

Liyana studied her. She'd seen that look in Raan's eyes once, the first time they'd met. She noted that Maara held a waterskin. "The emperor won't leave easily," Liyana said. "He believes that the mountains hold the key to his people's salvation."

Maara shook her head. "Trust me. No one is sticking around to face us after that display! Whoo, did you see those worms? One of them swallowed a soldier whole." As if to emphasize her point, she took a deep swig from the waterskin.

That soldier could have been one of the ones who Liyana had seen in the emperor's encampment. She pictured the pinched cheeks and gaunt bodies. She wondered who the soldier had been there for—had he had a wife at home? Mother? Sister? Brother?

"I think you have had enough to drink," Korbyn said to Maara. "Sober yourself up or sleep it off."

Maara leveled a finger at him. "You used to be fun."

You have changed him, Bayla said to Liyana.

Because he cares about more than himself? He— She broke off her own thought. *I don't want to fight right now.* She rubbed her eyes. She felt sore inside and out. *There's been enough fighting.* And then she knew what she had to do.

Without speaking to any of the deities, including Bayla, Liyana walked away from the camp. She stopped when the voices and music and celebration faded into a blur. She was a quarter of the way to the emperor's camp. Bending over, she ripped off the white bottom ruffle of her mother's dress. She broke off a stalk from one of the dead desert plants, and she wrapped the ruffle around the top.

Following her, Korbyn caught her arm. "Liyana, they'll kill you."

"The emperor wanted to parlay."

"With all the clan chiefs," he said. "And that was before. Now—"

Liyana faced him. With his hand on her arm, he was close. His eyes bored into hers. She was aware of his lips and how they frowned at her, and she remembered how they felt on hers. She felt Bayla stir inside, swirling. *I have had enough fighting,* Liyana told her again before she could say a word. Out loud she said to Korbyn, "He'll speak to me."

Chapter Thirty

Liyana waved the white flag as she walked across the expanse toward the emperor's camp. After a while her arm ached, but she continued to hold it high. She didn't want to be riddled with arrows.

You do know what you're doing, I hope, Bayla said.

You can hope that, Liyana said.

Lowering the flag, she climbed over a cluster of rocks. She raised it up high and waved it once she reached the other side. She watched each step, veering around clumps of brittle grasses, in case not all of the snakes and scorpions had dispersed after the battle.

Ahead she saw the tents in the neat rows that she remembered. It looked as if the emperor had scooped up the encampment from its location on the border and then deposited it intact in the middle of the desert.

You may control this body, but I have a vested interest in its continued health, Bayla said. *I do not like the way you are recklessly endangering us.*

Guards gathered at the edge. She'd been seen.

I'd like to know what you plan to say to the emperor, Bayla said.

Last time she'd told him a story. This time there was no relevant story. No one had ever done what had happened here. She caught a glimpse of a glint out of the corner of her eye. She looked up and saw two sky serpents wheeling overhead. Stars reflected off their scales. She wondered what they thought of the battle. She hoped they knew the desert people were keeping their gods' bargain. *I plan to talk to him,* Liyana said.

More specifics, please. This is an important conversation. I'll feed you the words, and you will repeat them. We can't afford to risk—

No, Bayla. You don't understand the emperor.

Liyana felt the goddess swirl inside. *And you, girl of the Goat Clan, understand him, the emperor of the Crescent Empire?* Scorn tinged her voice.

Liyana approached the guards. *Yes, I think I do.*

The guards clutched their swords. One had a bow with an arrow leveled at her chest. Liyana continued to hold the white flag. "I am here to accept the offer to parlay with His Imperial Majesty," she said. "I come in peace, and I expect to be treated with hospitality."

One guard had a gash on his cheek. Clotted blood still dotted his face.

Liyana spread her arms out. "I am unarmed."

Except for the knife in your sash, Bayla commented. *Ah, you* do *have a plan!*

Could you please feed me some magic? Slowly, so as not to alarm the soldier, she reached one hand toward the wounded man's face. Flinching, he pressed the tip of his sword to her sternum. She felt the metal through the fabric, and she froze. Magic poured into her. Without moving, she expanded her awareness to encompass his wound. She encouraged the skin to knit together.

He healed.

He lowered the tip of his sword.

"I am not your enemy," Liyana said. "Take me to the emperor."

✻   ✻   ✻

Ringed by guards, Liyana was led through the camp. Other soldiers joined them as they marched, until she could see only uniforms in every direction. She kept her eyes straight ahead, and she gripped the truce flag so hard that the wood dented her skin.

At last the guards parted, and she saw the emperor's tent. It matched her memory of it exactly, and for an instant she felt like she had weeks ago, when she first insisted on an audience with the emperor and demanded that he leave.

You failed before, Bayla said.

I will not fail again, Liyana said. Flanked by guards, she strode into the tent. Inside, the soldiers blocked her, and she waited, unable to see the emperor through them.

One of the soldiers bowed low. "This desert woman approached under a flag of truce. She wishes to parlay." The soldiers parted, and she saw him. His eyes locked on hers, and she felt her heart lurch. She hadn't expected to feel . . . She didn't know what she felt.

The emperor rose from behind his ridiculous wooden desk. She spotted the circles under his eyes, so dark that they looked like the smudge of a thumbprint. "Liyana or Bayla?" he asked.

Lie, Bayla whispered. *Do not tell him about me!*

"Both," she said. "But you speak to Liyana."

"Leave us," the emperor ordered his guards.

Bowing, the guards exited the tent. The emperor studied her for a moment and then crossed to the pillows and sat. He poured tea into two chalices. *Now I see your plan,* Bayla said. *You will kill him with the sky serpent knife. Without its leader the army will leave.*

Liyana froze. *I did not come here to assassinate the emperor!*

His death would solve our problem, Bayla thought. *One death to save many. It is the sacrifice that vessels have made over the generations, willingly or not.*

Liyana sat across from the emperor and accepted one of the chalices.

"Your people killed many of my soldiers," the emperor said. "I did not expect that. Congratulations."

The tea tasted sour. She set it down. "Three other vessels were with me when I came into your camp. All of them are dead now, displaced by deities. I do not celebrate deaths, ours or yours."

"And that is why you are here," the emperor said. It was a statement, not a question. "We are thousands. You do not want this much blood on your hands."

Only one man needs to die, Bayla thought. *It could be done with magic, if you don't want blood on your hands. Slow his heart. Block his breath. You could make it painless.*

"Bayla wants me to kill you," Liyana said.

Liyana!

"She should," the emperor said without changing his expression. "I ordered her imprisonment with the intent of causing suffering to her clan."

"But you intended to save them—and me," Liyana said.

"Yes, I did," he said. "Without their deities the clans would have welcomed an alliance with the empire. We could have worked together to survive the drought. It was a brilliant plan. You undid it."

"I won't apologize for that," Liyana said.

A brief smile crossed his lips. "I do not expect you to, any more than I will apologize to you for trying to save my people."

"You're still trying," she pointed out. "You haven't left."

"We are healing from the attack," he said. "Our focus has not been on packing."

"But you don't intend to leave."

"Once, there was a mosquito who—" the emperor began.

Liyana reached over and touched his hand. Inside her, Bayla crowed, *Now!* and flooded magic into her body. The magic filled her, but Liyana let her hand simply rest on his. "I am not here as an enemy, even if that is what you are," she said. "You cannot enter the mountains, but I believe I can convince my people to supply rations to you so you and your army can return to your lands. We don't want war."

The emperor covered her hand with his. His hand was soft and warm. "It is too late for a simple peace. You saw the fear in the eyes of my people. If I do not find a way to defeat that fear, it will eat at us as surely as hunger." His lips quirked into a smile. "When you walked into my tent that day, I never expected you held the power to destroy an empire."

"I didn't have a goddess in me then," Liyana said.

"You don't need one," the emperor said. "You are powerful on your own."

She looked into his eyes. He had sorrow inside, more sadness than he should have had to hold. "If our people fight again, more will die," she said. "We have magic, but you have numbers. You don't want more blood on your hands, either. I know that."

"You presume to know me."

"I *do* know you. We are alike."

He was silent, staring into her eyes, and she found herself holding her breath. It was presumptuous of her. Not so long ago she would not have dreamed of uttering such a statement. But it felt true.

"Become my wife," he said.

She stared as all words fled her mind. It felt as if the world slowed and faded away beyond the tent. She heard a roar of wind. *You cannot,* Bayla said.

He leaned forward and very gently kissed her. His lips felt like a butterfly on her lips. He drew back, and she touched her lips with her fingertips.

"We can save our people by uniting our people," he said.

"We . . . my people . . ." It felt difficult to think, as if she had to swim through sand. "We value our freedom."

"You would have it," he said. "As empress you could ensure that your people retain the independence they need. You would be joining the empire as an equal nation, not a conquered one."

Bayla roared inside her. Caught off guard, Liyana fell into darkness. The swirl of Bayla's presence surrounded her, and Liyana fought her way back to feel her body. She blinked her eyes. She was lying on the blankets. The emperor bent over her, his face merely inches from hers. He clutched her shoulders. "Liyana? Liyana! Can you hear me?"

"You care," she said, wonder filling her voice. The look in his eyes . . .

He loosened his grip and rocked back. Raising his head, he waved to the guards. "All is well. You may leave us. Tell the doctors to return to the wounded." He bent back over Liyana. "Are you well? Was it her—Bayla?"

She nodded, and she felt tears spill out of her eyes onto her cheeks.

You cannot consider this! Bayla howled. *It is a betrayal of all we are! To choose this stranger, this outsider—*

He's no outsider! He is human! Even more, he dreams of the lake! Liyana rubbed her forehead as if that would help the howls inside her head. "I . . . don't want anyone else to die." She let him help her sit up. He cradled her against his shoulder. For an instant she let him comfort her. His arms felt safe.

"No more bloodshed," he said.

He wants to use you, Bayla hissed.

"And the lake?" Liyana asked. "You cannot enter the mountains. United or not, that must never happen. The sky serpents will attack."

He took a deep breath. "If you can bring water to the desert, then summoning it to a once-fertile land . . . You could bring magic to the empire through what is inside you. We will not need the mountains or the lake." Kneeling, he held both her hands in his. "Come to my empire, Liyana. Come save us."

I will not feed you magic to save our enemy, Bayla said.

Why must they be our enemy? Liyana asked. *They're people too!*

We are the turtle's people, Bayla said. *We are of the desert.*

Liyana felt Bayla swirl faster and faster like a sandstorm. She heard the rush of wind inside of her. *What are you afraid of?*

I am a goddess! I fear nothing! But Liyana saw a glimpse of a thought, one that Bayla did not intend for her to see. An image of a raven.

This isn't about the desert or our people, Liyana realized. *This is about Korbyn!*

Bayla swirled inside her. *I love him! And I felt you care for him, as he cares for you. You cannot be contemplating this . . . this abomination! You cannot make me leave him! You promised me this body!*

I cannot allow more people to die, not when I can prevent it, Liyana said. She had planned to sacrifice herself to save her people. This fate . . . He was intelligent, passionate, and handsome.

One day this body will be mine, Bayla said. *One day you will lose control, and you will lose yourself as Raan did. And I will destroy this man and his empire, and I will return to my true love. All the deities will join me, and all the clans will rise up with me.*

Liyana felt as if her breath had been stolen away. She felt the full force of her goddess's anger rising inside her. It threatened to engulf her, but she clung to her body as if to a tree in a windstorm.

The emperor cupped her face in his hand. "Liyana?"

She took a breath and then another. "Your Imperial Majesty..."

"Jarlath," he said. "My parents called me Jarlath. You may as well."

She liked the name. "Jarlath, I cannot marry you." He lowered his hand, and she caught it in hers. "She will not allow it." But Bayla could not control all of her, despite her threats. Liyana leaned forward and kissed the emperor.

Chapter Thirty-One

Liyana lost herself in the emperor's arms. She didn't hear Bayla inside her as anything more than a distant storm. She was aware of every inch of her skin, the way his hands felt on her back and the way his lips tasted. It felt like magic, or the reverse of magic, the way every thought drifted away until she was only here and now, only herself with Jarlath.

And then the moment shattered. "Your Imperial Majesty!"

Releasing him, she shot up to her feet. He rose more gracefully, and his face stilled into his stonelike emperor expression. "Mulaf." The name was a greeting, a reprimand, and a question all at once.

Mulaf laughed and clapped his hands like a toddler. "I did it! I have them!"

Jarlath frowned, and he slid his hand around Liyana's fingers. Liyana wondered if he did so consciously or not. She held his hand. "Clarify, please," he said.

"Inside!" Mulaf thumped his chest and crowed. "Out of gratitude for the kindness that the empire has shown me, I have come to sever our relationship."

Liyana, look at him, Bayla said.

The magician looked crazed. He wore the bed shirt of an ill man, and his hair was gnarled and uncombed. He walked in tight knots around the tent.

The emperor raised his voice. "Guards."

No one entered.

Look inside, Bayla urged.

Liyana absorbed a spurt of magic and spread out to touch the magician's soul. She felt a swirling vortex, sparking like lightning. Suddenly she was flung backward. Her body blew back across the tent and she smacked into the tarp wall.

"Guards!" Jarlath shouted. He raced to Liyana and crouched in front of her, blocking her from Mulaf. "What did you do?" he demanded.

"Take your army home, boy-emperor," Mulaf said. "I no longer need you to reach the lake."

They're inside him, Bayla said. Horror colored her voice. *The others . . . They're inside him!*

Liyana grabbed Jarlath, and he helped her to her feet. She

pulled out the sky serpent blade, and she stepped in front of him.

"Equals, remember?" Jarlath said. "You don't guard me, desert princess." He stepped beside her. He had his own knife in his hand.

"Dear child, I would never hurt you," Mulaf said to Liyana. "If not for you, I would never have known the possibilities." He held out his hand palm up and giggled. "Look!" Air swirled on his palm faster and faster, and a whirlwind bloomed. He tossed it upward. It fed on the air and grew larger and larger. He then spread his hands, and the tornado dispersed. The air stilled. "Don't fear me, child. I promised you freedom, and I will deliver it. You will call me your hero when this is through."

He cannot go to the lake, Bayla said.

Liyana felt as if the air stilled around her. *The lake . . . It's real?*

It is raw magic, the source of all magic in the world, Bayla said. *It is essential to us—without its magic in the world, we cannot exist outside the Dreaming. He cannot be allowed to tamper with it!*

"Bayla says you cannot go to the lake," Liyana said. She asked Bayla, *You knew the lake was real and did not tell me? All the gods knew and never told their people?*

Speak for me: The lake cannot be used as you and the emperor envision. You cannot control it. You cannot even touch it. A single drop will send your soul to the Dreaming, leaving your body an empty shell that will soon die. It is death water for mortals! Liyana repeated her warning.

"Don't worry your pretty little head," Mulaf said. "Using it was never my intent."

"We had an agreement, Mulaf," Jarlath said. He drew himself to his full height, towering over the magician. His voice was pitched low but it carried, full of authority and reproach.

"I apologize for deceiving you, Your Imperial Majesty," Mulaf said with a mocking bow, "but Bayla speaks the truth. Saving your people was never possible."

Jarlath looked as if he had been stabbed. His stone face broke. For an instant Liyana saw the true Jarlath—the boy behind the emperor's mask—who only wanted to save his people.

"Then what do you want with the lake?" Liyana asked.

Mulaf smiled. "I want to destroy it, of course. It is time for the gods to die."

Liyana felt her throat dry. Stunned, she could think of no words to say. Knife in his hand, the emperor lunged forward.

With a rush of wind, Mulaf knocked him backward. "This is courtesy only, Your Imperial Majesty. And you, Liyana. Leave here. Live your lives. Honor me in your stories."

Liyana helped Jarlath to his feet. "Our stories?"

"Stories are the way people understand the world," Mulaf said. "And I am about to give the people of the turtle a new world." He spread his arms, and wind whipped around him in a tight circle. It lifted him up. He rose into the air. "At my command the mountains will fall, the lake will be buried, and the gods will leave this world forever. A new era will begin!"

"Wait!" Liyana called. "Don't!"

He touched the roof of the tent, and the fabric disintegrated as his palms touched it, as if the threads had instantly aged. The cyclone lifted him through the hole toward the night sky and then swept forward, ripping through the tarp. Tearing through more tents, it gouged a crater in the hard sand.

Around the remnants of the tent, the emperor's guards were strewn in every direction. Jarlath knelt by one and pressed his fingers to his neck. "He's unconscious," Jarlath said. "Mulaf didn't kill them."

Only because it is quicker to cause sleep, Bayla said.

How many deities are inside of him? Liyana asked.

She felt Bayla shudder. *Six. Somayo of the Falcon Clan, Keleena of the Sparrow Clan, Vakeen of the Wolf Clan . . .*

The cyclone stretched into the sky as if it wanted to scrape the moon. Liyana felt her stomach clench, and she wanted to be sick. "The sky serpents will attack once he crosses into the mountains," she said to Jarlath. "You need to evacuate. Flee east as fast as you can."

The emperor shouted to the nearest alert soldier, "Mobilize the army! We have to retreat!" He strode over the inert bodies of his guards and began issuing orders.

We have to warn the clans, Liyana said. She ran after the cyclone, following the path of destruction left in Mulaf's wake.

Climb onto that horse, Bayla said.

Liyana veered toward a saddled horse. She scooped up his reins, and she flung herself into the saddle. The horse sidestepped and snorted. Liyana felt power flow into her. Bayla issued instructions: fill the lungs, stretch the muscles, pump the heart, dry the sweat. *And hang on.*

The horse thundered out of the camp and into the darkness. Liyana clung to his neck as he pelted the desert. She felt sand hit her face, and the wind slapped her. She poured magic into the horse's heart, lungs, and legs. He ran faster. As the cyclone swerved, she passed it. She sent more strength into the horse's muscles, erased his fatigue, and urged him even faster.

In the clans' camps, the desert people were fleeing the approaching cyclone. It was headed for the mountains, straight through the camp. Grabbing children and animals, they abandoned the tents and ran. Liyana found Korbyn and Sendar in the center of it all, shouting orders. Slowing, Liyana leaped off the horse. She then used a burst of magic to encourage the empire's horse to flee to safety.

"The emperor's magician, the one who kidnapped the deities . . . He has six deities inside him." Liyana gasped between words, and she rested her hands on her knees. "He is headed for the mountains. He wants to destroy the lake."

"Without the lake, magic cannot exist here," Korbyn said.

Without the lake, we cannot remain here, Bayla said.

"We must stop him," Sendar said grimly. He strode forward,

hands outstretched, as if he would rend the cyclone from the earth. Liyana chased after him. Korbyn followed her.

"Sendar!" Liyana said.

He is stronger than six, Bayla said, *as you are stronger than one.*

The cyclone stretched toward the dark sky, smudging the stars. A few yards from the churning wind, Sendar halted. He entered a trance.

"We can't win on sheer magic!" Liyana shouted to him. "He's too powerful! Sendar, retreat!" Wind battered against her, and she shielded her face as she pressed forward, trying to reach Sendar.

Before them, the cyclone collapsed. Mulaf plummeted and then landed catlike on his feet. Instantly Mulaf's hand closed around Sendar's throat.

Liyana lunged forward. "No!"

Trance broken, Sendar opened his eyes. As he clawed at Mulaf's hand, Liyana heard a snap. Sendar crumpled to the ground.

Sendar! Bayla shrieked.

"Don't make me hurt you, child," Mulaf said. Liyana froze, afraid to move. Sendar was motionless. She couldn't see signs of breathing. "Liyana, you alone I do not wish to harm. Your companion, however . . ." He tightened his fist on empty air.

Beside her, Korbyn collapsed.

"And so you will not be tempted to follow me. . . ." Mulaf swirled his fingers in the air, and multiple man-size cyclones bore down on the camp. He rose into the air, and the wind swept him away.

Liyana heard herself screaming. Inside, Bayla screamed as well. Liyana fell to her knees next to Korbyn. "Don't die! Oh, sweet goddess, don't die!" *Bayla, magic, now!*

Bayla flooded her with magic.

Liyana plunged her awareness into Korbyn. She jolted his heart once, twice . . . "Please, oh please, Korbyn, wake up." He opened his eyes as his heart began to pump again.

Sendar, Bayla thought. *Heal Sendar!*

Liyana spun around. Sendar lay motionless. She leaped to her feet and ran to his side. Using the magic, she dove into his body. His neck had been snapped. She poured magic into the bones— slowly, then faster, they began to knit together. His heart! She should restart his heart. And he needed to breathe. She poured magic into him.

Suddenly his chest expanded, and he coughed.

Oh, my Sendar! Bayla's cry nearly wrenched Liyana in two. *I forgive you! I know you cared for me. And I . . . oh, forgive me!*

Liyana swayed. She felt Korbyn's hands on her shoulders, steadying her. But she didn't collapse. Around them, the other deities fought the cyclones. She watched Maara subdue one. "The magician escaped," Korbyn said quietly. He nodded toward the mountains. "He's entered the mountains. The sky serpents are coming."

Liyana rose to her feet.

Over the mountains she saw hundreds of serpents lift into the sky, their translucent bodies distorting the stars and multiplying their lights by the thousands. She also heard hoofbeats behind her, and she turned. Flanked by two men, Jarlath rode into camp. Behind him, his army marched toward the clans, across the expanse between the remaining whirlwinds.

Korbyn shoved Liyana behind him, shielding her.

"Jarlath! I thought you were fleeing," Liyana said.

"The empire's army will fight the sky serpents alongside the desert clans," Jarlath said. His eyes were on Liyana. "These are my generals, General Xevi and General Akkon." He indicated two men. "Give them your orders."

"I don't understand," Korbyn said.

"Give them your orders," Jarlath repeated. "I will accompany Liyana to stop Mulaf. He used me and the Crescent Empire to achieve his goals. It is my responsibility to stop him."

"Liyana isn't—" Korbyn began.

"Of course I am," Liyana said. She was going after Mulaf. Jarlath had known she would.

"Then I am as well," Korbyn said. He turned to Sendar. "Old friend, it falls to you. Will you protect our people? And theirs? You are best able to lead." For a moment the two gods stared at each other. Bayla stirred within Liyana but was silent. Liyana could almost feel the years stretching between them, these age-old relationships.

"I will protect them," Sendar said. He clasped Korbyn's arm, and then he faced the generals. "The sky serpents have few weak-nesses. Here is what we must do. . . ." He led them away.

Liyana turned to Korbyn. "How do we catch up to Mulaf? The mountains are too steep for horses, and we'll never catch him on foot."

Korbyn flashed a smile. "Thievery." He pointed to one of the magician's cyclones. The other deities had collapsed several so far. "Far easier to hijack one than to create one. Come with me!" He ran toward the closest cyclone. Grabbing Jarlath's hand, Liyana ran after him.

"Are you sure about this?" she said to Jarlath as they reached the swirl of wind. She had to shout to be heard over it. "Your people need you, and there's no guarantee—"

"I have failed my people," Jarlath said. "I will not fail you as well."

Undirected, the cyclone tore through tents, consuming the sand. "Liyana, you'll have to control it," Korbyn said. "We will have to ride it like Mulaf, and you are the only one of us who does not need to enter a trance to work magic."

"You don't?" Jarlath asked her. "Fascinating."

"Bayla pulls the magic," Liyana said. "I direct it."

"Yes, she's very impressive. She's also intelligent and beautiful, but perhaps now is not the best time to discuss it," Korbyn said dryly. "Let's move." From the side, he wrapped his arms around Liyana's waist. Jarlath mimicked him on the other side. She felt the breath of both boys on her neck.

Ready? Liyana asked Bayla.

Do it.

"Hold tight," Liyana said. She let the magic flow into her. She expanded herself into the cyclone. She became the cyclone. She played with the wind, raising it higher and sinking it lower. As it sank low and wide, she stepped on top of it, pulling Korbyn and Jarlath with her. The wind bashed into them, and they were shoved up into the air. Wind whipped under her feet, and she felt as if she were skimming over water. She held the boys as tightly as she could, and she steered the cyclone toward the mountains.

Ahead she saw a sky serpent glow fiery red and orange and then white. Cracks ran through its body, and it shattered with a sound like thunder. Glass shards flew in every direction.

"He's heating the sky serpents fast so they'll explode," Jarlath said.

Another sky serpent exploded, raining shards over the boulders below. Glass cascaded down the mountainside. *Fire is one of their few weaknesses,* Bayla said. *Sendar knows this as well.*

He has fought sky serpents before? Liyana asked.

Bayla was silent for a moment. *He knows the sky serpents because we created them.*

You . . . what?

We knew we could not protect the lake ourselves, not without a constant presence in the world, so we created the sky serpents to guard the mountains. It required the full strength of every deity outside of the Dreaming. We seeped magic into the sand, fused it with enough fire to harden. . . .

If you created them, then call them off! Two sky serpents dove at them. One skimmed near the top of the cyclone. Another plunged into it, and then spiraled up toward them. He spun out of the cyclone, roared, and dove again. *Tell them to attack Mulaf, not us!*

Alas, we cannot control them, Bayla said. *Like the sand wolves—*

You are to blame for them as well?

"Liyana!" Korbyn shouted in her ear.

Liyana saw a mountainside rushing toward them. She steered the cyclone to the left, around the serrated edge, and then she gasped at her first view of the mountain range.

Ahead was an expanse of peaks that stretched so high that they looked like they cut the night sky. Half the moon was visible behind one of them. It shed a silvery glow over the black rock mountains.

"Up ahead!" Jarlath cried. "The sky serpents are slowing him!" She veered through the peaks, around the rock faces and the spindly trees. In her wake, boulders rolled down the mountainsides and cliffs collapsed. She felt the wind pound her body as they rode the cyclone.

Suddenly Mulaf's cyclone disappeared.

Faster! Bayla shouted. She poured more and more magic into Liyana. Liyana felt as if her skin would burst open as the pressure increased faster than she could pour the magic out. The cyclone whipped beneath them.

She saw shards of bright glass fill the sky ahead as sky serpents exploded above the peaks. More circled in, diving down between the mountains.

Set us down on that cliff above the lake, Bayla ordered. *But do not miss. The lake water is death to the touch.*

Liyana let the wind slow and then die, and the cyclone slowly lowered them onto the cliff. Mulaf was directly below them on a wider cliff. All his concentration was fixed on the sky serpents. As each one dove at him, he roared at it and swept his arms. It heated to white hot and then exploded. Glass rained on the valley below.

Each flash of light illuminated the sheer, granite cliffs, the oval lake, and the overflow of greenery and flowers that existed nowhere else in the mountains or the desert. As the flare faded, the valley plunged into shadows, and then it flashed again as the next sky serpent died.

The lake looked exactly as she'd pictured it.

"It's beautiful," Jarlath breathed.

Liyana couldn't speak. She watched the white-hot glass scales rain on the lake and the valley. When a scale hit the water, the lake glowed for an instant. Steam curled up. And then it darkened as the scale sank beneath the surface.

"He hasn't seen us," Liyana whispered.

"Or he's too busy with the sky serpents to care," Korbyn said. "They seek to protect the lake. It is their purpose. They won't quit no matter how many of them he explodes."

"We need a plan," Liyana said. Her knees shook, and she was

grateful that Jarlath and Korbyn still held her. Without them, she thought she might fall into the deadly water below. The magic was gone, and she felt empty and breathless. She gripped their arms.

"Simple is best," Korbyn said. "He can outmagic us."

Attack him, Bayla said. Liyana repeated her words out loud.

Jarlath nodded. She couldn't see it, but she felt it. "On the count of three," he said. "One. Two . . ." Another sky serpent exploded. As its light faded to darkness, Jarlath said, "Three." They jumped from the cliff.

As another sky serpent dove to attack, they crashed down on top of Mulaf. He was knocked backward, with Korbyn pinning his legs. Looking past them, Mulaf raised his hand up, and the sky serpent exploded. Shards plummeted around them.

Liyana felt a shard graze her arm. She bit back a cry. Shielding her head from the falling glass, Liyana recoiled. Both Korbyn and Jarlath were forced to dodge as well.

Mulaf got to his feet and raised his hand to point at them. Korbyn and Jarlath lunged at him at the same time. Korbyn hit first, and then Jarlath knocked them all backward. They crashed onto the edge of the cliff. Mulaf's torso extended over open air. Liyana dove forward to catch Korbyn's legs, adding her weight to keep them from tumbling off the cliff.

Bayla yelled, *Watch for—*

Korbyn and Jarlath were tossed backward by wind. They slammed into the granite wall. Still prone, Mulaf defeated another sky serpent. He then rose and advanced on the two boys. "Fools!" Mulaf said. "You could have saved yourselves. Now, you and the lake will be buried in this valley."

"Don't hurt them!" Liyana stepped in front of them. She felt Bayla pour magic into her.

"Desert princess, your magic cannot hope to compete—"

He expected her to use magic against him. So she didn't. She slammed her fist into Mulaf's face. Blood stained his upper lip. As he teetered backward in surprise, she pulled out the sky serpent knife and stabbed him in the stomach.

Her hands shook as she stared at the blood that spread over his clothes. Dark, it blossomed over his torso. Releasing the hilt, she stumbled backward.

He pulled the blade from his stomach, and Korbyn and Jarlath dove at him. His flesh was beginning to heal as they both rammed into him. He toppled over the edge of the cliff, and they fell with him.

"No!" Liyana shouted. She ran to the edge and used Bayla's magic to send the wind screaming underneath them. It swept them toward the grasses and away from the deadly lake. She leaped into the wind, and it blew her down with them. She hit the ground and rolled.

Healed, Mulaf walked toward the edge of the water. It reflected the moon in its ripples. He raised his hands toward the cliffs. Rocks began to shake. Liyana got to her feet and ran toward him. Jarlath and Korbyn were on their feet and running too. Above, sky serpents circled and cried, looking for their prey.

Jarlath reached him first. He tackled Mulaf from behind.

Mulaf fell forward. His hands slapped the water. Ripples spread from them. His body submerged face-first, and then Jarlath's arms sank into the water, pushing Mulaf down. Jarlath's body stiffened, and he collapsed into the water. "No!" Liyana shouted. As she reached for him, the lake water splashed onto her hands.

She died.

Chapter Thirty-Two
Korbyn

Korbyn dragged Liyana's body away from the shore. She lay peacefully, as if sleeping in the greenery. Returning to the lake, he pulled the emperor by his ankles out of the water. Drops splashed onto Korbyn's hands, but as a god, he didn't need to fear the water. Dragging the body over the pebbles, Korbyn laid the emperor next to Liyana. He touched the emperor's neck.

There was no pulse.

Liyana opened her eyes. "She's gone," Bayla said with Liyana's voice.

"She'll return," Korbyn said. "She's resourceful."

"She is in the Dreaming," Bayla said gently.

"She will return with him, and she will not forgive me if he's dead." Korbyn judged that he had not been soulless too long. His skin was still warm.

Bayla knelt beside him. She wrapped her arms—Liyana's arms—around him. "He is already gone. It is over."

Korbyn shook his head.

"Even if he were to return, his body . . ." She trailed off. "No, Korbyn. Korbyn, look at me. We are together now. You cannot do this."

"We will be together in the Dreaming," Korbyn said. "We will be together forever." He closed his eyes. He had never tried this particular trick before. In theory it was sound. The emperor's body wasn't dying from any bodily harm, merely lack of a soul.

He gathered the magic that was his own soul, and he poured it into the emperor's body.

Korbyn took a breath and opened his eyes. His chest felt different. He was lying in the grasses. Water had dampened his face and his clothes. He opened his eyes and saw his former body in Liyana's—Bayla's—arms.

She was crying. "How could you do this to me?"

"She will return," Korbyn said. His voice sounded different, deeper. "I believe in her."

"You love her," Bayla said.

He thought about that. He remembered how he'd met her in the oasis. She'd been throwing sand and screaming at the desert. He remembered how she'd taught him to dance. He remembered guiding her through magic lessons. He remembered how he'd felt when she woke as herself, not as Bayla. "I think I do."

"You don't love me."

"I *know* I do," he said.

Bayla cradled his former body. "Your body will die in minutes if you do not return to it. And say that you are correct and your Liyana returns with her emperor's soul. . . . How will he inhabit that body if you are in it? He is not trained in magic. He will not be able to coexist with you. Your sacrifice will be for nothing."

"That body is not the sacrifice," Korbyn said gently.

Bayla stared at him, and he saw the realization spread over her face.

"Our time here is stolen and will come again. These people . . . they deserve to finish their natural lives. They deserve it more than we do. This is their world. These are their lives. We exist for them and because of them." He attempted a smile and tried to make his voice light. "Besides, you have never seen Liyana when she is angry. She would not like to go through the trouble of saving her emperor only to have him die again here."

"You truly trust her," Bayla said.

Korbyn watched the lake. "Yes, I do." Beside him, in his lover's arms, his body died.

Chapter Thirty-Three

Liyana was in the desert. She rotated slowly, scanning the horizon. To the east she saw a tamar tree with branches that stretched seemingly for miles. To the west she saw rock hills. It was day. The sun was directly above her. There were no shadows.

She felt no heat. The wind caressed her skin and touched her hair. She wore braids and her ceremony dress, even though she'd lost this dress in the emperor's camp.

"Jarlath!" she called.

There were no birds or creatures of any kind. She tried to expand her soul to sense others. . . . But she felt no excess magic, nor did she feel the familiar swirl that was her goddess. *Bayla?* she thought tentatively.

She heard no answer.

SARAH BETH DURST

"I'm dead," she said out loud. The words tasted strange in her mouth. She didn't feel dead. She rubbed the fabric of her skirt between her fingers and thumb. The skirt felt real, and it felt as soft as it had on the morning of her ceremony, without any of the rips or stains.

She walked toward the tamar tree. Around her, sand swirled in the air. She stared at the flecks of sand. Each glinted in the sun like a tiny jewel. Ruby, emerald, sapphire. She touched the glittering air, and she thought she heard the sound of laughter. It tinkled like broken glass and then dissolved. She inhaled the scent of milk and honey carried on the light breeze. Under her feet the sand felt warm, as if it had been heated but not scorched by the midday sun. Her feet, she noticed, wore the same beautiful shoes, tattered from her journey.

"Hello?" she called. "Jarlath? Pia? Fennik? I know you're here!" In fact, thousands of souls should have been there—all the deities who weren't in the desert plus all the dead from prior generations, including Jarlath. And Mulaf.

Mulaf sat on a rock with his face in his hands.

She halted. He had not been there an instant before. Staring at him, she wondered if she should speak to him. He hadn't noticed her. Stepping softly, she backed away.

"He can't hurt you here," Pia said. "I will not let him."

Liyana pivoted. Standing next to her, Pia smiled. She looked as beautiful as she had on the day that Liyana had met her, perhaps more beautiful. She seemed to glow with a soft light, like the aftereffect of staring at the sun. Her eyes did not focus on Liyana but instead seemed to drink in the entire desert. "You still cannot see," Liyana said. "I'd have thought . . ." She trailed off because Pia was smiling with a joy that lit her like a flame. Behind her, the sky rippled with amber, rose, and purple light before it returned to brilliant blue.

"I could always see," Pia said. "Just not with my eyes." She reached with a surety of what she would find, and she touched Liyana's face. "You, however, are blind. Like Oyri was. She needed true blindness before she could see beyond our clan."

"I can see him," Liyana said. "He wants to kill the gods."

"Gods cannot die," Pia said with her familiar conviction. Liyana had missed that certainty, even as she wanted to shake Pia and yell that this man was dangerous. Pia continued to smile, and her unseeing eyes sparkled like opals.

"But he could trap them here," Liyana said. "He planned to destroy the mountains and bury the lake in the rubble. Without the lake the deities cannot leave the Dreaming, and magic dies in the world."

"He cannot destroy anything from within the Dreaming, and I will not let his soul leave."

Liyana knelt in front of him. Mulaf did not seem to know she was there. She waved his hand in front of his face. He did not respond. He looked as if he was staring directly through her.

Tears ran down his face, curving into rivulets in his wrinkles. "He doesn't see me."

"He sees her," Pia said.

Liyana turned but saw no one, only desert stretching on and on.

"His lost love, the Cat Clan vessel who sacrificed herself, his reason for everything that followed," Pia said. "I found her, and we have been awaiting his arrival. Thank you for delivering him to us."

"But he could find a way to leave—"

"He won't," Pia said. "Not now that he has found her. Besides, as I said, I will not let him." She smiled again, and the glow around her brightened. She skipped around Mulaf and dropped into the sand next to him. She patted his shoulder, and he started. "Mulaf and I will become friends." Liyana thought her smile had a sharpness to it, as if she were a cat with a mouse.

Another voice spoke. "Here, you are as strong as your soul." Fennik walked toward them. He looked as he had on the day she'd met him, dressed in his clan's traditional body paint and loincloth. He had his bow and arrows strapped to his back, and he held a waterskin as if he had been on a hunt. "Pia's soul is very strong. She will contain him."

Pia beamed at Fennik. He planted a kiss on the top of her head. Reaching up, she looped her hand into his, and his hand enveloped hers. Their smiles at each other seemed to exclude all else. Pia had never smiled that fiercely when she was alive.

Here, she was not ephemeral.

"Fennik . . ." Liyana searched for the right words.

"The rules of the living world do not apply here. You should see the horses!" Fennik swept his arm open. Behind him, across the sands, a herd of horses ran. Their jewel-like hides gleamed in the sun, and their manes and tails streamed in the wind. "I am in the process of creating my own herd." He smiled at her, and Liyana thought he exuded light too, a leak around him that blurred the air. The horses vanished like smoke. "You will love it here, Liyana. Release your worries. You have finished your task."

"Nothing is finished!" Liyana said. "The sky serpents are attacking the clans and the empire's army. They will destroy everyone! I must find Jarlath. His people need him more than ever, and I cannot leave until I know my clan will be safe." A horrible thought occurred to her. "Jarlath's soul *is* here, isn't he? He dreamed of the lake. He must be a reincarnated soul. Please tell me he is here. And Raan. Where is Raan? Did she find her way?"

"Right here," Raan said with a wave. She was perched on a rock near Pia as if she'd been there the entire time. Lush grasses ringed her rock, and purple flowers grew beside her. The blossoms swayed in the wind, and the grasses were bright green, incongruous with the sand all around. "Glad you finally remembered me. I was beginning to feel unloved."

Liyana felt a tightness in her chest loosen. At least Raan was whole. "Don't tell me you forgive me, too, and that the Dreaming is happy meadows and bubbling brooks and that you've released your anger at your death and embraced eternity?"

"Of course not," Raan said. "But I can torment him until I feel better, so that helps." Raan punched Mulaf in his shoulder. He flinched, but he did not look at her. His eyes were fixed on an empty patch of desert. "He can see his lost love, but he can't talk to her or touch her. We won't let him—and truth be told, neither will she. She has watched him through the years and hates what he has done in her name."

Liyana studied the empty desert and tried to imagine what he saw, a woman he'd loved and lost so long ago. In the distance the dunes seemed to rise and fall, undulating like water—a trick of the light, or a trick of the Dreaming.

"Do you remember the stories of the Cat Clan? How they suffered tragedy after tragedy until they were extinct? He caused those tragedies, as revenge for her death," Raan said. "We will make sure he does not find peace too easily."

"But you will." Gracefully Pia rose and embraced Liyana. She smelled like honey. "If you try, you will find peace and understanding here. All you must do is look for it."

"I don't need to find peace," Liyana said, pulling away. "I need to find Jarlath, and I need to find a way to take him back."

"If finding him will grant you peace, then you will find him," Pia said serenely.

"But you can't take him back," Raan said. "It is . . . too difficult to return to one's body." Liyana heard the pain in her voice. "Besides, his body must be dead by now. Don't seek him for that reason. You'll only break your heart."

"I healed Sendar," Liyana said. "I can heal him." She strode away across the sands. She didn't want to hear any more about peace or the glorious wonders of the Dreaming. She wasn't finished with the real world yet. "Jarlath!"

Behind her, she heard Pia say, "Let her go. She will return soon enough."

"Jarlath, appear!" She felt tears on her cheeks, and she didn't wipe them away. *He must be here,* she thought. He'd dreamed of the lake.

She walked for miles. Above, the sun crossed the sky. Shadows blossomed over the sand dunes and then spread. The sand shifted in color from red to gold. She didn't feel the heat or thirst or hunger.

Liyana stopped. She took a deep breath. "You aren't real," she said to the desert. She thought of Korbyn. He'd raced Sendar across this desert, and he'd won by moving the finish line.

Cresting a sand dune, a gray mare trotted toward her. She could have been a twin of Gray Luck. Her saddle and bridle were already in place. She slowed in front of Liyana and whickered in her hair. Liyana felt the horse's hot breath on her ear and neck, and the tickle of the horse's lips as Gray Luck's twin nipped her shoulder. Liyana patted the horse's neck, and then she swung herself into the saddle.

It felt so familiar to ride across the sands, and yet at the same time so foreign to ride alone. Ahead she saw an oasis—it shimmered into view as if the wind had blown it into existence. She saw a collection of tents, familiar tents in the style of the Goat Clan. Liyana kneed Gray Luck's twin into a trot, and then she reined in.

"I want Jarlath," she told the desert firmly. She would reunite with her clan in the real world. The oasis wavered as if it were a mirage, and then it vanished.

In its place she saw a solitary figure sitting with his back toward her. She nudged Gray Luck's twin into a canter. Reaching the figure, Liyana dismounted. As she moved to care for the mare, the horse vanished. She spun around, afraid that Jarlath would have disappeared too. But he remained, unmoving.

He sat by a pool of water. The water was a perfect circle in the sand. Its surface reflected the sky. "Jarlath?" She placed her hand on his shoulder. "Can you hear me?"

He did not look up. "You're dead. I had hoped you weren't. Too many are." Jarlath pointed to the water. Distorted, she saw the clans' camp in its reflection.

Bodies were strewn between the tents. Sky serpents attacked the living from above. She couldn't hear the screams, but she could see the faces twisted in pain and fear. Children were plucked from the ground, and warriors lay beside their elders in pools of blood and dust. Soldiers plunged into the mountains only to die at the talons and teeth of more sky serpents. But worst of all, as the serpents continued their relentless attack, squadrons of soldiers and desert warriors fought one another.

"What are they doing?" Liyana cried.

"Some in my army blame the clans for the fact that I haven't returned. . . . Perhaps my guards remember my order: If you kill me, they slaughter." His voice was wooden. Dead. "Others seek to find me, further enraging the sky serpents."

"Come with me," Liyana said. "We have to leave."

"You cannot leave death."

"Our souls have left before," Liyana said. She put her hands on his shoulders, wanting to shake him into life again.

A sad smile ghosted across his face. "Always so brave and so stubborn. I am not a fool, though. I know what happens when a soul leaves a body. I have no living body to return to." Then his eyes lit up. "But you do! Bayla is in your body, keeping it alive. You could return!" He grasped his arms. "Yes! You must stop my people from fighting yours. . . ." The light faded from his eyes. "Until the sky serpents kill them all."

Both of them watched through the pool.

"The gods must stop this," Liyana said.

He pointed at Maara. Sweat poured down her face. Deep in a trance, she deflected a sky serpent from above her. "Even they are not strong enough."

"All the gods must stop this." Liyana rose to her feet as an idea shaped within her. She scanned the desert around her. "We need an amphitheatre with stone steps. Cascades of flowers. And the sound of birds." Closing her eyes, she visualized it exactly as Bayla had once described it—the gathering place of the deities. She placed the steps in a semicircle around them. She chose every desert flower she'd ever seen plus some from the valley, and she pictured them spilling down the sides of the steps. She imagined the trill of birds.

Hearing birds, she opened her eyes.

The amphitheatre was around her, rising out of the desert sands, exactly as she'd pictured it. But it was empty. Wind blew across the steps.

"Summon the gods," Jarlath said. "Dance."

Liyana spread her arms wide and imagined she was sending her voice across the sands. *"Ebuci o nanda wadi. Ebuci o yenda. Vessa oenda nasa we."* She repeated it. And then she began to dance. Spinning, she heard bells—the silver bells were again in her hair. She twisted and twirled in silence.

Drums began. Steady as a heartbeat.

A syncopated rhythm joined it.

She danced faster, her arms swirling with the rhythm, her feet pounding to the heart drum. A melody soared above. Pia was singing, she realized. And Fennik and Raan were drumming. Jarlath spoke the words as Liyana danced. *"Ebuci o nanda wadi. Ebuci o yenda. Vessa oenda nasa we!"*

All of a sudden the drums fell silent, and the melody ceased. Liyana stopped dancing. Around her and Jarlath, the amphitheatre was filled with gods.

Some of the deities shone like soft moonlight. Others blazed. Above them the light shifted and waved like an aurora. Liyana saw that the sky had darkened to a deep blue.

One of the goddesses lifted her hand, and the birds fell silent. All eyes fixed on Liyana. She felt her throat go dry, as if it had never known moisture. The eyes of the deities burned her. Liyana tried to find the words, or perhaps a story. . . . Her mind felt blank.

Jarlath laid his hand on her shoulder. "Perhaps *this* is why I am here," he said. He walked past her and stood in front of the gods and goddesses. His face was as calm as stone. He raised his voice. "Deities of the desert, children of the children of the turtle, I am not your enemy."

He talked, and the words flowed out of him like water from a stream. He told them of families whose fields had died, whose children with hungry eyes were thin as sticks, whose parents had to choose who to save. He told of the desperation and the terrible hope that drove him with his army into the desert. And he told the story of his parents' deaths. "We came to the desert to find life, not death. Yet now my people are killing and dying on the desert sands. Please, you must end this. Save us from the sky serpents and one another."

One god rose. His eyes gleamed like stars against his night black skin. "Your words are eloquent, and we are not deaf to your plea. But we in the Dreaming cannot affect the world of the living no matter how much we may wish it. Indeed, that is the purpose of vessels. Only from within a vessel can our magic touch the world."

A goddess whose hair wound in coils to her feet spoke next. "Already there are several deities with vessels in the desert, and they are ineffective to halt the slaughter. I do not know what you expect us to do without vessels."

Others nodded in agreement.

Liyana touched Jarlath on the shoulder as he began to speak. "And *this* is why I am here," she said. She raised her voice. "Once, there was a desert girl who saved her goddess. . . ." She told them how Bayla had entered her but Liyana hadn't left. She told them how they had worked magic together—and how the power was amplified when conducted through a human mind. "And that was with only one deity inside. Add more . . ." She told them about Mulaf.

Gasps and whispers spread through the deities. Many did not believe her. Others suspected exaggeration. Only a few thought it could be truth. She scanned the amphitheatre, trying to spot the gods who had been inside Mulaf. She doubted they'd remained in his body once the lake water had forced him to leave.

"If you don't believe her, ask Mulaf," Jarlath said.

"Bring him before us," one of the gods commanded.

Pia vanished for an instant. When she reappeared, Mulaf was with her. He blinked at the assembly of deities. "You!" He pointed. "Filthy parasites! Plague upon our world!" He spat on the ground before them.

"You will tell us of your experience—" one god began.

"I will tell you nothing!"

Pia vanished and reappeared again, this time with a woman.

The woman was as lovely as a bird, with a delicate face and soft hair that flowed over her shoulders. She stepped in front of Mulaf, and all his rage drained away to be replaced by naked anguish. Her hand touched Mulaf's cheek, and he let out an inarticulate cry, like a small animal in pain.

"I would have avenged you, Serra," Mulaf said.

Gently Serra said, "I never needed to be avenged. I went willingly into death."

He looked as if she had stabbed him. "But . . . you had no choice."

Her smile was sad. "There is always choice. I wanted to help our people. I believed, as did we all, that the death of the vessel was the only way." She cupped her hands around his face and leaned her forehead against his. "My love, you have caused much pain in my name. I do not know if I can forgive you for what you have done or for what you almost did." Her voice was as hard as her face was sweet.

Liyana put her hand on the woman's shoulder. "He can begin

to make amends right now. He must tell the gods how he nearly destroyed the lake."

"Tell them, my love," Serra said, still cradling his face in her hands.

He yanked away as if her touch hurt him. "Do not ask this of me! Please, Serra. . . . These parasites caused your death. Needlessly!"

Liyana spoke again. "Once the truth is known, no vessel will ever need to choose to die. Gods will never again freely walk the world in a stolen body. Isn't that a kind of revenge?"

She saw the emotions play across his face.

She pushed harder. "Besides, doesn't your story deserve to be told?"

"Indeed, it does." Mulaf faced the assembly of deities. He pointed to six of them. "You, you, you, you, you, and you . . . I captured you inside of me." He went on to describe how he had trapped them in false vessels, summoned them into his body, controlled them, and then used them. "Their power was combined and then magnified through me. Speak the truth to your fellow parasites!"

One by one, the six humiliated deities, including Somayo of the Falcon Clan, whose statue Liyana had held and not broken, confirmed his story with hatred in their eyes for how they had been used. After they sank into their seats again, Mulaf clasped Serra's hands to his chest. "Now can you forgive me?"

She removed her hands. "With time. Perhaps."

"It is fortunate, then, that we have eternity."

Pia tapped Mulaf's shoulder and he disappeared. Serra vanished as well.

"So here's the trick," Liyana said to the deities. She hoped Korbyn would approve of what she was about to do. She thought he would. "I return to my body. All of you come with me. And through me, we end this."

Chapter Thirty-Four

L iyana took Jarlath's hand. "You are coming with me."

He raised her hand to his lips and kissed her knuckles. "My body is dead. I cannot."

"You do not say no to the girl with the deities." She wrapped her arms around his waist and then yanked him off-balance. Together, they fell into the pool of water.

Light swirled around her. Colors sparkled, shifting as they shimmered. She imagined the feel of her skin, the shape of her body, the throb of blood pulsing through her veins, and the rush of air into her lungs. It was the reverse of how it felt when she used to picture the lake. Carefully she poured her soul into her body.

Liyana? Bayla's mental voice was stunned.

I'm not alone, Liyana said. *Ready yourself.*

The other deities filled her. Liyana was engulfed in wind, buffeted by a storm within. She clung to the familiar contours of her body, grounding herself in her muscles and bones. She drew on everything she had practiced in all the lessons with Korbyn, and she seized control of herself before the other minds could establish themselves.

The other souls jostled inside her, but she held on, not relinquishing control. All the pounding by Bayla had prepared her for this onslaught, though this was far worse than anything Bayla had ever tried. She felt as if she were being ripped apart inside out by wild dogs.

Bayla!

Yes, Liyana? Bayla's voice rose from the vortex of other voices.

Slowly, painfully, Liyana reached into the chaos toward Bayla's voice. She felt Bayla move through the souls as well, shepherding them into semicohesion. Liyana coaxed the spinning souls to swirl in the same direction. Together, the two of them swept the other deities into a single cyclone inside her.

Are you ready? Bayla asked.

Yes, Liyana said.

Voices spoke in unison, echoing her. *Yes. Yes. Yes!* She felt them speed up inside her, all their emotions and thoughts tumbling in a thick storm.

Feed me magic, Liyana ordered them.

She felt them all still for a moment.

And then the magic dumped into her, more and more, like an ocean pouring into a bowl. She pushed her soul wider, expanding it as fast as she could as the magic flowed in. She flowed through the valley. She sank into the earth and felt the life of the plants, the strength of the stone, and the heat of the dirt. She swept through the mountains, into their hearts and over their peaks. The magic surged within her, forcing her faster and wider and deeper.

Oh, sweet goddess, it's too much! she cried.

You can do this, Liyana, Jarlath whispered within the deities. *You are strong.*

She pushed herself harder, and she became the wind in the mountains. It was her breath. She breathed out and spread into the desert. She felt the souls of the soldiers and the clans like bursts of fire in the wind. She felt their deaths as their souls flickered past her, en route to the Dreaming.

You must end this tragedy, Jarlath said.

She targeted one of the sky serpents. As Mulaf had done, she focused the heat of the sun on its glass body, and she intensified the heat rapidly, as if a year's worth of sun pounded on it at once. The heart of the sky serpent heated to white-hot, and then the sky serpent cracked and shattered in an explosion that rained down on the clans and army below.

She focused on the next sky serpent. . . . But there were hundreds.

You're killing them, Jarlath said. *Our people. Find another way!*

The shards that fell below were as deadly as the serpents themselves. She needed to make them vanish, not explode. Only then would her people be safe.

I need more magic, she said as an idea occurred to her.

Liyana stirred the wind high above the clans and army. She controlled the wind in a tight cyclone, keeping it from touching the humans, and then she widened her whirlwind. Pouring magic into it, she swept the wind into the sky serpents. She caught them in a net of air. The sky serpents tumbled head over tail. Their glass scales caught the sunlight and twisted it until the sky looked as if it were filled with thousands of jewels.

Fueled by the gods' magic, Liyana propelled the sky serpents across the mountains and then beyond, a hundred miles west over empty desert. She let the wind die, and she flew her soul back to the clans and the army, leaving the sky serpents far behind her.

They will return to their mountains, Bayla said. *It is how we made them. They must guard the lake.*

When they return, they will find no one to kill, Liyana said. She spun the wind again, and this time she aimed it down at the army and the clans. She ripped through the sands, splitting the clans from the army.

She added more whirlwinds. It felt like stirring a soup with her finger. She guided each one carefully, using the wind to gently separate the combatants. She plucked a soldier up midbattle and blew him north to his encampment, and she removed a desert man from the encampment and returned him to the clan tents. She scooped up a clump of desert children and delivered them safely away from an advancing soldier, and then she delivered the soldier to his army. Jarlath helped direct her, pointing out his people and steering her toward them. After nearly an hour of intense concentration, she had corralled the empire's army with their tents and the clans with theirs.

She then broadened the wind and blew the entire army eastward, across the desert and into the hills, over the border, and into the Crescent Empire. She left them on a golden plain— soldiers, horses, tents, and all.

Done, she returned to the clans. She narrowed her focus to locate the Horse Clan god. She found him, a spiky soul mounted on a bleeding horse. She sent words toward him, wrapping her thoughts in magic as if they were a summoning chant. *Sendar, tell the clans that it is over. Tell them to leave the mountains before the sky serpents come back. Tell them to return to their oases and their lives.*

You? His voice was as loud as a horse's bray. *You eliminated the sky serpents?*

I am not alone, she said simply. She sank back toward the valley where her body waited. She felt herself lying in the grasses, sun on her skin and the smell of flowers around her. The voices within her faded. She reached for them. . . . The magic felt like a tiny pool inside her. *What's happening?*

You have done well, vessel, Bayla said.

Wait! I do not understand—

Jarlath, listen for your voice. It chants for you. Follow it, Bayla said. To Liyana she said, *Do not be angry with Korbyn. Or yourself.*

She lost the feel of the wind inside of her. She no longer touched the valley or the mountains or the desert. She had her own human arms and legs again. *Bayla—*

The feel of the deities was faint, like a whisper on skin. *It has been an honor,* Bayla said. *An uncomfortable honor, perhaps, but still . . . You were worthy of me.*

And then they were gone.

❋   ❋   ❋

Liyana woke to silence. She felt the earth on her back, and she stared up at the sky. It was day, and the bleached blue sky was empty. The sky serpents were gone. *Bayla? Jarlath? Anyone?*

Only quiet, inside and out.

She inhaled and felt her ribs expand. She ached in every muscle. Stretching, she tested her arms and legs. She clenched and unclenched her hands. She was whole and alive. But she felt as empty as the sky.

"Liyana." Jarlath's voice. Close. Outside her.

She turned her head. He lay beside her in the grass. He reached out his hand, and his fingers twined around hers. "You're alive," she said.

"As are you."

Cheek against the ground, she smelled the dirt and the grass. She also smelled flowers, sweet as honey. She watched Jarlath as he pushed himself up to sitting. She saw his eyes widen and his lips part. He opened his mouth as if to speak and then shut it, wordless.

Gingerly she also pushed herself up to sitting. "Oh, sweet goddess," she said.

The lake was dry.

All that remained was a perfect oval of jewel-like pebbles. On its edge, Mulaf's body lay facedown where he had fallen into the water. Liyana rose and walked, her legs shaking like a newborn calf, to the shore. She didn't look at Mulaf.

"Liyana, don't—"

Kneeling, she laid her hands palms down on the pebbles. She felt only dry stones.

She heard Jarlath walk over the pebbles and halt behind her. He placed his hands on her shoulders. Picking up the pebbles, she held them in her palm. She rolled them so that they sparkled in the sun, and then she let them drop onto the lake bed. They pinged as they hit, and then rolled until they settled. She stood and walked across the pebbles to what was once the center of the lake.

"It's gone," she said. She heard her voice, and it sounded as empty as she felt. Breathing deeply, she tried to concentrate, to drop herself into the familiar trance and picture the lake to draw its magic—but she saw only a memory and felt nothing.

She tried again. And again.

"The magic is gone," she said. She wondered if the gods had known this would happen. If she had realized that—*oh no*, she thought. "The gods . . ." She saw a shape in the grass, lying still. She ran toward it. She barely heard Jarlath follow her.

She collapsed in the grass next to Korbyn's body. Hand shaking, she touched his face. He felt cold. Like touching the pebbles. She drew her hand back. She stared at his chest as if she could will it to rise and breathe! But he did not move.

She sat there for a long time. Silent, Jarlath sat beside her.

At last she and Jarlath carried Korbyn to the lake. They laid him in the center and piled pebbles on him to bury him. Without tools it was the best they could do. Liyana cried silently as she piled the pebbles higher and higher.

After, they buried Mulaf in the same way.

When they finished, the sky was gray. Liyana stood between the two mounds of rocks in the dry lake bed, and she looked across the green expanse of the valley, shadowed by the cliffs. Birds were calling to one another from the trees. She wondered if they had eggs in their nests. She'd seen plants with berries and a few of the trees looked as though they had fresh dates. Others had nuts, and others she recognized had edible bark. She could fashion new waterskins out of snakeskins—this valley had to have snakes. And they could find water within the succulent plants and cacti.

Quietly Jarlath asked, "What are you thinking?"

"He wanted us to live," Liyana said.

She took his hand, and they walked out of the lake.

Epilogue
Three years later . . .

The sky serpents circled above the mountains. Glass scales split the sun into a thousand shards of colors, and their wings reflected the blueness of the morning sky. Liyana kept an eye on them as she urged Gray Luck up the slope.

Behind her she heard the clan warriors and the imperial soldiers jostle for position. She didn't have to look back to know that the more sure-footed desert horses had taken the lead.

She crested the top of the ridge and reined in Gray Luck. She looked down into the valley. Green cascaded from the rock slopes and stopped where the pebbles began. The lake was still an oval of pebbles.

"I thought that the valley would have died without the lake," Jarlath said beside her.

SARAH BETH DURST

She didn't answer. Instead she coaxed Gray Luck to descend. The horse trampled flowers and bushes as she zigzagged down the slope toward the base of the valley. At the bottom, she let the horse graze on the soft grass until Jarlath and their guard joined them. "Watch for the sky serpents," she ordered. They hadn't attacked anyone since their return from across the desert. With the lake gone, their purpose had ended. The sky serpents had no need to guard the mountains anymore. But no one had forgotten the damage they could do. Her father had lost a hand, sliced by one of their scales. Many, unbearably many, had lost their lives, including the Silk Clan's magician Ilia and the chief of the Horse Clan. Countless soldiers and desert people had been injured before she had swept away the sky serpents.

A few of the soldiers on their horses began to press forward through the green toward the lake. Liyana held up her hand. "I wish to proceed alone," she said.

They halted. "Yes, Empress."

She slid off her horse and handed the reins to one of the warriors. Jarlath dismounted and crossed to her. He looked as handsome as he had on the day that she had first met him, but his face was no longer unreadable stone, at least not to her. "Whatever you find," he said, "know this."

She waited for him to continue.

But instead of speaking, he gathered her in his arms and

kissed her. It felt as soft as summer rain. She let it wash away every worry, every fear, and every thought.

He released her, and neither spoke. Alone, she walked through the blankets of white and blue flowers, around the bushes covered in butterflies, and under trees that rang with the cries of birds. At last she reached the lake.

The pebbles were perfectly smooth except for the two mounds in the center of the lake. She walked toward the one on the right, and she opened the silk purse that she'd tied to her sash. She upended it into her palm, and silver bells fell into her hand. She spread them over Korbyn's grave.

She saw a patch of yellow flowers that had burst through the pebbles beyond the grave. She reached to pick one to add to her offering, but she stopped. A few of the pebbles around the blooms lay beneath a sheen of water. She drew her hand back and stared at the tiny but unmistakable pool of water.

Overhead, a raven cried.

Liyana smiled. And then she rose and walked back through the valley to Jarlath.

SARAH BETH DURST